LITTLE WOMEN

Little Women

OR MEG, JO, BETH, AND AMY

BY LOUISA MAY ALCOTT

ILLUSTRATED BY REISIE LONETTE

ABRIDGED FOR MODERN READING

CHILDREN'S CLASSICS
GARDEN CITY, NEW YORK

PREFACE

"Go, then, my little Book, and show to all
That entertain and bid thee welcome shall,
What thou dost keep close shut up in thy breast;
And wish what thou dost show them may be blest
To them for good, may make them choose to be
Pilgrims better, by far, than thee or me.
Tell them of Mercy; she is one
Who early hath her pilgrimage begun.
Yea, let young damsels learn of her to prize
The world which is to come, and so be wise;
For little tripping maids may follow God
Along the ways which saintly feet have trod."

ADAPTED FROM JOHN BUNYAN

PART FIRST

PLAYING PILGRIMS, 3

A MERRY CHRISTMAS, 12

THE LAURENCE BOY, 20

BURDENS, 29

BEING NEIGHBORLY, 37

BETH FINDS THE PALACE BEAUTIFUL, 46

AMY'S VALLEY OF HUMILIATION, 53

JO MEETS APOLLYON, 59

MEG GOES TO VANITY FAIR, 68

THE P.C. AND P.O., 81

EXPERIMENTS, 88

CAMP LAURENCE, 97

CASTLES IN THE AIR, 112

SECRETS, 120

A TELEGRAM, 126

LEFT WITHOUT MARMEE, 134

LITTLE FAITHFUL, 136

DARK DAYS, 141

AMY'S WILL, 145

CONFIDENTIAL, 150

LAURIE MAKES MISCHIEF, AND JO MAKES PEACE, 154

PLEASANT MEADOWS, 158

AUNT MARCH SETTLES THE QUESTION, 164

PART SECOND

GOSSIP, 177

THE FIRST WEDDING, 184

ARTISTIC ATTEMPTS, 189

LITERARY LESSONS, 197

DOMESTIC EXPERIENCES, 204

CALLS, 217

CONSEQUENCES, 228

OUR FOREIGN CORRESPONDENT, 237

TENDER TROUBLES, 244

JO'S JOURNAL, 253

A FRIEND, 264

HEARTACHE, 276

BETH'S SECRET, 284

NEW IMPRESSIONS, 287

ON THE SHELF, 295

LAZY LAURENCE, 306

THE VALLEY OF THE SHADOW, 317

LEARNING TO FORGET, 321

ALL ALONE, 330

SURPRISES, 336

MY LORD AND LADY, 348

DAISY AND DEMI, 350

UNDER THE UMBRELLA, 355

HARVESTTIME, 367

PART 1

PLAYING PILGRIMS

"Christmas won't be Christmas without any presents," grumbled Jo, lying on the rug.

"It's so dreadful to be poor!" sighed Meg, looking down at her old dress.

"I don't think it's fair for some girls to have plenty of pretty things and other girls nothing at all," added little Amy, with an injured sniff.

"We've got Father and Mother and each other," said Beth contentedly, from her corner.

The four young faces on which the firelight shone brightened at the cheerful words, but darkened again as Jo said sadly:

"We haven't got Father, and shall not have him for a long time." She didn't say "perhaps never," but each silently added it, thinking of Father far away, where the fighting was.

Nobody spoke for a minute, then Meg said in an altered tone: "You know the reason Mother proposed not having any presents this Christmas was because it is going to be a hard winter for everyone and she thinks we ought not to spend money for pleasure when our men are suffering so in the army. We can't do much, but we can make our little sacrifices, and ought to do it gladly. But I am afraid I don't." And Meg shook her head as she thought regretfully of all the pretty things she wanted.

"But I don't think the little we should spend would do any good. We've each got a dollar, and the army wouldn't be much helped by our giving that. I agree not to expect anything from Mother or you, but I do want to buy *Undine and Sintram* for myself. I've wanted it *so* long," said Jo, who was a bookworm.

"I have planned to spend mine in new music," said Beth, with a little sigh.

"I shall get a nice box of Faber's drawing pencils. I really need them," said Amy decidedly.

3

"Mother didn't say anything about our money, and she won't wish us to give up everything. Let's each buy what we want, and have a little fun. I'm sure we work hard enough to earn it," cried Jo, examining the heels of her shoes in a gentlemanly manner.

"I know I do—teaching those tiresome children nearly all day when I'm longing to enjoy myself at home," began Meg, in the complaining tone again.

"You don't have half such a hard time as I do," said Jo. "How would you like to be shut up for hours with a nervous, fussy old lady who keeps you trotting, is never satisfied, and worries you till you're ready to fly out of the window or cry?"

"It's naughty to fret, but I do think washing dishes and keeping things tidy is the worst work in the world. It makes me cross, and my hands get so stiff I can't practice well at all." And Beth looked at her rough hands.

"I don't believe any of you suffer as I do," cried Amy; "for you don't have to go to school with impertinent girls who plague you if you don't know your lessons, and laugh at your dresses, and label your father if he isn't rich, and insult you when your nose isn't nice."

"If you mean *libel*, I'd say say so, and not talk about *labels* as if Papa was a pickle bottle," advised Jo, laughing.

"I know what I mean, and you needn't be *statirical* about it. It's proper to use good words, and improve your *vocabilary*," returned Amy with dignity.

"Don't peck at one another, children. Don't you wish we had the money Papa lost when we were little, Jo? Dear me, how happy and good we'd be if we had no worries!" said Meg, who could remember better times.

"You said the other day you thought we were a deal happier than the King children, for they were fighting and fretting all the time, in spite of their money."

"So I did, Beth. Well, I think we are; for though we do have to work, we make fun for ourselves, and are a pretty jolly set, as Jo would say."

"Jo does use such slang words!" observed Amy, with a reproving look at the long figure stretched on the rug. Jo immediately sat up, put her hands in her pockets, and began to whistle. "Don't, Jo—it's so boyish!"

"That's why I do it."

"I detest rude, unladylike girls!"

"I hate affected, niminy-piminy chits!"

" 'Birds in their little nests agree,' " sang Beth, the peacemaker, with

4

such a funny face that both sharp voices softened to a laugh, and the "pecking" ended for that time.

"Really, girls, you are both to be blamed," said Meg, beginning to lecture in her elder-sisterly fashion. "You are old enough to leave off boyish tricks, and to behave better, Josephine. It didn't matter so much when you were a little girl; but now you are so tall, and turn up your hair, you should remember that you are a young lady."

"I'm not! And if turning up my hair makes me one, I'll wear it in two tails till I'm twenty," cried Jo, pulling off her net and shaking down a chestnut mane. "I hate to think I've got to grow up, and be Miss March, and wear long gowns, and look as prim as a China aster. It's bad enough to be a girl, anyway, when I like boys' games and work and manners! I can't get over my disappointment in not being a boy; and it's worse than ever now, for I'm dying to go and fight with Papa, and I can only stay at home and knit, like a poky old woman!"

"Poor Jo! It's too bad, but it can't be helped; so you must try to be contented with making your name boyish, and playing brother to us girls," said Beth, stroking the rough head at her knee with a hand that all the dishwashing and dusting in the world could not make ungentle in its touch.

"As for you, Amy," continued Meg, "you are altogether too particular and prim. Your airs are funny now, but you'll grow up an affected little goose if you don't take care. I like your nice manners and refined ways of speaking when you don't try to be elegant, but your absurd words are as bad as Jo's slang."

"If Jo is a tomboy and Amy a goose, what am I, please?" asked Beth, ready to share the lecture.

"You're a dear, and nothing else," answered Meg warmly.

The four sisters sat knitting away in the twilight while the December snow fell quietly without and the fire crackled cheerfully within. It was a comfortable old room, though the carpet was faded and the furniture very plain; for a good picture or two hung on the walls, books filled the recesses, chrysanthemums and Christmas roses bloomed in the windows, and a pleasant atmosphere of home peace pervaded it.

Margaret, the eldest of the four, was sixteen, and very pretty, being plump and fair, with large eyes, plenty of soft brown hair, a sweet mouth, and white hands, of which she was rather vain. Fifteen-year-old Jo was very tall, thin, and brown, and reminded one of a colt; for she never seemed to know what to do with her long limbs, which were very much in her way. She had a decided mouth, a comical nose, and sharp gray eyes which appeared to see everything, and were by turns fierce, funny, or thoughtful. Her long, thick hair was her one beauty, but it was usually bundled into a net, to be out of her way. Round shoulders had Jo, big hands and feet, a flyaway look to her clothes, and the uncomfortable appearance of a girl who was rapidly shooting up into a woman and didn't like it. Elizabeth—or Beth, as everyone called her—was a rosy, smooth-haired, bright-eyed girl of thirteen, with a shy manner, a timid voice, and a peaceful expression, which was seldom disturbed. Her father called her "Little Tranquillity," and the name suited her excellently, for she seemed to live in a happy world of her own, only venturing out to meet the few whom she trusted and loved. Amy, though the youngest, was a most important person—in her own opinion at least. A regular snow maiden, with blue eyes and yellow hair curling on her shoulders, pale and slender, and always carrying herself like a young lady mindful of her manners.

The clock struck six, and having swept up the hearth, Beth put a pair of slippers down to warm. Somehow the sight of the old shoes had a good effect upon the girls; for Mother was coming, and everyone brightened to welcome her. Meg stopped lecturing and lighted the lamp, Amy got out of the easy chair without being asked, and Jo forgot how tired she was as she sat up to hold the slippers nearer to the blaze.

"They are quite worn out. Marmee must have a new pair."

"I thought I'd get her some with my dollar," said Beth.

"No, I shall!" cried Amy.

"I'm the oldest," began Meg, but Jo cut in with a decided:

"I'm the man of the family now Papa is away, and I shall provide the slippers, for he told me to take special care of Mother while he was gone."

"I'll tell you what we'll do," said Beth. "Let's each get her something for Christmas, and not get anything for ourselves."

"That's like you, dear! What will we get?" exclaimed Jo.

Everyone thought soberly for a minute, then Meg announced, as if the idea was suggested by the sight of her own pretty hands, "I shall give her a nice pair of gloves."

"Army shoes, best to be had," cried Jo.

"Some handkerchiefs, all hemmed," said Beth.

"I'll get a little bottle of cologne. It won't cost much, so I'll have some left to buy my pencils," added Amy.

"Let Marmee think we are getting things for ourselves, and then surprise her. We must go shopping tomorrow afternoon, Meg; there is so much to do about the play for Christmas night," said Jo.

"I don't mean to act any more after this time. I'm getting too old for such things," observed Meg, who was as much a child as ever about "dressing-up" frolics.

"You won't stop, I know, as long as you can trail round in a white gown with your hair down, and wear gold-paper jewelry. You are the best actress we've got, and there'll be an end of everything if you quit the

boards," said Jo. "We ought to rehearse tonight. Come here, Amy, and do the fainting scene, for you are as stiff as a poker in that."

"I can't help it. I never saw anyone faint, and I don't choose to make myself all black-and-blue tumbling flat as you do. If I can go down easily, I'll drop; if I can't, I shall fall into a chair and be graceful. I don't care if Hugo does come at me with a pistol," returned Amy, who was not gifted with dramatic power, but was chosen because she was small enough to be borne out shrieking by the villain of the piece.

"Do it this way—clasp your hands so, and stagger across the room crying frantically, 'Roderigo! Save me! Save me!'" And away went Jo with a melodramatic scream which was truly thrilling.

Amy followed, but she poked her hands out stiffly before her, and jerked herself along as if she went by machinery, and her "Ow!" was more suggestive of pins being run into her than of fear and anguish. Jo gave a despairing groan, and Meg laughed outright.

"It's no use! Do the best you can when the time comes, and if the audience laugh, don't blame me. Come on, Meg."

Then things went smoothly, for Don Pedro defied the world in a speech of two pages without a single break; Hagar, the witch, chanted an awful incantation over her kettleful of simmering toads with weird effect; Roderigo rent his chains asunder manfully; and Hugo died in agonies of remorse and arsenic, with a wild "Ha! Ha!"

"It's the best we've had yet," said Meg as the dead villain sat up and rubbed his elbows.

"I don't see how you can write and act such splendid things, Jo. You're a regular Shakespeare!" exclaimed Beth.

"Not quite," replied Jo modestly. "I do think *The Witch's Curse, an Operatic Tragedy*, is rather a nice thing; but I'd like to try *Macbeth*, if we only had a trapdoor for Banquo. I always wanted to do the killing part. 'Is that a dagger that I see before me?'" muttered Jo, rolling her eyes and clutching at the air as she had seen a famous tragedian do, and the rehearsal ended in a general burst of laughter.

"Glad to find you so merry, my girls," said a cheery voice at the door, and actors and audience turned to welcome a tall, motherly lady with a "can-I-help-you" look about her. She was not elegantly dressed, but a noble-looking woman, and the girls thought the gray cloak and unfashionable bonnet covered the most splendid mother in the world.

"Well, dearies, how have you got on today? There was so much to do getting the boxes ready to go tomorrow that I didn't come home to dinner. Has anyone called, Beth? How is your cold, Meg? Jo, you look tired to death. Come and kiss me, baby."

While making these maternal inquiries Mrs. March got her wet things off, her warm slippers on, and sitting down in the easy chair, drew Amy to her lap, preparing to enjoy the happiest hour of her busy day. The girls flew about trying to make things comfortable. Meg arranged the tea table; Jo brought wood and set chairs, dropping, overturning, and clattering everything she touched; Beth trotted to and fro between parlor and kitchen, quiet and busy; while Amy gave directions to everyone as she sat with her hands folded.

As they gathered about the table, Mrs. March said, with a particularly happy face, "I've got a treat for you after supper."

8

A quick, bright smile went round like a streak of sunshine. Beth clapped her hands, regardless of the biscuit she held, and Jo tossed up her napkin, crying: "A letter! A letter! Three cheers for Father!"

"Yes, a nice long letter. He is well, and thinks he shall get through the cold season better than we feared. He sends all sorts of loving wishes for Christmas, and an especial message to you girls," said Mrs. March, patting her pocket as if she had got a treasure there.

"Hurry and get done! Don't stop to quirk your little finger and simper over your plate, Amy," cried Jo.

Beth ate no more, but crept away to sit in her shadowy corner and brood over the delight to come.

"I think it was so splendid in Father to go as a chaplain when he was too old to be drafted, and not strong enough for a soldier," said Meg warmly.

"Don't I wish I could go as a drummer, a vivan—what's its name? Or a nurse, so I could be near him and help him," exclaimed Jo with a groan.

"It must be very disagreeable to sleep in a tent, and eat all sorts of bad-tasting things, and drink out of a tin mug," sighed Amy.

"When will he come home, Marmee?" asked Beth.

"Not for many months, dear, unless he is sick. He will stay and do his work faithfully as long as he can, and we won't ask for him back a minute sooner than he can be spared. Now come and hear the letter."

They all drew to the fire, Mother in the big chair with Beth at her feet, Meg and Amy perched on either arm of the chair, and Jo leaning on the back, where no one would see any sign of emotion if the letter should happen to be touching. Very few letters were written in those hard times that were not touching, especially those which fathers sent home. In this one little was said of the hardships endured, the dangers faced, or the homesickness conquered; it was a cheerful, hopeful letter, and only at the end did the writer's heart overflow with fatherly love and longing for the little girls at home.

"Give them all my dear love and a kiss. Tell them I think of them by day, pray for them by night, and find my best comfort in their affection at all times. A year seems very long to wait before I see them, but remind them that while we wait we may all work, so that these hard days need not be wasted. I know they will remember all I said to them, that they will be loving children to you, will do their duty faithfully, fight their bosom enemies bravely, and conquer themselves so beautifully that when

I come back to them I may be fonder and prouder than ever of my little women."

Everybody sniffed when they came to that part. Jo wasn't ashamed of the great tear that dropped off the end of her nose, and Amy never minded the rumpling of her curls as she hid her face on her mother's shoulder and sobbed out: "I *am* a selfish girl! But I'll truly try to be better, so he mayn't be disappointed in me by and by."

"We all will!" cried Meg. "I think too much of my looks, and hate to work, but I won't any more, if I can help it."

"I'll try and be what he loves to call me, 'a little woman,' and not be rough and wild, but do my duty here instead of wanting to be somewhere else," said Jo, thinking that keeping her temper at home was a much harder task than facing a rebel or two down South.

Beth said nothing, but wiped away her tears with the blue army sock, and began to knit with all her might, losing no time in doing the duty that lay nearest her, while she resolved in her quiet little soul to be all that Father hoped to find her when the year brought round the happy coming-home.

Mrs. March broke the silence that followed Jo's words by saying in her cheery voice: "Do you remember how you used to play *Pilgrim's Progress* when you were little things? Nothing delighted you more than to have me tie my piece bags on your backs for burdens, give you hats and sticks and rolls of paper, and let you travel through the house from the cellar, which was the City of Destruction, up, up, to the housetop, where you had all the lovely things you could collect to make a Celestial City."

"What fun it was, especially going by the lions, fighting Apollyon, and passing through the valley where the hobgoblins were!" said Jo.

"I liked the place where the bundles fell off and tumbled downstairs," said Meg.

"My favorite part was when we came out on the flat roof where our flowers and arbors and pretty things were, and all stood and sang for joy up there in the sunshine," said Beth.

"I don't remember much about it, except that I was afraid of the cellar and the dark entry, and always liked the cake and milk we had up at the top. If I wasn't too old for such things, I'd rather like to play it over again," said Amy, who began to talk of renouncing childish things at the mature age of twelve.

"We never are too old for this, because it is a play we are playing all the time in one way or another. Our burdens are here, our road is before us, and the longing for goodness and happiness is the guide that leads us through many troubles and mistakes to the peace which is a true Celestial City. Now, my little pilgrims, suppose you begin again, not in play, but in earnest, and see how far on you can get before Father comes home."

"Really, Mother? Where are our bundles?" asked Amy.

"Each of you told what your burden was just now, except Beth. I rather think she hasn't got any," said her mother.

"Yes I have. Mine is dishes and dusters, and envying girls with nice pianos, and being afraid of people."

Beth's bundle was such a funny one that everybody wanted to laugh, but nobody did, for it would have hurt her feelings.

"Let us do it," said Meg thoughtfully. "It is only another name for trying to be good, and the story may help us; for though we do want to be good, it's hard work, and we forget, and don't do our best."

"We were in the Slough of Despond tonight, and Mother came and pulled us out as Help did in the book. We ought to have our roll of directions, like Christian. What shall we do about that?" asked Jo.

"Look under your pillows Christmas morning and you will find your guidebook," replied Mrs. March.

They talked over the new plan while old Hannah cleared the table; then out came the four little workbaskets, and the needles flew as the girls made sheets for Aunt March. It was uninteresting sewing, but tonight no one grumbled. They adopted Jo's plan of dividing the long seams into four parts and calling the quarters Europe, Asia, Africa, and America, and in that way got on capitally.

At nine they stopped work, and sang, as usual, before they went to bed. No one but Beth could get much music out of the old piano; but she had a way of softly touching the yellow keys and making a pleasant accompaniment to the simple songs they sang. Meg had a voice like a flute, and she and her mother led the little choir. Amy chirped like a cricket, and Jo wandered through the airs at her own sweet will, always coming out at the wrong place with a croak or a quaver that spoiled the most pensive tune. They had always done this from the time they could lisp "Crinkle, crinkle, 'ittle 'tar," and it had become a household custom, for the mother was a born singer. The first sound in the morning was her voice as she went about the house singing like a lark, and the last sound at night was the same cheery sound, for the girls never grew too old for that familiar lullaby.

A MERRY CHRISTMAS

Jo was the first to wake in the gray dawn of Christmas morning. No stockings hung at the fireplace, and for a moment she felt as much disappointed as she did long ago when her little sock fell down because it was so crammed with goodies. Then she remembered her mother's promise, and slipping her hand under her pillow, drew out a little crimson-covered book. She knew it very well, for it was that beautiful old story of the best life ever lived, and Jo felt that it was a true guidebook for any pilgrim going the long journey. She woke Meg with a "Merry Christmas," and bade her see what was under her pillow. A green-covered book appeared, with the same picture inside, and a few words written by their mother which made their one present very precious in their eyes. Presently Beth and Amy woke, to rummage and find their little books also—one dove-colored, the other blue.

"Girls," said Meg seriously, looking from the tumbled head beside her to the two little nightcapped ones in the room beyond, "Mother wants us to read and love and mind these books, and we must begin at once. We used to be faithful about it; but since Father went away, and all this war trouble unsettled us, we have neglected many things. You can do as you please, but I shall keep my book on the table here and read a little every morning as soon as I wake, for I know it will do me good, and help me through the day."

Then she opened her new book and began to read. Jo put her arm round her and, leaning cheek to cheek, read also, with the quiet expression so seldom seen on her restless face.

"How good Meg is! Come, Amy, let's do as they do. I'll help you with the hard words, and they'll explain things if we don't understand," whispered Beth.

"I'm glad mine is blue," said Amy. And then the rooms were very still while the pages were softly turned, and the winter sunshine crept in to touch the bright heads and serious faces with a Christmas greeting.

"Where is Mother?" asked Meg as she and Jo ran down to thank her for their gifts, half an hour later.

"Goodness only knows. Some poor creeter come a-beggin', and your ma went straight off to see what was needed. There never *was* such a woman for givin' away vittles and drink, clothes and firin'," replied Hannah, who had lived with the family since Meg was born, and was considered by them all more as a friend than a servant.

"She will be back soon, I think, so fry your cakes and have everything ready," said Meg, looking over the presents which were collected in a basket and kept under the sofa, ready to be produced at the proper time. "Why, where is Amy's bottle of cologne?" she added as the little flask did not appear.

"She took it out a minute ago, and went off with it to put a ribbon on it, or some such notion," replied Jo.

"How nice my handkerchiefs look, don't they? Hannah washed and ironed them for me, and I marked them all myself," said Beth, looking proudly at the somewhat uneven letters which had cost her such labor.

"There's Mother. Hide the basket, quick!" cried Jo as a door slammed and steps sounded in the hall.

Amy came in hastily, and looked rather abashed when she saw her sisters all waiting for her.

"Where have you been, and what are you hiding behind you?" asked Meg, surprised to see by her hood and cloak that lazy Amy had been out so early.

"Don't laugh at me, Jo! I didn't mean anyone should know till the time came. I only meant to change the little bottle for a big one, and I gave *all* my money to get it, and I'm truly trying not to be selfish any more."

As she spoke, Amy showed the handsome flask which replaced the cheap one, and looked so earnest and humble in her little effort to forget herself that Meg hugged her on the spot, Jo pronounced her "a trump," and Beth ran to the window and picked her finest rose to ornament the stately bottle.

Another bang of the street door sent the basket under the sofa and the girls to the table, eager for breakfast.

"Merry Christmas, Marmee! Many of them! Thank you for our books. We read some, and mean to every day," they cried in chorus.

"Merry Christmas, little daughters! I'm glad you began at once, and hope you will keep on. But I want to say one word before we sit down. Not far away from here lies a poor woman with a little newborn baby. Six children are huddled into one bed to keep from freezing, for they have no fire. There is nothing to eat over there, and the oldest boy came to tell me they were suffering hunger and cold. My girls, will you give them your breakfast as a Christmas present?"

They were all unusually hungry, having waited nearly an hour, and for a minute no one spoke—only a minute, for Jo exclaimed impetuously:

"I'm so glad you came before we began!"

"May I go and help carry the things to the poor little children?" asked Beth eagerly.

"I shall take the cream and the muffins," added Amy, heroically giving up the articles she most liked.

Meg was already covering the buckwheats, and piling the bread into one big plate.

"I thought you'd do it," said Mrs. March, smiling as if satisfied. "You shall all go and help me, and when we come back we will have bread and milk for breakfast, and make it up at dinnertime."

They were soon ready, and the procession set out. Fortunately it was early, and they went through back streets, so few people saw them, and no one laughed at the queer party.

A poor, bare, miserable room it was, with broken windows, no fire, ragged bedclothes, a sick mother, a wailing baby, and a group of pale, hungry children cuddled under one old quilt trying to keep warm. How the big eyes stared and the blue lips smiled as the girls went in!

"Ach, mein Gott! It is good angels come to us!" said the poor woman, crying for joy.

"Funny angels in hoods and mittens," said Jo, and set them laughing.

In a few minutes it really did seem as if kind spirits had been at work there. Hannah, who had carried wood, made a fire, and stopped up the broken panes with old hats and her own cloak. Mrs. March gave the mother tea and gruel, and comforted her with promises of help, while she dressed the little baby as tenderly as if it had been her own. The girls, meantime, spread the table, set the children round the fire, and fed them like so many hungry birds.

"Das ist gut!" "Die Engelkinder!" cried the poor things as they ate, and warmed their purple hands at the comfortable blaze.

The girls had never been called angel children before, and thought it very agreeable, especially Jo, who had been considered a "Sancho" ever since she was born. That was a very happy breakfast, though they didn't get any of it; and when they went away leaving comfort behind, I think there were not in all the city four merrier people than the hungry little girls who gave away their breakfasts and contented themselves with bread and milk on Christmas morning.

"That's loving our neighbor better than ourselves, and I like it," said Meg as they set out their presents while their mother was upstairs collecting clothes for the poor Hummels.

Not a very splendid show, but there was a great deal of love done up in the few little bundles; and the tall vase of red roses, white chrysanthemums, and trailing vines which stood in the middle gave quite an elegant air to the table.

"She's coming! Strike up, Beth! Open the door, Amy! Three cheers for Marmee!" cried Jo, prancing about while Meg went to conduct Mother to the seat of honor.

Beth played her gayest march, Amy threw open the door, and Meg enacted escort with great dignity. Mrs. March was both surprised and touched, and smiled with her eyes full as she examined her presents and read the little notes which accompanied them. The slippers went on at once, a new handkerchief was slipped into her pocket, well scented with Amy's cologne, the rose was fastened in her bosom, and the nice gloves were pronounced a "perfect fit." There was a good deal of laughing and kissing and explaining, in the simple, loving fashion which makes these home festivals so pleasant at the time, so sweet to remember long afterward, and then all fell to work.

The morning charities and ceremonies took so much time that the rest of the day was devoted to preparations for the evening festivities. Being still too young to go often to the theater, and not rich enough to afford any great outlay for private performances, the girls put their wits to work, and—necessity being the mother of invention—made whatever they needed. Very clever were some of their productions—pasteboard guitars, antique lamps made of old-fashioned butter boats covered with silver paper, gorgeous robes of old cotton glittering with tin spangles from a pickle factory, and armor covered with the same useful diamond-shaped bits, left in sheets when the lids of tin preserve pots were cut out. The furniture was used to being turned topsy-turvy, and the big chamber was the scene of many innocent revels.

No gentlemen were admitted, so Jo played male parts to her heart's content, and took immense satisfaction in a pair of russet-leather boots given her by a friend who knew a lady who knew an actor. These boots, an old foil, and a slashed doublet once used by an artist for some picture were Jo's chief treasures, and appeared on all occasions. The smallness of the company made it necessary for the two principal actors to take several parts apiece; and they certainly deserved some credit for the hard work they did in learning three or four different parts, whisking in and out of various costumes, and managing the stage besides.

On Christmas night, a dozen girls piled onto the bed which was the dress circle, and sat before the blue-and-yellow chintz curtains in a most flattering state of expectancy. There was a good deal of rustling and whispering behind the curtain, a trifle of lamp smoke, and an occasional giggle from Amy, who was apt to get hysterical in the excitement of the moment. Presently a bell sounded, the curtains flew apart, and the *Operatic Tragedy* began.

"A gloomy wood," according to the one playbill, was represented by a few shrubs in pots, green baize on the floor, and a cave in the distance. This cave was made with a clotheshorse for a roof, bureaus for walls; and in it was a small furnace in full blast, with a black pot on it and an old witch bending over it. The stage was dark, and the glow of the furnace had a fine effect, especially as real steam issued from the kettle when the witch took off the cover. A moment was allowed for the first thrill to subside; then Hugo, the villain, stalked in with a clanking sword at his side, a slouched hat, black beard, mysterious cloak, and the boots. After pacing to and fro in much agitation, he struck his forehead and burst out in a wild strain, singing of his hatred to Roderigo, his love for Zara, and his pleasing resolution to kill the one and win the other. The gruff tones of Hugo's voice, with an occasional shout when his feelings overcame him, were very impressive, and the audience applauded the moment he paused for breath. Bowing with the air of one accustomed to public praise, he stole to the cavern and ordered Hagar to come forth with a commanding "What ho, minion! I need thee!"

Out came Meg, with gray horsehair hanging about her face, a red-and-black robe, a staff, and cabalistic signs on her cloak. Hugo demanded a potion to make Zara adore him, and one to destroy Roderigo. Hagar, in a fine dramatic melody, promised both, and proceeded to call up the spirit who would bring the love philter:

> "Hither, hither, from thy home,
> Airy sprite, I bid thee come!
> Born of roses, fed on dew,
> Charms and potions canst thou brew?
> Bring me here, with elfin speed,
> The fragrant philter which I need;

> Make it sweet and swift and strong,
> Spirit, answer now my song!"

A soft strain of music sounded, and then at the back of the cave appeared a little figure in cloudy white, with glittering wings, golden hair, and a garland of roses on its head. Waving a wand, it sang:

> "Hither I come
> From my airy home,
> Afar in the silver moon.
> Take the magic spell,
> And use it well,
> Or its power will vanish soon!"

And, dropping a small, gilded bottle at the witch's feet, the spirit vanished. Another chant from Hagar produced another apparition—not a lovely one; for, with a bang, an ugly black imp appeared, and having croaked a reply, tossed a dark bottle at Hugo and disappeared with a mocking laugh. Having warbled his thanks and put the potions in his boots, Hugo departed; and Hagar informed the audience that as he had killed a few of her friends in times past, she has cursed him, and intends to thwart his plans, and be revenged on him. Then the curtain fell, and the audience reposed and ate candy while discussing the merits of the play.

A good deal of hammering went on before the curtain rose again; but when it became evident what a masterpiece of stage carpentering had been got up, no one murmured at the delay. It was truly superb! A tower rose to the ceiling; halfway up appeared a window with a lamp burning at it, and behind the white curtain appeared Zara in a lovely blue-and-silver dress, waiting for Roderigo. He came in gorgeous array, with plumed cap, red cloak, chestnut lovelocks, a guitar, and the boots, of course. Kneeling at the foot of the tower, he sang a serenade in melting tones. Zara replied, and after a musical dialogue, consented to fly. Then came the grand effect of the play. Roderigo produced a rope ladder with five steps to it, threw up one end, and invited Zara to descend. Timidly she crept from her lattice, put her hand on Roderigo's shoulder, and was about to leap gracefully down when, "Alas! Alas for Zara!" she forgot her train. It caught in the window; the tower tottered, leaned forward, fell with a crash, and buried the unhappy lovers in the ruins! A universal shriek arose as the

17

russet boots waved wildly from the wreck, and a golden head emerged, exclaiming, "I told you so! I told you so!" With wonderful presence of mind, Don Pedro, the cruel sire, rushed in, dragged out his daughter, with a hasty aside: "Don't laugh! Act as if it was all right!" and, ordering Roderigo up, banished him from the kingdom with wrath and scorn. Though decidedly shaken by the fall of the tower upon him, Roderigo defied the old gentleman and refused to stir. This dauntless example fired Zara. She also defied her sire, and he ordered them both to the deepest dungeons of the castle. A stout little retainer came in with chains and led them away, looking very much frightened and evidently forgetting the speech he ought to have made.

Act Third was the castle hall, and here Hagar appeared, having come to free the lovers and finish Hugo. She hears him coming, and hides; sees him put the potions into two cups of wine and bid the timid little servant "Bear them to the captives in their cells, and tell them I shall come anon." The servant takes Hugo aside to tell him something, and Hagar changes the cups for two others which are harmless. Ferdinando, the "minion," carries them away, and Hagar puts back the cup which holds the poison meant for Roderigo. Hugo, getting thirsty after a long warble, drinks it, loses his wits, and, after a good deal of clutching and stamping, falls flat and dies while Hagar informs him what she has done in a song of exquisite power and melody.

Act Fourth displayed the despairing Roderigo on the point of stabbing himself because he has been told that Zara has deserted him. Just as the dagger is at his heart, a lovely song is sung under his window informing him that Zara is true, but in danger, and he can save her, if he will. A key is thrown in, which unlocks the door, and in a spasm of rapture he tears off his chains and rushes away to find and rescue his ladylove.

Act Fifth opened with a stormy scene between Zara and Don Pedro. He wishes her to go into a convent, but she won't hear of it and, after a touching appeal, is about to faint when Roderigo dashes in and demands her hand. Don Pedro refuses, because he is not rich. They shout and gesticulate tremendously, but cannot agree, and Roderigo is about to bear away the exhausted Zara when the timid servant enters with a letter and a bag from Hagar, who has mysteriously disappeared. The latter informs the party that she bequeaths untold wealth to the young pair, and an awful doom to Don Pedro if he doesn't make them happy. The bag is opened, and several quarts of tin money shower down upon the stage, till it is quite glorified with the glitter. This entirely softens the "stern sire." He consents without a murmur, all join in a joyful chorus, and the curtain falls upon the lovers kneeling to receive Don Pedro's blessing in attitudes of the most romantic grace.

Tumultuous applause followed, but received an unexpected check; for the cot bed on which the "dress circle" was built suddenly shut up, and extinguished the enthusiastic audience. Roderigo and Don Pedro flew to the rescue, and all were taken out unhurt, though many were speechless with laughter. The excitement had hardly subsided when Hannah appeared, with Mrs. March's compliments, and would the ladies walk down to supper.

This was a surprise, even to the actors, and when they saw the table, they looked at one another in rapturous amazement. It was like Marmee to get up a little treat for them; but anything so fine as this was unheard-of-since the departed days of plenty. There was ice cream and cake and fruit and distracting French bonbons, and in the middle of the table four great bouquets of hothouse flowers! It quite took their breath away, and they stared first at the table and then at their mother.

"Is it fairies?" asked Amy.

"It's Santa Claus," said Beth.

"Mother did it." And Meg smiled her sweetest, in spite of her gray beard and white eyebrows.

"Aunt March had a good fit, and sent the supper," cried Jo.

"All wrong. Old Mr. Laurence sent it," replied Mrs. March.

"The Laurence boy's grandfather! What in the world put such a thing into his head? We don't know him!" exclaimed Meg.

"Hannah told one of his servants about your breakfast party. He is an odd old gentleman, but that pleased him. He knew my father years ago, and he sent me a polite note this afternoon saying he hoped I would allow him to express his friendly feeling toward my children by sending them a few trifles in honor of the day. I could not refuse, and so you have a little feast at night to make up for the bread-and-milk breakfast."

"That boy put it into his head, I know he did! He's a capital fellow, and I wish we could get acquainted. He looks as if he'd like to know us, but he's bashful, and Meg is so prim she won't let me speak to him when we pass," said Jo.

"You mean the people who live in the big house next door?" asked one of the girls. "My mother knows old Mr. Laurence, but says he's very proud, and doesn't like to mix with his neighbors. He keeps his grandson shut up when he isn't riding or walking with his tutor, and makes him study very hard. We invited him to our party, but he didn't come. Mother says he's very nice, though he never speaks to us girls."

"Our cat ran away once, and he brought her back, and we talked over the fence, and were getting on capitally—all about cricket, and so on— when he saw Meg coming, and walked off. I mean to know him some day, for he needs fun, I'm sure he does," said Jo decidedly.

"I like his manners, and he looks like a little gentleman, so I've no objection to your knowing him, if a proper opportunity comes. He brought the flowers himself, and I should have asked him in if I had been sure what was going on upstairs. He looked so wistful as he went away, hearing the frolic, and evidently having none of his own."

"It's a mercy you didn't, Mother!" laughed Jo, looking at her boots. "But we'll have another play sometime that he *can* see. Perhaps he'll help act. Wouldn't that be jolly?"

THE LAURENCE BOY

"Jo! Jo! Where are you?" cried Meg at the foot of the garret stairs.

"Here!" answered a husky voice from above and running up, Meg found her sister eating apples and crying over *The Heir of Redclyffe*, wrapped up in a comforter on an old three-legged sofa by the sunny window. This was Jo's favorite refuge, and here she loved to retire with half a dozen russets and a nice book, to enjoy the quiet and the society of a pet rat who lived near by, and didn't mind her a particle. As Meg appeared, Scrabble whisked into his hole. Jo shook the tears off her cheeks, and waited to hear the news.

"Such fun! Only see! A regular note of invitation from Mrs. Gardiner for tomorrow night!" cried Meg, waving the precious paper, and then proceeding to read it with girlish delight.

"'Mrs. Gardiner would be happy to see Miss March and Miss Josephine at a little dance on New Year's Eve.' Marmee is willing we should go. Now what *shall* we wear?"

"What's the use of asking that when you know we shall wear our poplins because we haven't got anything else?" answered Jo with her mouth full.

"If I only had a silk!" sighed Meg. "Mother says I may when I'm eighteen, perhaps, but two years is an everlasting time to wait."

"I'm sure our pops look like silk, and they are nice enough for us. Yours is as good as new, but I forgot the burn and the tear in mine. Whatever shall I do? The burn shows badly, and I can't take any out."

"You must sit still all you can, and keep your back out of sight; the front is all right. I shall have a new ribbon for my hair, and Marmee will lend me her little pearl pin, and my new slippers are lovely, and my gloves will do, though they aren't as nice as I'd like."

"Mine are spoiled with lemonade, and I can't get any new ones, so I shall have to go without," said Jo, who never troubled herself much about dress.

"You *must* have gloves, or I won't go," cried Meg decidedly. "Gloves are more important than anything else; you can't dance without them, and if you don't I should be so mortified."

"Then I'll stay still. I don't care much for company dancing; it's no fun to go sailing round. I like to fly about and cut capers."

"You can't ask Mother for new ones, they are so expensive, and you are so careless. She said when you spoiled the others that she shouldn't get you any more this winter. Can't you make them do?" asked Meg anxiously.

"I can hold them crumpled up in my hand, so no one will know how stained they are—that's all I can do. No! I'll tell you how we can manage —each wear one good one and carry a bad one, don't you see?"

"Your hands are bigger than mine, and you will stretch my glove dreadfully," began Meg, whose gloves were a tender point with her.

"Then I'll go without. I don't care what people say!" cried Jo, taking up her book.

"You may have it, you may! Only don't stain it, and do behave nicely. Don't put your hands behind you, or stare, or say 'Christopher Columbus!' will you?"

"Don't worry about me. I'll be as prim as I can, and not get into any scrapes, if I can help it. Now go and answer your note, and let me finish this splendid story."

So Meg went away to "accept with thanks," look over her dress, and sing blithely as she did up her one real-lace frill, while Jo finished her story and her four apples, and had a game of romps with Scrabble.

On New Year's Eve the parlor was deserted, for the two younger girls played dressing maids, and the two elder were absorbed in the all-important business of "getting ready for the party." Simple as the toilets were, there was a great deal of running up and down, laughing and talking, and at one time a strong smell of burned hair pervaded the house. Meg wanted a few curls about her face, and Jo undertook to pinch the papered locks with a pair of hot tongs.

"Ought they to smoke like that?" asked Beth from her perch on the bed.

"It's the dampness drying," replied Jo.

"What a queer smell! It's like burned feathers," observed Amy, smoothing her own pretty curls with a superior air.

"There, now I'll take off the papers and you'll see a cloud of little ringlets," said Jo, putting down the tongs.

She did take off the papers, but no cloud of ringlets appeared, for the hair came with the papers, and the horrified hairdresser laid a row of little scorched bundles on the bureau before her victim.

"Oh, oh, oh! What *have* you done? I'm spoiled! I can't go! My hair, oh, my hair!" wailed Meg, looking with despair at the uneven frizzle on her forehead.

"Just my luck! You shouldn't have asked me to do it, I always spoil everything. I'm so sorry, but the tongs were too hot, and so I've made a mess," groaned poor Jo, regarding the black pancakes with tears of regret.

"It isn't spoiled. Just frizzle it, and tie your ribbon so the ends come on your forehead a bit, and it will look like the last fashion. I've seen many girls do it so," said Amy consolingly.

"Serves me right for trying to be fine. I wish I'd let my hair alone," cried Meg petulantly.

"So do I, it was so smooth and pretty. But it will soon grow out again," said Beth, coming to kiss and comfort the shorn sheep.

After various lesser mishaps, Meg was finished at last, and by the united exertions of the family Jo's hair was got up and her dress on. They looked very well in their simple suits—Meg in silvery drab, with a blue-velvet snood, lace frills, and the pearl pin; Jo in maroon, with a stiff, gentlemanly linen collar, and a white chrysanthemum or two for her only ornament. Each put on one nice light glove and carried one soiled one. Meg's high-heeled slippers were very tight, and hurt her, though she would not own it, and Jo's nineteen hairpins all seemed stuck straight into her head, which was not exactly comfortable; but, dear me, let us be elegant or die!

"Have a good time, dearies!" said Mrs. March as the sisters went daintily down the walk. "Don't eat much supper, and come away at eleven, when I send Hannah for you." As the gate clashed behind them, a voice cried from a window: "Girls, girls! *Have* you both got nice pocket handkerchiefs?"

"Yes, yes, spendy nice, and Meg has cologne on hers," cried Jo, adding with a laugh as they went on, "I do believe Marmee would ask that if we were all running away from an earthquake."

"It is one of her aristocratic tastes, and quite proper, for a real lady is always known by neat boots, gloves, and handkerchief," replied Meg, who had a good many little "aristocratic tastes" of her own.—"Now don't forget to keep the bad breadth out of sight, Jo. Is my sash right? And does my hair look *very* bad?" said Meg as she turned from the glass in Mrs. Gardiner's dressing room, after a prolonged prink.

"I know I shall forget. If you see me doing anything wrong, just remind me by a wink, will you?" returned Jo.

"No, winking isn't ladylike. I'll lift my eyebrows if anything is wrong, and nod if you are all right. Now hold your shoulders straight, and take short steps, and don't shake hands if you are introduced to anyone. It isn't the thing."

Down they went, feeling a trifle timid, for they seldom went to parties, and informal as this little gathering was, it was an event to them. Mrs. Gardiner, a stately old lady, greeted them kindly, and handed them over to the eldest of her six daughters. Meg knew Sallie, and was at her ease very soon; but Jo, who didn't care much for girls or girlish gossip, stood about with her back carefully against the wall, and felt as much out of place as a colt in a flower garden. Half a dozen jovial lads were talking about skates in another part of the room, and she longed to go and join them, for skating was one of the joys of her life. She telegraphed her wish to Meg, but the eyebrows went up so alarmingly that she dared not stir. No one came to talk to her, and one by one the group near her dwindled away till she was left alone. She could not roam about and amuse herself, for the burned breadth would show, so she stared at people rather forlornly till the dancing began. Meg was asked at once, and the tight slippers tripped about so briskly that none would have guessed the pain their wearer suffered smilingly. Jo saw a big redheaded youth approaching her corner, and fearing he meant to engage her, she slipped into a curtained recess, intending to peep and enjoy herself in peace. Another bashful person had chosen the same refuge; for as the curtain fell behind her, she found herself face to face with the "Laurence boy."

"Dear me, I didn't know anyone was here!" stammered Jo, preparing to back out as speedily as she had bounced in.

But the boy laughed, and said pleasantly, though he looked a little startled, "Don't mind me. Stay, if you like."

"Shan't I disturb you?"

"Not a bit. I only came here because I don't know many people, and felt rather strange at first, you know."

"So did I. Don't go away, please, unless you'd rather."

The boy sat down again and looked at his pumps till Jo said, trying to be polite and easy: "I think I've had the pleasure of seeing you before. You live near us, don't you?"

"Next door." And he looked up and laughed outright, for Jo's prim manner was rather funny when he remembered how they had chatted about cricket when he brought the cat home.

That put Jo at her ease, and she laughed too as she said, "We did have such a good time over your nice Christmas present."

"Grandpa sent it."

"But you put it into his head, didn't you now?"

"How is your cat, Miss March?" asked the boy, trying to look sober while his black eyes shone with fun.

"Nicely, thank you, Mr. Laurence. But I am not Miss March, I'm only Jo," returned the young lady.

"I'm not Mr. Laurence, I'm only Laurie."

"Laurie Laurence—what an odd name!"

"My first name is Theodore, but I don't like it, for the fellows called me Dora, so I made them say Laurie instead."

"I hate my name, too—so sentimental! I wish everyone would say Jo instead of Josephine. How did you make the boys stop calling you Dora?"

"I thrashed 'em."

"I can't thrash Aunt March, so I suppose I shall have to bear it." And Jo resigned herself with a sigh.

"Don't you like to dance, Miss Jo?" asked Laurie.

"I like it well enough if there is plenty of room, and everyone is lively. In a place like this I'm sure to upset something, tread on people's toes, or do something dreadful, so I keep out of mischief and let Meg sail about. Don't you dance?"

"Sometimes. You see I've been abroad a good many years, and haven't been into company enough yet to know how you do things here."

"Abroad!" cried Jo. "Oh, tell me about it! I love dearly to hear people describe their travels."

Laurie didn't seem to know where to begin, but Jo's eager questions soon set him going, and he told her how he had been at school in Vevay, where the boys never wore hats, and had a fleet of boats on the lake, and for holiday fun went on walking trips about Switzerland with their teachers.

"Don't I wish I'd been there! Did you go to Paris?"

"We spent last winter there."

"Can you talk French?"

"We were not allowed to speak anything else at Vevay."

"Do say some! I can read it, but can't pronounce."

"*Quel nom a cette jeune demoiselle en les pantoufles jolis?*" said Laurie good-naturedly.

"How nicely you do it! Let me see—you said, 'Who is the young lady in the pretty slippers,' didn't you?"

"*Oui, mademoiselle.*"

"It's my sister Margaret, and you knew it was! Do you think she is pretty?"

"Yes. She makes me think of the German girls, she looks so fresh and quiet, and dances like a lady."

Jo quite glowed with pleasure at this boyish praise of her sister, and stored it up to repeat to Meg. Both peeped and criticized and chatted till they felt like old acquaintances. Laurie's bashfulness soon wore off, for Jo's gentlemanly demeanor amused him and set him at his ease, and Jo was her merry self again, because her dress was forgotten, and nobody lifted their eyebrows at her. She liked the "Laurence boy" better than ever, and took several good looks at him, so that she might describe him to the girls, for they had no brothers, very few male cousins, and boys were almost unknown creatures to them.

"Curly black hair; brown skin; big black eyes; handsome nose; fine teeth; small hands and feet; taller than I am; very polite, for a boy, and altogether jolly. Wonder how old he is?" It was on the tip of Jo's tongue to ask, but she checked herself in time, and, with unusual tact, tried to find out in a roundabout way. "I suppose you are going to college soon? I see you pegging away at your books—no, I mean studying hard." And Jo blushed at the dreadful "pegging" which had escaped her.

Laurie smiled, but didn't seem shocked, and answered, with a shrug: "Not for a year or two. I won't go before seventeen, anyway."

"Aren't you but fifteen?" asked Jo.

"Sixteen next month."

"How I wish I was going to college! You don't look as if you liked it."

"I hate it! Nothing but grinding or skylarking. And I don't like the way fellows do either, in this country."

"What do you like?"

"To live in Italy, and to enjoy myself in my own way."

Jo wanted very much to ask what his own way was; but his black brows looked rather threatening as he knit them, so she changed the subject by saying, as her foot kept time:

"That's a splendid polka! Why don't you go and try it?"

"If you will come too," he answered, with a gallant little bow.

"I can't, for I told Meg I wouldn't, because——" There Jo stopped, and looked undecided whether to tell or to laugh.

"Because what?" asked Laurie curiously.

"You won't tell?"

"Never!"

"Well, I have a bad trick of standing before the fire, and so I burn my frocks, and I scorched this one. And though it's nicely mended, it shows, and Meg told me to keep still, so no one would see it. You may laugh, if you want to; it is funny, I know."

But Laurie didn't laugh; he only looked down a minute, and the expression of his face puzzled Jo when he said very gently: "Never mind that—I'll tell you how we can manage—there's a long hall out there, and we can dance grandly and no one will see us. Please come?"

Jo thanked him, and gladly went. The hall was empty, and they had a grand polka; for Laurie danced well, and taught her the German step, which delighted Jo, being full of swing and spring. When the music stopped, they sat down on the stairs to get their breath, and Laurie was in the midst of an account of a students' festival at Heidelberg when Meg appeared in search of her sister. She beckoned, and Jo reluctantly followed her into a side room, where she found her on a sofa, holding her foot and looking pale.

"I've sprained my ankle. That stupid high heel turned, and gave me a sad wrench. It aches so I can hardly stand, and I don't know how I'm ever going to get home," she said, rocking to and fro in pain.

"I knew you'd hurt your feet with those silly shoes. I'm sorry. But I don't see what you can do, except get a carriage, or stay here all night," answered Jo, softly rubbing the poor ankle as she spoke.

"I can't have a carriage without its costing ever so much. I dare say I can't get one at all, for most people come in their own, and it's a long way to the stable, and no one to send."

"I'll go."

"No indeed! It's past nine, and dark as Egypt. I can't stop here, for the house is full. Sallie has some girls staying with her. I'll rest till Hannah comes, and then do the best I can."

"I'll ask Laurie. He will go," said Jo, looking relieved as the idea occurred to her.

"Mercy no! Don't ask or tell anyone. Get me my rubbers, and put these slippers with our things. I can't dance any more, but as soon as supper is over, watch for Hannah, and tell me the minute she comes."

"They are going out to supper now. I'll stay with you. I'd rather."

"No, dear, run along, and bring me some coffee. I'm so tired I can't stir!"

So Meg reclined, with rubbers well hidden, and Jo went blundering away to the dining room, which she found after going into a china closet and opening the door of a room where old Mr. Gardiner was taking a little private refreshment. Making a dart at the table, she secured the coffee, which she immediately spilled, thereby making the front of her dress as bad as the back.

"Oh dear, what a blunderbuss I am!" exclaimed Jo, finishing Meg's glove by scrubbing her gown with it.

"Can I help you?" said a friendly voice, and there was Laurie, with a full cup in one hand and a plate of ice in the other.

"I was trying to get something for Meg, who is very tired, and someone shook me and here I am in a nice state," answered Jo, glancing dismally from the stained skirt to the coffee-colored glove.

"Too bad! I was looking for someone to give this to. May I take it to your sister?"

"Oh, thank you! I'll show you where she is. I don't offer to take it myself, for I should only get into another scrape if I did."

Jo led the way, and as if used to waiting on ladies, Laurie drew up a little table, brought a second installment of coffee and ice for Jo, and was so obliging that even particular Meg pronounced him a "nice boy." They were in the midst of a quiet game of Buzz with two or three other young people who had strayed in when Hannah appeared. Meg forgot her foot, and rose so quickly that she was forced to catch hold of Jo, with an exclamation of pain.

"Hush! Don't say anything," she whispered, adding aloud: "It's nothing. I turned my foot a little, that's all," and limped upstairs to put her things on.

Hannah scolded, Meg cried, and Jo was at her wit's end till she decided to take things into her own hands. Slipping out, she ran down and, finding a servant, asked if he could get her a carriage. It happened to be a hired waiter who knew nothing about the neighborhood, and Jo was looking round for help, when Laurie, who had heard what she said, came up and offered his grandfather's carriage, which had just come for him, he said.

"It's so early! You can't mean to go yet?" began Jo.

"I always go early—I do, truly! Please let me take you home, it's all on my way, you know, and it rains, they say."

That settled it, and telling him of Meg's mishap, Jo gratefully accepted, and rushed up to bring down the rest of the party. So they rolled away in the luxurious closed carriage feeling very festive and elegant. Laurie went on the box, and the girls talked over their party in freedom.

"I had a capital time. Did you?" asked Jo.

"Yes, till I hurt myself. Sallie's friend Annie Moffat took a fancy to me, and asked me to come and spend a week with her when Sallie does. She is going in the spring, when the opera comes, and it will be perfectly splendid, if Mother only lets me go," answered Meg, cheering up at the thought. "What *were* you about all that time?"

Jo told her adventures, and by the time she had finished they were at home. With many thanks, they said "Good night," and crept in, hoping to disturb no one; but the instant their door creaked, two little nightcaps bobbed up, and two sleepy but eager voices cried out:

"Tell about the party! Tell about the party!"

With what Meg called "a great want of manners," Jo had saved some bonbons for the little girls, and they soon subsided, after hearing the most thrilling events of the evening.

"I declare it really seems like being a fine young lady to come home from the party in a carriage, and sit in my dressing gown with a maid to wait on me," said Meg as Jo bound up her foot with arnica, and brushed her hair.

"I don't believe fine young ladies enjoy themselves a bit more than we do, in spite of our burned hair, old gowns, one glove apiece, and tight slippers that sprain our ankles when we are really silly enough to wear them."

Burdens

"Oh dear, how hard it does seem to take up our packs and go on," sighed Meg the morning after the party; for now the holidays were over, the week of merrymaking did not fit her for going on easily with the task she never liked.

"I wish it was Christmas or New Year all the time. Wouldn't it be fun?" answered Jo, yawning dismally.

"We shouldn't enjoy ourselves half so much as we do now. But it does seem so nice to have little suppers and bouquets, and go to parties, and drive home, and read and rest, and not work. It's like other people, you know, and I always envy girls who do such things. I'm so fond of luxury," said Meg.

"Well, we can't have it, so don't let us grumble, but shoulder our bundles and trudge along as cheerfully as Marmee does. I'm sure Aunt March is a regular Old Man of the Sea to me, but I suppose when I've learned to carry her without complaining, she will tumble off, or get so light that I shan't mind her."

This idea tickled Jo's fancy, and put her in good spirits; but Meg didn't brighten, for her burden of four spoiled children seemed heavier than ever. She hadn't heart enough even to make herself pretty, as usual, by putting on a blue neck ribbon and dressing her hair in the most becoming way.

"Where's the use of looking nice when no one sees me but those cross midgets, and no one cares whether I'm pretty or not?" she muttered, shutting her drawer with a jerk. "I shall have to toil and moil all my days, with only little bits of fun now and then, and get old and ugly and sour, because I'm poor, and can't enjoy my life as other girls do. It's a shame!"

So Meg went down wearing an injured look, and wasn't at all agreeable at breakfast time. Everyone seemed rather out of sorts, and inclined to croak. Beth had a headache, and lay on the sofa trying to comfort herself with the cat and three kittens; Amy was fretting because her lessons were not learned, and she couldn't find her rubbers; Jo *would* whistle and make a great racket getting ready; Mrs. March was very busy trying to finish a letter which must go at once; and Hannah had the grumps, for being up late didn't suit her.

"There never *was* such a cross family!" cried Jo, losing her temper when she had upset an inkstand, broken both boot lacings, and sat down on her hat.

"You're the crossest person in it!" returned Amy, washing out the sum that was all wrong with the tears that had fallen on her slate.

"Beth, if you don't keep these horrid cats down cellar I'll have them drowned," exclaimed Meg angrily as she tried to get rid of the kitten which had scrambled up her back, and stuck like a burr just out of reach. Jo laughed, Meg scolded, Beth implored, and Amy wailed because she couldn't remember how much nine times twelve was.

"Girls, girls, do be quiet one minute! I *must* get this off by the early mail, and you drive me distracted with your worry," cried Mrs. March, crossing out the third spoiled sentence in her letter.

There was a momentary lull, broken by Hannah, who stalked in, laid two hot turnovers on the table, and stalked out again. These turnovers were an institution, and the girls called them "muffs," for they had no others, and found the hot pies very comforting to their hands on cold mornings. Hannah never forgot to make them, no matter how busy or grumpy she might be, for the walk was long and bleak; the poor things got no other lunch, and were seldom home before two.

"Cuddle your cats, and get over your headache, Bethy. Good-by, Marmee. We are a set of rascals this morning, but we'll come home regular angels. Now then, Meg!" and Jo tramped away.

They always looked back before turning the corner, for their mother was always at the window, to nod and smile and wave her hand to them; whatever their mood might be, the last glimpse of that motherly face was sure to affect them like sunshine.

"If Marmee shook her fist instead of kissing her hand to us, it would serve us right, for more ungrateful wretches than we are were never seen," cried Jo, taking a remorseful satisfaction in the snowy walk and bitter wind.

"Don't use such dreadful expressions," said Meg from the depths of the veil in which she had shrouded herself like a nun sick of the world.

"I like good strong words that mean something," replied Jo, catching her hat as it took a leap off her head preparatory to flying away altogether.

"Call yourself any names you like, but I am neither a rascal nor a wretch, and I don't choose to be called so."

"You're a blighted being, and decidedly cross today because you can't sit in the lap of luxury all the time. Poor dear, just wait till I make my fortune, and you shall revel in carriages and ice cream and high-heeled slippers and posies."

"How ridiculous you are, Jo!" But Meg laughed at the nonsense, and felt better in spite of herself.

"Lucky for you I am, for if I put on crushed airs and tried to be dismal, as you do, we should be in a nice state. Thank goodness I can always find something funny to keep me up. Don't croak any more, but come home jolly, there's a dear."

Jo gave her sister an encouraging pat on the shoulder as they parted for the day, each going a different way, each hugging her little warm turnover, and each trying to be cheerful in spite of wintry weather, hard work, and the unsatisfied desires of pleasure-loving youth.

When Mr. March lost his property in trying to help an unfortunate friend, the two oldest girls begged to be allowed to do something toward their own support, at least. Believing that they could not begin too early to cultivate energy, industry, and independence, their parents consented, and both fell to work with the hearty goodwill which in spite of all obstacles is sure to succeed at last. Margaret found a place as nursery governess, and felt rich with her small salary. As she said, she *was* "fond of luxury," and her chief trouble was poverty. She found it harder to bear than the others, because she could remember a time when home was beautiful, life full of ease and pleasure, and want of any kind unknown. At the Kings' she daily saw all she wanted, for the children's older sisters were just out, and Meg caught frequent glimpses of dainty ball dresses and bouquets, heard lively gossip about theaters, concerts, sleighing parties, and merrymakings of all kinds, and saw money lavished on trifles which would have been so precious to her.

Jo happened to suit Aunt March, who was lame and needed an active person to wait on her. The childless old lady had offered to adopt one of the girls when the troubles came, and was much offended because her offer was declined. Other friends told the Marches that they had lost all chance of being remembered in the rich old lady's will, but the unworldly Marches only said:

"We can't give up our girls for a dozen fortunes. Rich or poor, we will keep together and be happy in one another."

The old lady wouldn't speak to them for a time, but happening to meet Jo at a friend's, something in her comical face and blunt manners struck the old lady's fancy, and she proposed to take her for a companion. This did not suit Jo at all; but she accepted the place, since nothing better appeared, and to everyone's surprise, got on remarkably well with her irascible relative. There was an occasional tempest, and once Jo had marched home declaring she couldn't bear it any longer; but Aunt March always cleared up quickly, and sent for her back again with such urgency that she could not refuse, for in her heart she rather liked the peppery old lady.

I suspect that the real attraction was a large library of fine books, which was left to dust and spiders since Uncle March died. Jo remembered the kind old gentleman, who used to let her build railroads and bridges with his big dictionaries, tell her stories about the queer pictures in his Latin books, and buy her cards of gingerbread whenever he met her in the street. The dim, dusty room, with the busts staring down from the tall bookcases, the cozy chairs, the globes, and best of all, the wilderness of books, in which she could wander where she liked, made the library a region of bliss to her. The moment Aunt March took her nap, or was busy with company, Jo hurried to this quiet place, and curling herself up in the easy chair, devoured poetry, romance, history, travels, and pictures like a regular bookworm. But, like all happiness, it did not last long; for as sure as she had just reached the heart of the story, the sweetest verse of the song, or the most perilous adventure of her traveler, a shrill voice called "Josy-phine! Josy-phine!" and she had to leave her paradise to wind yarn, wash the poodle, or read Belsham's *Essays* by the hour together.

Jo's ambition was to do something very splendid. What it was she had no idea as yet, but left it for time to tell her, and meanwhile found her greatest affliction in the fact that she couldn't read, run, and ride as much as she liked. A quick temper, a sharp tongue, and a restless spirit were always getting her into scrapes, and her life was a series of ups and downs which were both comic and pathetic. But the training she received at Aunt March's was just what she needed, and the thought that she was doing something to support herself made her happy in spite of the perpetual "Josy-phine!"

Beth was too bashful to go to school; it had been tried, but she suffered so much that it was given up, and she did her lessons at home with her father. Even when he went away Beth went faithfully on by herself, and did the best she could. She was a housewifely little creature, and helped Hannah keep home neat and comfortable for the workers, never thinking of any reward but to be loved. Long, quiet days she spent, not lonely nor idle, for her little world was peopled with imaginary friends, and she was by nature a busy bee. There were six dolls to be taken up and dressed every morning, for Beth was a child still. Not one whole or handsome one among them—all were outcasts till Beth took them in; for when her sisters outgrew these idols, they passed to her because Amy would have nothing old or ugly. Beth cherished them all the more tenderly for that very reason, and set up a hospital for infirm dolls. No pins were ever stuck into their cotton vitals; no harsh words or blows were ever given them; no neglect ever saddened the heart of the most repulsive; but all were fed and clothed, nursed and caressed, with an affection which never failed.

Beth had her troubles as well as the others, and not being an angel, but a very human little girl, she often "wept a little weep," as Jo said, because she couldn't take music lessons and have a fine piano. She loved music so dearly, tried so hard to learn, and practiced away so patiently at the jingling old instrument, that it did seem as if someone (not to hint Aunt

March) ought to help her. Nobody did, however, and nobody saw Beth wipe the tears off the yellow keys that wouldn't keep in tune, when she was all alone. She sang like a little lark about her work, and day after day said hopefully to herself, "I know I'll get my music sometime, if I'm good."

If anybody had asked Amy what the greatest trial of her life was, she would have answered at once, "My nose." When she was a baby, Jo had accidentally dropped her into the coal hod, and Amy insisted that the fall had ruined her nose forever. It was not big, nor red like poor "Petrea's"; it was only rather flat, and all the pinching in the world could not give it an aristocratic point. No one minded it but herself, and it was doing its best to grow, but Amy felt deeply the want of a Grecian nose, and drew whole sheets of handsome ones to console herself.

"Little Raphael," as her sisters called her, had a decided talent for drawing, and was never so happy as when copying flowers, designing fairies, or illustrating stories with queer specimens of art. Her teachers complained that instead of doing her sums, she covered her slate with animals; the blank pages of her atlas were used to copy maps on; and caricatures of the most ludicrous description came fluttering out of all her books at unlucky moments. She got through her lessons as well as she could, and managed to escape reprimands by being a model of deportment. She was a great favorite with her mates, being good-tempered, and possessing the happy art of pleasing without effort. Her little airs and graces were much admired, so were her accomplishments; for beside her drawing, she could play twelve tunes, crochet, and read French without mispronouncing more than two-thirds of the words.

Amy was in a fair way to be spoiled, for everyone petted her, and her small vanities and selfishnesses were growing nicely. One thing, however, rather quenched the vanities; she had to wear her cousin's clothes. Now Florence's mamma hadn't a particle of taste, and Amy suffered deeply at having to wear a red instead of a blue bonnet, unbecoming gowns, and fussy aprons that did not fit. Everything was good, well made, and little worn; but Amy's artistic eyes were much afflicted, especially this winter, when her school dress was a dull purple with yellow dots and no trimming.

"My only comfort," she said to Meg, with tears in her eyes, "is that Mother don't take tucks in my dresses whenever I'm naughty, as Maria Parks's mother does. My dear, it's really dreadful, for sometimes she is so bad her frock is up to her knees, and she can't come to school. When

34

I think of this *deggerredation*, I feel that I can bear even my flat nose and purple gown with yellow skyrockets on it."

Meg was Amy's confidant and monitor, and by some strange attraction of opposites, Jo was gentle Beth's. To Jo alone did the shy child tell her thoughts, and over her big harum-scarum sister Beth unconsciously exercised more influence than anyone else in the family. The two older girls were a great deal to one another, but each took one of the younger into her keeping, and watched over her in her own way; "playing mother," they called it.

"Has anybody got anything to tell? It's been such a dismal day I'm really dying for some amusement," said Meg as they sat sewing together that evening.

"I had a queer time with Aunt today, and as I got the best of it, I'll tell you about it," began Jo, who dearly loved to tell stories. "I was reading that everlasting Belsham, and droning away as I always do, for Aunt soon drops off and then I take out some nice book and read like fury till she wakes up. I actually made myself sleepy, and before she began to nod, I gave such a gape that she asked me what I meant by opening my mouth wide enough to take the whole book in at once.

"'I wish I could, and be done with it,' said I, trying not to be saucy.

"Then she gave me a long lecture on my sins, and told me to sit and think them over while she just 'lost' herself for a moment. She never finds herself very soon, so the minute her cap began to bob like a top-heavy dahlia, I whipped *The Vicar of Wakefield* out of my pocket and read away, with one eye on him and one on Aunt. I'd just got to where they all tumbled into the water when I forgot, and laughed out loud. Aunt woke up, and being more good-natured after her nap, told me to read a bit, and show what frivolous work I preferred to the worthy and instructive Belsham. I did my very best, and she liked it, though she only said: 'I don't understand what it's all about. Go back and begin it, child.'

"Back I went, and made the Primroses as interesting as ever I could. Once I was wicked enough to stop in a thrilling place and say meekly, 'I'm afraid it tires you, ma'am. Shan't I stop now?' She caught up her knitting, which she had dropped out of her hands, gave me a sharp look, and said, in her short way: 'Finish the chapter, and don't be impertinent, miss.'"

"Did she own she liked it?" asked Meg.

"Oh bless you no! But she let old Belsham rest, and when I ran back after my gloves this afternoon, there she was, so hard at the V*icar* that she didn't hear me laugh as I danced a jig in the hall because of the good time coming. I don't envy her much, in spite of her money," added Jo.

"That reminds me," said Meg, "that I've got something to tell. It isn't funny, like Jo's story, but I thought about it a good deal as I came home. At the Kings' today I found everybody in a flurry, and one of the children said that her oldest brother had done something dreadful, and Papa had sent him away. I heard Mrs. King crying and Mr. King talking very loud, and Grace and Ellen turned away their faces when they passed me, so I shouldn't see how red their eyes were. I felt so sorry for them, and was rather glad I hadn't any wild brothers to do wicked things and disgrace the family."

"I think being disgraced in school is a great deal try*inger* than anything bad boys can do," said Amy, shaking her head as if her experience of life had been a deep one. "Susie Perkins came to school today with a lovely red carnelian ring. I wanted it dreadfully, and wished I was her with all my might. Well, she drew a picture of Mr. Davis with a monstrous nose and a hump, and the words, 'Young ladies, my eye is upon you!' coming out of his mouth in a balloon thing. We were laughing over it when all of a sudden his eye *was* on us, and he ordered Susie to bring up her slate. She was *parry*lized with fright, but she went, and oh, what *do* you think he did? He took her by the ear—the ear! Just fancy how horrid!—and led her to the recitation platform, and made her stand there half an hour holding that slate so everyone could see."

"Didn't the girls laugh at the picture?" asked Jo.

"Laugh? Not one! They sat as still as mice, and Susie cried quarts, I know she did. I didn't envy her then, for I felt that millions of carnelian rings wouldn't have made me happy after that. I never, never should have got over such a agonizing mortification." And Amy went on with her work, in the proud consciousness of virtue and the successful utterance of two long words in a breath.

"I saw something that I liked this morning, and I meant to tell it at dinner, but I forgot," said Beth, putting Jo's topsy-turvy basket in order as she talked. "When I went to get some oysters for Hannah, Mr. Laurence was in the fish shop; but he didn't see me, for I kept behind a barrel. A poor woman came in with a pail and a mop, and asked Mr. Cutter if he would let her do some scrubbing for a bit of fish, because she hadn't any dinner for her children, and had been disappointed of a day's work. Mr. Cutter was in a hurry, and said 'No,' rather crossly; so she was going away, looking hungry and sorry, when Mr. Laurence hooked up a big fish with the crooked end of his cane and held it out to her. She was so glad and surprised she took it right in her arms, and thanked him over and over. He told her to 'go along and cook it,' and she hurried off, so happy! Wasn't it good of him? Oh, she did look so funny hugging the big, slippery fish and hoping Mr. Laurence's bed in Heaven would be 'aisy.' "

BEING NEIGHBORLY

"What in the world are you going to do now, Jo?" asked Meg one snowy afternoon as her sister came tramping through the hall in rubber boots, old sack and hood, with a broom in one hand and a shovel in the other.

"Going out for exercise," answered Jo.

"I should think two long walks this morning would have been enough! It's cold and dull out, and I advise you to stay warm and dry by the fire, as I do," said Meg with a shiver.

"Never take advice! Can't keep still all day, and not being a pussycat, I don't like to doze by the fire. I like adventures, and I'm going to find some."

Meg went back to toast her feet and read *Ivanhoe*, and Jo began to dig paths with great energy. The snow was light, and with her broom she soon swept a path all round the garden. Now the garden separated the Marches' house from that of Mr. Laurence. Both stood in a suburb of the city, which was still countrylike, with groves and lawns, large gardens, and quiet streets. A low hedge parted the two estates. On one side was an old brown house, looking rather bare and shabby robbed of the vines that in summer covered its walls and the flowers which then surrounded it. On the other side was a stately stone mansion, plainly betokening every sort of comfort and luxury, from the big coach house and well-kept grounds to the conservatory. Yet it seemed a lonely, lifeless sort of house; for no children frolicked on the lawn, no motherly face ever smiled at the windows, and few people went in and out except the old gentleman and his grandson.

To Jo's lively fancy, this fine house seemed a kind of enchanted palace, full of splendors and delights which no one enjoyed. She had long wanted to behold these hidden glories, and to know the "Laurence boy," who looked as if he would like to be known if he only knew how to begin. Since the party, she had been more eager than ever, and had planned many ways of making friends with him; but he had not been seen lately, and Jo began to think he had gone away when she one day spied a brown face at the upper window, looking wistfully down into their garden, where Beth and Amy were snowballing one another.

"That boy is suffering for society and fun," she said to herself. "His grandpa does not know what's good for him, and keeps him shut up all alone. He needs a party of jolly boys to play with, or somebody young and lively. I've a great mind to go over and tell the old gentleman so!"

The idea amused Jo, who liked to do daring things and was always scandalizing Meg by her queer performances. The plan of "going over" was not forgotten, and when the snowy afternoon came, Jo resolved to try what could be done. She saw Mr. Laurence drive off, and then sallied out to dig her way down to the hedge, where she paused and took a survey. All quiet—curtains down at the lower windows, servants out of sight, and nothing human visible but a curly black head leaning on a thin hand at the upper window.

"There he is," thought Jo, "poor boy! All alone and sick this dismal day. It's a shame! I'll toss up a snowball and make him look out, and then say a kind word to him."

Up went a handful of soft snow, and the head turned at once, showing a face which lost its listless look in a minute. Jo nodded and laughed, and flourished her broom as she called out: "How do you do? Are you sick?"

Laurie opened the window, and croaked out as hoarsely as a raven: "Better, thank you. I've had a bad cold and been shut up a week."

"I'm sorry. What do you amuse yourself with?"

"Nothing. It's as dull as tombs up here."

"Don't you read?"

"Not much. They won't let me."

"Can't somebody read to you?"

"Grandpa does, sometimes; but my books don't interest him, and I hate to ask Brooke all the time."

"Have someone come and see you, then."

"There isn't anyone I'd like to see. Boys make such a row, and my head is weak."

"Isn't there some nice girl who'd read and amuse you? Girls are quiet, and like to play nurse."

"Don't know any."

"You know us," began Jo, then laughed, and stopped.

"So I do! Will you come, please?" cried Laurie.

"I'm not quiet and nice, but I'll come if Mother will let me. I'll go ask her. Shut that window, like a good boy, and wait till I come."

With that, Jo shouldered her broom and marched into the house, wondering what they would all say to her. Laurie was in a flutter of excitement at the idea of having company, and flew about to get ready. Presently there came a loud ring, then a decided voice asking for "Mr. Laurie," and a surprised-looking servant came running up to announce a young lady.

"All right, show her up. It's Miss Jo," said Laurie, going to the door of his little parlor to meet Jo, who appeared with a covered dish in one hand and Beth's three kittens in the other.

"Here I am, bag and baggage," she said briskly. "Mother sent her love, and was glad if I could do anything for you. Meg wanted me to bring some of her blancmange—she makes it very nicely—and Beth thought her cats would be comforting. I knew you'd laugh at them, but I couldn't refuse, she was so anxious to do something."

It so happened that Beth's funny loan was just the thing, for in laughing over the kits Laurie forgot his bashfulness, and grew sociable at once.

"That looks too pretty to eat," he said, smiling with pleasure as Jo uncovered the dish and showed the blancmange, surrounded by a garland of green leaves and the scarlet flowers of Amy's pet geranium.

"It isn't anything, only they all felt kindly, and wanted to show it. Tell the girl to put it away for your tea. It's so simple you can eat it, and it will slip down without hurting your sore throat. What a cozy room this is!"

"It might be if it was kept nice, but the maids are lazy, and I don't know how to make them mind. It worries me."

"I'll right it up in two minutes; for it only needs to have the hearth brushed, so—and the things made straight on the mantelpiece, so—and the books put here, and the bottles there, and your sofa turned from the light, and the pillows plumped up a bit. Now then, you're fixed."

And so he was, for as she laughed and talked Jo had whisked things into place, and given quite a different air to the room. Laurie watched her in respectful silence and when she beckoned him to his sofa, he sat down with a sigh of satisfaction, saying gratefully: "How kind you are!

39

Yes, that's what it wanted. Now please take the big chair, and let me do something to amuse my company."

"No—I came to amuse you. Shall I read aloud?" And Jo looked affectionately toward some inviting books near by.

"Thank you, I've read all those, and if you don't mind, I'd rather talk," answered Laurie.

"Not a bit. I'll talk all day if you'll only set me going. Beth says I never know when to stop."

"Is Beth the rosy one who stays at home a good deal, and sometimes goes out with a little basket?" asked Laurie.

"Yes, that's Beth. She's my girl, and a regular good one she is, too."

"The pretty one is Meg, and the curly-haired one is Amy, I believe?"

"How did you find that out?"

Laurie colored up, but answered frankly: "Why, you see I often hear you calling to one another, and when I'm alone up here, I can't help looking over at your house, you always seem to be having such good times. I beg your pardon for being so rude, but sometimes you forget to put down the curtain at the window where the flowers are; and when the lamps are lighted, it's like looking at a picture to see the fire, and you all round the table with your mother. Her face is right opposite, and it looks so sweet behind the flowers I can't help watching it. I haven't got any mother, you know."

The solitary, hungry look in his eyes went straight to Jo's warm heart. She had been so simply taught that there was no nonsense in her head, and at fifteen she was as innocent and frank as any child. Laurie was sick and lonely, and feeling how rich she was in home love and happiness, she gladly tried to share it with him. Her face was very friendly and her sharp voice unusually gentle as she said:

"We'll never draw that curtain any more, and I give you leave to look as much as you like. I just wish, though, instead of peeping, you'd come over and see us. Mother is so splendid she'd do you heaps of good, and Beth would sing to you if I begged her to, and Amy would dance, Meg and I would make you laugh over our funny stage properties, and we'd have jolly times. Wouldn't your grandpa let you?"

"I think he would, if your mother asked him. He's very kind, though he does not look so; and he lets me do what I like, pretty much, only he's afraid I might be a bother to strangers," began Laurie, brightening more and more.

"We are not strangers, we are neighbors, and you needn't think you'd be a bother. We *want* to know you, and I've been trying to do it this ever so long. We haven't been here a great while, you know, but we have got acquainted with all our neighbors but you."

"You see Grandpa lives among his books, and doesn't mind much what happens outside. Mr. Brooke, my tutor, doesn't stay here, you know, and I have no one to go about with me, so I just stop at home and get on as I can."

"That's bad. You ought to make an effort, and go visiting everywhere you are asked. Then you'll have plenty of friends, and pleasant places to go to. Never mind being bashful; it won't last long if you keep going."

Laurie turned red again, but wasn't offended at being accused of bashfulness, for there was so much goodwill in Jo it was impossible not to take her blunt speeches as kindly as they were meant.

"Do you like your school?" asked the boy, changing the subject.

"Don't go to school. I'm a businessman—girl, I mean. I go to wait on my great-aunt, and a dear, cross old soul she is, too," answered Jo.

Laurie opened his mouth to ask another question, but remembering just in time that it wasn't manners to make too many inquiries into people's affairs, he shut it again, and looked uncomfortable. Jo liked his good breeding, and didn't mind having a laugh at Aunt March, so she gave him a lively description of the fidgety old lady, her fat poodle, the parrot, and the library where she reveled. Laurie enjoyed that immensely.

"Oh, that does me no end of good! Tell on, please."

Much elated with her success, Jo did "tell on," all about their plays and plans, their hopes and fears for Father, and the most interesting events of the little world in which the sisters lived. Then they got to talking about books, and to Jo's delight, she found that Laurie loved them as well as she did, and had read even more than herself.

"If you like them so much, come down and see ours. Grandpa is out, so you needn't be afraid," said Laurie.

"I'm not afraid of anything," returned Jo, with a toss of the head.

"I don't believe you are!" exclaimed the boy, looking at her with much admiration, though he privately thought she would have good reason to be a trifle afraid of the old gentleman if she met him in some of his moods.

The atmosphere of the whole house being summerlike, Laurie led the way from room to room, letting Jo stop to examine whatever struck her fancy; and so at last they came to the library, where she clapped her hands, and pranced, as she always did when especially delighted. It was lined with books, and there were pictures and statues, and distracting little cabinets full of coins and curiosities, and sleepy-hollow chairs, and queer tables, and bronzes; and best of all, a great open fireplace, with quaint tiles all round it.

"What richness!" sighed Jo, sinking into the depth of a velvet chair and gazing about her with an air of intense satisfaction. "Theodore Laurence, you ought to be the happiest boy in the world," she added impressively.

"A fellow can't live on books," said Laurie, shaking his head.

Before he could say more, a bell rang, and Jo flew up, exclaiming with alarm: "Mercy me! It's your grandpa!"

"Well, what if it is? You are not afraid of anything, you know," returned the boy, looking wicked.

"I think I am a little bit afraid of him, but I don't know why I should be. Marmee said I might come, and I don't think you're any the worse for it," said Jo, composing herself.

"I'm a great deal better for it, and ever so much obliged. I'm only afraid you are very tired talking to me. It was so pleasant I couldn't bear to stop," said Laurie gratefully.

"The doctor to see you, sir," and the maid beckoned as she spoke.

"Would you mind if I left you for a minute? I suppose I must see him," said Laurie.

"Don't mind me. I'm as happy as a cricket here."

Laurie went away, and his guest amused herself in her own way. She was standing before a fine portrait of the old gentleman when the door opened again, and, without turning, she said decidedly: "I'm sure now that I shouldn't be afraid of him, for he's got kind eyes, though his mouth is grim and he looks as if he had a tremendous will of his own. He isn't as handsome as *my* grandfather, but I like him."

"Thank you, ma'am," said a gruff voice behind her, and there, to her great dismay, stood old Mr. Laurence.

Poor Jo blushed till she couldn't blush any redder, and her heart began to beat uncomfortably fast as she thought what she had said. For a minute a wild desire to run away possessed her; but that was cowardly, and the girls would laugh at her, so she resolved to stay and get out of the scrape as she could. A second look showed her that the living eyes under the bushy gray eyebrows were kinder even than the painted ones, and there was a sly twinkle in them which lessened her fear a good deal. The gruff voice was gruffer than ever as the old gentleman said abruptly, "So you're not afraid of me, hey?"

"Not much, sir."

"And you don't think me as handsome as your grandfather?"

"Not quite, sir."

"And I've got a tremendous will, have I?"

"I only said I thought so."

"But you like me, in spite of it?"

"Yes, I do, sir."

That answer pleased the old gentleman. He gave a short laugh, shook hands with her, and putting his finger under her chin, turned up her face, examined it gravely, and let it go, saying with a nod:

"You've got your grandfather's spirit, if you haven't his face. He *was* a fine man, my dear, but what is better, he was a brave and an honest one, and I was proud to be his friend."

"Thank you, sir."

"What have you been doing to this boy of mine, hey?" was the next question, sharply put.

"Only trying to be neighborly, sir." And Jo told how her visit came about.

"You think he needs cheering up a bit, do you?"

"Yes, sir. He seems a little lonely, and young folks would do him good perhaps. We are only girls, but we should be glad to help if we could, for we don't forget the splendid Christmas present you sent us," said Jo eagerly.

"I shall come and see your mother some fine day. Tell her so. There's the tea bell; we have it early, on the boy's account. Come down, and go on being neighborly."

"If you'd like to have me, sir."

"Shouldn't ask you if I didn't." And Mr. Laurence offered her his arm with old-fashioned courtesy.

"What *would* Meg say to this?" thought Jo as she was marched away.

"Hey! Why, what the dickens has come to the fellow?" said the old gentleman as Laurie came running downstairs and brought up with a start of surprise at the astonishing sight of Jo arm-in-arm with his redoubtable grandfather.

"I didn't know you'd come, sir."

"That's evident by the way you racket downstairs. Come to your tea, sir, and behave like a gentleman." And having pulled the boy's hair by

43

way of a caress, Mr. Laurence walked on, while Laurie went through a series of comic evolutions behind their backs which nearly produced an explosion of laughter from Jo.

The old gentleman did not say much as he drank his four cups of tea, but he watched the young people, who soon chatted away like old friends, and the change in his grandson did not escape him. There was color, light, and life in the boy's face now, vivacity in his manner, and genuine merriment in his laugh.

"She's right, the lad *is* lonely. I'll see what these little girls can do for him," thought Mr. Laurence. He liked Jo, for her odd, blunt ways suited him, and she seemed to understand the boy almost as well as if she had been one herself.

If the Laurences had been what Jo called "prim and poky," she would not have got on at all, for such people always made her shy and awkward; but finding them free and easy, she was so herself, and made a good impression. When they rose she proposed to go, but Laurie said he had something more to show her and took her away to the conservatory. It seemed quite fairylike to Jo as she went up and down the walks enjoying the blooming walls on either side, the soft light, the damp sweet air, and the wonderful vines and trees that hung above her. Her new friend cut the finest flowers till his hands were full; then he tied them up, saying, with the happy look Jo liked to see: "Please give these to your mother, and tell her I like the medicine she sent me very much."

They found Mr. Laurence standing before the fire in the great drawing room, but Jo's attention was entirely absorbed by a grand piano, which stood open.

"Do you play?" she asked, turning to Laurie with a respectful expression.

"Sometimes," he answered modestly.

"Please do now. I want to hear it, so I can tell Beth."

"Won't you first?"

"Don't know how—too stupid to learn—but I love music dearly."

So Laurie played, and Jo listened, with her nose luxuriously buried in heliotrope and tea roses. Her respect and regard for the "Laurence boy" increased very much, for he played remarkably well, and didn't put on any airs. She wished Beth could hear him, but she did not say so, only praised him till he was quite abashed and his grandfather came to the rescue.

"That will do, that will do, young lady. Too many sugarplums are not good for him. His music isn't bad, but I hope he will do as well in more important things. Going? Well, I'm much obliged to you, and I hope you'll come again. My respects to your mother. Good night, Dr. Jo."

He shook hands kindly, but looked as if something did not please him. When they got into the hall, Jo asked Laurie if she had said anything amiss. He shook his head.

"No, it was me. He doesn't like to hear me play."

"Why not?"

"I'll tell you someday. You will come again, I hope?"

"If you promise to come and see us after you are well."

"I will."

"Good night, Laurie!"

"Good night, Jo, good night!"

When all the afternoon's adventures had been told, the family felt inclined to go visiting in a body, for each found something very attractive in the big house on the other side of the hedge. Mrs. March wanted to talk of her father with the old man who had not forgotten him; Meg longed to walk in the conservatory; Beth sighed for the grand piano; and Amy was eager to see the fine pictures and statues.

"Mother, why didn't Mr. Laurence like to have Laurie play?" asked Jo, who was of an inquiring disposition.

"I am not sure, but I think it was because his son, Laurie's father, married an Italian lady, a musician, which displeased the old man, who is very proud. The lady was good and lovely and accomplished, but he did not like her, and never saw his son after he married. They both died when Laurie was a little child, and then his grandfather took him home. I fancy the boy, who was born in Italy, is not very strong, and the old man is afraid of losing him, which makes him so careful. Laurie comes naturally by his love of music, for he is like his mother, and I dare say his grandfather fears that he may want to be a musician. At any rate, his skill reminds him of the woman he did not like, and so he 'glowered,' as Jo said."

"Dear me, how romantic!" exclaimed Meg.

"How silly!" said Jo. "Let him be a musician, if he wants to, and not plague his life out sending him to college when he hates to go."

"That's why he has such handsome black eyes and pretty manners, I suppose. Italians are always nice," said Meg, who was a little sentimental.

"What do you know about his eyes and his manners? You never spoke to him, hardly," cried Jo, who was *not* sentimental.

"I saw him at the party, and what you tell shows that he knows how to behave. That was a nice little speech about the medicine mother sent him."

"He meant the blancmange, I suppose."

"How stupid you are, child! He meant you, of course."

"Did he?" And Jo opened her eyes as if it had never occurred to her before.

"I never saw such a girl! You don't know a compliment when you get it," said Meg.

"I think they are great nonsense, and I'll thank you not to be silly, and spoil my fun. Laurie's a nice boy, and I like him, and I won't have any sentimental stuff about compliments and such rubbish. We'll all be good to him, because he hasn't got any mother, and he *may* come over and see us, mayn't he, Marmee?"

"Yes, Jo, your friend is very welcome, and I hope Meg will remember that children should be children as long as they can."

"I don't call myself a child, and I'm not in my teens yet," observed Amy. "What do you say, Beth?"

"I was thinking about our *Pilgrim's Progress,*" answered Beth, who had not heard a word. "How we got out of the Slough and through the Wicket Gate by resolving to be good, and up the steep hill by trying, and that maybe the house over there, full of splendid things, is going to be our Palace Beautiful."

"We have got to get by the lions first," said Jo, as if she rather liked the prospect.

ᗷETH FINDS THE PALACE BEAUTIFUL

The big house did prove a Palace Beautiful, though it took some time for all to get in, and Beth found it very hard to pass the lions. Old Mr. Laurence was the biggest one; but after he had called, said something funny or kind to each one of the girls, and talked over old times with their mother, nobody felt much afraid of him except timid Beth. The other lion was the fact that they were poor and Laurie rich, for this made them shy of accepting favors which they could not return. But after a while they found that he considered them the benefactors, and could not do enough to show how grateful he was for Mrs. March's motherly welcome, their cheerful society, and the comfort he took in that humble home of theirs. So they soon forgot their pride, and interchanged kindnesses without stopping to think which was the greater.

All sorts of pleasant things happened about that time, for the new friendship flourished like grass in spring. Everyone liked Laurie, and he privately informed his tutor that the Marches were "regularly splendid girls." With the delightful enthusiasm of youth, they took the solitary boy into their midst, and made much of him, and he found something very charming in the innocent companionship of these simplehearted girls. He was tired of books, and found people so interesting now that Mr. Brooke was obliged to make very unsatisfactory reports; for Laurie was always playing truant and running over to the Marches'.

"Never mind. Let him take a holiday, and make it up afterward," said the old gentleman. "The good lady next door says he is studying too hard, and needs young society, amusement, and exercise. I suspect she is right, and that I've been coddling the fellow as if I'd been his grandmother. Let him do what he likes as long as he is happy. He can't get into mischief in that little nunnery over there."

What good times they had, to be sure! Such plays and tableaux, such sleigh rides and skating frolics, such pleasant evenings in the old parlor, and now and then such gay little parties at the great house. Meg could walk in the conservatory whenever she liked, and revel in bouquets; Jo browsed over the new library voraciously, and convulsed the old gentleman with her criticisms; Amy copied pictures, and enjoyed beauty to her heart's content; and Laurie played "lord of the manor" in the most delightful style.

But Beth, though yearning for the grand piano, could not pluck up courage to go to the "Mansion of Bliss," as Meg called it. She went once with Jo; but the old gentleman, not being aware of her infirmity, stared at her so hard from under his heavy eyebrows, and said "Hey!" so loud, that he frightened her so much her "feet chattered on the floor," she told her mother, and she ran away, declaring she would never go there any more, not even for the dear piano. No persuasions or enticements could overcome her fear till, the fact coming to Mr. Laurence's ear in some mysterious way, he set about mending matters. During one of the brief calls he made, he artfully led the conversation to music, and talked away about great singers whom he had seen, fine organs he had heard, and told such charming ancedotes that Beth found it impossible to stay in her distant corner, but crept nearer and nearer, as if fascinated. At the back of his chair she stopped and stood listening, with her great eyes wide-open. Taking no more notice of her than if she had been a fly, Mr. Laurence talked on about Laurie's lessons and teachers, and presently, as if the idea had just occurred to him, he said to Mrs. March:

"The boy neglects his music now, and I'm glad of it, for he was getting too fond of it. But the piano suffers for want of use. Wouldn't some of your girls like to run over and practice on it now and then, just to keep it in tune, you know, ma'am?"

Beth took a step forward and pressed her hands tightly together to keep from clapping them, for this was an irresistible temptation. Before Mrs. March could reply, Mr. Laurence went on with an odd little nod and smile: "They needn't see or speak to anyone, but run in at any time; for I'm shut up in my study at the other end of the house, Laurie is out a great deal, and the servants are never near the drawing room after nine o'clock."

Here he rose, as if going, and Beth made up her mind to speak, for that last arrangement left nothing to be desired. "Please tell the young ladies what I say; and if they don't care to come, why, never mind." Here a little hand slipped into his, and Beth looked up at him with a face full of gratitude as she said, "O sir, they do care, very, very much!"

"Are you the musical girl?" he asked, without any startling "Hey!" as he looked down at her kindly.

"I'm Beth. I love it dearly, and I'll come if you are quite sure nobody will hear me—and be disturbed."

"Not a soul, my dear. The house is empty half the day, so come and drum away as much as you like."

"How kind you are, sir!"

Beth blushed like a rose under the friendly look he wore; but she was not frightened now, and gave the big hand a grateful squeeze, because she had no words to thank him for the precious gift he had given her. The old gentleman softly stroked the hair off her forehead and, stooping down, he kissed her, saying, in a tone few people ever heard: "I had a little girl once, with eyes like these. God bless you, my dear! Good day, madam." And away he went, in a great hurry.

Beth had a rapture with her mother, and then rushed up to impart the glorious news to her family of invalids, as the girls were not at home. How blithely she sang that evening, and how they all laughed at her because she woke Amy in the night by playing the piano on her face in her sleep. Next day, having seen both the old and young gentleman out of the house, Beth, after two or three retreats, fairly got in at the side door and made her way as noiselessly as any mouse to the drawing room, where her idol stood. Quite by accident, of course, some pretty, easy music lay on the piano; and with trembling fingers, and frequent stops to listen and look about, Beth at last touched the great instrument, and straightway forgot her fear, herself, and everything else but the unspeakable delight which the music gave her. She stayed till Hannah came to take her home to dinner, but she had no appetite, and could only sit and smile upon everyone in a general state of beatitude.

After that, the little brown hood slipped through the hedge nearly every day, and the great drawing room was haunted by a tuneful spirit that came and went unseen. She never knew that Mr. Laurence often opened his study door to hear the old-fashioned airs he liked; she never saw Laurie mount guard in the hall to warn the servants away; she never suspected that the exercise books and new songs which she found in the rack were put there for her especial benefit; and when he talked to her about music at home, she only thought how kind he was to tell things that helped her so much. So she enjoyed herself heartily, and found, what isn't always the case, that her granted wish was all she had hoped.

"Mother, I'm going to work Mr. Laurence a pair of slippers. He is so kind to me I must thank him, and I don't know any other way. Can I do it?" asked Beth, a few weeks after that eventful call of his.

"Yes, dear. It will please him very much, and be a nice way of thanking him. The girls will help you about them, and I will pay for the making up," replied Mrs. March.

After many serious discussions with Meg and Jo, the pattern was chosen, the materials bought, and the slippers begun. A cluster of grave yet cheerful pansies, on a deeper purple ground, was pronounced very appropriate and pretty; and Beth worked away early and late, with occasional lifts over hard parts. She was a nimble little needlewoman, and they were finished before anyone got tired of them. Then she wrote a very short, simple note and, with Laurie's help, got them smuggled onto the study table one morning before the old gentleman was up.

When this excitement was over, Beth waited to see what would happen. All that day passed, and a part of the next, before any acknowledgment arrived, and she was beginning to fear she had offended her crotchety friend. On the afternoon of the second day, she went out to do an errand, and give poor Joanna, the invalid doll, her daily exercise. As she came up the street on her return, she saw three—yes, four—heads popping in and out of the parlor windows, and the moment they saw her, several hands were waved, and several joyful voices screamed: "Here's a letter from the old gentleman! Come quick and read it!"

"O Beth, he's sent you——" began Amy; but she got no further, for Jo quenched her by slamming down the window.

Beth hurried on in a flutter of suspense. At the door, her sisters seized and bore her to the parlor in a triumphal procession, all pointing, and all saying at once, "Look there! Look there!" Beth did look, and turned pale with delight and surprise; for there stood a little cabinet piano, with a letter lying on the glossy lid, directed to "Miss Elizabeth March."

"For me?" gasped Beth, holding onto Jo, and feeling as if she should tumble down.

"Yes, all for you, my precious! Isn't it splendid of him? Here's the key in the letter. We didn't open it, but we are dying to know what he says," cried Jo, hugging her sister, and offering the note.

"You read it! I can't, I feel so queer! Oh, it is too lovely!" And Beth hid her face in Jo's apron, quite upset by her present.

Jo opened the paper and began to laugh, for the first words she saw were,

Miss March:
Dear Madam,

"How nice it sounds! I wish someone would write to me so!" said Amy.

" 'I have had many pairs of slippers in my life, but I never had any that suited me so well as yours,' " continued Jo. " 'Heartsease is my favorite flower, and these will always remind me of the gentle giver. I like to pay my debts, so I know you will allow "the old gentleman" to send you something which once belonged to the little granddaughter he lost. With hearty thanks and best wishes, I remain

" 'Your grateful friend and humble servant,

" 'James Laurence' "

"There, Beth, that's an honor to be proud of, I'm sure! Laurie told me how fond Mr. Laurence used to be of the child who died, and how he kept all her little things carefully. Just think, he's given you her piano. That comes of having big blue eyes and loving music," said Jo, trying to soothe Beth, who trembled, and looked more excited than she had ever been before.

"See the cunning brackets to hold candles, and the nice green silk, puckered up, with a gold rose in the middle, and the pretty rack and stool, all complete," added Meg, opening the instrument and displaying its beauties.

" 'Your humble servant, James Laurence'—only think of his writing that to you," said Amy, much impressed by the note.

"Try it, honey," said Hannah, who always took a share in the family joys and sorrows.

So Beth tried it, and everyone pronounced it the most remarkable piano ever heard. It had evidently been newly tuned and put in apple-pie order; but, perfect as it was, I think the real charm of it lay in the happiest of all happy faces which leaned over it as Beth lovingly touched the beautiful black and white keys and pressed the bright pedals.

"You'll have to go and thank him," said Jo, by way of a joke, for the idea of the child's really going never entered her head.

"Yes, I mean to. I guess I'll go now, before I get frightened thinking about it." And, to the utter amazement of the assembled family, Beth walked deliberately down the garden, through the hedge, and in at the Laurences' door.

"Well, I wish I may die if it ain't the queerest thing I ever see! The pianny has turned her head! She'd never have gone in her right mind," cried Hannah, staring after her, while the girls were rendered quite speechless by the miracle.

They would have been still more amazed if they had seen what Beth did afterward. If you will believe me, she went and knocked at the study door before she gave herself time to think, and when a gruff voice called out "Come in!" she did go in, right up to Mr. Laurence, who looked quite taken aback, and held out her hand, saying, with only a small quaver in her voice, "I came to thank you, sir, for——" But she didn't finish; for he looked so friendly that she forgot her speech, and only remembering that he had lost the little girl he loved, she put both arms round his neck and kissed him.

If the roof of the house had suddenly flown off, the old gentleman wouldn't have been more astonished; but he liked it—oh dear yes, he liked it amazingly!—and was so touched and pleased by that confiding little kiss that all his crustiness vanished, and he just set her on his knee and laid his wrinkled cheek against her rosy one, feeling as if he had got his own little granddaughter back again. Beth ceased to fear him from that moment, and sat there talking to him as cozily as if she had known him all her life. When she went home, he walked with her to her own gate, shook hands cordially, and touched his hat as he marched back again, looking very stately and erect, like a handsome, soldierly old gentleman, as he was.

When the girls saw that performance, Jo began to dance a jig by way of expressing her satisfaction; Amy nearly fell out of the window in her surprise; and Meg exclaimed, "Well, I do believe the world is coming to an end!"

MY'S VALLEY OF HUMILIATION

"That boy is a perfect Cyclops, isn't he?" said Amy, one day as Laurie clattered by on horseback.

"How dare you say so when he's got both his eyes? And very handsome ones they are, too," cried Jo, who resented any slighting remarks about her friend.

"I didn't say anything about his eyes, and I don't see why you need fire up when I admire his riding."

"Oh my goodness! That little goose means a centaur, and she called him a Cyclops," exclaimed Jo.

"You needn't be so rude; it's only a 'lapse of lingy,' as Mr. Davis says," retorted Amy, finishing Jo with her Latin. "I just wish I had a little of the money Laurie spends on that horse."

"Why?" asked Meg kindly, for Jo had gone off in another laugh at Amy's second blunder.

"I need it so much. I'm dreadfully in debt, and it won't be my turn to have the rag money for a month."

"In debt, Amy? What do you mean?" And Meg looked sober.

"Why, I owe at least a dozen pickled limes, and I can't pay them, you know, till I have money, for Marmee forbade my having anything charged at the shop."

"Tell me all about it. Are limes the fashion now? It used to be pricking bits of rubber to make balls." And Meg tried to keep her countenance, Amy looked so grave and important.

"Why, you see the girls are always buying them, and unless you want to be thought mean, you must do it too. It's nothing but limes now, for everyone is sucking them in their desks in schooltime, and trading them off for pencils, bead rings, paper dolls, or something else, at recess. If one girl likes another, she gives her a lime; if she's mad with her, she eats one before her face and don't offer even a suck. They treat by turns, and I've had ever so many, but haven't returned them; and I ought, for they are debts of honor, you know."

53

"How much will pay them off and restore your credit?" asked Meg, taking out her purse.

"A quarter would more than do it, and leave a few cents over for a treat for you. Don't you like limes?"

"Not much. You may have my share. Here's the money. Make it last as long as you can."

"Oh thank you! It must be so nice to have pocket money! I'll have a grand feast, for I haven't tasted a lime this week. I felt delicate about taking any, as I couldn't return them, and I'm actually suffering for one."

Next day Amy was rather late at school, but could not resist the temptation of displaying, with pardonable pride, a moist brown-paper parcel before she consigned it to the inmost recesses of her desk. During the next few minutes the rumor that Amy March had got twenty-four delicious limes (she ate one on the way), and was going to treat, circulated through her "set," and the attentions of her friends became quite overwhelming. Katy Brown invited her to her next party on the spot; Mary Kingsley insisted on lending her her watch till recess; and Jenny Snow, a satirical young lady who had basely twitted Amy upon her limeless state, promptly buried the hatchet and offered to furnish answers to certain appalling sums. But Amy had not forgotten Miss Snow's cutting remarks about "some persons whose noses were not too flat to smell other people's limes, and stuck-up people who were not too proud to ask for them," and she instantly crushed "that Snow girl's" hopes by the withering telegram, "You needn't be so polite all of a sudden, for you won't get any."

A distinguished personage happened to visit the school that morning, and Amy's beautiful maps received praise, which honor to her foe rankled in the soul of Miss Snow, and caused Miss March to assume the airs of a studious young peacock. But, alas, alas! pride goes before a fall, and the revengeful Snow turned the tables with disastrous success. No sooner had the guest bowed himself out than Jenny, under pretense of asking an important question, informed Mr. Davis, the teacher, that Amy March had pickled limes in her desk.

Now Mr. Davis had declared limes a contraband article, and solemnly vowed to publicly ferule the first person who was found breaking the law. This much-enduring man had done all that one man could do to keep half a hundred rebellious girls in order. It was a most unfortunate moment for denouncing Amy, and Jenny knew it. Mr. Davis had evidently taken his coffee too strong that morning; there was an east wind, which always affected his neuralgia; and his pupils had not done him the credit which he felt he deserved; therefore, to use the expressive, if not elegant, language of a schoolgirl, he was "as nervous as a witch and as cross as a bear." The word "limes" was like fire to powder; his yellow face flushed, and he rapped on his desk with an energy which made Jenny skip to her seat with unusual rapidity.

"Young ladies, attention, if you please!" At the stern order the buzz ceased, and fifty pairs of blue, black, gray, and brown eyes were obediently fixed upon his awful countenance. "Miss March, come to the desk." Amy rose to comply with outward composure, but a secret fear oppressed her, for the limes weighed upon her conscience. "Bring with you the limes you have in your desk" was the unexpected command which arrested her before she got out of her seat.

"Don't take all," whispered her neighbor, a young lady of great presence of mind.

Amy hastily shook out half a dozen, and laid the rest down before Mr. Davis, feeling that any man possessing a human heart would relent when that delicious perfume met his nose. Unfortunately, Mr. Davis particularly detested the odor of the fashionable pickle, and disgust added to his wrath.

"Is that all?"

"Not quite," stammered Amy.

"Bring the rest immediately." With a despairing glance at her set, she obeyed. "You are sure there are no more?"

"I never lie, sir."

"So I see. Now take these disgusting things two by two, and throw them out of the window."

There was a simultaneous sigh, which created quite a little gust, as the last hope fled and the treat was ravished from their longing lips. Scarlet with shame and anger, Amy went to and fro, and as each doomed couple —looking oh! so plump and juicy—fell from her reluctant hands, a shout from the street completed the anguish of the girls, for it told them that their feast was being exulted over by the little Irish children who were their sworn foes.

As Amy returned from her last trip, Mr. Davis said, in his most impressive manner: "Young ladies, you remember what I said to you a week ago. I am sorry this has happened, but I never allow my rules to be infringed, and I *never* break my word. Miss March, hold out your hand."

Amy started, and put both hands behind her, turning on him an imploring look which pleaded for her better than the words she could not utter. She was rather a favorite with "old Davis," as of course he was called, and it's my private belief that he *would* have broken his word if the indignation of one irrepressible young lady had not found vent in a hiss. That hiss irritated the irascible gentleman, and sealed the culprit's fate.

"Your hand, Miss March!" was the only answer her mute appeal received; and, too proud to cry or beseech, Amy set her teeth, threw back her head defiantly, and bore without flinching several tingling blows on her little palm. They were neither many nor heavy, but that made no difference to her. For the first time in her life she had been struck, and the disgrace, in her eyes, was as deep as if he had knocked her down.

"You will now stand on the platform till recess," said Mr. Davis, resolved to do the thing thoroughly, since he had begun.

That was dreadful. It would have been bad enough to go to her seat and see the pitying faces of her friends, or the satisfied ones of her few enemies; but to face the whole school with that shame fresh upon her seemed impossible, and for a second she felt as if she could only drop down where she stood, and break her heart with crying. A bitter sense of wrong, and the thought of Jenny Snow, helped her to bear it; and, taking the ignominious place, she stood there so motionless and white that the girls found it very hard to study with that pathetic figure before them.

During the fifteen minutes that followed, the proud and sensitive little girl suffered a shame and pain which she never forgot. To others it might seem a ludicrous or trivial affair, but to her it was a hard experience; for during the twelve years of her life she had been governed by love alone, and a blow of that sort had never touched her before. The smart of her hand and the ache of her heart were forgotten in the sting of the thought: "I shall have to tell at home, and they will be so disappointed in me!"

The fifteen minutes seemed an hour, but they came to an end at last, and the word "Recess!" had never seemed so welcome to her before.

"You can go, Miss March," said Mr. Davis, looking, as he felt, uncomfortable.

He did not soon forget the reproachful glance Amy gave him as she went, without a word to anyone, straight into the anteroom, snatched her things, and left the place "forever," as she passionately declared to herself. She was in a sad state when she got home, and when the older girls arrived, sometime later, an indignation meeting was held at once. Mrs. March did not say much, but looked disturbed, and comforted her afflicted little daughter in her tenderest manner. Meg bathed the insulted hand with glycerine and tears; Beth felt that even her beloved kittens would fail as a balm for griefs like this; Jo wrathfully proposed that Mr. Davis be arrested without delay; and Hannah shook her fist at the "villain," and pounded potatoes for dinner as if she had him under her pestle.

No notice was taken of Amy's flight except by her mates, but the sharp-eyed demoiselles discovered that Mr. Davis was quite benignant in the afternoon, also unusually nervous. Just before school closed, Jo appeared, wearing a grim expression as she stalked up to the desk and delivered a letter from her mother, then collected Amy's property and departed, carefully scraping the mud from her boots on the door mat, as if she shook the dust of the place off her feet.

"Yes, you can have a vacation from school, but I want you to study a little every day, with Beth," said Mrs. March that evening. "I don't approve of corporal punishment, especially for girls. I dislike Mr. Davis's manner of teaching, and don't think the girls you associate with are doing you any good, so I shall ask your father's advice before I send you anywhere else."

"That's good! I wish all the girls would leave, and spoil his old school. It's perfectly maddening to think of those lovely limes," sighed Amy, with the air of a martyr.

"I am not sorry you lost them, for you broke the rules, and deserved some punishment for disobedience," was the severe reply, which rather disappointed the young lady, who expected nothing but sympathy.

"Do you mean you are glad I was disgraced before the whole school?" cried Amy.

"I should not have chosen that way of mending a fault," replied her mother, "but I'm not sure that it won't do you more good than a milder method. You are getting to be rather conceited, my dear, and it is quite time you set about correcting it. You have a good many little gifts and virtues, but there is no need of parading them, for conceit spoils the finest genius. There is not much danger that real talent or goodness will be overlooked long, and the great charm of all power is modesty."

"So it is!" cried Laurie, who was playing chess in a corner with Jo. "I knew a girl once who had a really remarkable talent for music, and she didn't know it—never guessed what sweet little things she composed when she was alone, and wouldn't have believed it if anyone had told her."

"I wish I'd known that nice girl. Maybe she would have helped me, I'm so stupid," said Beth.

"You do know her, and she helps you better than anyone else could," answered Laurie, looking at her with such mischievous meaning in his merry black eyes that Beth suddenly turned very red, and hid her face in the sofa cushion, quite overcome by such an unexpected discovery.

Beth could not be prevailed upon to play for them after her compliment. So Laurie did his best, and sang delightfully, being in a particularly lively humor, for to the Marches he seldom showed the moody side of his character. When he was gone, Amy, who had been pensive all the evening, said suddenly, as if busy over some new idea: "Is Laurie an accomplished boy?"

"Yes. He has had an excellent education, and has much talent; he will make a fine man, if not spoiled by petting," replied her mother.

"And he isn't conceited, is he?" asked Amy.

"Not in the least. That is why he is so charming, and we all like him so much."

"I see. It's nice to have accomplishments, and be elegant, but not to show off, or get perked up," said Amy thoughtfully.

"These things are always seen and felt in a person's manner and conversation, if modestly used, but it is not necessary to display them," said Mrs. March.

"Any more than it's proper to wear all your bonnets and gowns and ribbons at once, that folks may know you've got them," added Jo, and the lecture ended in a laugh.

JO MEETS APOLLYON

"Girls, where are you going?" asked Amy, coming into their room one Saturday afternoon and finding them getting ready to go out with an air of secrecy which excited her curiosity.

"Never mind. Little girls shouldn't ask questions," returned Jo sharply.

Now if there *is* anything mortifying to our feelings when we are young, it is to be told that; and to be bidden to "run away, dear," is still more trying to us. Amy bridled up at this insult, and determined to find out the secret if she teased for an hour. Turning to Meg, who never refused her anything very long, she said coaxingly: "Do tell me! I should think you might let me go too; for I haven't got anything to do, and am *so* lonely."

"I can't, dear, because you aren't invited," began Meg, but Jo broke in impatiently: "Now, Meg, be quiet. You can't go, Amy, so don't be a baby and whine about it."

"You are going somewhere with Laurie, I know you are. You were whispering and laughing together on the sofa last night, and you stopped when I came in. Aren't you going with him?"

"Yes, we are. Now do be still, and stop bothering."

Amy held her tongue, but used her eyes, and saw Meg slip a fan into her pocket.

"I know! I know! You're going to the theater to see *The Seven Castles!*" she cried, adding resolutely, "and I *shall* go, for Mother said I might see it, and I've got my rag money."

"Just listen to me a minute, and be a good child," said Meg soothingly. "Mother doesn't wish you to go this week, because your eyes are not well enough yet to bear the light of this fairy piece. Next week you can go with Beth and Hannah."

"I don't like that half as well as going with you and Laurie. Please let me. I've been sick with this cold so long, and shut up, I'm dying for some fun. Do, Meg! I'll be ever so good," pleaded Amy, looking as pathetic as she could.

"Suppose we take her. I don't believe Mother would mind, if we bundle her up well," began Meg.

"If she goes I shan't! And if I don't, Laurie won't like it, and it will be very rude, after he invited only us, to go and drag in Amy. I should think she'd hate to poke herself where she isn't wanted," said Jo crossly.

Her tone and manner angered Amy, who began to put her boots on, saying in her most aggravating way: "I *shall* go. Meg says I may, and if I pay for myself, Laurie hasn't anything to do with it."

"You can't sit with us, for our seats are reserved, and you mustn't sit alone; so Laurie will give you his place, and that will spoil our pleasure, or he'll get another seat for you, and that isn't proper, when you weren't asked. You shan't stir a step, so you may just stay where you are," scolded Jo.

Sitting on the floor, with one boot on, Amy began to cry and Meg to reason with her, when Laurie called from below, and the two girls hurried down, leaving their sister wailing. Just as the party was setting out, Amy called over the banisters in a threatening tone: "You'll be sorry for this, Jo March, see if you ain't."

"Fiddlesticks," returned Jo, slamming the door.

They had a charming time, for *The Seven Castles of the Diamond Lake* were as brilliant and wonderful as heart could wish. But in spite of the comical red imps, sparkling elves, and gorgeous princes and princesses, Jo's pleasure had a drop of bitterness in it; the fairy queen's yellow curls reminded her of Amy, and between the acts she amused herself with wondering what her sister would do to make her "sorry for it." She and Amy had had many lively skirmishes in the course of their lives, for both had quick tempers and were apt to be violent when fairly roused. Amy teased Jo, and Jo irritated Amy, and semioccasional explosions occurred of which both were much ashamed afterward. Although the older, Jo had the least self-control, and had hard times trying to curb the fiery spirit which was continually getting her into trouble. Her anger never lasted long, and having humbly confessed her fault, she sincerely repented, and tried to do better. Poor Jo tried desperately to be good, but her bosom enemy was always ready to flame up and defeat her, and it took years of patient effort to subdue it.

When they got home, they found Amy reading in the parlor. She assumed an injured air as they came in, never lifted her eyes from her book, or asked a single question. Perhaps curiosity might have conquered resentment if Beth had not been there to inquire and receive a glowing description of the play. On going up to put away her best hat, Jo's first look was toward the bureau, for in their last quarrel Amy had soothed her feelings by turning Jo's top drawer upside down on the floor. Everything was in its place, however, and after a hasty glance into her various closets, bags, and boxes, Jo decided that Amy had forgiven and forgotten her wrongs. There Jo was mistaken, for next day she made a discovery which produced a tempest. Meg, Beth, and Amy were sitting together, late in the afternoon, when Jo burst into the room looking excited, and demanding breathlessly: "Has anyone taken my book?"

Meg and Beth said "No," at once, and looked surprised. Amy poked the fire, and said nothing. Jo saw her color rise, and was down upon her in a minute.

"Amy, you've got it!"

"No I haven't."

"You know where it is, then!"

"No I don't."

"That's a fib!" cried Jo, taking her by the shoulders, and looking fierce enough to frighten a much braver child than Amy.

"It isn't. I haven't got it, don't know where it is now, and don't care."

"You know something about it, and you'd better tell at once or I'll make you." And Jo gave her a slight shake.

"Scold as much as you like, you'll never see your silly old book again," cried Amy, getting excited in her turn.

"Why not?"

"I burned it up."

"What! My little book I was so fond of, and worked over, and meant to finish before Father got home? Have you really burned it?" said Jo, turning very pale.

"Yes, I did! I told you I'd make you pay for being so cross yesterday, and I have, so——"

Amy got no farther, for Jo's hot temper mastered her, and she shook Amy till her teeth chattered in her head, crying in a passion of grief and anger: "You wicked, wicked girl! I'll never forgive you as long as I live."

Meg flew to rescue Amy, and Beth to pacify Jo, but Jo was quite beside herself; and she rushed out of the room up to the old sofa in the garret, and finished her fight alone.

The storm cleared up below, for Mrs. March came home, and having heard the story, soon brought Amy to a sense of the wrong she had done her sister. Jo's book was the pride of her heart, and was regarded by her family as a literary sprout of great promise. It was only half a dozen little fairy tales, but Jo had worked over them patiently, putting her whole heart into her work, hoping to make something good enough to print. She had just copied them with great care, and had destroyed the old manuscript, so that Amy's bonfire had consumed the loving work of several years. It seemed a small loss to others, but to Jo it was a dreadful calamity, and she felt that it never could be made up to her. Beth mourned and Meg refused to defend her pet. Mrs. March looked grave and grieved, and Amy felt that no one would love her till she had asked pardon for the act which she now regretted more than any of them.

When the tea bell rang, Jo appeared looking so grim and unapproachable that it took all Amy's courage to say meekly: "Please forgive me, Jo. I'm very, very sorry."

"I never shall forgive you," was Jo's stern answer, and from that moment she ignored Amy entirely.

No one spoke of the great trouble—not even Mrs. March—for all had learned by experience that when Jo was in that mood words were wasted, and the wisest course was to wait till some little accident, or her own generous nature, softened Jo's resentment and healed the breach. It was not a happy evening; for though they sewed as usual while their mother read aloud from Bremer, Scott, or Edgeworth, something was wanting, and the sweet home peace was disturbed. They felt this most when singing time came; for Beth could only play, Jo stood dumb as a stone, and Amy broke down, so Meg and Mother sang alone. As Jo received her good-night kiss, Mrs. March whispered gently: "My dear, don't let the sun go down upon your anger. Forgive each other, help each other, and begin again tomorrow."

Jo wanted to lay her head down on that motherly bosom and cry her grief and anger all away; but tears were an unmanly weakness, and she felt so deeply injured that she really *couldn't* quite forgive yet. So she winked hard, shook her head, and said, gruffly because Amy was listening: "It was an abominable thing, and she don't deserve to be forgiven."

With that she marched off to bed, and there was no merry or confidential gossip that night.

Amy was much offended that her overtures of peace had been repulsed, and began to wish she had not humbled herself, to feel more injured than ever, and to plume herself on her superior virtue in a way which was particularly exasperating. Jo still looked like a thundercloud, and nothing went well all day. It was bitter cold in the morning; she dropped her precious turnover in the gutter; Aunt March had an attack of fidgets; Meg was pensive; Beth *would* look grieved and wistful when she got home; and Amy kept making remarks about people who were always talking about being good, and yet wouldn't try when other people set them a virtuous example.

"Everybody is so hateful I'll ask Laurie to go skating. He is always kind and jolly, and will put me to rights, I know," said Jo to herself, and off she went.

Amy heard the clash of skates, and looked out with an impatient exclamation: "There! She promised I should go next time, for this is the last ice we shall have. But it's no use to ask such a crosspatch to take me."

"Don't say that. You *were* very naughty, and it *is* hard to forgive the loss of her precious little book; but I think she might do it now, and I guess she will, if you try her at the right minute," said Meg. "Go after them. Don't say anything till Jo has got good-natured with Laurie, then take a quiet minute and just kiss her, or do some kind thing, and I'm sure she'll be friends again, with all her heart."

"I'll try," said Amy, for the advice suited her, and after a flurry to get ready, she ran after the friends.

It was not far to the river, but both were ready before Amy reached them. Jo saw her coming and turned her back. Laurie did not see, for he was carefully skating along the shore, sounding the ice, for a warm spell had preceded the cold snap.

"I'll go on to the first bend, and see if it's all right, before we begin to race," Amy heard him say as he shot away.

Jo heard Amy panting after her run, stamping her feet and blowing her fingers as she tried to put her skates on; but Jo never turned, and went slowly zigzagging down the river, taking a bitter, unhappy sort of satisfaction in her sister's troubles. She had cherished her anger till it grew strong, and took possession of her. As Laurie turned the bend, he shouted back: "Keep near the shore. It is not safe in the middle."

Jo heard, but Amy was just struggling to her feet and did not catch a word. Jo glanced over her shoulder, and the little demon she was harboring said in her ear: "No matter whether she heard or not. Let her take care of herself."

Laurie had vanished round the bend, Jo was just at the turn, and Amy, far behind, striking out toward the smoother ice in the middle of the river. For a minute Jo stood still, with a strange feeling at her heart; then she resolved to go on, but something held her and turned her round just in time to see Amy throw up her hands and go down, with the sudden crash of rotten ice, the splash of water, and a cry that made Jo's heart

stand still with fear. She tried to call Laurie, but her voice was gone; she tried to rush forward, but her feet seemed to have no strength in them; and for a second she could only stand motionless, staring with a terror-stricken face at the little blue hood above the black water. Something rushed swiftly by her, and Laurie's voice cried out: "Bring a rail—quick, quick!"

How she did it she never knew; but for the next few minutes she worked as if possessed, blindly obeying Laurie, who was quite self-possessed and, lying flat, held Amy up by his arm till Jo dragged a rail from the fence, and together they got the child out, more frightened than hurt.

"Now then, we must walk her home as fast as we can. Pile our things on her while I get off these confounded skates," cried Laurie, wrapping his coat round Amy.

Shivering, dripping, and crying, they got Amy home; and, after an exciting time of it, she fell asleep, rolled in blankets, before a hot fire. During the bustle Jo had scarcely spoken, but flown about looking pale and wild, with her things half off, her dress torn, and her hands cut and bruised by ice and rails and refractory buckles. When Amy was comfortably asleep, the house quiet, and Mrs. March sitting by the bed, she called Jo to her and began to bind up the hurt hands.

"Are you sure she is safe?" whispered Jo, looking remorsefully at the golden head which might have been swept away from her sight forever under the treacherous ice.

"Quite safe, dear. She is not hurt, and won't even take cold, I think, you were so sensible in covering her and getting her home quickly," replied her mother cheerfully.

"Laurie did it all, I only let her go. Mother, if she *should* die, it would be my fault." And Jo dropped down beside the bed in a passion of penitent tears, telling all that had happened, bitterly condemning her hardness of heart, and sobbing out her gratitude for being spared the heavy punishment which might have come upon her. "It's my dreadful temper! I try to cure it. I think I have, and then it breaks out worse than ever. O Mother, what shall I do? What shall I do?" cried poor Jo.

"Watch and pray, dear, never get tired of trying, and never think it is impossible to conquer your fault," said Mrs. March, drawing the blowzy head to her shoulder and kissing the wet cheek so tenderly that Jo cried harder than ever.

"You don't know, you can't guess how bad it is! It seems as if I could do anything when I'm in a passion. I get so savage I could hurt anyone and enjoy it. I'm afraid I *shall* do something dreadful some day, and spoil my life, and make everybody hate me. O Mother, help me, do help me!"

"I will, my child, I will. Don't cry so bitterly, but remember this day, and resolve with all your soul that you will never know another like it. Jo dear, we all have our temptations, some far greater than yours, and it often takes us all our lives to conquer them. You think your temper is the worst in the world, but mine used to be just like it."

"Yours, Mother? Why, you are never angry!" And for the moment Jo forgot remorse in surprise.

"I've been trying to cure it for forty years, and have only succeeded in controlling it. I am angry nearly every day of my life, Jo; but I have learned not to show it, and I still hope to learn not to feel it, though it may take me another forty years to do so."

The patience and the humility of the face she loved so well was a better lesson to Jo than the wisest lecture, the sharpest reproof. The knowledge that her mother had a fault like hers, and tried to mend it, made her own easier to bear and strengthened her resolution to cure it— though forty years seemed rather a long time to watch and pray, to a girl of fifteen.

"Mother, are you angry when you fold your lips tight together and go out of the room sometimes, when Aunt March scolds or people worry you?" asked Jo.

"Yes, I've learned to check the hasty words that rise to my lips; and when I feel that they mean to break out against my will, I just go away a minute, and give myself a little shake for being so weak and wicked," answered Mrs. March with a sigh and a smile.

"How did you learn to keep still? That is what troubles me—for the sharp words fly out before I know what I'm about. And the more I say, the worse I get, till it's a pleasure to hurt people's feelings, and say dreadful things. Tell me how you do it, Marmee dear."

"My good mother used to help me——"

"As you do us," interrupted Jo, with a grateful kiss.

"But I lost her when I was a little older than you are, and for years had to struggle on alone, for I was too proud to confess my weakness to anyone else. I had a hard time, Jo, and shed a good many bitter tears over my failures; for in spite of my efforts, I never seemed to get on. Then your father came, and I was so happy that I found it easy to be good. But by and by, when I had four little daughters, and we were poor, the old trouble began again; for I am not patient by nature, and it tried me very much to see my children wanting anything."

"Poor Mother! What helped you then?"

"Your father, Jo. He never loses patience—never doubts or complains, but always hopes, and works and waits so cheerfully that one is ashamed to do otherwise before him. He helped and comforted me, and showed me that I must try to practice all the virtues I would have my little girls possess, for I was their example. It was easier to try for your sakes than for my own; a startled or surprised look from one of you when I spoke sharply rebuked me more than any words could have done."

"O Mother, if I'm ever half as good as you, I shall be satisfied," cried Jo, much touched.

"I hope you will be a great deal better, dear; but you must keep watch over your 'bosom enemy,' as Father calls it, or it may sadden if not spoil your life. You have had a warning. Remember it, and try with heart and soul to master this quick temper before it brings you greater sorrow and regret than you have known today."

"I will try, Mother, I truly will. But you must help me, remind me, and keep me from flying out. I used to see Father sometimes put his finger on his lips and look at you with a very kind but sober face, and you always folded your lips tight or went away. Was he reminding you then?"

"Yes. I asked him to help me so, and he never forgot it, but saved me from many a sharp word by that little gesture and kind look."

Jo saw that her mother's eyes filled and her lips trembled as she spoke; and fearing that she had said too much, she whispered anxiously: "Was it wrong to watch you, and to speak of it? I didn't mean to be rude, but it's so comfortable to say all I think to you, and feel so safe and happy here."

"My Jo, you may say anything to your mother, for it is my greatest happiness and pride to feel that my girls confide in me, and know how much I love them."

"I thought I'd grieved you."

"No, my dear. But speaking of Father reminded me how much I miss him, how much I owe him, and how faithfully I should watch and work to keep his little daughters safe and good for him."

"Yet you told him to go, Mother, and didn't cry when he went, and never complain now, or seem as if you needed any help," said Jo, wondering.

"I gave my best to the country I love, and kept my tears till he was gone. Why should I complain when we both have merely done our duty and will surely be the happier for it in the end? If I don't seem to need help, it is because I have a better Friend even than Father to comfort and sustain me. My child, the troubles and temptations of your life are beginning, and may be many; but you can overcome and outlive them all if you learn to feel the strength and tenderness of your Heavenly Father as you do that of your earthly one. His love and care never tire or change, can never be taken from you, but may become the source of lifelong peace, happiness, and strength. Believe this heartily, and go to God with all your little cares, and hopes, and sins, and sorrows as freely and confidingly as you come to your mother."

Jo's only answer was to hold her mother close, and in the silence which followed, the sincerest prayer she had ever prayed left her heart without words; for in that sad yet happy hour she had learned not only the bitterness of remorse and despair, but the sweetness of self-denial and self-control; and, led by her mother's hand, she had drawn nearer to the Friend who welcomes every child with a love stronger than that of any father, tenderer than that of any mother.

Amy stirred, and sighed in her sleep, and Jo looked up with an expression on her face which it had never worn before. "I let the sun go down on my anger. I wouldn't forgive her, and today, if it hadn't been for Laurie, it might have been too late! How could I be so wicked?" said Jo half aloud as she leaned over her sister, softly stroking the wet hair scattered on the pillow.

Amy opened her eyes and held out her arms, with a smile that went straight to Jo's heart. Neither said a word, but they hugged one another close, in spite of the blankets, and everything was forgiven and forgotten in one hearty kiss.

MEG GOES TO VANITY FAIR

"I do think it was the most fortunate thing in the world that those children should have the measles just now," said Meg one April day as she stood packing the "go-abroady" trunk in her room, surrounded by her sisters.

"And so nice of Annie Moffat not to forget her promise. A whole fortnight of fun will be regularly splendid," replied Jo.

"And such lovely weather. I'm so glad of that," added Beth, tidily sorting neck and hair ribbons in her best box, lent for the great occasion.

"I wish I was going to have a fine time, and wear all these nice things," said Amy, with her mouth full of pins.

"I wish you were all going, but as you can't, I shall keep my adventures to tell you when I come back. I'm sure it's the least I can do when you have been so kind, lending me things, and helping me get ready," said Meg.

"What did Mother give you out of the treasure box?" asked Amy, who

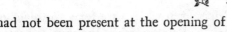

had not been present at the opening of a certain cedar chest in which Mrs. March kept a few relics of past splendor as gifts for her girls when the proper time came.

"A pair of silk stockings, that pretty carved fan, and a lovely blue sash."

"I wish I hadn't smashed my coral bracelet, for you might have had it," said Jo, who loved to give and lend, but whose possessions were usually too dilapidated to be of much use.

"There is a lovely old-fashioned pearl set in the treasure box, but Mother said real flowers were the prettiest ornament for a young girl, and Laurie promised to send me all I want," replied Meg. "Now, let me see. There's my new gray walking suit—just curl up the feather in my hat, Beth—then my poplin, for Sunday, and the small party."

"You've got the tarlatan for the big party, and you always look like an angel in white," said Amy.

"It isn't low-necked, and it doesn't sweep enough, but it will have to do. My blue house dress looks so well turned and freshly trimmed that I feel as if I'd got a new one. My silk sack isn't a bit the fashion, and my bonnet doesn't look like Sallie's."

"Change it," advised Jo.

"I won't be so silly, or hurt Marmee's feelings when she took so much pains to get my things. It's a nonsensical notion of mine, and I'm not going to give up to it. My silk stockings and two pairs of new gloves are my comfort. You are a dear to lend me yours, Jo. I feel so rich, and sort of elegant, with two new pairs and the old ones cleaned up for common." And Meg took a refreshing peep at her glove box.

"Annie Moffat has blue and pink bows on her nightcaps. Would you put some on mine?" she asked as Beth brought up a pile of snowy muslins fresh from Hannah's hands.

"No, I wouldn't, for the smart caps won't match the plain gowns. Poor folks shouldn't rig," said Jo decidedly.

"I wonder if I shall *ever* be happy enough to have real lace on my clothes, and bows on my caps?" said Meg impatiently.

"You said the other day that you'd be perfectly happy if you could only go to Annie Moffat's," observed Beth in her quiet way.

"So I did! Well, I *am* happy, and I *won't* fret; but it does seem as if the more one gets the more one wants, doesn't it? There now, the trays are ready, and everything in but my ball dress, which I shall leave for Mother to pack," said Meg, cheering up as she glanced from the half-filled trunk to the many-times pressed and mended white tarlatan.

The next day was fine, and Meg departed in style for a fortnight of novelty and pleasure. Mrs. March had consented to the visit rather reluctantly, fearing that Margaret would come back more discontented than she went. But she had begged so hard, and a little pleasure seemed so delightful after a winter of irksome work, that the mother yielded, and the daughter went to take her first taste of fashionable life.

The Moffats *were* very fashionable, and simple Meg was rather daunted at first by the splendor of the house and the elegance of its occupants. But they were kindly people, in spite of the frivolous life they led, and soon put their guest at her ease. Perhaps Meg felt, without understanding why, that they were not particularly cultivated or intelligent people, and that all their gilding could not quite conceal the ordinary material of which they were made. It certainly was agreeable to fare sumptuously, drive in a fine carriage, wear her best frock every day, and do nothing but enjoy herself. It suited her exactly, and soon she began to imitate the manners and conversation of those about her—to put on little airs and graces, use French phrases, crimp her hair, take in her dresses, and talk about the fashions as well as she could. The more she saw of Annie Moffat's pretty things, the more she envied her, and sighed to be rich.

She had not much time for repining, however, for the three young girls were busily employed in "having a good time." They shopped, walked, rode, and called all day; went to theaters and operas or frolicked at home in the evening, for Annie had many friends, and knew how to entertain them. Her older sisters were very fine young ladies, and one was engaged. Mr. Moffat was a fat, jolly old gentleman who knew her father, and Mrs. Moffat, a fat, jolly old lady who took as great a fancy to Meg as her daughter had done. Everyone petted her, and "Daisy," as they called her, was in a fair way to have her head turned.

When the evening for the "small party" came, she found that the poplin wouldn't do at all, for the other girls were putting on thin dresses, and making themselves very fine indeed. So out came the tarlatan, looking older, limper, and shabbier than ever beside Sallie's crisp new one. Meg saw the girls glance at it and then at one another, and her cheeks began to burn, for with all her gentleness she was very proud. No one said a word about it, but Sallie offered to dress her hair, and Annie to tie her sash, and Belle, the engaged sister, praised her white arms. But in their kindness Meg saw only pity for her poverty, and her heart felt very heavy as she stood by herself while the others laughed, chattered, and flew about like gauzy butterflies. The hard, bitter feeling was getting pretty bad when the maid brought in a box of flowers. Before she could speak, Annie had the cover off, and all were exclaiming at the lovely roses, heath, and fern within.

"It's for Belle, of course. George always sends her some, but these are altogether ravishing," cried Annie.

"They are for Miss March, the man said. And here's a note," put in the maid, holding it out to Meg.

"What fun! Who are they from? Didn't know you had a lover," cried the girls.

"The note is from Mother, and the flowers from Laurie."

"Oh indeed!" said Annie, with a funny look as Meg slipped the note into her pocket.

Feeling almost happy again, she laid by a few ferns and roses for herself, and quickly made up the rest in dainty bouquets for the breasts, hair, or skirts of her friends, offering them so prettily that Clara, the older sister, told her she was "the sweetest little thing" she ever saw. Somehow the kind act finished her despondency; and when all the rest went to show themselves to Mrs. Moffat, she saw a happy, bright-eyed face in the mirror as she laid her ferns against her rippling hair and fastened the roses in the dress that didn't strike her as so *very* shabby now.

She enjoyed herself very much that evening, for she danced to her heart's content, everyone was very kind, and she had three compliments. Annie made her sing, and someone said she had a remarkably fine voice. Major Lincoln asked who "the fresh little girl, with the beautiful eyes," was, and Mr. Moffat insisted on dancing with her, because she "didn't dawdle, but had some spring in her." So altogether she had a very nice time—till she overheard a bit of a conversation which disturbed her extremely. She was sitting just inside the conservatory, waiting for her partner to bring her an ice, when she heard a voice ask on the other side of the flowery wall:

"How old is he?"

"Sixteen or seventeen, I should say," replied another voice.

"It would be a grand thing for one of those girls, wouldn't it? Sallie says they are very intimate now, and the old man quite dotes on them."

"Mrs. M. has made her plans, I dare say, and will play her cards well, early as it is. The girl evidently doesn't think of it yet," said Mrs. Moffat.

"She told that fib about her mamma as if she did know, and colored up when the flowers came, quite prettily. Poor thing! She'd be so nice if she was only got up in style. Do you think she'd be offended if we offered to lend her a dress for Thursday?" asked another voice.

"She's proud, but I don't believe she'd mind, for that dowdy tarlatan is all she has got. She may tear it tonight, and that will be a good excuse for offering a decent one."

"We'll see. I shall ask young Laurence, as a compliment to her, and we'll have fun about it afterward."

Here Meg's partner appeared, to find her looking much flushed and rather agitated. She *was* proud, and her pride was useful just then, for it helped her hide her mortification, anger, and disgust at what she had just heard. She tried to forget it, but could not, and kept repeating to herself "Mrs. M. has made her plans," "that fib about her mamma," and "dowdy tarlatan," till she was ready to cry, and rush home to tell her troubles and ask for advice. As that was impossible, she did her best to seem gay, and being rather excited, she succeeded so well that no one dreamed what an effort she was making. Those foolish yet well-meant words had opened a new world to Meg, and much disturbed the peace of the old one, in which till now she had lived as happily as a child. Her innocent friendship with Laurie was spoiled by the silly speeches she had overheard; her faith in her mother was a little shaken by the worldly plans attributed to her by Mrs. Moffat, who judged others by herself; and the sensible resolution to be contented with the simple wardrobe which suited a poor man's daughter was weakened by the unnecessary pity of girls who thought a shabby dress one of the greatest calamities under heaven.

Poor Meg had a restless night, and got up heavy-eyed, unhappy, half resentful toward her friends, and half ashamed of herself for not speaking out frankly and setting everything right. Something in the manner of her friends struck Meg at once. They treated her with more respect, she thought, took quite a tender interest in what she said, and looked at her with eyes that plainly betrayed curiosity. All this surprised and flattered her, though she did not understand it till Miss Belle looked up from her writing and said, with a sentimental air: "Daisy dear, I've sent an invitation to your friend Mr. Laurence for Thursday. We should like to know him, and it's only a proper compliment to you."

Meg colored, but a mischievous fancy to tease the girls made her reply demurely: "You are very kind, but I'm afraid he won't come."

"Why not, *chérie?*" asked Miss Belle.

"He's too old."

"My child, what do you mean? What is his age, I beg to know!" cried Miss Clara.

"Nearly seventy, I believe," answered Meg, counting stitches to hide the merriment in her eyes.

"You sly creature! Of course we meant the young man," exclaimed Miss Belle, laughing.

"There isn't any. Laurie is only a little boy."

"About your age," Nan said.

"Nearer my sister Jo's. *I* am seventeen in August," returned Meg, tossing her head.

"It's very nice of him to send you flowers, isn't it?" said Annie, looking wise about nothing.

"Yes, he often does, to all of us; we are so fond of them. My mother and old Mr. Laurence are friends, you know, so it is quite natural that we children should play together."

"It's evident Daisy isn't out yet," said Miss Clara to Belle.

"Quite a pastoral state of innocence all around," returned Miss Belle, with a shrug.

"I'm going out to get some little matters for my girls. Can I do anything for you, young ladies?" asked Mrs. Moffat, lumbering in like an elephant in silk and lace.

"No thank you, ma'am," replied Sallie. "I've got my new pink silk for Thursday, and don't want a thing."

"Nor I——" began Meg, but stopped, because it occurred to her that she *did* want several things, and could not have them.

"What shall you wear?" asked Sallie.

"My old white one again, if I can mend it fit to be seen. It got sadly torn last night," said Meg, trying to speak quite easily, but feeling very uncomfortable.

"Why don't you send home for another?" said Sallie.

"I haven't got any other." It cost Meg an effort to say that, but Sallie did not see it, and exclaimed, in amiable surprise: "Only that? How funny——" Belle shook her head at her, and broke in, saying kindly: "Not at all. Where is the use of having a lot of dresses when she isn't out? There's no need of sending home, Daisy, even if you had a dozen, for I've got a sweet blue silk laid away which I've outgrown, and you shall wear it, to please me, won't you, dear?"

"You are very kind, but I don't mind my old dress if you don't. It does well enough for a little girl like me," said Meg.

"Now do let me please myself by dressing you up in style. You'd be a regular little beauty, with a touch here and there. I shan't let anyone see you till you are done, and then we'll burst upon them like Cinderella and her godmother going to the ball," said Belle in her persuasive tone.

Meg couldn't refuse the offer so kindly made, for a desire to see if she would be "a little beauty" after "touching up" caused her to accept, and to forget all her former uncomfortable feelings toward the Moffats.

On the Thursday evening, Belle shut herself up with her maid, and between them they turned Meg into a fine lady. They crimped and curled her hair, they polished her neck and arms with some fragrant powder, touched her lips with coralline salve to make them redder. They laced her into a sky-blue dress which was so tight she could hardly breathe, and so low in the neck that modest Meg blushed at herself in the mirror. A set of silver filigree was added, bracelets, necklace, brooch, and even earrings, for Hortense tied them on with a bit of pink silk which did not show. A cluster of tea rosebuds at the bosom, and a ruche, reconciled Meg to the display of her pretty white shoulders, and a pair of high-heeled blue-silk boots satisfied the last wish of her heart. A laced handkerchief, a plumy fan, and a bouquet in a silver holder finished her off, and Miss Belle surveyed her with the satisfaction of a little girl with a newly dressed doll.

"Come and show yourself," said Miss Belle, leading the way to the room where the others were waiting. As Meg went rustling after, with her long skirts trailing, her earrings tinkling, her curls waving, and her heart beating, she felt as if her "fun" had really begun at last, for the mirror had plainly told her that she *was* "a little beauty." Her friends repeated the pleasing phrase enthusiastically; and for several minutes she stood, like the jackdaw in the fable, enjoying her borrowed plumes.

"While I dress, do you drill her, Nan, in the management of her skirt, and those French heels, or she will trip herself up. Take your silver butterfly and catch up that long curl on the left side of her head, Clara, and don't any of you disturb the charming work of my hands," said Belle.

"I'm afraid to go down, I feel so queer and stiff and half-dressed," said Meg to Sallie as the bell rang and Mrs. Moffat sent to ask the young ladies to appear at once.

"You don't look a bit like yourself, but you are very nice. I'm nowhere beside you, for Belle has heaps of taste, and you're quite French, I assure you. Let your flowers hang, don't be so careful of them, and be sure you don't trip," returned Sallie.

Keeping that warning carefully in mind, Margaret got safely downstairs and sailed into the drawing rooms, where the Moffats and a few early guests were assembled. She very soon discovered that there is a charm about fine clothes which attracts a certain class of people, and secures their respect. Several young ladies who had taken no notice of her before were very affectionate all of a sudden; several young gentlemen who had only stared at her at the other party now not only stared, but asked to be introduced, and said all manner of foolish but agreeable things to her; and several old ladies who sat on sofas and criticized the rest of the party inquired who she was.

The "queer feeling" did not pass away, but she imagined herself acting the new part of fine lady, and so got on pretty well, though the tight dress gave her a side ache, the train kept getting under her feet, and she was in constant fear lest her earrings should fly off and get lost or broken. She was flirting her fan, and laughing at the feeble jokes of a young gentleman who tried to be witty, when she suddenly stopped laughing and looked confused; for, just opposite, she saw Laurie. He was staring at her with undisguised surprise, and disapproval also, she thought; for though he bowed and smiled, yet something in his honest eyes made her blush, and wish she had her old dress on. To complete her confusion, she saw Belle nudge Annie, and both glance from her to Laurie.

"Silly creatures, to put such thoughts into my head! I won't care for it, or let it change me a bit," thought Meg, and rustled across the room to shake hands with her friend.

"I'm glad you came. I was afraid you wouldn't," she said, with her most grown-up air.

"Jo wanted me to come and tell her how you looked, so I did," answered Laurie, without turning his eyes upon her.

"What shall you tell her?" asked Meg, full of curiosity to know his opinion of her, yet feeling ill at ease with him.

"I shall say I didn't know you, for you look so grown-up and unlike yourself I'm quite afraid of you," he said.

"How absurd of you! The girls dressed me up for fun, and I rather like it. Wouldn't Jo stare if she saw me?"

"Yes, I think she would," returned Laurie gravely.

"Don't you like me so?" asked Meg.

"No, I don't," was the blunt reply.

"Why not?" in an anxious tone.

He glanced at her frizzled head, bare shoulders, and fantastically trimmed dress with an expression that abashed her more than his answer, which had not a particle of his usual politeness about it. "I don't like fuss and feathers."

That was altogether too much from a lad younger than herself, and Meg walked away, saying petulantly, "You are the rudest boy I ever saw."

Feeling very much ruffled, she went and stood at a quiet window to cool her cheeks. As she stood there, Major Lincoln passed by, and a minute after she heard him saying to his mother: "They are making a fool of that little girl. I wanted you to see her, but they have spoiled her entirely. She's nothing but a doll tonight."

"Oh dear!" sighed Meg. "I wish I'd been sensible and worn my own things; then I should not have disgusted other people or felt so uncomfortable and ashamed myself."

She leaned her forehead on the cool pane, and stood half-hidden by the curtains never minding that her favorite waltz had begun till someone touched her, and, turning, she saw Laurie, looking penitent as he said, with his very best bow: "Please forgive my rudeness and come and dance with me."

"I'm afraid it will be too disagreeable to you," said Meg, trying to look offended, and failing entirely.

"Not a bit of it. I'm dying to do it. Come, I'll be good. I don't like your gown, but I do think you are—just splendid." And he waved his hands, as if words failed to express his admiration.

Meg smiled and relented, and whispered as they stood waiting to catch the time: "Take care my skirt don't trip you up. It's the plague of my life, and I was a goose to wear it."

"Pin it round your neck, and then it will be useful," said Laurie.

Away they went, fleeting and gracefully; for, having practiced at home, they were well matched, and the blithe young couple were a pleasant sight to see as they twirled merrily round and round feeling more friendly than ever after their small tiff.

"Laurie, I want you to do me a favor, will you?" said Meg as he stood fanning her when her breath gave out.

"Won't I!" said Laurie with alacrity.

"Please don't tell them at home about my dress tonight. They won't understand the joke, and it will worry Mother."

"Then why did you do it?" said Laurie's eyes, so plainly that Meg hastily added: "I shall tell them myself all about it, and ''fess' to Mother how silly I've been. But I'd rather do it myself, so you'll not tell, will you?"

"I'll give you my word I won't. Only what shall I say when they ask me?"

"Just say I looked pretty well, and was having a good time."

"I'll say the first, with all my heart, but how about the other? You don't look as if you were having a good time. Are you?" And Laurie looked at her with an expression which made her answer, in a whisper: "No, not just now. Don't think I'm horrid. I only wanted a little fun, but this sort doesn't pay, I find, and I'm getting tired of it."

He did not speak to her again till suppertime, when he saw her drinking champagne with Ned Moffat and his friend Fisher, who were behaving "like a pair of fools," as Laurie said to himself, for he felt a brotherly sort of right to watch over the Marches, and fight their battles whenever a defender was needed.

"You'll have a splitting headache tomorrow if you drink much of that.

I wouldn't, Meg. Your mother doesn't like it, you know," he whispered, leaning over her chair.

"I'm not Meg tonight, I'm 'a doll.' Tomorrow I shall put away my 'fuss and feathers' and be desperately good again," she answered, with an affected little laugh.

"Wish tomorrow was here, then," muttered Laurie, walking off ill-pleased at the change he saw in her.

Meg danced and flirted, chattered and giggled, as the other girls did. After supper she undertook the German, and blundered through it, nearly upsetting her partner with her long skirt, and romping in a way that scandalized Laurie, who looked on and meditated a lecture. But he got no chance to deliver it, for Meg kept away from him till he came to say good night.

"Remember!" she said, trying to smile, for the splitting headache had already begun.

"Silence à la mort," replied Laurie with a melodramatic flourish as he went away.

Meg went to bed feeling as if she had been to a masquerade and hadn't enjoyed herself as much as she expected. She was sick all the next day, and on Saturday went home quite used up with her fortnight's fun, and feeling that she had sat "in the lap of luxury" long enough.

"It does seem pleasant to be quiet, and not have company manners on all the time. Home is a nice place, though it isn't splendid," said Meg, looking about her with a restful expression as she sat with her mother and Jo on the Sunday evening.

"I'm glad to hear you say so, dear, for I was afraid home would seem dull and poor to you after your fine quarters," replied her mother.

Meg had told her adventures gaily, and said over and over what a charming time she had had; but something still seemed to weigh upon her spirits, and when the younger girls were gone to bed, she sat thoughtfully staring at the fire, saying little and looking worried. As the clock struck nine and Jo proposed bed, Meg suddenly left her chair, and taking Beth's stool, leaned her elbows on her mother's knee, saying bravely:

"Marmee, I want to ''fess.'"

"I thought so. What is it, dear?"

"Shall I go away?" asked Jo discreetly.

"Of course not. Don't I always tell you everything? I was ashamed to speak of it before the children, but I want you to know all the dreadful things I did at the Moffats'."

"We are prepared," said Mrs. March, smiling, but looking a little anxious.

"I told you they dressed me up, but I didn't tell you they powdered and squeezed and frizzled, and made me look a fashion plate. Laurie thought I wasn't proper, I know he did, though he didn't say so, and one man called me 'a doll.' I knew it was silly, but they flattered me, and said I was a beauty, and quantities of nonsense, so I let them make a fool of me."

"Is that all?" asked Jo as Mrs. March looked silently at the downcast face of her pretty daughter.

"No. I drank champagne and romped and tried to flirt, and was altogether abominable," said Meg self-reproachfully.

"There is something more, I think."

Meg answered slowly: "Yes—it's very silly, but I want to tell it, because I hate to have people say and think such things about us and Laurie."

Then she told the various bits of gossip she had heard at the Moffats', and as she spoke Jo saw her mother fold her lips tightly, as if ill-pleased that such ideas should be put into Meg's innocent mind.

"Well, if that isn't the greatest rubbish I ever heard," cried Jo indignantly. "Why didn't you pop out and tell them so, on the spot?"

"I couldn't, it was so embarrassing for me. I couldn't help hearing at first, and then I was so angry and ashamed I didn't remember that I ought to go away."

"Just wait till I see Annie Moffat and I'll show you how to settle such ridiculous stuff. The idea of having 'plans,' and being kind to Laurie, because he's rich, and may marry us by and by! Won't he shout when I tell him what those silly things say about us poor children?"

"If you tell Laurie, I'll never forgive you! She mustn't, must she, Mother?" said Meg, looking distressed.

"No. Never repeat that foolish gossip, and forget it as soon as you can," said Mrs. March gravely. "I was very unwise to let you go among people of whom I know so little—kind, I dare say, but worldly, ill-bred, and full of these vulgar ideas about young people. I am more sorry than I can express for the mischief this visit may have done you, Meg."

"Don't be sorry, I won't let it hurt me. I'll forget all the bad, and remember only the good; for I did enjoy a great deal, and thank you very much for letting me go. I'll not be sentimental or dissatisfied, Mother. I know I'm a silly little girl, and I'll stay with you till I'm fit to take care of myself. But it *is* nice to be praised and admired, and I can't help saying I like it," said Meg, looking half-ashamed of the confession.

"That is perfectly natural, and quite harmless if the liking does not become a passion and lead one to do foolish or unmaidenly things. Learn to know and value the praise which is worth having, and to excite the admiration of excellent people by being modest as well as pretty, Meg."

Margaret sat thinking a moment while Jo stood with her hands behind her, looking both interested and a little perplexed; for it was a new thing to see Meg blushing and talking about admiration, lovers, and things of that sort, and Jo felt as if her sister had grown up amazingly, and was drifting away from her into a world where she could not follow.

"Mother, do you have 'plans,' as Mrs. Moffat said?" asked Meg bashfully.

"Yes, my dear, I have a great many. All mothers do, but mine differ somewhat from Mrs. Moffat's, I suspect. I will tell you some of them, for the time has come when a word may set this romantic little head and heart of yours right on a very serious subject. You are young, Meg, but not too young to understand me. Jo, your turn will come in time, perhaps, so listen to my 'plans,' and help me carry them out if they are good."

Jo went and sat on one arm of the chair, looking as if she thought they were about to join in some very solemn affair. Holding a hand of each, and watching the two young faces wistfully, Mrs. March said, in her serious yet cheery way:

"I want my daughters to be beautiful, accomplished, and good; to be admired, loved, and respected; to have a happy youth, to be well and wisely married, and to lead useful pleasant lives, with as little care and sorrow to try them as God sees fit to send. To be loved and chosen by a good man is the best and sweetest thing which can happen to a woman and I sincerely hope my girls may know this beautiful experience. It is natural to think of it, Meg—right to hope and wait for it, and wise to prepare for it so that when the happy time comes, you may feel ready for the duties and worthy of the joy. My dear girls, I *am* ambitious for you, but not to have you make a dash in the world—marry rich men merely because they are rich, or have splendid houses which are not homes because love is wanting. Money is a needful and precious thing—and when well used a noble thing—but I never want you to think it is the first or only prize to strive for. I'd rather see you poor men's wives, if you were happy, beloved, contented, than queens on thrones without self-respect and peace."

"Poor girls don't stand any chance, Belle says, unless they put themselves forward," sighed Meg.

"Then we'll be old maids," said Jo stoutly.

"Right, Jo. Better be happy old maids than unhappy wives, or unmaidenly girls running about to find husbands," said Mrs. March decidedly. "Don't be troubled, Meg. Poverty seldom daunts a sincere lover. Leave these things to time. Make this home happy, so that you may be fit for homes of your own if they are offered you, and contented here if they are not. One thing remember, my girls: Mother is always ready to be your confidante, Father to be your friend, and both of us trust and hope that our daughters, whether married or single, will be the pride and comfort of our lives."

"We will, Marmee, we will!" cried both with all their hearts as she bade them good night.

THE P.C. AND P.O.

As spring came on, a new set of amusements became the fashion, and the lengthening days gave long afternoons for work and play of all sorts. The garden had to be put in order, and each sister had a quarter of the little plot to do what she liked with. Hannah used to say, "I'd know which each of them gardings belong to ef I see 'em in Chiny," and so she might, for the girls' tastes differed as much as their characters. Meg's had roses and heliotrope, myrtle, and a little orange tree in it. Jo's bed was never alike two seasons, for she was always trying experiments; this year it was to be a plantation of sunflowers, the seeds of which cheerful and aspiring plant were to feed "Aunt Cockletop" and her family of chicks. Beth had old-fashioned, fragrant flowers in her garden—sweet peas and mignonette, larkspur, pinks, pansies, and southernwood, with chickweed for the bird, and catnip for the pussies. Amy had a bower in hers—rather small and earwiggy, but very pretty to look at—with honeysuckles and morning-glories hanging their colored horns and bells in graceful wreaths all over it, tall, white lilies, delicate ferns, and as many brilliant, picturesque plants as would consent to blossom there.

Gardening, walks, rows on the river, and flower hunts employed the fine days; and for rainy ones, they had house diversions—some old, some new, all more or less original. One of these was the "P.C."; for as secret societies were the fashion, it was thought proper to have one, and as all of the girls admired Dickens, they called themselves the Pickwick Club. With a few interruptions, they had kept this up for a year, and met every Saturday evening in the big garret, on which occasions the ceremonies were as follows: Three chairs were arranged in a row before a table on which was a lamp, also four white badges, with a big "P.C." in different colors on each, and the weekly newspaper, called "The Pickwick Portfolio," to which all contributed something, while Jo, who reveled in pens and ink, was the editor. At seven o'clock, the four members ascended to the clubroom, tied their badges round their heads, and took their seats with great solemnity. Meg, as the eldest, was Samuel Pickwick; Jo, being of a literary turn, Augustus Snodgrass; Beth, because she was round and rosy, Tracy Tupman; and Amy, who was always trying to do what she couldn't, was Nathaniel Winkle. Pickwick, the president, read the paper, which was filled with original tales, poetry, local news, funny advertisements, and hints in which they good-naturedly reminded each other of their faults and shortcomings. On one occasion, Mr. Pickwick put on a pair of spectacles without any glasses, rapped upon the table, hemmed, and, having stared hard at Mr. Snodgrass, who was tilting back in his chair, till he arranged himself properly, began to read:

The Pickwick Portfolio

May 20, 18—

Poet's Corner

ANNIVERSARY ODE

———

Again we meet to celebrate
　With badge and solemn rite,
Our fifty-second anniversary,
　In Pickwick Hall, tonight.

We all are here in perfect health,
　None gone from our small band:
Again we see each well-known face,
　And press each friendly hand.

Our Pickwick, always at his post,
　With reverence we greet,

As, spectacles on nose, he reads
　Our well-filled weekly sheet.

Although he suffers from a cold,
　We joy to hear him speak,
For words of wisdom from him fall,
　In spite of croak or squeak.

Old six-foot Snodgrass looms on high,
　With elephantine grace,
And beams upon the company,
　With brown and jovial face.

Poetic fire lights up his eye,
　He struggles 'gainst his lot.
Behold ambition on his brow,
　And on his nose a blot!

Next our peaceful Tupman comes,
So rosy, plump, and sweet,
Who chokes with laughter at the puns,
And tumbles off his seat.

Prim little Winkle too is here,
With every hair in place,
A model of propriety,
Though he hates to wash his face.

The year is gone, we still unite
To joke and laugh and read,
And tread the path of literature
That doth to glory lead.

Long may our paper prosper well,
Our club unbroken be,
And coming years their blessings pour
On the useful, gay "P.C."

A. SNODGRASS

THE MASKED MARRIAGE

A TALE OF VENICE

———

Gondola after gondola swept up to the marble steps, and left its lovely load to swell the brilliant throng that filled the stately halls of Count de Adelon. Knights and ladies, elves and pages, monks and flower girls, all mingled gaily in the dance. Sweet voices and rich melody filled the air; and so with mirth and music the masquerade went on.

"Has your Highness seen the Lady Viola tonight?" asked a gallant troubadour of the fairy queen who floated down the hall upon his arm.

"Yes; is she not lovely, though so sad! Her dress is well chosen, too, for in a week she weds Count Antonio, whom she passionately hates."

"By my faith, I envy him. Yonder he comes, arrayed like a bridegroom, except the black mask. When that is off we shall see how he regards the fair maid whose heart he cannot win, though her stern father bestows her hand," returned the troubadour.

" 'Tis whispered that she loves the young English artist who haunts her steps, and is spurned by the old Count," said the lady as they joined the dance.

The revel was at its height when a priest appeared, and, withdrawing the young pair to an alcove hung with purple velvet, he motioned them to kneel. Instant silence fell upon the gay throng, and not a sound but the dash of fountains or the rustle of orange groves sleeping in the moonlight broke the hush as Count de Adelon spoke thus:

"My lords and ladies, pardon the ruse by which I have gathered you here to witness the marriage of my daughter. Father, we wait your services."

All eyes turned toward the bridal party; and a low murmur of amazement went through the throng, for neither bride nor groom removed their masks. Curiosity and wonder possessed all hearts, but respect restrained all tongues till the holy rite was over. Then the eager spectators gathered round the Count, demanding an explanation.

"Gladly would I give it if I could; but I only know that it was the whim of my timid Viola, and I yielded to it. Unmask, and receive my blessing."

But neither bent the knee; for the young bridegroom replied, in a tone that startled all listeners as the mask fell disclosing the noble face of Ferdinand Devereux, the artist lover; and, leaning on the breast where now flashed the star of an English earl, was the lovely Viola radiant with joy and beauty.

"My lord, you scornfully bade me claim your daughter when I could boast as high a name and vast a fortune as the Count Antonio. I can do more; for even your ambitious soul cannot refuse the Earl of Devereux and De Vere when he gives his ancient name and boundless wealth in return for the beloved hand of this fair lady, now my wife."

The Count stood like one changed to stone, and, turning to the bewildered crowd, Ferdinand added, with a gay smile of triumph, "To you, my gallant friends, I can only wish that your wooing may prosper as mine has done; and that you may all win as fair a bride as I have by this masked marriage."

S. PICKWICK

Why is the P.C. like the Tower of Babel? It is full of unruly members.

THE HISTORY OF A SQUASH

Once upon a time a farmer planted a little seed in his garden, and after a while it sprouted and became a vine, and bore many squashes. One day in October, when they were ripe, he picked one and took it to market. A grocerman bought and put it in his shop. That same morning, a little girl in a brown hat and blue dress, with a round face and snub nose, went and bought it for her mother. She lugged it home, cut it up, and boiled it in the big pot; mashed some of it with salt and butter for dinner; and to the rest she added a pint of milk, two eggs, four spoons of sugar, nutmeg, and some crackers, put it in a deep dish, and baked it till it was brown and nice; and next day it was eaten by a family named March.

T. TUPMAN

MR. PICKWICK, Sir:
I address you upon the subject of sin the sinner I mean is a man named Winkle who makes trouble in his club by laughing and sometimes won't write Now, my children, let the play end. his piece in this fine paper I hope you will pardon his badness and let him send a French fable because he can't write out of his head as he has so many lessons to do and no brains in future I will try to take time by the fetlock and prepare some work which will be all commy la fo that means all right I am in haste as it is nearly schooltime
Yours respectably,   N. WINKLE

[The above is a manly and handsome acknowledgment of past misdemeanors. If our young friend studied punctuation, it would be well.]

A SAD ACCIDENT

On Friday last, we were startled by a violent shock in our basement, followed by cries of distress. On rushing, in a body, to the cellar, we discovered our beloved President prostrate upon the floor, having tripped and fallen while getting wood for domestic purposes. A perfect scene of ruin met our eyes; for in his fall Mr. Pickwick had plunged his head and shoulders into a tub of water, upset a keg of soft soap upon his manly form, and torn his garments badly. On being removed from this perilous situation, it was discovered that he had suffered no injury but several bruises; and, we are happy to add, is now doing well.

ED.

THE PUBLIC BEREAVEMENT

It is our painful duty to record the sudden and mysterious disappearance of our cherished friend Mrs. Snowball Pat Paw. This lovely and beloved cat was the pet of a large circle of warm and admiring friends; for her beauty attracted all eyes, her graces and virtues endeared her to all hearts, and her loss is deeply felt by the whole community.

When last seen, she was sitting at the gate, watching the butcher's cart; and it is feared that some villain, tempted by her charms, basely stole her. Weeks have passed, but no trace of her has been discovered; and we relinquish all hope, tie a black ribbon to her basket, set aside her dish, and weep for her as one lost to us forever.

A sympathizing friend sends the following gem:

A LAMENT

FOR S. B. PAT PAW

We mourn the loss of our little pet,
　And sigh o'er her hapless fate,
For never more by the fire she'll sit,
　Nor play by the old green gate.

The little grave where her infant sleeps
　Is 'neath the chestnut tree;
But o'er her grave we may not weep,
　We know not where it may be.

Her empty bed, her idle ball,
　Will never see her more;
No gentle tap, no loving purr
　Is heard at the parlor door.

Another cat comes after her mice,
　A cat with a dirty face;
But she does not hunt as our darling did,
　Nor play with her airy grace.

Her stealthy paws tread the very hall
　Where Snowball used to play,
But she only spits at the dogs our pet
　So gallantly drove away.

She is useful and mild, and does her best,
　But she is not fair to see;
And we cannot give her your place, dear,
　Nor worship her as we worship thee.

　　　　　　　　　　　　A. S.

ADVERTISEMENTS

Miss ORANTHY BLUGGAGE, the accomplished Strong-Minded Lecturer, will deliver her famous Lecture on "WOMAN AND HER POSITION," at Pickwick Hall, next Saturday Evening, after the usual performances.

A WEEKLY MEETING will be held at Kitchen Place, to teach young ladies how to cook. Hannah Brown will preside, and all are invited to attend.

THE DUSTPAN SOCIETY will meet on Wednesday next, and parade in the upper story of the Clubhouse. All members to appear in uniform and shoulder their brooms at nine precisely.

MRS. BETH BOUNCER will open her new assortment of Doll's Millinery next week. The latest Paris Fashions have arrived, and orders are respectfully solicited.

A NEW PLAY will appear at the Barnville Theater in the course of a few weeks, which will surpass anything ever seen on the American stage. "THE GREEK SLAVE, or Constantine the Avenger," is the name of this thrilling drama! ! !

HINTS

If S. P. didn't use so much soap on his hands, he wouldn't always be late at breakfast. A. S. is requested not to whistle in the street. T. T., please don't forget Amy's napkin. N. W. must not fret because his dress has not nine tucks.

WEEKLY REPORT

Meg—Good
Jo—Bad
Beth—Very good
Amy—Middling

As the president finished reading the paper a round of applause followed, and then Mr. Snodgrass rose to make a proposition.

"Mr. President and gentlemen," he began, assuming a parliamentary attitude and tone, "I wish to propose the admission of a new member—

85

one who highly deserves the honor, would be deeply grateful for it, and would add immensely to the spirit of the club, the literary value of the paper, and be no end jolly and nice. I propose Mr. Theodore Laurence as an honorary member of the P.C. Come now, do have him."

Jo's sudden change of tone made the girls laugh, but all looked rather anxious, and no one said a word as Snodgrass took his seat.

"We'll put it to vote," said the president. "All in favor of this motion please to manifest it by saying 'Aye.'"

A loud response from Snodgrass, followed, to everybody's surprise, by a timid one from Beth.

"Contrary-minded say 'No.'"

Meg and Amy were contrary-minded, and Mr. Winkle rose to say, with great elegance:

"We don't wish any boys; they only joke and bounce about."

"I'm afraid he'll laugh at our paper, and make fun of us afterward," observed Pickwick.

Up rose Snodgrass, very much in earnest. "Sir, I give you my word as a gentleman Laurie won't do anything of the sort. He likes to write, and he'll give a tone to our contributions, and keep us from being sentimental, don't you see? We can do so little for him, and he does so much for us, I think the least we can do is to offer him a place here, and make him welcome if he comes."

This artful allusion to benefits conferred brought Tupman to his feet, looking as if he had quite made up his mind.

"Yes, we ought to do it, even if we *are* afraid. I say he *may* come, and his grandpa too, if he likes."

This spirited burst from Beth electrified the club, and Jo left her seat to shake hands approvingly. "Now then, vote again. Everybody remember it's our Laurie, and say 'Aye!'"

"Aye! Aye! Aye!" replied three voices at once.

"Good! Bless you! Now, as there's nothing like 'taking Time by the *fetlock*,' as Winkle characteristically observes, allow me to present the new member." And, to the dismay of the rest of the club, Jo threw open the door of the closet and displayed Laurie sitting on a ragbag, flushed and twinkling with suppressed laughter.

"You rogue! You traitor! Jo, how could you?" cried the three girls as Snodgrass led her friend triumphantly forth.

"The coolness of you two rascals is amazing," began Mr. Pickwick, trying to get up an awful frown, and only succeeding in producing an

86

amiable smile. But the new member was equal to the occasion, and, rising, with a grateful salutation to the Chair, said in the most engaging manner: "Mr. President and ladies—I beg pardon, gentlemen—allow me to introduce myself as Sam Weller, the very humble servant of the club."

"Good! Good!" cried Jo, pounding with the handle of the old warming pan on which she leaned.

"My faithful friend and noble patron," continued Laurie, with a wave of the hand, "who has so flatteringly presented me, is not to be blamed for the base stratagem of tonight. I planned it, and she only gave in after lots of teasing."

"Come now, don't lay it all on yourself. You know I proposed the cupboard," broke in Snodgrass.

"Never you mind what she says. I'm the wretch that did it, sir," said the new member, with a Welleresque nod to Mr. Pickwick. "But on my honor, I never will do so again, and henceforth *dewote* myself to the interest of this immortal club."

"Hear! Hear!" cried Jo, clashing the lid of the warming pan like a cymbal.

"Go on, go on!" added Winkle and Tupman.

"I merely wish to say that as a slight token of my gratitude for the honor done me, and as a means of promoting friendly relations between adjoining nations, I have set up a post office in the hedge in the lower corner of the garden, a fine, spacious building with padlocks on the doors, and every convenience for the mails—also the females, if I may be allowed the expression. It's the old martin house, but I've stopped up the door, and made the roof open, so it will hold all sorts of things, and save our valuable time. Letters, manuscripts, books, and bundles can be passed in there. Allow me to present the club key and, with many thanks for your favor, take my seat."

Great applause as Mr. Weller deposited a little key on the table, and subsided. The warming pan clashed and waved wildly, and it was some time before order could be restored. A long discussion followed, and everyone came out surprisingly, for everyone did her best, so it was an unusually lively meeting. No one ever regretted the admittance of Sam Weller, for a more devoted, well-behaved, and jovial member no club could have. He certainly did add "spirit" to the meetings, and "a tone" to the paper; for his orations convulsed his hearers, and his contributions were excellent, being patriotic, classical, comical, or dramatic, but never sentimental.

The P.O. was a capital little institution, and flourished wonderfully, for nearly as many queer things passed through it as through the real office. Tragedies and cravats, poetry and pickles, garden seeds and long letters, music and gingerbread; rubbers, invitations, scoldings, and puppies. The old gentleman liked the fun, and amused himself by sending odd bundles, mysterious messages, and funny telegrams.

EXPERIMENTS

"The first of June! The Kings are off to the seashore tomorrow, and I'm free. Three months' vacation—how I shall enjoy it!" exclaimed Meg, coming home one warm day to find Jo laid upon the sofa in an unusual state of exhaustion while Beth took off her dusty boots, and Amy made lemonade for the refreshment of the whole party.

"Aunt March went today, for which, oh be joyful!" said Jo. "I was mortally afraid she'd ask me to go with her. If she had, I should have felt as if I ought to do it, but Plumfield is about as gay as a churchyard, you know, and I'd rather be excused. We had a flurry getting the old lady off, and I had a fright every time she spoke to me, for I was in such a hurry to be through that I was uncommonly helpful and sweet, and feared she'd find it impossible to part from me. I quaked till she was fairly in the carriage, and had a final fright, for as it drove off she popped out her head, saying, 'Josyphine, won't you——?' I didn't hear any more, for I basely turned and fled."

"Poor old Jo! She came in looking as if bears were after her," said Beth as she cuddled her sister's feet with a motherly air.

"Aunt March is a regular samphire, is she not?" observed Amy, tasting her mixture critically.

"She means *vampire*, not seaweed, but it doesn't matter, it's too warm to be particular about one's parts of speech," murmured Jo.

"What shall you do all your vacation?" asked Amy, changing the subject with tact.

"I shall lie abed late, and do nothing," replied Meg from the depths of the rocking chair. "I've been routed up early all winter, and had to

spend my days working for other people, so now I'm going to rest and revel to my heart's content."

"No," said Jo, "that dozy way wouldn't suit me. I've laid in a heap of books, and I'm going to improve my shining hours reading on my perch in the old apple tree."

"Don't let us do any lessons, Beth, for a while, but play all the time, and rest, as the girls mean to," proposed Amy.

"Well, I will, if Mother doesn't mind. I want to learn some new songs, and my children need fitting up for the summer."

"May we, Mother?" asked Meg, turning to Mrs. March, who sat sewing in what they called "Marmee's corner."

"You may try your experiment for a week and see how you like it. I think by Saturday night you will find that all play and no work is as bad as all work and no play."

"I now propose a toast, as my 'friend and pardner, Sairy Gamp,' says. Fun forever, and no grubbing!" cried Jo, raising glass in hand as the lemonade went round.

They all drank it merrily, and began the experiment by lounging for the rest of the day. Next morning, Meg did not appear till ten o'clock. Her solitary breakfast did not taste nice, and the room seemed lonely and untidy, for Jo had not filled the vases, Beth had not dusted, and Amy's books lay scattered about. Nothing was neat and pleasant but Marmee's corner, which looked as usual, and there Meg sat to "rest and read," which meant yawn and imagine what pretty summer dresses she would get with her salary. Jo spent the morning on the river with Laurie, and the afternoon reading and crying over *The Wide, Wide World* up in the apple tree. Beth began by rummaging everything out of the big closet where her family resided; but, getting tired before half-done, she left her establishment topsy-turvy and went to her music, rejoicing that she had no dishes to wash. Amy arranged her bower, put on her best white frock, smoothed her curls, and sat down to draw under the honeysuckles, hoping someone would see and inquire who the young artist was. As no one appeared but an inquisitive daddy longlegs, who examined her work with interest, she went to walk, got caught in a shower, and came home dripping.

At teatime they compared notes, and all agreed that it had been a delightful though unusually long day. Meg, who went shopping in the afternoon and got a "sweet blue muslin," had discovered after she had cut the breadths off that it wouldn't wash, which mishap made her slightly cross. Jo had burned the skin off her nose boating, and got a raging headache by reading too long. Beth was worried by the confusion of her closet and the difficulty of learning three or four songs at once; and Amy deeply regretted the damage done her frock, for Katy Brown's party was to be the next day, and now, like Flora McFlimsey, she had "nothing to wear." But these were mere trifles, and they assured their mother that the experiment was working finely. She smiled, said nothing, and with Hannah's help did their neglected work, keeping home pleasant and the domestic machinery running smoothly.

It was astonishing what a peculiar and uncomfortable state of things was produced by the "resting and reveling" process. The days kept getting longer and longer; the weather was unusually variable, and so were tempers; an unsettled feeling possessed everyone, and Satan found plenty of mischief for the idle hands to do. As the height of luxury, Meg put out some of her sewing, and then found time hang so heavily that she fell to snipping and spoiling her clothes in her attempts to furbish them up à la Moffat. Jo read till her eyes gave out and she was sick of books, got so fidgety that even good-natured Laurie had a quarrel with her, and so reduced in spirits that she desperately wished she had gone with Aunt March. Beth got on pretty well, for she was constantly forgetting that it was to be *all play, and no work,* and fell back into her old ways now and then; but something in the air affected her, and more than once her tranquillity was much disturbed. Amy fared worst of all, for her resources were small, and when her sisters left her to amuse and care for herself she soon found that accomplished and important little self a great burden. She didn't like dolls, fairy tales were childish, and one couldn't draw all the time; tea parties didn't amount to much, neither did picnics, unless very well conducted.

No one would own that they were tired of the experiment, but by Friday night each acknowledged to herself that she was glad the week was nearly done. Hoping to impress the lesson more deeply, Mrs. March, who had a good deal of humor, resolved to finish off the trial in an appropriate manner, so she gave Hannah a holiday and let the girls enjoy the full effect of the play system. When they got up on Saturday morning, there was no fire in the kitchen, no breakfast in the dining room, and no mother anywhere to be seen.

"Mercy on us! What *has* happened?" cried Jo, staring about her in dismay.

Meg ran upstairs, and soon came back again looking relieved, but rather bewildered, and a little ashamed. "Mother isn't sick, only very tired, and she says she is going to stay quietly in her room all day, and let us do the best we can. She doesn't act a bit like herself, but she says it has been a hard week for her, so we must take care of ourselves."

"That's easy enough, and I like the idea. I'm aching for something to do—that is, some new amusement, you know," added Jo quickly.

In fact it *was* an immense relief to them all to have a little work, and they took hold with a will, but soon realized the truth of Hannah's saying "Housekeeping ain't no joke." There was plenty of food in the larder, and while Beth and Amy set the table, Meg and Jo got breakfast.

"I shall take some up to Mother, though she said we were not to think of her, for she'd take care of herself," said Meg, who presided and felt quite matronly behind the teapot.

So a tray was fitted out before anyone began, and taken up, with the cook's compliments. The boiled tea was very bitter, the omelet scorched, and the biscuits speckled with saleratus; but Mrs. March received her repast with thanks, and laughed heartily over it after Jo was gone.

"Poor little souls, they will have a hard time, I'm afraid; but they won't suffer, and it will do them good," she said, producing the more palatable viands with which she had provided herself, and disposing of the bad breakfast, so that their feelings might not be hurt. Many were the complaints below, and great the chagrin of the head cook at her failures. "Never mind, I'll get the dinner, and be servant. You be mistress, keep your hands nice, see company, and give orders," said Jo, who knew still less than Meg about culinary affairs.

This obliging offer was gladly accepted, and Margaret retired to the parlor, which she hastily put in order by whisking the litter under the sofa and shutting the blinds, to save the trouble of dusting. Jo, with perfect faith in her own powers, and a friendly desire to make up the quarrel, immediately put a note in the office inviting Laurie to dinner.

"You'd better see what you have got before you think of having company," said Meg when informed of the hospitable but rash act.

"Oh, there's corned beef and plenty of potatoes, and I shall get some asparagus and a lobster, 'for a relish,' as Hannah says. We'll make a salad. I don't know how, but the books tell. I'll have blancmange and strawberries for dessert, and coffee too, if you want to be elegant."

"Don't try too many messes, Jo, for you can't make anything but gingerbread and molasses candy fit to eat. I wash my hands of the dinner party, and since you have asked Laurie on your own responsibility, you may just take care of him."

"I don't want you to do anything but be civil to him, and help with the pudding. You'll give me your advice if I get in a muddle, won't you?" asked Jo, rather hurt.

"Yes, but I don't know much, except about bread, and a few trifles. You had better ask Mother's leave before you order anything," returned Meg prudently.

"Of course I shall. I'm not a fool." And Jo went off in a huff at the doubts expressed of her powers.

"Get what you like, and don't disturb me. I'm going out to dinner, and can't worry about things at home," said Mrs. March when Jo spoke to her.

The unusual spectacle of her busy mother rocking comfortably and reading early in the morning made Jo feel as if some unnatural phenomenon had occurred; for an eclipse, an earthquake, or a volcanic eruption would hardly have seemed stranger.

"Everything is out of sorts, somehow," she said to herself, going downstairs. "There's Beth crying; that's a sure sign that something is wrong with this family. If Amy is bothering, I'll shake her."

Feeling very much out of sorts herself, Jo hurried into the parlor to find Beth sobbing over Pip, the canary, who lay dead in the cage, with his little claws pathetically extended as if imploring the food for want of which he had died.

"It's all my fault—I forgot him—there isn't a seed or a drop left. O Pip! O Pip! How could I be so cruel to you?" cried Beth, taking the poor thing in her hands and trying to restore him.

Jo peeped into his half-open eye, felt his little heart, and finding him stiff and cold, shook her head, and offered her domino box for a coffin.

"Put him in the oven, and maybe he will get warm and revive," said Amy hopefully.

"He's been starved, and he shan't be baked now he's dead. I'll make him a shroud, and he shall be buried in the garden; and I'll never have another bird, never, my Pip! for I am too bad to own one," murmured Beth.

"The funeral shall be this afternoon, and we will all go. Now don't cry, Bethy; it's a pity, but nothing goes right this week, and Pip has had the worst of the experiment. Make the shroud, and lay him in my box, and after the dinner party we'll have a nice little funeral," said Jo.

Leaving the others to console Beth, she departed to the kitchen, which was in a most discouraging state of confusion. Putting on a big apron, she fell to work, and got the dishes piled up ready for washing when she discovered that the fire was out. "Here's a sweet prospect!" muttered Jo, slamming the stove door open and poking vigorously among the cinders.

Having rekindled the fire, she thought she would go to market while the water heated. The walk revived her spirits and, flattering herself that she had made good bargains, she trudged home again after buying a very young lobster, some very old asparagus, and two boxes of acid strawberries. By the time she got cleared up, the dinner arrived, and the stove was red-hot. Hannah had left a pan of bread to rise, Meg had worked it up early, set it on the hearth for a second rising, and forgotten it. Meg was entertaining Sallie Gardiner in the parlor when the door flew open, and a floury, crocky, flushed, and disheveled figure appeared, demanding tartly: "I say, isn't bread 'riz' enough when it runs over the pans?"

Sallie began to laugh, but Meg nodded, and lifted her eyebrows as high as they would go, which caused the apparition to vanish and put the sour bread into the oven without further delay. Mrs. March went out, after peeping here and there to see how matters went, also saying a word of comfort to Beth, who sat making a winding sheet, while the dear departed lay in state in the domino box. A strange sense of helplessness fell upon the girls as the gray bonnet vanished round the corner, and despair seized them when, a few minutes later, Miss Crocker appeared, and said she'd come to dinner. Now this lady was a thin, yellow spinster with a sharp nose and inquisitive eyes who saw everything, and gossiped about all she saw. They disliked her, but had been taught to be kind to her, simply because she was old and poor, and had few friends. So Meg gave her the easy chair, and tried to entertain her, while she asked questions, criticized everything, and told stories of the people whom she knew.

Language cannot describe the anxieties, experiences, and exertions which Jo underwent that morning, and the dinner she served up became a standing joke. Fearing to ask any more advice, she did her best alone, and discovered that something more than energy and goodwill is necessary to make a cook. She boiled the asparagus for an hour, and was grieved to find the heads cooked off and the stalks harder than ever. The bread burned black, for the salad dressing so aggravated her that she let everything else go till she had convinced herself that she could not make it fit to eat. The lobster was a scarlet mystery to her, but she hammered and poked till it was unshelled, and its meager proportions concealed in a grove of lettuce leaves. The potatoes had to be hurried, not to keep the asparagus waiting, and were not done at last. The blancmange was lumpy, and the strawberries not as ripe as they looked.

"Well, they can eat beef, and bread and butter, if they are hungry; only it's mortifying to have to spend your whole morning for nothing," thought Jo as she rang the bell half an hour later than usual, and stood, hot, tired, and dispirited, surveying the feast spread for Laurie, accustomed to all sorts of elegance, and Miss Crocker, whose curious eyes would mark all failures, and whose tattling tongue would report them far and wide.

Poor Jo would gladly have gone under the table as one thing after another was tasted and left, while Amy giggled, Meg looked distressed, Miss Crocker pursed up her lips, and Laurie talked and laughed with all his might, to give a cheerful tone to the festive scene. Jo's one strong point was the fruit, for she had sugared it well, and had a pitcher of rich cream to eat with it. Her hot cheeks cooled a trifle, and she drew a long breath as the pretty glass plates went round, and everyone looked graciously at the little rosy islands floating in a sea of cream. Miss Crocker tasted first, made a wry face, and drank some water hastily. Jo, who had refused, thinking there might not be enough—for they dwindled sadly after the picking over—glanced at Laurie, but he was eating away manfully, though there was a slight pucker about his mouth and he kept his eyes fixed on his plate. Amy took a heaping spoonful, choked, hid her face in her napkin, and left the table precipitately.

"Oh, what is it?" exclaimed Jo, trembling.

"Salt instead of sugar, and the cream is sour," replied Meg.

Jo uttered a groan and fell back in her chair, remembering that she had given a last hasty powdering to the berries out of the two boxes on the kitchen table, and had neglected to put the milk in the refrigerator. She turned scarlet, and was on the verge of crying when she met Laurie's eyes, which *would* look merry in spite of his heroic efforts. The comical side of the affair suddenly struck her, and she laughed till the tears ran down her cheeks. So did everyone else, even "Croaker," as the girls called the old lady, and the unfortunate dinner ended gaily, with bread and butter, olives, and fun.

"I haven't strength of mind enough to clear up now, so we will sober ourselves with a funeral," said Jo as they rose and Miss Crocker made ready to go.

They did sober themselves, for Beth's sake. Laurie dug a grave under the ferns in the grove, little Pip was laid in with many tears by his tender-hearted mistress, and covered with moss, while a wreath of violets and chickweed was hung on the stone which bore his epitaph, composed by Jo while she struggled with the dinner:

> Here lies Pip March,
> Who died the 7th of June;
> Loved and lamented sore,
> And not forgotten soon.

Mrs. March came home to find the three older girls hard at work in the middle of the afternoon, and a glance at the closet gave her an idea of the success of one part of the experiment. As twilight fell, dewy and still, one by one they gathered in the porch, where the June roses were budding beautifully, and each groaned or sighed as she sat down, as if tired or troubled.

"What a dreadful day this has been!" began Jo.

"It has seemed shorter than usual, but so uncomfortable," said Meg.

"Not a bit like home," added Amy.

"It can't seem so without Marmee and little Pip," sighed Beth, glancing with full eyes at the empty cage above her head.

"Here's Mother, dear, and you shall have another bird tomorrow, if you want it." As she spoke, Mrs. March came and took her place among them, looking as if her holiday had not been much pleasanter than theirs. "Are you satisfied with your experiment, girls, or do you want another week of it?" she asked.

"I don't!" cried Jo decidedly.

"Nor I," echoed the others.

"You think, then, that it is better to have a few duties, and live a little for others, do you?"

"Lounging and larking doesn't pay," observed Jo, shaking her head. "I'm tired of it, and mean to go to work at something right off."

"Suppose you learn plain cooking. That's a useful accomplishment which no woman should be without," said Mrs. March, laughing inaudibly at the recollection of Jo's dinner party, for she had met Miss Crocker, and heard her account of it.

"Mother, did you go away and let everything be just to see how we'd get on?" cried Meg.

"Yes. I wanted you to see how the comfort of all depends on each doing her share faithfully. While Hannah and I did your work, you got on pretty well, though I don't think you were very happy or amiable; so I thought I would show you what happens when everyone thinks only of herself. Don't you feel that it is pleasanter to help one another, to have daily duties which make leisure sweet when it comes, and to bear and forbear, that home may be comfortable and lovely to us all?"

"We do, Mother, we do!" cried the girls.

"Then let me advise you to take up your little burdens again; for though they seem heavy sometimes, they are good for us, and lighten as we learn to carry them. Work is wholesome."

"We'll work like bees, and love it too, see if we don't!" said Jo. "I'll learn plain cooking for my holiday task, and the next dinner party I have shall be a success."

"I'll make the set of shirts for Father instead of letting you do it, Marmee. That will be better than fussing over my own things, which are plenty nice enough as they are," said Meg.

"I'll do my lessons every day, and not spend so much time with my music and dolls," was Beth's resolution, while Amy followed their example by heroically declaring, "I shall learn to make buttonholes, and attend to my parts of speech."

"Very good! Then I am quite satisfied with the experiment, and fancy that we shall not have to repeat it. Only don't go to the other extreme and delve like slaves. Have regular hours for work and play, make each day both useful and pleasant, and prove that you understand the worth of time by employing it well. Then youth will be delightful, old age will bring few regrets, and life become a beautiful success, in spite of poverty."

"We'll remember, Mother!" And they did.

CAMP LAURENCE

Beth was postmistress, for, being most at home, she could attend to it regularly, and dearly liked the daily task of unlocking the little door and distributing the mail. One July day she came in with her hands full, and went about the house leaving letters and parcels, like the penny post.

"Here's your posy, Mother! Laurie never forgets that," she said, putting the fresh nosegay in the vase that stood in Marmee's corner, and was kept supplied by the affectionate boy.

"Miss Meg March, one letter and a glove," continued Beth, delivering the articles to her sister.

"Why, I left a pair over there, and here is only one."

"Didn't you drop the other in the garden?"

"No, I'm sure I didn't. I hate to have odd gloves! Never mind, the other may be found. My letter is only a translation of the German song I wanted. I think Mr. Brooke did it, for that isn't Laurie's writing."

Mrs. March glanced at Meg, who was looking very pretty in her gingham morning gown, with the little curls blowing about her forehead, and very womanly as she sat sewing at her little work table full of tidy white rolls—so unconscious of the thought in her mother's mind that Mrs. March smiled, and was satisfied.

"A letter for Doctor Jo, a book, and a funny old hat, which covered the whole post office, stuck outside," said Beth, laughing, as she went into the study where Jo sat writing.

"What a sly fellow Laurie is! I said I wished bigger hats were the fashion, because I burn my face every hot day. He said, 'Why mind the fashion? Wear a big hat, and be comfortable!' I said I would if I had one, and he has sent me this, to try me. I'll wear it, for fun, and show him I *don't* care for the fashion." And, hanging the antique broad brim on a bust of Plato, Jo read her letter.

In a big, dashing hand, Laurie wrote:

Dear Jo,
What ho!

Some English girls and boys are coming to see me tomorrow and I want to have a jolly time. If it's fine, I'm going to pitch my tent in Longmeadow, and row up the whole crew to lunch and croquet—have a fire, make messes, gypsy-fashion, and all sorts of larks. They are nice people, and like such things. Brooke will go, to keep us boys steady, and Kate Vaughn will play propriety for the girls. I want you all to come. Can't let Beth off at any price, and nobody shall worry her. Don't bother about rations—I'll see to that, and everything else—only do come, there's a good fellow!

In a tearing hurry,
Yours ever, Laurie

"Here's richness!" cried Jo, flying in to tell the news to Meg.

"Of course we can go, Mother? It will be such a help to Laurie, for I can row, and Meg see to the lunch, and the children be useful in some way."

"I hope the Vaughns are not fine, grown-up people. Do you know anything about them, Jo?" asked Meg.

"Only that there are four of them. Kate is older than you, Fred and Frank (twins) about my age, and a little girl (Grace), who is nine or ten. Laurie knew them abroad, and liked the boys. I fancied, from the way he primmed up his mouth in speaking of her, that he didn't admire Kate much."

"I'm so glad my French print is clean. It's just the thing, and so becoming!" observed Meg complacently. "Have you anything decent, Jo?"

"Scarlet and gray boating suit, good enough for me. I shall row and tramp about, so I don't want any starch to think of. You'll come, Betty?"

"If you won't let any of the boys talk to me."

"Not a boy!"

"I like to please Laurie, and I'm not afraid of Mr. Brooke, he is so kind. But I don't want to play, or sing, or say anything. You'll take care of me, Jo, so I'll go."

"That's my good girl. Thank you, Mother." And Jo gave the thin cheek a grateful kiss.

"I had a box of chocolate drops, and the picture I wanted to copy," said Amy, showing her mail.

"And I got a note from Mr. Laurence asking me to come over and play to him tonight before the lamps are lighted, and I shall go," added Beth, whose friendship with the old gentleman prospered finely.

"Now let's fly round and do double duty today, so that we can play tomorrow with free minds," said Jo.

When the sun peeped into the girls' rooms early next morning, to promise them a fine day, he saw a comical sight. Each had made such preparation for the fete as seemed necessary and proper. Meg had an extra row of little curl papers across her forehead, Jo had copiously anointed her afflicted face with cold cream. Beth had taken Joanna to bed with her to atone for the approaching separation, and Amy had capped the climax by putting a clothespin on her nose, to uplift the offending feature. It was one of the kind artists use to hold the paper on their drawing boards, therefore quite appropriate and effective for the purpose to which it was now put. This funny spectacle appeared to amuse the sun, for he burst out with such radiance that Jo woke up and roused all her sisters by a hearty laugh at Amy's ornament. Sunshine and laughter were good omens for a pleasure party, and soon a lively bustle began in both houses. Beth, who was ready first, kept reporting what went on next door, and enlivened her sisters' toilets by frequent telegrams from the window.

"There goes the man with the tent! I see Mrs. Barker doing up the lunch in a hamper and a great basket. Now Mr. Laurence is looking up at the sky, and the weathercock. I wish he would go too. There's Laurie, looking like a sailor—nice boy! Oh mercy me! Here's a carriage full of people—a tall lady, a little girl, and two dreadful boys. One is lame—poor thing, he's got a crutch. Laurie didn't tell us that. Be quick, girls! It's getting late. Why, there is Ned Moffat, I do declare. Look, Meg, isn't that the man who bowed to you one day when we were shopping?"

"So it is. How queer that he should come. I thought he was at the mountains. There is Sallie. I'm glad she got back in time. Am I all right, Jo?" cried Meg, in a flutter.

"A regular daisy. Hold up your dress and put your hat straight. Now then, come on!"

"O Jo, you are not going to wear that awful hat? It's too absurd! You shall *not* make a guy of yourself," remonstrated Meg.

"I just will, though, for it's capital—so shady, light, and big. It will make fun, and I don't mind being a guy if I'm comfortable." With that Jo marched straight away, and the rest followed.

Laurie ran to meet them and present them to his friends. The lawn was the reception room, and for several minutes a lively scene was enacted there. Meg was grateful to see that Miss Kate, though twenty, was dressed with a simplicity which American girls would do well to imitate, and she was much flattered by Mr. Ned's assurances that he came especially to see her. Jo understood why Laurie "primmed up his mouth" when speaking of Kate, for that young lady had a stand-off-don't-touch-me air which contrasted strongly with the free-and-easy demeanor of the other girls. Beth took an observation of the new boys, and decided that the lame one was not "dreadful," but gentle and feeble, and she would be kind to him on that account. Amy found Grace a well-mannered, merry little person, and after staring dumbly at one another for a few minutes, they suddenly became very good friends.

Tents, lunch, and croquet utensils having been sent on beforehand, the party was soon embarked, and the two boats pushed off together, leaving Mr. Laurence waving his hat on the shore. Laurie and Jo rowed one boat, Mr. Brooke and Ned the other, while Fred Vaughn, the riotous twin, did his best to upset both by paddling about in a wherry like a disturbed water bug. Jo's funny hat deserved a vote of thanks, for it was of general utility; it broke the ice in the beginning by producing a laugh; it created quite a refreshing breeze, flapping to and fro as she rowed; and would make an excellent umbrella for the whole party if a shower came up, she said. Kate looked rather amazed at Jo's proceedings, especially as she exclaimed "Christopher Columbus!" when she lost her oar, and Laurie said, "My dear fellow, did I hurt you?" when he tripped over her feet in taking his place. But after putting up her glass to examine the queer girl several times, Miss Kate decided that she was "odd, but rather clever," and smiled upon her from afar.

Meg, in the other boat, was delightfully situated, face to face with the rowers, who both admired the prospect. Mr. Brooke was a grave, silent young man with handsome brown eyes and a pleasant voice. Meg liked his quiet manners, and considered him a walking encyclopedia of useful knowledge. He never talked to her much, but he looked at her a good deal, and she felt sure that he did not regard her with aversion. Ned, being in college, of course put on all the airs which freshmen think it their bounden duty to assume; he was not very wise, but very good-natured, and altogether an excellent person to carry on a picnic. Sallie Gardiner was absorbed in keeping her white piqué dress clean and chattering with the ubiquitous Fred, who kept Beth in constant terror by his pranks.

It was not far to Longmeadow, but the tent was pitched and the wickets down by the time they arrived. A pleasant green field, with three wide-spreading oaks in the middle, and a smooth strip of turf for croquet.

"Welcome to Camp Laurence!" said the young host as they landed with exclamations of delight. "Brooke is commander in chief. I am commissary general, the other fellows are staff officers, and you, ladies, are company. The tent is for your especial benefit, and that oak is your drawing room, this is the messroom, and the third is the camp kitchen. Now let's have a game before it gets hot."

Frank, Beth, Amy, and Grace sat down to watch the game played by the other eight. Mr. Brooke chose Meg, Kate, and Fred; Laurie took Sallie, Jo, and Ned. The Englishers played well, but the Americans played better, and contested every inch of the ground as strongly as if the spirit of '76 inspired them. Jo and Fred had several skirmishes, and once narrowly escaped high words. Jo was through the last wicket, and had missed the stroke, which failure ruffled her a good deal. Fred was close behind her, and his turn came before hers; he gave a stroke, his ball hit the wicket and stopped an inch on the wrong side. No one was very near, and running up, he gave it a sly nudge with his toe, which put it just an inch on the right side.

"I'm through! Now, Miss Jo, I'll settle you and get in first," cried the young gentleman.

"You pushed it, I saw you. It's my turn now," said Jo sharply.

"Upon my word, I didn't move it. It rolled a bit, perhaps, but that is allowed, so stand off, please, and let me have a go at the stake."

"We don't cheat in America, but you can, if you choose," said Jo angrily.

"Yankees are a deal the most tricky, everybody knows. There you go!" returned Fred, croqueting her ball far away.

Jo opened her lips to say something rude, but checked herself in time, colored up to her forehead, and stood a minute hammering down a wicket with all her might while Fred hit the stake, and declared himself out with much exultation. She went off to get her ball, and was a long time finding it among the bushes; but she came back looking cool and quiet, and waited her turn patiently. It took several strokes to regain the place she had lost, and when she got there, the other side had nearly won, for Kate's ball was the last but one, and lay near the stake.

"By George, it's all up with us! Good-by, Kate. Miss Jo owes me one, so you are finished," cried Fred excitedly.

"Yankees have a trick of being generous to their enemies," said Jo, with a look that made the lad redden, "especially when they beat them," she added as, leaving Kate's ball untouched, she won the game by a clever stroke.

Laurie threw up his hat, then remembered that it wouldn't do to exult over the defeat of his guests, and stopped in the middle of a cheer to whisper to his friend: "Good for you, Jo! He did cheat, I saw him. We can't tell him so, but he won't do it again, take my word for it."

Meg drew her aside, under pretense of pinning up a loose braid, and said approvingly: "It was dreadfully provoking, but you kept your temper, and I'm so glad, Jo."

"Don't praise me, Meg, for I could box his ears this minute. I should certainly have boiled over if I hadn't stayed among the nettles till I got my rage under enough to hold my tongue. It's simmering now, so I hope he'll keep out of my way," returned Jo, biting her lips.

"Time for lunch," said Mr. Brooke. "Commissary general, will you make the fire and get water while Miss March, Miss Sallie, and I spread the table? Who can make good coffee?"

"Jo can," said Meg, glad to recommend her sister. So Jo, feeling that her late lessons in cookery were to do her honor, went to preside over the coffeepot.

The commander in chief and his aides soon spread the tablecloth with an inviting array of eatables and drinkables, prettily decorated with green leaves. Jo announced that the coffee was ready, and everyone settled themselves to a hearty meal. A very merry lunch it was. There was a pleasing inequality in the table, which produced many mishaps to cups and plates; acorns dropped into the milk, little black ants partook of the refreshments without being invited, and fuzzy caterpillars swung down from the tree to see what was going on.

"There's salt here, if you prefer it," said Laurie as he handed Jo a saucer of berries.

"Thank you, I prefer spiders," she replied, fishing up two unwary little ones who had gone to a creamy death. "How dare you remind me of that horrid dinner party when yours is so nice in every way?" added Jo as they both laughed.

"I had an uncommonly good time that day, and haven't got over it yet. This is no credit to me, you know. I don't do anything; it's you and Meg and Brooke who make it go. What shall we do when we can't eat any more?" asked Laurie.

"Have games—till it's cooler. I brought Authors, and I dare say Miss Kate knows something new and nice. Go and ask her. She's company, and you ought to stay with her more."

"Aren't you company too? I thought she'd suit Brooke, but he keeps talking to Meg. I'm going, so you needn't try to preach propriety, for you can't do it, Jo."

Miss Kate did know several new games, and as the girls would not, and the boys could not, eat any more, they all adjourned to the drawing room to play Rigmarole.

"One person begins a story, any nonsense you like, and tells as long as he pleases, only taking care to stop short at some exciting point, when the next takes it up and does the same. It's very funny when well done, and makes a perfect jumble of tragical-comical stuff to laugh over. Please start it, Mr. Brooke," said Kate.

Lying on the grass at the feet of the two young ladies, Mr. Brooke obediently began the story, with the handsome brown eyes steadily fixed upon the sunshiny river.

"Once on a time, a knight went out into the world to seek his fortune, for he had nothing but his sword and his shield. He traveled a long while, nearly eight and twenty years, and had a hard time of it till he came to the palace of a good old king, who had offered a reward to anyone who would tame and train a fine but unbroken colt of which he was very fond. The knight agreed to try, and got on slowly but surely; for the colt was a gallant fellow, and soon learned to love his new master, though he was freakish and wild. Every day when he gave his lessons to this pet of the king's the knight rode him through the city, and as he rode he looked everywhere for a certain beautiful face, which he had seen many times in his dreams, but never found. One day, as he went prancing down a quiet street he saw at the window of a ruinous castle the lovely face. He was delighted, inquired who lived in this old castle, and was told that several captive princesses were kept there by a spell, and spun all day to lay up money to buy their liberty. The knight wished intensely that he could free them, but he was poor, and could only go by each day, watching for the sweet face. At last he resolved to get into the castle and ask how he could help them. He went and knocked, the great door flew open, and he beheld——"

"A ravishingly lovely lady, who exclaimed, with a cry of rapture, 'At last! At last!'" continued Kate, who had read French novels, and admired the style. "''Tis she!' cried Count Gustave, and fell at her feet in an ecstasy of joy. 'Oh, rise!' she said, extending a hand of marble fairness. 'Never!—till you tell me how I may rescue you," swore the knight, still kneeling. 'Alas! my cruel fate condemns me to remain here till my tyrant is destroyed.' 'Where is the villain?' 'In the mauve salon. Go, brave heart, and save me from despair.' 'I obey, and return victorious or dead!' With these thrilling words he rushed away, and flinging open the door of the mauve salon, was about to enter, when he received——"

"A stunning blow from the big Greek lexicon which an old fellow in a black gown fired at him," said Ned. "Instantly Sir What's-his-name recovered himself, pitched the tyrant out of the window, and turned to join the lady, victorious, but with a bump on his brow; found the door locked, tore up the curtains, made a rope ladder, got halfway down when the ladder broke, and he went headfirst into the moat, sixty feet below. Could swim like a duck, paddled round the castle till he came to a little door guarded by two stout fellows; knocked their heads together till they cracked like a couple of nuts, then he smashed in the door, went up a pair of stone steps covered with dust a foot thick, toads as big as your fist, and spiders that would frighten you into hysterics, Miss March. At the top of these steps he came plump upon a sight that took his breath away and chilled his blood——"

"A tall figure, all in white with a veil over its face and a lamp in its wasted hand," went on Meg. "It beckoned, gliding noiselessly before him down a corridor as dark and cold as any tomb. Shadowy effigies in armor stood on either side, a dead silence reigned, the lamp burned blue, and the ghostly figure ever and anon turned its face toward him, showing the glitter of awful eyes through its white veil. They reached a curtained door, behind which sounded lovely music. He sprang forward to enter, but the specter plucked him back, and waved threateningly before him a——"

"Snuffbox," said Jo, in a sepulchral tone which convulsed the audience. "'Thankee,' said the knight politely as he took a pinch, and sneezed seven times so violently that his head fell off. 'Ha! Ha!' laughed the ghost, and having peeped through the keyhole at the princesses spinning away for dear life, the evil spirit picked up her victim and put him in a large tin box, where there were eleven other knights packed together without their heads, like sardines, who all rose and began to——"

"Dance a hornpipe," cut in Fred as Jo paused for breath, "and as they danced the rubbishy old castle turned to a man-of-war in full sail. 'Up with the jib, reef the tops'l halliards, helm hard alee, and man the guns!' roared the captain as a Portuguese pirate hove in sight, with a flag black as ink flying from her foremast. 'Go in and win, my hearties!' says the captain, and a tremendous fight began. Of course the British beat—they always do."

"No they don't!" cried Jo, aside.

"Having taken the pirate captain prisoner, sailed slap over the schooner, whose decks were piled with dead and lee scuppers ran blood. 'Bosun's mate, take a bight of the flying-jib sheet, and start this villain if he don't confess his sins double-quick,' said the British captain. The Portuguese held his tongue like a brick, and walked the plank while the jolly tars cheered like mad. But the sly dog dived, came up under the man-of-war, scuttled her, and down she went, with all sail set, 'To the bottom of the sea, sea, sea,' where——"

"Oh gracious! What *shall* I say?" cried Sallie as Fred ended his rigmarole, in which he had jumbled together, pell-mell, nautical phrases and facts out of one of his favorite books. "Well, they went to the bottom, and a nice mermaid welcomed them, but was much grieved on finding the box of headless knights, and kindly pickled them in brine, hoping to discover the mystery about them. By and by a diver came down, and the mermaid said, 'I'll give you this box of pearls if you can take it up,' for she wanted to restore the poor things to life, and couldn't raise the heavy load herself. So the diver hoisted it up, and was much disappointed on opening it to find no pearls. He left it in a great lonely field, where it was found by a——"

"Little goose girl, who kept a hundred fat geese in the field," said Amy when Sallie's invention gave out. "The little girl was sorry for them, and asked an old woman what she should do to help them. 'Your geese will tell you, they know everything,' said the old woman. So she asked what she should use for new heads, since the old ones were lost, and all the geese opened their hundred mouths and screamed——"

"'Cabbages!'" continued Laurie promptly. "'Just the thing,' said the girl, and ran to get twelve fine ones from her garden. She put them on, the knights revived at once, thanked her, and went on their way rejoicing, never knowing the difference, for there were so many other heads like them in the world that no one thought anything of it. The knight in whom I'm interested went back to find the pretty face, and learned that the princesses had spun themselves free, and all gone to be married but one. He was in a great state of mind at that, and mounting the colt, who stood by him through thick and thin, rushed to the castle to see which was left. Peeping over the hedge, he saw the queen of his affections picking flowers in her garden. 'Will you give me a rose?' said he. 'You must come and get it. I can't come to you. It isn't proper,' said she, as sweet as honey. He tried to climb over the hedge, but it seemed to grow higher and higher; then he tried to push through, but it grew thicker and thicker, and he was in despair. So he patiently broke twig after twig till he had made a little hole, through which he peeped, saying imploringly, 'Let me in! Let me in!' But the pretty princess did not seem to understand, for she picked her roses quietly, and left him to fight his way in. Whether he did or not, Frank will tell you."

"I can't. I'm not playing, I never do," said Frank, dismayed at the sentimental predicament out of which he was to rescue the absurd couple.

"So the poor knight is to be left sticking in the hedge, is he?" asked Mr. Brooke, still watching the river.

"I guess the princess gave him a posy, and opened the gate, after a while," said Laurie, smiling to himself.

"What a piece of nonsense we have made! With practice we might do something quite clever. Do you know Truth?" asked Sallie, after they had laughed over their story.

"I hope so," said Meg soberly.

"The game, I mean?"

"What is it?" said Fred.

"Why, you pile up your hands, choose a number and draw out in turn, and the person who draws the number has to answer truly any questions put by the rest. It's great fun."

"Let's try it," said Jo, who liked new experiments.

Miss Kate and Mr. Brooke, Meg, and Ned declined, but Fred, Sallie, Jo, and Laurie piled and drew, and the lot fell to Laurie.

"Who are your heroes?" asked Joe.

"Grandfather and Napoleon."

"Which lady here do you think prettiest?" said Sallie.

"Margaret."

"Which do you like best?" from Fred.

"Jo, of course."

"What silly questions you ask!" And Jo gave a disdainful shrug as the rest laughed at Laurie's matter-of-fact tone.

"Try again. Truth isn't a bad game," said Fred.

"It's a very good one for you," retorted Jo, in a low voice. Her turn came next.

"What is your greatest fault?" asked Fred, by way of testing in her the virtue he lacked himself.

"A quick temper."

"What do you wish for?" said Laurie.

"A pair of boot lacings," returned Jo, guessing and defeating his purpose.

"Not a true answer. You must say what you really do want most."

"Genius. Don't you wish you could give it to me, Laurie?" And she slyly smiled in his disappointed face.

"What virtues do you most admire in a man?" asked Sallie.

"Courage and honesty."

"Now my turn," said Fred, as his hand came last.

"Let's give it to him," whispered Laurie to Jo, who nodded, and asked at once, "Didn't you cheat at croquet?"

"Well, yes, a little bit."

"Good! Didn't you take your story out of *The Sea Lion?*" said Laurie.

"Rather."

"Don't you think the English nation perfect in every respect?" asked Sallie.

"I should be ashamed of myself if I didn't."

"He's a true John Bull. Now, Miss Sallie, you shall have a chance without waiting to draw. I'll harrow up your feelings first by asking if you don't think you are something of a flirt," said Laurie.

"You impertinent boy! Of course I'm not," exclaimed Sallie, with an air that proved the contrary.

"What do you hate most?" asked Fred.

"Spiders and rice pudding."

"What do you like best?" asked Jo.

"Dancing and French gloves."

"Well, *I* think Truth is a very silly play. Let's have a sensible game of Authors, to refresh our minds," proposed Jo.

Ned, Frank, and the little girls joined in this, and while it went on, the three elders sat apart, talking. Miss Kate took out her sketch again, and Margaret watched her, while Mr. Brooke lay on the grass with a book, which he did not read.

"How beautifully you do it! I wish I could draw," said Meg, with mingled admiration and regret in her voice.

"Why don't you learn? I should think you had taste and talent for it," replied Miss Kate graciously.

"I haven't time."

"Your mamma prefers other accomplishments, I fancy. So did mine, but I proved to her that I had talent by taking a few lessons privately, and then she was quite willing I should go on. Can't you do the same with your governess?"

"I have none."

"I forgot. Young ladies in America go to school more than with us. Very fine schools they are, too, Papa says. You go to a private one, I suppose?"

"I don't go at all. I am a governess myself."

"Oh, indeed!" said Miss Kate, but she might as well have said, "Dear me, how dreadful!" for her tone implied it.

Mr. Brooke looked up, and said quickly, "Young ladies in America love independence as much as their ancestors did, and are admired and respected for supporting themselves."

"Oh yes, of course it's very nice and proper in them to do so. We have many most respectable and worthy young women who do the same and are employed by the nobility because, being the daughters of gentlemen, they are both well-bred and accomplished, you know," said Miss Kate in a patronizing tone that hurt Meg's pride, and made her work seem not only more distasteful, but degrading.

"Did the German song suit, Miss March?" inquired Mr. Brooke, breaking an awkward pause.

"Oh yes! It was very sweet, and I'm much obliged to whoever translated it for me."

"Don't you read German?" asked Miss Kate, with a look of surprise.

"Not very well. My father, who taught me, is away, and I don't get on very fast alone."

"Try a little now. Here is Schiller's *Mary Stuart*, and a tutor who loves to teach," and Mr. Brooke laid his book on her lap, with an inviting smile.

"It's so hard I'm afraid to try," said Meg, grateful, but bashful in the presence of the accomplished young lady beside her.

"I'll read a bit to encourage you," and Miss Kate read one of the most beautiful passages, in a perfectly correct but perfectly expressionless manner.

Mr. Brooke made no comment as she returned the book to Meg, who said innocently: "I thought it was poetry."

"Some of it is. Try this passage." There was a queer smile about Mr. Brooke's mouth as he opened at poor Mary's lament.

Meg, obediently following the long grass-blade which her new tutor used to point with, read slowly and timidly, unconsciously making poetry of the hard words by the soft intonation of her musical voice. Down the page went the green guide, and presently, forgetting her listener in the beauty of the sad scene, Meg read as if alone, giving a little touch of tragedy to the words of the unhappy queen. If she had seen the brown eyes then, she would have stopped short, but she never looked up, and the lesson was not spoiled for her.

"Very well indeed!" said Mr. Brooke as she paused, quite ignoring her many mistakes, and looking as if he did indeed "love to teach."

Miss Kate put up her glass and, having taken a survey of the little tableau before her, shut her sketchbook, saying with condescension:

"You've a nice accent, and, in time, will be a clever reader. I advise you to learn, for German is a valuable accomplishment to teachers. I must look after Grace, she is romping." And Miss Kate strolled away, adding to herself, with a shrug: "I didn't come to chaperon a governess, though she *is* young and pretty. What odd people these Yankees are. I'm afraid Laurie will be quite spoiled among them."

"I forgot that English people rather turn up their noses at governesses, and don't treat them as we do," said Meg.

"Tutors, also, have rather a hard time of it there, as I know to my sorrow. There's no place like America for us workers, Miss Margaret." And Mr. Brooke looked so contented and cheerful that Meg was ashamed to lament her hard lot.

"I'm glad I live in it, then. I don't like my work, but I get a good deal of satisfaction out of it after all, so I won't complain. I only wish I liked teaching as you do."

"I think you would if you had Laurie for a pupil. I shall be sorry to lose him next year," said Mr. Brooke.

"Going to college, I suppose?" Meg's lips asked that question, but her eyes added, "And what becomes of you?"

"Yes. It's high time he went, for he is ready. And as soon as he is off, I shall turn soldier. I am needed."

"I am glad of that!" exclaimed Meg. "I should think every young man would want to go—though it is hard for the mothers and sisters who stay at home," she added sorrowfully.

"I have neither, and very few friends, to care whether I live or die," said Mr. Brooke rather bitterly.

"Laurie and his grandfather would care a great deal, and we should all be very sorry to have any harm happen to you," said Meg heartily.

"Thank you. That sounds pleasant," began Mr. Brooke, looking cheerful again, but before he could finish his speech, Ned, mounted on the old horse, came lumbering up to display his equestrian skill before the young ladies.

"Don't you love to ride?" asked Grace of Amy as they stood resting after a race round the field with the others, led by Ned.

"I dote upon it. My sister Meg used to ride when Papa was rich, but we don't keep any horses now, except Ellen Tree," added Amy, laughing.

"Tell me about Ellen Tree. Is it a donkey?" asked Grace curiously.

"Why, you see Jo is crazy about horses, and so am I, but we've only got an old side saddle, and no horse. Out in our garden is an apple tree that has a nice low branch; so Jo put the saddle on it, fixed some reins on the part that turns up, and we bounce away on Ellen Tree whenever we like."

"How funny!" laughed Grace. "I have a pony at home, and ride nearly every day in the park with Fred and Kate. It's very nice, for my friends go too, and the Row is full of ladies and gentlemen."

"Dear, how charming! I hope I shall go abroad some day, but I'd rather go to Rome than the Row," said Amy, who had not the remotest idea what the Row was, and wouldn't have asked for the world.

Frank, sitting just behind the little girls, heard what they were saying, and pushed his crutch away from him with an impatient gesture as he watched the active lads going through all sorts of comical gymnastics. Beth, who was collecting the scattered Author cards, said in her shy yet friendly way: "I'm afraid you are tired. Can I do anything for you?"

"Talk to me, please. It's dull sitting by myself," answered Frank, who had evidently been used to being made much of at home.

If he had asked her to deliver a Latin oration, it would not have seemed a more impossible task to bashful Beth; but there was no place to run to, no Jo to hide behind now, and the poor boy looked so wistfully at her that she bravely resolved to try.

"What do you like to talk about?" she asked.

"Well, I like to hear about cricket and boating and hunting," said Frank, who had not yet learned to suit his amusements to his strength.

"My heart! What shall I do? I don't know anything about them," thought Beth, and, forgetting the boy's misfortune in her flurry, she said, hoping to make him talk, "I never saw any hunting, but I suppose you know all about it."

"I did once, but I can never hunt again, for I got hurt leaping a confounded five-barred gate; so there are no more horses and hounds for me," said Frank, with a sigh that made Beth hate herself for her innocent blunder.

"Your deer are much prettier than our ugly buffaloes," she said, turning to the prairies for help, and feeling glad that she had read one of the boys' books in which Jo delighted.

Buffaloes proved soothing and satisfactory, and in her eagerness to amuse another Beth forgot herself, and was quite unconscious of her sisters' surprise and delight at the unusual spectacle of Beth talking away to one of the dreadful boys against whom she had begged protection.

"Bless her heart! She pities him, so she is good to him," said Jo, beaming at her from the croquet ground.

"I always said she was a little saint," added Meg.

"I haven't heard Frank laugh so much for ever so long," said Grace to Amy as they sat discussing dolls.

"My sister Beth is a very *fastidious* girl when she likes to be," said Amy, well pleased at Beth's success. She meant "fascinating," but as Grace didn't know the exact meaning of either word, "fastidious" sounded well, and made a good impression.

At sunset the tent was struck, hampers packed, wickets pulled up, boats loaded, and the whole party floated down the river singing at the tops of their voices. Ned, getting sentimental, warbled a serenade with the pensive refrain—"Alone, alone, ah! woe, alone."—and at the lines

> "We each are young, we each have a heart,
> Oh, why should we stand thus coldly apart?"

he looked at Meg with such a lackadaisical expression that she laughed outright and spoiled his song.

"How can you be so cruel to me?" he whispered, under cover of a lively chorus. "You've kept close to that starched-up Englishwoman all day, and now you snub me."

"I didn't mean to, but you looked so funny I really couldn't help it," replied Meg, passing over the first part of his reproach, for it was quite true that she *had* shunned him, remembering the Moffat party and the talk after it.

Ned was offended, and turned to Sallie for consolation, saying to her rather pettishly: "There isn't a bit of flirt in that girl, is there?"

"Not a particle, but she's a dear," returned Sallie.

CASTLES IN THE AIR

Laurie lay luxuriously swinging to and fro in his hammock one warm September afternoon, wondering what his neighbors were about, but too lazy to go and find out. He was in one of his moods, for the day had been both unprofitable and unsatisfactory, and he was wishing he could live it over again. The hot weather made him indolent, and he had shirked his studies, tried Mr. Brooke's patience to the utmost, displeased his grandfather by practicing half the afternoon, frightened the maid-servants half out of their wits by mischievously hinting that one of his dogs was going mad, and after high words with the stableman about some fancied neglect of his horse, he had flung himself into his hammock to fume over the stupidity of the world in general till the peace of the lovely day quieted him in spite of himself. Staring up into the green gloom of the horse-chestnut trees above him, he dreamed dreams of all sorts, and was just imagining himself tossing on the ocean in a voyage round the world when the sound of voices brought him ashore in a flash. Peeping through the meshes of the hammock, he saw the Marches coming out as if bound on some expedition.

"What in the world are those girls about now?" thought Laurie, opening his sleepy eyes to take a good look, for there was something rather peculiar in the appearance of his neighbors. Each wore a large, flapping hat, a brown-linen pouch slung over one shoulder, and carried a long staff. Meg had a cushion, Jo a book, Beth a basket, and Amy a portfolio. All walked quietly through the garden, out at the back gate, and began to climb the hill that lay between the house and the river.

"Well, that's cool!" said Laurie to himself. "To have a picnic and never ask me. They can't be going in the boat, for they haven't got the key. Perhaps they forgot it. I'll take it to them, and see what's going on."

Though possessed of half a dozen hats, it took him some time to find one, then there was a hunt for the key, so that the girls were quite out of sight when he leaped the fence and ran after them. Taking the shortest way to the boathouse, he waited for them to appear, but no one came, and he went up the hill to take an observation. A grove of pines covered one part of it, and from the heart of this green spot came a clearer sound than the soft sigh of the pines or the drowsy chirp of the crickets.

"Here's a landscape!" thought Laurie, peeping through the bushes, and looking wide-awake and good-natured already.

It *was* rather a pretty little picture, for the sisters sat together in the shady nook, with sun and shadow flickering over them, the aromatic wind lifting their hair and cooling their hot cheeks, and all the little wood people going on with their affairs as if these were no strangers but old friends. Meg sat on her cushion, sewing daintily with her white hands, and looking as fresh and sweet as a rose in her pink dress among the green. Beth was sorting the cones that lay thick under the hemlock near by, for she made pretty things of them. Amy was sketching a group of ferns, and Jo was knitting as she read aloud. A shadow passed over the boy's face as he watched them, feeling that he ought to go away because uninvited, yet lingering because home seemed very lonely, and this quiet party in the woods most attractive to his restless spirit. He stood so still that a squirrel busy with its harvesting ran down a pine close beside him, saw him suddenly and skipped back, scolding so shrilly that Beth looked up, espied the wistful face behind the birches, and beckoned with a reassuring smile.

"May I come in, please? Or shall I be a bother?" he asked.

Meg lifted her eyebrows, but Jo scowled at her defiantly and said at once: "Of course you may. We should have asked you before, only we thought you wouldn't care for such a girl's game as this."

"I always liked your games, but if Meg doesn't want me, I'll go away."

"I've no objection if you do something; it's against the rules to be idle here," replied Meg, gravely but graciously.

"Much obliged. I'll do anything if you'll let me stop a bit, for it's as dull as the Desert of Sahara down there. Shall I sew, read, cone, draw, or do all at once? Bring on your bears, I'm ready." And Laurie sat down with a submissive expression delightful to behold.

"Finish this story while I set my heel," said Jo, handing him the book.

"Yes'm," was the meek answer as he began, doing his best to prove his gratitude for the favor of an admission into the "Busy Bee Society." The story was not a long one, and when it was finished, he ventured to ask a few questions as a reward of merit. "Please, ma'am, could I inquire if this highly instructive and charming institution is a new one?"

"Would you tell him?" asked Meg of her sisters.

"He'll laugh," said Amy warningly.

"Who cares?" said Jo.

"I guess he'll like it," added Beth.

"Of course I shall! I give you my word I won't laugh. Tell away, Jo, and don't be afraid."

"The idea of being afraid of you! Well, you see we used to play *Pilgrim's Progress*, and we have been going on with it in earnest, all winter and summer."

"Yes, I know," said Laurie, nodding wisely.

"Who told you?" demanded Jo.

"Spirits."

"No, I did. I wanted to amuse him one night when you were all away, and he was rather dismal. He did like it, so don't scold, Jo," said Beth meekly.

"You can't keep a secret. Never mind, it saves trouble now."

"Go on, please," said Laurie.

"Oh, didn't she tell you about this new plan of ours? Well, we have tried not to waste our holiday, but each has had a task. The vacation is nearly over, the stints are all done, and we are ever so glad that we didn't dawdle."

"Yes, I should think so." And Laurie thought regretfully of his own idle days.

"Mother likes to have us out of doors as much as possible, so we bring our work here. For the fun of it we bring our things in these bags, wear the old hats, use poles to climb the hill, and play pilgrims, as we used to do years ago. We call this hill the Delectable Mountain, for we can look far away and see the country where we hope to live sometime."

Jo pointed, and Laurie sat up to examine; for through an opening in the wood one could look across the wide blue river, the meadows on the other side, far over the outskirts of the great city to the green hills that rose to meet the sky. The sun was low, and the heavens glowed with the splendor of an autumn sunset. Gold and purple clouds lay on the hilltops, and rising high into the ruddy light were silvery white peaks that shone like the airy spires of some Celestial City.

"How beautiful that is!" said Laurie softly, for he was quick to see and feel beauty of any kind.

"It's often so, and we like to watch it, for it is never the same, but always splendid," replied Amy.

"Jo talks about the country where we hope to live sometime—the real country, she means, with pigs and chickens and haymaking. It would be nice, but I wish the beautiful country up there was real, and we could ever go to it," said Beth musingly.

"There is a lovelier country even than that, where we *shall* go by and by, when we are good enough," answered Meg.

"It seems so long to wait, so hard to do. I want to fly away at once, as those swallows fly, and go in at that splendid gate."

"You'll get there, Beth, sooner or later, no fear of that," said Jo. "I'm the one that will have to fight and work, and climb and wait, and maybe never get in after all."

"You'll have me for company, if that's any comfort. I shall have to do a deal of traveling before I come in sight of your Celestial City. If I arrive late, you'll say a good word for me, won't you, Beth?"

Something in the boy's face troubled his little friend, but she said cheerfully, with her quiet eyes on the changing clouds: "If people really want to go, and really try all their lives, I think they will get in; for I don't believe there are any locks on that door, or any guards at the gate. I always imagine it is as it is in the picture where the shining ones stretch out their hands to welcome poor Christian as he comes up from the river."

"Wouldn't it be fun if all the castles in the air which we make could come true, and we could live in them?" said Jo after a little pause.

"I've made such quantities it would be hard to choose which I'd have," said Laurie, lying flat, and throwing cones at the squirrel who had betrayed him.

"You'd have to take your favorite one. What is it?" asked Meg.

"If I tell mine, will you tell yours?"

"Yes, if the girls will too."

"We will. Now, Laurie."

"After I'd seen as much of the world as I want to, I'd like to settle in Germany, and have just as much music as I choose. I'm to be a famous musician myself, and all creation is to rush to hear me; and I'm never to be bothered about money or business, but just enjoy myself, and live for what I like. That's my favorite castle. What's yours, Meg?"

Margaret seemed to find it a little hard to tell hers. She said slowly: "I should like a lovely house, full of all sorts of luxurious things—nice food, pretty clothes, handsome furniture, pleasant people, and heaps of money. I am to be mistress of it, and manage it as I like, with plenty of servants, so I never need work a bit. How I should enjoy it! For I wouldn't be idle, but do good, and make everyone love me dearly."

"Wouldn't you have a master for your castle in the air?" asked Laurie slyly.

"I said 'pleasant people,' you know." And Meg carefully tied up her shoes as she spoke, so that no one saw her face.

"Why don't you say you'd have a splendid, wise, good husband, and some angelic little children? You know your castle wouldn't be perfect without," said blunt Jo.

"You'd have nothing but horses, inkstands, and novels in yours," answered Meg petulantly.

"Wouldn't I, though? I'd have a stable full of Arabian steeds, rooms piled with books, and I'd write out of a magic inkstand, so that my works should be as famous as Laurie's music. I want to do something splendid before I go into my castle—something heroic or wonderful that won't be forgotten after I'm dead. I don't know what, but I'm on the watch for it. I think I shall write books, and get rich and famous. That would suit me, so that is *my* favorite dream."

"Mine is to stay at home safe with Father and Mother, and help take care of the family," said Beth contentedly.

"Don't you wish for anything else?" asked Laurie.

"Since I had my little piano, I am perfectly satisfied. I only wish we may all keep well and be together—nothing else."

"I have ever so many wishes, but the pet one is to be an artist, and go to Rome, and do fine pictures, and be the best artist in the whole world," was Amy's modest desire.

"We're an ambitious set, aren't we? Every one of us but Beth wants to be rich and famous, and gorgeous in every respect. I do wonder if any of us will ever get our wishes," said Laurie, chewing grass like a meditative calf.

"I've got the key to my castle in the air, but whether I can unlock the door remains to be seen," observed Jo mysteriously.

"I've got the key to mine, but I'm not allowed to try it. Hang college!" muttered Laurie, with an impatient sigh.

"Here's mine!" And Amy waved her pencil.

"I haven't got any," said Meg forlornly.

"Yes you have," said Laurie at once.

"Where?"

"In your face."

"Nonsense. That's of no use."

"Wait and see if it doesn't bring you something worth having," replied the boy, laughing at the thought of a charming little secret which he fancied he knew. Meg colored behind the brake, but asked no questions and looked across the river with the same expectant expression which Mr. Brooke had worn when he told the story of the knight.

"If we are all alive ten years hence, let's meet, and see how many of us have got our wishes, or how much nearer we are then than now," said Jo, always ready with a plan.

"Bless me! How old I shall be—twenty-seven!" exclaimed Meg, who felt grown-up already, having just reached seventeen.

"You and I will be twenty-six, Teddy, Beth twenty-four, and Amy twenty-two. What a venerable party!" said Jo.

"I hope I shall have done something to be proud of by that time, but I'm such a lazy dog I'm afraid I shall 'dawdle,' Jo."

"You need a motive, Mother says, and when you get it, she is sure you'll work splendidly."

"Is she? By Jupiter I will, if I only get the chance!" cried Laurie, sitting up with sudden energy. "I ought to be satisfied to please Grandfather, and I do try, but it's working against the grain, you see, and comes hard. He wants me to be an India merchant, as he was, and I'd rather be shot. I hate tea and silk and spices, and every sort of rubbish his old ships bring, and I don't care how soon they go to the bottom when I own them. Going to college ought to satisfy him, for if I give him four years he ought to let me off from the business; but he's set, and I've got to do just as he did—unless I break away and please myself, as my father did. If there was anyone left to stay with the old gentleman, I'd do it tomorrow."

Laurie spoke excitedly, and looked ready to carry his threat into execution on the slightest provocation; for he was growing up very fast, and in spite of his indolent ways, had a young man's restless longing to try the world for himself.

"I advise you to sail away in one of your ships and never come home again till you have tried your own way," said Jo, whose imagination was fired by the thought of such a daring exploit.

"That's not right, Jo. You mustn't talk in that way, and Laurie mustn't take your bad advice. You should do just what your grandfather wishes, my dear boy," said Meg, in her most maternal tone. "Do your best at college, and when he sees that you try to please him, I'm sure he won't be hard or unjust to you. As you say, there is no one else to stay with and love him, and you'd never forgive yourself if you left him without his permission. Don't be dismal or fret, but do your duty, and you'll get your reward, as good Mr. Brooke has, by being respected and loved."

"What do you know about him?" asked Laurie, grateful for the good advice, but objecting to the lecture.

"Only what your grandpa told us about him—how he took good care of his own mother till she died, and wouldn't go abroad as tutor to some nice person because he wouldn't leave her; and how he provides now for an old woman who nursed his mother, and never tells anyone, but is just as generous and patient and good as he can be."

"So he is, dear old fellow!" said Laurie heartily as Meg paused, looking flushed and earnest with her story. "It's like Grandpa to find out all about him without letting him know, and to tell all his goodness to others. Brooke couldn't understand why your mother was so kind to him, asking him over with me, and treating him in her beautiful friendly way. He thought she was just perfect, and talked about it for days and days, and went on about you all in flaming style. If ever I do get my wish, you see what I'll do for Brooke."

"Begin to do something now, by not plaguing his life out," said Meg sharply.

"How do you know I do, miss?"

"I can always tell by his face when he goes away. If you have been good, he looks satisfied and walks briskly; if you have plagued him, he's sober and walks slowly, as if he wanted to go back and do his work better."

"Well, I like that! So you keep an account of my good and bad marks in Brooke's face, do you?"

"Don't be angry, and oh, don't tell him I said anything! It was only to show that I cared how you get on, and what is said here is said in confidence, you know," cried Meg.

"I don't tell tales," replied Laurie with his "high-and-mighty" air, as Jo called a certain expression which he occasionally wore.

"Please don't be offended. I didn't mean to preach or tell tales or be silly. I only thought Jo was encouraging you in a feeling which you'd be sorry for by and by. You are so kind to us we feel as if you were our brother, and say just what we think. Forgive me, I meant it kindly." And Meg offered her hand with a gesture both affectionate and timid.

Ashamed of his momentary pique, Laurie squeezed the kind little hand, and said frankly: "I'm the one to be forgiven. I'm cross. I like to have you tell me my faults and be sisterly, so don't mind if I am grumpy sometimes. I thank you all the same."

Bent on showing that he was not offended, he made himself as agreeable as possible—wound cotton for Meg, recited poetry to please Jo, shook down cones for Beth, and helped Amy with her ferns, proving himself a fit person to belong to the Busy Bee Society. The faint sound of a bell warned them that Hannah had put the tea to "draw," and they would just have time to get home to supper.

"May I come again?" asked Laurie.

"Yes, if you are good, and love your book, as the boys in the primer are told to do," said Meg, smiling.

"I'll try."

"Then you may come, and I'll teach you to knit as the Scotchmen do. There's a demand for socks just now," added Jo, waving hers like a big blue worsted banner as they parted at the gate.

That night when Beth played to Mr. Laurence in the twilight, Laurie, standing in the shadow of the curtain, listened to the little David, whose simple music always quieted his moody spirit, and watched the old man, who sat with his gray head on his hand thinking tender thoughts of the dead child he had loved so much. Remembering the conversation of the afternoon, the boy said to himself, with the resolve to make the sacrifice cheerfully:

"I'll let my castle go, and stay with the dear old gentleman while he needs me, for I am all he has."

SECRETS

Jo was very busy in the garret, for the October days began to grow chilly, and the afternoons were short. For two or three hours the sun lay warmly in the high window, showing Jo seated on the old sofa writing busily, with her papers spread out upon a trunk before her. Quite absorbed in her work, Jo scribbled away till the last page was filled, when she signed her name with a flourish, and threw down her pen, exclaiming: "There, I've done my best! If this won't suit, I shall have to wait till I can do better."

Lying back on the sofa, she read the manuscript carefully through, making dashes here and there, and putting in many exclamation points. Then she tied it up with a smart red ribbon, and sat a minute looking at it with a sober, wistful expression which plainly showed how earnest her work had been. Jo's desk up here was an old tin kitchen, which hung against the wall. In it she kept her papers and a few books. From this tin receptacle Jo produced another manuscript, and putting both in her pocket, crept quietly downstairs.

She put on her hat and jacket as noiselessly as possible, and going to the back-entry window, got out on the roof of a low porch, swung herself down to the grassy bank, and took a roundabout way to the road. Once there, she composed herself, hailed a passing omnibus, and rolled away to town looking very merry and mysterious.

If anyone had been watching her, he would have thought her movements decidedly peculiar; for on alighting she went off at a great pace till she reached a certain number in a certain busy street. Having found the place with some difficulty, she went into the doorway, looked up the dirty stairs, and after standing stock-still a minute, suddenly dived into the street and walked away as rapidly as she came. This maneuver she repeated several times, to the great amusement of a black-eyed young gentleman lounging in the window of a building opposite. On returning for the third time, Jo gave herself a shake, pulled her hat over her eyes, and walked up the stairs looking as if she were going to have all her teeth out.

There was a dentist's sign, among others, which adorned the entrance, and after staring a moment at the pair of artificial jaws which slowly opened and shut to draw attention to a fine set of teeth, the young gentleman put on his coat, took his hat, and went down to post himself in the opposite doorway, saying, with a smile and a shiver: "It's like her to come alone, but if she has a bad time she'll need someone to help her home."

In ten minutes Jo came running down stairs with a very red face, and the general appearance of a person who had just passed through a trying ordeal of some sort. When she saw the young gentleman, she looked anything but pleased, and passed him with a nod, but he followed, asking with an air of sympathy: "Did you have a bad time?"

"Not very."

"You got through quickly."

"Yes, thank goodness!"

"Why did you go alone?"

"Didn't want anyone to know."

"You're the oddest fellow I ever saw. How many did you have out?"

Jo looked at her friend as if she did not understand him, then began to laugh. "There are two which I want to have come out, but I must wait a week."

"What are you laughing at? You are up to some mischief, Jo," said Laurie, looking mystified. "I'd like to walk with you, and tell you a secret, and if I tell you, you must tell me yours."

"I haven't got any," began Jo, but stopped suddenly, remembering that she had.

"You know you have—you can't hide anything, so up and 'fess, or I won't tell," cried Laurie.

"Is your secret a nice one?"

"Oh, isn't it! All about people you know, and such fun! You ought to hear it, and I've been aching to tell it this long time. Come, you begin."

"You'll not say anything about it at home, will you?"

"Not a word."

"Well, I've left two stories with a newspaperman, and he's to give his answer next week," whispered Jo.

"Hurrah for Miss March, the celebrated American authoress!" cried Laurie, throwing up his hat and catching it again.

"Hush! It won't come to anything, I dare say. But I couldn't rest till I had tried, and I said nothing about it, because I didn't want anyone else to be disappointed."

"It won't fail. Why, Jo, your stories are works of Shakespeare compared to half the rubbish that is published every day. Won't it be fun to see them in print, and shan't we feel proud of our authoress?"

Jo's eyes sparkled. "Where's *your* secret? Play fair, Teddy, or I'll never believe you again," she said.

"I may get into a scrape for telling; but I didn't promise not to, so I will, for I never feel easy in my mind till I've told you any plummy bit of news I get. I know where Meg's glove is."

"Is that all?" said Jo, looking disappointed.

"It's quite enough for the present, as you'll agree when I tell you where it is."

"Tell, then."

Laurie bent and whispered three words in Jo's ear which produced a comical change. She stood and stared at him for a minute, looking both surprised and displeased, then walked on, saying sharply: "How do you know?"

"Saw it."

"Where?"

"Pocket."

"All this time?"

"Yes. Isn't that romantic?"

"No, it's horrid."

"Don't you like it?"

"Of course I don't. It's ridiculous. It won't be allowed. My patience! What would Meg say?"

"You are not to tell anyone, mind that."

"I didn't promise."

"That was understood, and I trusted you."

"Well, I won't for the present, anyway. But I'm disgusted, and wish you hadn't told me."

"I thought you'd be pleased."

"At the idea of anybody coming to take Meg away? No thank you."

"You'll feel better about it when somebody comes to take you away."

"I'd like to see anyone try it," cried Jo fiercely.

"So should I!" And Laurie chuckled at the idea.

"I don't think secrets agree with me. I feel rumpled up in my mind since you told me that," said Jo, rather ungratefully.

"Race down this hill with me and you'll be all right."

No one was in sight, the smooth road sloped invitingly before her, and finding the temptation irresistible, Jo darted away, soon leaving hat and comb behind her and scattering hairpins as she ran. Laurie reached the goal first, and was quite satisfied with the success of his treatment; for his Atalanta came panting up with flying hair, bright eyes, ruddy cheeks, and no signs of dissatisfaction in her face.

"I wish I was a horse; then I could run for miles in this splendid air and not lose my breath. It was capital, but see what a guy it's made me. Go pick up my things, like a cherub as you are," said Jo, dropping down under a maple tree which was carpeting the bank with crimson leaves.

Laurie leisurely departed to recover the lost property, and Jo bundled up her braids, hoping no one would pass by till she was tidy again. But someone did pass, and who should it be but Meg, looking particularly ladylike in her state and festival suit, for she had been making calls.

"What in the world are you doing here?" she asked, regarding her disheveled sister with well-bred surprise.

"Getting leaves," meekly answered Jo, sorting the rosy handful she had just swept up.

"And hairpins," added Laurie, throwing half a dozen into Jo's lap. "They grow on this road, Meg; so do combs and brown straw hats."

"You have been running, Jo. How could you? When *will* you stop such romping ways?" said Meg reprovingly.

"Never till I'm stiff and old, and have to use a crutch. Don't try to make me grow up before my time, Meg. It's hard enough to have you change all of a sudden; let me be a little girl as long as I can."

As she spoke, Jo bent over the leaves to hide the trembling of her lips, for lately she had felt that Margaret was fast getting to be a woman, and Laurie's secret made her dread the separation which must surely come sometime, and now seemed very near. He saw the trouble in her face, and drew Meg's attention from it by asking quickly:

"Where have you been calling, all so fine?"

"At the Gardiners', and Sallie has been telling me all about Belle Moffat's wedding. It was very splendid, and they have gone to spend the winter in Paris. Just think how delightful that must be!"

"Do you envy her, Meg?" said Laurie.

"I'm afraid I do."

"I'm glad of it!" muttered Jo, tying on her hat with a jerk.

"Why?" asked Meg, looking surprised.

"Because if you care much about riches, you will never go and marry a poor man," said Jo.

"I shall never 'go and marry' anyone," observed Meg, walking on with great dignity while the others followed, laughing, whispering, skipping stones, and "behaving like children," as Meg said to herself.

For a week or two, Jo behaved so queerly that her sisters were quite bewildered. She rushed to the door when the postman rang; was rude to Mr. Brooke whenever they met; would sit looking at Meg with a woebegone face, occasionally jumping up to shake and then to kiss her, in a very mysterious manner; Laurie and she were always making signs to one another, and talking about *Spread Eagles* till the girls declared they had both lost their wits. On the second Saturday after Jo got out of the window, Meg, as she sat sewing at her window, was scandalized by the sight of Laurie chasing Jo all over the garden, and finally capturing her in Amy's bower. What went on there Meg could not see, but shrieks of laughter were heard, followed by the murmur of voices and a great flapping of newspapers.

"What shall we do with that girl? She never *will* behave like a young lady," sighed Meg.

"It's very trying, but we never can make her *commy la fo*," added Amy.

In a few minutes Jo bounced in, laid herself on the sofa, and affected to read.

"Have you anything interesting there?" asked Meg with condescension.

"Nothing but a story! Won't amount to much, I guess," returned Jo, carefully keeping the name of the paper out of sight.

"You'd better read it aloud. That will amuse us and keep you out of mischief," said Amy in her most grown-up tone.

"What's the name?" asked Beth, wondering why Jo kept her face behind the sheet.

" 'The Rival Painters.' "

"That sounds well. Read it," said Meg.

With a loud "Hem!" and a long breath, Jo began to read very fast. The girls listened with interest, for the tale was romantic, and somewhat pathetic, as most of the characters died in the end.

"I like that about the splendid picture," was Amy's approving remark as Jo paused.

"I prefer the lovering part. Viola and Angelo are two of our favorite names. Isn't that queer?" said Meg.

"Who wrote it?" asked Beth, who had caught a glimpse of Jo's face.

The reader suddenly sat up, cast away the paper, displaying a flushed countenance, and with a funny mixture of solemnity and excitement replied in a loud voice: "Your sister."

"You?" cried Meg, dropping her work.

"It's very good," said Amy critically.

"I knew it! I knew it! O my Jo, I *am* so proud!" and Beth ran to hug her sister and exult over this splendid success.

Dear me, how delighted they all were, to be sure! How Meg wouldn't believe it till she saw the words "Miss Josephine March" actually printed in the paper; how graciously Amy criticized the artistic parts of the story, and offered hints for a sequel, which unfortunately couldn't be carried out, as the hero and heroine were dead; how Beth got excited, and skipped and sang with joy; how proud Mrs. March was when she knew it; how Jo laughed with tears in her eyes as she declared she might as well be a peacock and done with it; and how the *Spread Eagle* might be said to flap his wings triumphantly over the House of March as the paper passed from hand to hand.

"Tell us all about it." "When did it come?" "How much did you get for it?" "What *will* Father say?" "Won't Laurie laugh?" cried the family, all in one breath, as they clustered about Jo.

"Stop jabbering, girls, and I'll tell you everything," said Jo, wondering if Miss Burney felt any grander over her *Evelina* than she did over her "Rival Painters." Having told how she disposed of her tales, Jo added:

"And when I went to get my answer, the man said he liked them both, but didn't pay beginners, only let them print in his paper, and noticed the stories. It was good practice, he said, and when the beginners improved, anyone would pay. So I let him have the two stories, and today this was sent to me, and Laurie caught me with it and insisted on seeing it, so I let him; and he said it was good, and I shall write more, and he's going to get the next paid for, and I *am* so happy, for in time I may be able to support myself and help the girls."

Jo's breath gave out here, and wrapping her head in the paper, she bedewed her little story with a few natural tears; for to be independent and earn the praise of those she loved were the dearest wishes of her heart, and this seemed to be the first step toward that happy end.

 TELEGRAM

"November is the most disagreeable month in the whole year," said Margaret, standing at the window one dull afternoon looking out at the frostbitten garden.

"That's the reason I was born in it," observed Jo pensively.

"If something very pleasant should happen now, we should think it a delightful month," said Beth, who took a hopeful view of everything, even November.

"I dare say, but nothing pleasant ever *does* happen in this family," said Meg, who was out of sorts. "We go grubbing along day after day, without a bit of change, and very little fun. We might as well be in a treadmill."

"My patience, how blue we are!" cried Jo. "I don't much wonder, poor dear, for you see other girls having splendid times while you grind, grind, year in and year out. Oh, don't I wish I could manage things for you as I do for my heroines! You're pretty enough and good enough already, so I'd have some rich relation leave you a fortune unexpectedly; then you'd dash out as an heiress, scorn everyone who has slighted you, go abroad, and come home My Lady Something, in a blaze of splendor and elegance."

"People don't have fortunes left them in that style nowadays; men have to work, and women to marry for money. It's a dreadfully unjust world," said Meg bitterly.

"Jo and I are going to make fortunes for you all. Just wait ten years and see if we don't," said Amy, who sat in a corner making mud pies, as Hannah called her little clay models of birds, fruit, and faces.

"Can't wait, and I'm afraid I haven't much faith in ink and dirt, though I'm grateful for your intentions."

Meg sighed, and turned to the frostbitten garden again. Jo groaned, and leaned both elbows on the table in a despondent attitude. But Amy spatted away energetically, and Beth, who sat at the other window, said, smiling: "Two pleasant things are going to happen right away: Marmee is coming down the street, and Laurie is tramping through the garden as if he had something nice to tell."

In they both came, Mrs. March with her usual question, "Any letter from Father, girls?" and Laurie to say in his persuasive way:

"Won't some of you come for a drive? I've been working away at mathematics till my head is in a muddle, and I'm going to freshen my wits by a brisk turn. I'm going to take Brooke home. Come, Jo, you and Beth will go, won't you?"

"Of course we will."

"Much obliged, but I'm busy." And Meg whisked out her workbasket, for she had agreed with her mother that it was best, for her at least, not to drive often with the young gentleman.

"We three will be ready in a minute," cried Amy, running away to wash her hands.

"Can I do anything for you, Madam Mother?" asked Laurie leaning over Mrs. March's chair with the affectionate look and tone he always gave her.

"No thank you, except call at the office, if you'll be so kind, dear. It's our day for a letter, and the postman hasn't been. Father is as regular as the sun."

A sharp ring interrupted her, and a minute after Hannah came in with a letter. "It's one of them horrid telegraph things, mum," she said, handing it as if she was afraid it would explode and do some damage.

At the word "telegraph," Mrs. March snatched it, read the two lines it contained, and dropped back into her chair as white as if the little paper had sent a bullet to her heart. Laurie dashed downstairs for water while Meg and Hannah supported her, and Jo read aloud, in a frightened voice:

> "'YOUR HUSBAND IS VERY ILL. COME AT ONCE.
> S. HALE, BLANK HOSPITAL, WASHINGTON.'"

How still the room was as they listened breathlessly, how strangely the day darkened outside, and how suddenly the whole world seemed to change as the girls gathered about their mother feeling as if all the happiness and support of their lives was about to be taken from them. Mrs. March was herself again directly, read the message over, and stretched out her arms to her daughters, saying in a tone they never forgot:

"I shall go at once, but it may be too late. O children, children; help me to bear it!"

For several minutes there was nothing but the sound of sobbing in the room, mingled with broken words of comfort, tender assurances of help, and hopeful whispers that died away in tears. Poor Hannah was the first to recover, and with unconscious wisdom she set all the rest a good example; for with her, work was the panacea for most afflictions.

"The Lord keep the dear man! I won't waste no time a cryin', but git your things ready right away, mum," she said heartily as she wiped her face on her apron and went away to work like three women in one.

"She's right. There's no time for tears now. Be calm, girls, and let me think." They tried to be calm, poor things, as their mother sat up, looking pale but steady, and put away her grief to think and plan for them. "Where's Laurie?" she asked presently, when she had collected her thoughts and decided on the first duties to be done.

"Here, ma'am. Oh, let me do something!" cried the boy, hurrying from the next room, whither he had withdrawn, feeling that their first sorrow was too sacred for even his friendly eyes to see.

"Send a telegram saying I will come at once. The next train goes early in the morning. I'll take that."

"What else? The horses are ready. I can go anywhere, do anything," he said, looking ready to fly to the ends of the earth.

"Leave a note at Aunt March's. Jo, give me that pen and paper." Tearing off the blank side of one of her newly copied pages, Jo drew the table before her mother, well knowing that money for the long, sad journey must be borrowed, and feeling as if she could do anything to add a little to the sum for her father. "Now go, dear, but don't kill yourself driving at a desperate pace. There is no need of that."

Mrs. March's warning was evidently thrown away, for five minutes later Laurie tore by the window riding as if for his life.

"Jo, run and get these things. I'll put them down. They'll be needed, and I must go prepared for nursing. Beth, go and ask Mr. Laurence for a couple of bottles of old wine. I'm not too proud to beg for Father; he shall have the best of everything. Amy, tell Hannah to get down the black trunk, and Meg, come and help me find my things."

Everyone scattered like leaves before a gust of wind, and the quiet, happy household was broken up as suddenly as if the paper had been an evil spell. Mr. Laurence came hurrying back with Beth, bringing every comfort the kind old gentleman could think of for the invalid, and friendliest promises of protection for the girls during the mother's absence. There was nothing he didn't offer, from his own dressing gown to himself as escort. But Mrs. March would not hear of the old gentleman's undertaking the long journey; yet an expression of relief was visible when he spoke of it. He saw the look, knit his heavy eyebrows, rubbed his hands, and marched abruptly away, saying he'd be back directly. No one had time to think of him again till as Meg ran through the entry with a pair of rubbers in one hand and a cup of tea in the other, she came suddenly upon Mr. Brooke.

"I'm very sorry to hear of this, Miss March," he said. "I came to offer myself as escort to your mother. Mr. Laurence has commissions for me in Washington, and it will give me real satisfaction to be of service to her there."

Down dropped the rubbers, and the tea was very near following as Meg put out her hand, with a face so full of gratitude that Mr. Brooke would have felt repaid for a much greater sacrifice than the trifling one of time and comfort which he was about to make.

"How kind you all are! Mother will accept, I'm sure, and it will be such a relief to know that she has someone to take care of her. Thank you very, very much!"

Everything was arranged by the time Laurie returned with a note from Aunt March enclosing the desired sum and a few lines repeating what she had often said before—that she had always told them it was absurd for March to go into the army, always predicted that no good would come of it, and she hoped they would take her advice next time. Mrs. March put the note in the fire, the money in her purse, and went on with her preparations.

The short afternoon wore away. All the other errands were done, and Meg and her mother busy at some necessary needlework while Beth and Amy got tea. But still Jo did not come. They began to get anxious, and Laurie went off to find her, for no one ever knew what freak Jo might take into her head. He missed her, however, and she came walking in with a very queer expression of countenance, for there was a mixture of fun and fear, satisfaction and regret, in it which puzzled the family as much as did the roll of bills she laid before her mother, saying, with a little choke in her voice: "That's my contribution toward making Father comfortable and bringing him home!"

"My dear, where did you get it? Twenty-five dollars! Jo, I hope you haven't done anything rash?"

"No, it's mine honestly. I didn't beg, borrow, or steal it. I earned it! And I don't think you'll blame me, for I only sold what was my own."

As she spoke, Jo took off her bonnet, and a general outcry arose, for all her abundant hair was cut short.

"Your hair!" "Oh Jo, how could you? Your one beauty!" "My dear girl, there was no need of this." "She doesn't look like my Jo any more, but I love her dearly for it!"

As everyone exclaimed, and Beth hugged the cropped head tenderly, Jo assumed an indifferent air, which did not deceive anyone a particle, and said, rumpling up the brown bush and trying to look as if she liked it: "It doesn't affect the fate of the nation, so don't wail, Beth. It will be good for my vanity. I was getting too proud of my wig. It will do my brains good to have that mop taken off; my head feels deliciously light and cool, and the barber said I could soon have a curly crop, which will be boyish, becoming, and easy to keep in order. I'm satisfied, so please take the money, and let's have supper."

"Tell me all about it, Jo. I am not quite satisfied, but I can't blame you, for I know how willingly you sacrificed your vanity, as you call it, to your love. But, my dear, it was not necessary, and I'm afraid you will regret it one of these days," said Mrs. March.

"No I won't!" returned Jo stoutly.

"What made you do it?" asked Amy, who would as soon have thought of cutting off her head as her pretty hair.

"Well, I was wild to do something for Father," replied Jo as they gathered about the table. "I hate to borrow as much as Mother does, and I knew Aunt March would croak; she always does if you ask for a nine-pence. Meg gave all her quarterly salary toward the rent, and I only got some clothes with mine, so I felt wicked, and was bound to have some money if I sold the nose off my face to get it.

"I hadn't the least idea of selling my hair at first, but as I went along I kept thinking what I could do. In a barber's window I saw tails of hair with the prices marked, and one black tail not so thick as mine was forty dollars. It came over me all of a sudden that I had one thing to make money out of, and without stopping to think, I walked in, asked if they bought hair, and what they would give for mine."

"I don't see how you dared to do it," said Beth.

"Oh, he was a little man who looked as if he merely lived to oil his hair. He rather stared at first, as if he wasn't used to having girls bounce into his shop and ask him to buy their hair. He said he didn't care about mine, it wasn't the fashionable color. It was getting late, and I was afraid if it wasn't done right away that I shouldn't have it done at all, and you know when I start to do a thing, I hate to give it up; so I begged him to take it, and told him why I was in such a hurry. It was silly, I dare say, but it changed his mind, for I got rather excited, and told the story in my topsy-turvy way, and his wife heard, and said so kindly:

"'Take it, Thomas, and oblige the young lady. I'd do as much for our Jimmy any day if I had a spire of hair worth selling.'"

"Who was Jimmy?" asked Amy.

"Her son, she said, who was in the army. How friendly such things make strangers feel, don't they? She talked away all the time the man clipped, and diverted my mind nicely."

"Didn't you feel dreadfully when the first cut came?" asked Meg, with a shiver.

"I took a last look at my hair while the man got his things, and that was the end of it. I never snivel over trifles like that. I will confess, though, I felt queer when I saw the dear old hair laid out on the table, and felt only the short, rough ends on my head. The woman saw me look at it, and picked out a long lock for me to keep. I'll give it to you, Marmee, just to remember past glories by, for a crop is so comfortable I don't think I shall ever have a mane again."

Mrs. March folded the wavy chestnut lock and laid it away with a short gray one in her desk. She only said "Thank you, dearie," but something in her face made the girls change the subject, and talk as cheerfully as they could about Mr. Brooke's kindness, the prospect of a fine day tomorrow, and the happy times they would have when Father came home to be nursed.

No one wanted to go to bed when, at ten o'clock, Mrs. March put by the last finished job and said, "Come, girls." Beth went to the piano, and played the father's favorite hymn. All began bravely, but broke down one by one, till Beth was left alone, singing with all her heart, for to her music was always a sweet consoler.

"Go to bed and don't talk, for we must be up early and shall need all the sleep we can get. Good night, my darlings," said Mrs. March as the hymn ended, for no one cared to try another.

They kissed her quietly, and went to bed as silently as if the dear invalid lay in the next room. Beth and Amy soon fell asleep in spite of the great trouble, but Meg lay awake, thinking the most serious thoughts she had ever known in her short life. Jo lay motionless, and her sister fancied that she was asleep till a stifled sob made her exclaim as she touched a wet cheek: "Jo dear, what is it? Are you crying about Father?"

"No, not now."

"What then?"

"My—my hair!" burst out poor Jo, trying vainly to smother her emotion in the pillow.

It did not sound at all comical to Meg, who kissed and caressed the afflicted heroine in the tenderest manner.

"I'm not sorry," protested Jo, with a choke. "I'd do it again tomorrow, if I could. It's only the vain selfish part of me that goes and cries in this silly way. Don't tell anyone, it's all over now. I thought you were asleep, so I just made a little private moan for my one beauty. How came you to be awake?"

"I can't sleep, I'm so anxious," said Meg.

"Think about something pleasant, and you'll soon drop off."

"I tried it, but felt wider awake than ever."

"What did you think of?"

"Handsome faces—eyes particularly," answered Meg, smiling to herself in the dark.

"What color do you like best?"

"Brown—that is, sometimes. Blue are lovely."

Jo laughed, and Meg sharply ordered her not to talk, then amiably promised to make her hair curl, and fell asleep to dream of living in her castle in the air.

The clocks were striking midnight, and the rooms were very still, as a figure glided quietly from bed to bed, smoothing a coverlid here, settling a pillow there, and pausing to look long and tenderly at each unconscious face, to kiss each with lips that mutely blessed, and to pray the fervent prayers which only mothers utter. As she lifted the curtain to look out into the dreary night, the moon broke suddenly from behind the clouds and shone upon her like a bright, benignant face, which seemed to whisper in the silence: "Be comforted, dear soul! There is always light behind the clouds."

LEFT WITHOUT MARMEE

In the cold gray dawn the sisters lit their lamp, and read their chapter with an earnestness never felt before; for now the shadow of a real trouble had come, the little books were full of help and comfort. And as they dressed, they agreed to say good-by cheerfully and hopefully, and send their mother on her anxious journey unsaddened by tears or complaints from them. Everything seemed very strange when they went down—so dim and still outside, so full of light and bustle within. The big trunk stood ready in the hall, Mother's cloak and bonnet lay on the sofa, and Mother herself sat trying to eat, but looking so pale and worn with sleeplessness and anxiety that the girls found it very hard to keep their resolution.

Nobody talked much, but as the time drew very near, and they sat waiting for the carriage, Mrs. March said to the girls:

"Children, I leave you to Hannah's care and Mr. Laurence's protection. Hannah is faithfulness itself, and our good neighbor will guard you as if you were his own. I have no fears for you, yet I am anxious that you should take this trouble rightly. Don't grieve and fret when I am gone, or think that you can comfort yourselves by being idle and trying to forget. Go on with your work as usual, for work is a blessed solace. Hope and keep busy, and whatever happens, remember that you never can be fatherless.

"Meg, dear, be prudent, watch over your sisters, consult Hannah, and in any perplexity go to Mr. Laurence. Be patient, Jo, don't get despondent or do rash things; write to me often, and be my brave girl. Beth, comfort yourself with your music, and be faithful to the little home duties; and you, Amy, help all you can, be obedient, and keep happy safe at home."

"We will, Mother! We will!"

They kissed their mother quietly, clung about her tenderly, and tried to wave their hands cheerfully when she drove away. Laurie and his grandfather came over to see her off, and Mr. Brooke looked so strong and sensible and kind that the girls christened him "Mr. Greatheart" on the spot.

"Good-by, my darlings! God bless and keep us all!" whispered Mrs. March as she kissed one dear little face after the other and hurried into the carriage.

As she rolled away, the sun came out, and looking back, she saw it shining on the group at the gate, like a good omen, and the last thing she beheld as she turned the corner was the four bright faces, and behind them, like a bodyguard, old Mr. Laurence, faithful Hannah, and devoted Laurie.

"I feel as if there had been an earthquake," said Jo as their neighbors went home to breakfast.

"It seems as if half the house was gone," added Meg forlornly, and they all broke down and cried bitterly.

Hannah wisely allowed them to relieve their feelings, and when the shower showed signs of clearing up, she came to the rescue, armed with a coffeepot. "Now, my dear young ladies, remember what your ma said, and don't fret. Come and have a cup of coffee all round, and then let's fall to work, and be a credit to the family."

They drew up to the table, exchanged their handkerchiefs for napkins, and in ten minutes were all right again.

" 'Hope and keep busy'—that's the motto for us, so let's see who will remember it best. I shall go to Aunt March, as usual. Oh, won't she lecture though!" said Jo.

"I shall go to my Kings, though I'd much rather stay at home and attend to things here," said Meg.

"No need of that. Beth and I can keep house perfectly well," put in Amy, with an important air.

"Hannah will tell us what to do, and we'll have everything nice when you come home," added Beth, getting out her mop and dishtub without delay.

"I think anxiety is very interesting," observed Amy, eating sugar pensively.

The girls couldn't help laughing, and felt better for it, though Meg shook her head at the young lady who could find consolation in the sugar bowl.

The sight of the turnovers made Jo sober again, and when the two went out to their daily tasks, they looked sorrowfully back at the window where they were accustomed to see their mother's face. It was gone, but Beth had remembered the little household ceremony, and there she was, nodding away at them like a rosy-faced mandarin.

"That's so like my Beth!" said Jo, waving her hat, with a grateful face. "Good-by, Meggy. I hope the Kings won't train today. Don't fret about Father, dear," she added as they parted.

"And I hope Aunt March won't croak. Your hair *is* becoming, and it looks very boyish and nice," returned Meg, trying not to smile at the curly head, which looked comically small on her tall sister's shoulders.

"That's my only comfort." And, touching her hat à la Laurie, away went Jo, feeling like a shorn sheep on a wintry day.

News from their father comforted the girls very much; for though dangerously ill, the presence of the best and tenderest of nurses had already done him good. Mr. Brooke sent a bulletin every day, and as the head of the family Meg insisted on reading the dispatches, which grew more and more cheering as the week passed.

LITTLE FAITHFUL

For a week the amount of virtue in the old house would have supplied the neighborhood. It was really amazing, for everyone seemed in a heavenly frame of mind, and self-denial was all the fashion. Relieved of their first anxiety about their father, the girls insensibly relaxed their praiseworthy efforts a little, and began to fall back into the old ways. They did not forget their motto, but hoping and keeping busy seemed to grow easier; and after such tremendous exertions, they felt that Endeavor deserved a holiday, and gave it a good many.

Jo caught a bad cold through neglect to cover the shorn head enough, and was ordered to stay at home till she was better, for Aunt March didn't like to hear people read with colds in their heads. Jo liked this, and after an energetic rummage from garret to cellar, subsided on the sofa to nurse her cold with arsenicum and books. Amy found that housework and art did not go well together, and returned to her mud pies. Meg went daily to her pupils, and sewed, or thought she did, at home, but much time was spent in writing long letters to her mother, or reading the Washington dispatches over and over. Beth kept on, with only slight relapses into idleness or grieving.

All the little duties were faithfully done each day, and many of her sisters' also, for they were forgetful, and the house seemed like a clock whose pendulum was gone a-visiting. When her heart got heavy with longings for Mother or fears for Father, she went away into a certain closet, hid her face in the folds of a certain dear old gown, and made her little moan and prayed her little prayer quietly by herself.

All were unconscious that this experience was a test of character, and when the first excitement was over, felt that they had done well, and deserved praise. So they did, but their mistake was in ceasing to do well, and they learned this lesson through much anxiety and regret.

"Meg, I wish you'd go and see the Hummels. You know Mother told us not to forget them," said Beth, ten days after Mrs. March's departure.

"I'm too tired to go this afternoon," replied Meg.

"Can't you, Jo?" asked Beth.

"Too stormy for me with my cold."

"I thought it was almost well."

"It's well enough for me to go out with Laurie, but not well enough to go to the Hummels'," said Jo, laughing, but looking a little ashamed of her inconsistency.

"Why don't you go yourself?" asked Meg.

"I *have* been every day, but the baby is sick, and I don't know what to do for it. Mrs. Hummel goes away to work, and Lottchen takes care of it; but it gets sicker and sicker, and I think you or Hannah ought to go."

Beth spoke earnestly, and Meg promised she would go tomorrow.

"Ask Hannah for some nice little mess and take it round, Beth. The air will do you good," said Jo, adding apologetically, "I'd go, but I want to finish my writing."

"My head aches and I'm tired, so I thought maybe some of you would go," said Beth.

"Amy will be in presently, and she will run down for us," suggested Meg.

"Well, I'll rest a little and wait for her."

So Beth lay down on the sofa, the others returned to their work, and the Hummels were forgotten. An hour passed. Amy did not come; Meg went to her room to try on a new dress; Jo was absorbed in her story, and Hannah was sound asleep before the kitchen fire, when Beth quietly put on her hood, filled her basket with odds and ends for the poor children, and went out into the chilly air with a heavy head, and a grieved look in her patient eyes. It was late when she came back, and no one saw her creep upstairs and shut herself into her mother's room. Half an hour after Jo went to "Mother's closet" for something, and there found Beth sitting on the medicine chest, looking very grave, with red eyes, and a camphor bottle in her hand.

"Christopher Columbus! What's the matter?" cried Jo as Beth put out her hand as if to warn her off, and asked quickly: "You've had the scarlet fever, haven't you?"

"Years ago, when Meg did. Why?"

"Then I'll tell you. Oh, Jo, the baby's dead!"

"What baby?"

"Mrs. Hummel's. It died in my lap before she got home," cried Beth, with a sob.

"My poor dear, how dreadful for you! I ought to have gone," said Jo, taking her sister in her arms.

"It wasn't dreadful, Jo, only so sad! I saw in a minute that it was sicker, but Lottchen said her mother had gone for a doctor, so I took the baby and let Lotty rest. It seemed asleep, but all of a sudden it gave a little cry, and trembled, and then lay very still. I tried to warm its feet, and Lotty gave it some milk, but it didn't stir, and I knew it was dead."

"Don't cry, dear! What did you do?"

"I just sat and held it softly till Mrs. Hummel came with the doctor. He said it was dead, and looked at Heinrich and Minna, who have got sore throats. 'Scarlet fever, ma'am. Ought to have called me before,' he said crossly. He turned round all of a sudden and told me to go home and take belladonna right away, or I'd have the fever."

"No you won't!" cried Jo, hugging her close, with a frightened look. "O Beth, if you should be sick I never could forgive myself! What *shall* we do?"

"Don't be frightened. I guess I shan't have it badly. I looked in Mother's book, and saw that it begins with headache, sore throat, and queer feelings like mine, so I did take some belladonna, and I feel better," said Beth.

"If Mother was only at home!" exclaimed Jo, seizing the book, and feeling that Washington was an immense way off. She read a page, looked at Beth, felt her head, peeped into her throat, and then said gravely: "You've been over the baby every day for more than a week, and among the others who are going to have it, so I'm afraid *you* are going to have it, Beth. I'll call Hannah, she knows all about sickness."

The good soul was wide-awake in a minute, and took the lead at once, assuring Jo that there was no need to worry. Everyone had scarlet fever, and if rightly treated, nobody died.

"Now I'll tell you what we'll do," said Hannah when she had examined and questioned Beth. "We will have Dr. Bangs, just to take a look at you, dear, and see that we start right. Then we'll send Amy off to Aunt March's for a spell, to keep her out of harm's way, and one of you girls can stay at home and amuse Beth for a day or two."

"I shall stay, of course, I'm oldest," began Meg, looking anxious and self-reproachful.

"I shall, because it's my fault she is sick. I told Mother I'd do the errands, and I haven't," said Jo decidedly.

"Which will you have, Beth? There ain't no need of but one," said Hannah.

"Jo, please." And Beth leaned her head against her sister.

"I'll go and tell Amy," said Meg, feeling a little hurt, yet rather relieved, on the whole, for she did not like nursing.

Amy rebelled outright, and passionately declared that she had rather have the fever than go to Aunt March. Meg reasoned, pleaded, and commanded—all in vain. Amy protested that she would *not* go, and Meg left her in despair, to ask Hannah what should be done. Before she came back, Laurie walked into the parlor to find Amy sobbing, with her head in the sofa cushions. She told her story, expecting to be consoled, but Laurie only put his hands in his pockets and walked about the room whistling softly as he knit his brows in deep thought. Presently he sat down beside her, and said in his most wheedlesome tone: "Now be a sensible little woman, and do as they say. No, don't cry, but hear what a jolly plan I've got. You go to Aunt March's, and I'll come and take you out every day, driving or walking, and we'll have capital times."

"I don't wish to be sent off as if I was in the way," began Amy in an injured voice.

"Bless your heart, child, it's to keep you well. You don't want to be sick, do you?"

"No, I'm sure I don't. But I dare say I shall be, for I've been with Beth all the time."

"That's the very reason you ought to go away at once, so that you may escape it. I advise you to be off as soon as you can, for scarlet fever is no joke, miss."

"Well—I guess—I will," said Amy slowly.

"Good girl! Call Meg, and tell her you'll give in," said Laurie. Meg and Jo came running down to behold the miracle which had been wrought, and Amy, feeling very precious and self-sacrificing, promised to go if the doctor said Beth was going to be ill. "How is the little dear?" asked Laurie, for Beth was his especial pet, and he felt more anxious about her than he liked to show.

"She is lying down on Mother's bed, and feels better," answered Meg.

"What a trying world it is!" said Jo, rumpling up her hair in a fretful sort of way. "No sooner do we get out of one trouble than down comes another. There doesn't seem to be anything to hold onto when Mother's gone, so I'm all at sea."

"Well, don't make a porcupine of yourself, it isn't becoming. Settle your wig, Jo, and tell me, shall I telegraph to your mother, or do anything?" asked Laurie.

"That is what troubles me," said Meg. "I think we ought to tell her if Beth is really ill, but Hannah says we mustn't, for Mother can't leave Father, and it will only make them anxious, but it doesn't seem quite right to me. Jo, go and get Dr. Bangs at once," commanded Meg. "We can't decide anything till he has been."

"Stay where you are, Jo. I'm errand boy to this establishment," said Laurie, taking up his cap.

Dr. Bangs came, said Beth had symptoms of the fever, but thought she would have it lightly, though he looked sober over the Hummel story. Amy was ordered off at once, and she departed in great state, with Jo and Laurie as escort.

Aunt March received them with her usual hospitality.

"What do you want now?" she asked, looking sharply over her spectacles while the parrot, sitting on the back of her chair, called out: "Go away. No boys allowed here."

Laurie retired to the window, and Jo told her story.

"No more than I expected if you are allowed to go poking about among poor folks. Amy can stay and make herself useful if she isn't sick, which I've no doubt she will be—looks like it now. Don't cry, child, it worries me to hear people sniff."

Amy *was* on the point of crying, but Laurie slyly pulled the parrot's tail, which caused Polly to utter an astonished croak, and call out "Bless my boots!" in such a funny way that she laughed instead.

"What do you hear from your mother?" asked the old lady gruffly.

"Father is much better," replied Jo, trying to keep sober.

"Oh, is he? Well, that won't last long, I fancy. March never had any stamina," was the cheerful reply.

"I don't think I *can* bear it, but I'll try," thought Amy as she was left alone with Aunt March.

DARK DAYS

Beth did have the fever, and was much sicker than anyone but Hannah and the doctor suspected. The girls knew nothing about illness, and Mr. Laurence was not allowed to see her, so Hannah did everything all her own way, and busy Dr. Bangs did his best, but left a good deal to the excellent nurse. Meg stayed at home, lest she should infect the Kings, and kept house, feeling very anxious and a little guilty when she wrote letters in which no mention was made of Beth's illness. She could not think it right to deceive her mother, but she had been bidden to mind Hannah, and Hannah wouldn't hear of "Mrs. March bein' told, and worried just for sech a trifle." Jo devoted herself to Beth day and night—not a hard task, for Beth was very patient, and bore her pain uncomplainingly as long as she could control herself. But there came a time when during the fever fits she began to talk in a hoarse, broken voice, to play on the coverlet as if on her beloved little piano, and try to sing with a throat so swollen that there was no music left; a time when she did not know the familiar faces round her, but addressed them by wrong names, and called imploringly for her mother. A letter from Washington added to their trouble, for Mr. March had had a relapse, and could not think of coming home for a long while.

Everyone missed Beth. The milkman, baker, grocer, and butcher inquired how she did; poor Mrs. Hummel came to beg pardon for her thoughtlessness, and to get a shroud for Minna; the neighbors sent all sorts of comforts and good wishes, and even those who knew her best were surprised to find how many friends shy little Beth had made. Meanwhile she lay hour after hour tossing to and fro with incoherent words on her lips, or sank into a heavy sleep which brought her no refreshment.

The first of December was a wintry day indeed to them, for a bitter wind blew, snow fell fast, and the year seemed getting ready for its death. When Dr. Bangs came that morning, he looked long at Beth, held the hot hand in both his own a minute, and laid it gently down, saying in a low tone to Hannah: "If Mrs. March *can* leave her husband, she'd better be sent for."

Hannah nodded without speaking, for her lips twitched nervously. Meg dropped down into a chair as the strength seemed to go out of her limbs at the sound of those words; and Jo, after standing with a pale face for a minute, ran to the parlor, and throwing on her things, rushed out into the storm. She was soon back, and while noiselessly taking off her cloak, Laurie came in with a letter saying that Mr. March was mending again. Jo read it thankfully, but the heavy weight did not seem lifted off her heart, and her face was so full of misery that Laurie asked quickly:

"What is it? Is Beth worse?"

"I've sent for Mother," said Jo.

"Good for you, Jo! Did you do it on your own responsibility?" asked Laurie.

"No, the doctor told us to."

"O Jo, it's not so bad as that?" cried Laurie.

"Yes, it is. She doesn't know us, she doesn't even talk about the flocks of green doves, as she calls the vine leaves on the wall. She doesn't look like my Beth, and there's nobody to help us bear it; Mother and Father both gone, and God seems so far away I can't find Him."

As the tears streamed fast down poor Jo's cheeks, she stretched out her hand in a helpless sort of way, as if groping in the dark, and Laurie took it in his, whispering with a lump in his throat: "I'm here. Hold on to me, Jo dear!"

She could not speak, but she did "hold on," and the warm grasp of the friendly human hand comforted her sore heart, and seemed to lead her nearer to the Divine arm which alone could uphold her in her trouble. Laurie longed to say something tender and comfortable, but no fitting words came to him, so he stood silent, gently stroking her bent head as her mother used to do. Soon she dried the tears which had relieved her, and looked up with a grateful face.

"Thank you, Teddy, I'm better now."

"Keep hoping for the best; that will help you, Jo. Soon your mother will be here, and then everything will be right."

"I'm so glad Father is better; now she won't feel so bad about leaving him. Oh me! It does seem as if all the troubles came in a heap," sighed Jo. "Beth is my conscience, and I *can't* give her up. I can't! I can't!"

Down went Jo's face, and she cried despairingly, for she had kept up bravely till now, and never shed a tear. Laurie drew his hand across his eyes, but could not speak till he had subdued the choky feeling in his throat and steadied his lips.

"Poor girl, you're worn out. Stop a bit. I'll hearten you up in a jiffy."

Laurie went off two stairs at a time, and Jo laid her wearied head down on Beth's little brown hood, which no one had thought of moving from the table where she left it. It must have possessed some magic, for the submissive spirit of its gentle owner seemed to enter into Jo, and when Laurie came running down with a glass of wine, she took it with a smile, and said bravely:

"I drink—Health to my Beth! You are a good doctor, Teddy, and *such* a comfortable friend. How can I ever pay you?"

"I'll send in my bill by and by, and tonight I'll give you something that will warm the cockles of your heart better than quarts of wine," said Laurie, beaming at her.

"What is it?" cried Jo, forgetting her woes for a minute.

"I telegraphed to your mother yesterday, and Brooke answered she'd come at once, and she'll be here tonight, and everything will be all right. Aren't you glad I did it?"

Laurie spoke very fast, and turned red and excited all in a minute, for he had kept his plot a secret, for fear of disappointing the girls or harming Beth. Jo grew quite white, flew out of her chair, and the moment he stopped speaking she electrified him by throwing her arms round his neck and crying out, with a joyful cry: "O Laurie! O Mother! I *am* so glad!"

Laurie, though decidedly amazed, behaved with great presence of mind. He patted her back soothingly, and finding that she was recovering, followed it up by a bashful kiss or two, which brought Jo round at once. Holding onto the banisters, she put him gently away, saying breathlessly:

"Oh, don't! I didn't mean to, it was dreadful of me; but you were such a dear to do it in spite of Hannah that I couldn't help flying at you."

"I don't mind," laughed Laurie as he settled his tie. "You see I got fidgety, and so did Grandpa. We thought Hannah was overdoing the authority business, and your mother ought to know. She'd never forgive us if Beth—well, if anything happened, you know. So I got Grandpa to say it was high time we did something, and off I pelted to the office yesterday, for the doctor looked sober. Your mother will come, I know, and the late train is in at 2 A.M. I shall go for her."

"Laurie, you're an angel! How shall I ever thank you?"

Every time the girls met, their pale faces broke into smiles as they hugged one another, whispering encouragingly, "Mother's coming, dear! Mother's coming!" Everyone rejoiced but Beth; she lay in that heavy stupor, alike unconscious of hope and joy, doubt and danger. The doctor had been in to say that some change, for better or worse, would probably take place about midnight, at which time he would return.

The girls never forgot that night, for no sleep came to them as they kept their watch with that dreadful sense of powerlessness which comes to us in hours like those. The house was still as death, and nothing but the wailing of the wind broke the deep hush.

It was past two when Jo, who stood at the window thinking how dreary the world looked in its winding sheet of snow, heard a movement by the bed, and turning quickly, saw Meg kneeling before their mother's easy chair, with her face hidden. A dreadful fear passed coldly over Jo as she thought, "Beth is dead, and Meg is afraid to tell me." She was back at her post in an instant, and to her excited eyes a great change seemed to have taken place. The fever flush and the look of pain were gone, and the beloved little face looked pale and peaceful in its utter repose. Leaning low over this dearest of her sisters, she kissed the damp forehead with her heart on her lips, and softly whispered, "Good-by, my Beth, good-by!"

Hannah hurried to the bed, looked at Beth, felt her hands, listened at her lips, and then, throwing her apron over her head, sat down to rock to and fro, exclaiming under her breath: "The fever's turned, she's sleepin' nat'ral, her skin's damp, and she breathes easy. Praise be given! Oh my goodness me!"

Before the girls could believe the happy truth, the doctor came to confirm it. "Yes, my dears, I think the little girl will pull through this time. Keep the house quiet, let her sleep, and when she wakes, give her——"

What they were to give neither heard; for both crept into the dark hall, and sitting on the stairs, held each other close, rejoicing with hearts too full for words. When they went back to be kissed and cuddled by faithful Hannah, they found Beth lying with her cheek pillowed on her hand, the dreadful pallor gone, and breathing quietly, as if just fallen asleep.

Never had the sun risen so beautifully, and never had the world seemed so lovely, as it did to the heavy eyes of Meg and Jo as they looked out in the early morning when their long, sad vigil was done.

"It looks like a fairy world," said Meg, smiling to herself as she stood behind the curtain watching the dazzling sight.

"Hark!" cried Jo, starting to her feet.

Yes, there was a sound of bells at the door below, a cry from Hannah, and then Laurie's voice saying in a joyful whisper:

"Girls, she's come! She's come!"

AMY'S WILL

While these things were happening at home, Amy was having hard times at Aunt March's. She felt her exile deeply, and for the first time in her life realized how much she was beloved and petted at home. Aunt March never petted anyone, she did not approve of it; but she meant to be kind, for the well-behaved little girl pleased her very much, and Aunt March had a soft place in her old heart for her nephew's children, though she didn't think proper to confess it. She really did her best to make Amy happy, but she worried Amy very much with her rules and orders, her prim ways and long, prosy talks.

If it had not been for Laurie, and old Esther, the maid, she felt that she never could have got through that dreadful time. The parrot alone was enough to drive her distracted, for he soon felt that she did not admire him, and revenged himself by being as mischievous as possible. He pulled her hair whenever she came near him, upset his bread and milk to plague her when she had newly cleaned his cage, made Mop bark by pecking at him while Madam dozed, called her names before company, and behaved in all respects like a reprehensible old bird. Then she could not endure the dog—a fat, cross beast, who snarled and yelped at her when she made his toilet, and who lay on his back, with all his legs in the air and a most idiotic expression of countenance, when he wanted something to eat, which was about a dozen times a day. The cook was bad-tempered, the old coachman deaf, and Esther the only one who ever took any notice of the young lady.

Esther was a Frenchwoman who had lived with "Madame," as she called her mistress, for many years, and who rather tyrannized over the old lady, who could not get along without her. She took a fancy to Mademoiselle, and amused her very much with odd stories of her life in France. She also allowed her to roam about the great house and examine the curious and pretty things stored away in the big wardrobes and the ancient chests, for Aunt March hoarded like a magpie. Amy's chief delight was an Indian cabinet full of queer drawers, little pigeonholes, and secret places, in which were kept all sorts of ornaments, some precious, some merely curious, all more or less antique. To examine and arrange these things gave Amy great satisfaction, especially the jewel cases, in which, on velvet cushions, reposed the ornaments which had adorned a belle forty years ago.

"I wish I knew where all these pretty things would go when Aunt March dies," she said as she shut the jewel cases one by one.

"To you and your sisters. I know it. Madame confides in me. I witnessed her will, and it is to be so," whispered Esther, smiling.

"How nice! But I wish she'd let us have them now. Pro-cras-ti-nation is not agreeable," observed Amy.

"It is too soon yet for the young ladies to wear these things. The first one who is affianced will have the pearls—Madame has said it. And I have a fancy that the little turquoise ring will be given to you when you go, for Madame approves your good behavior and charming manners."

"Do you think so? Oh, I'll be a lamb if I can only have that lovely ring!" And Amy tried on the blue ring with a delighted face, and a firm resolve to earn it.

In her first effort at being very, very good, she decided to make her will, as Aunt March had done, so that if she *did* fall ill and die, her possessions might be justly and generously divided. During one of her play hours she wrote out the important document as well as she could, with some help from Esther as to certain legal terms, and when the good-natured Frenchwoman had signed her name, Amy felt relieved, and laid it by to show Laurie, whom she wanted as a second witness. As it was a rainy day, she went upstairs to amuse herself in one of the large chambers, and took Polly with her for company. In this room there was a wardrobe full of old-fashioned costumes, with which Esther allowed her to play, and it was her favorite amusement to array herself in the faded brocades and parade up and down before the long mirror, making stately curtsies, and sweeping her train about with a rustle which delighted her ears. So busy was she on this day that she did not hear Laurie's ring, nor see his face peeping in at her, as she gravely promenaded to and fro, flirting her fan and tossing her head, on which she wore a great pink turban, contrasting oddly with her blue brocade dress and yellow quilted petticoat. She was obliged to walk carefully, for she had on high-heeled shoes, and as Laurie told Jo afterward, it was a comical sight to see her mince along in her gay suit, with Polly sidling and bridling just behind her, imitating her as well as he could, and occasionally stopping to laugh or exclaim: "Ain't we fine? Get along, you fright! Hold your tongue! Kiss me, dear! Ha! Ha!" Having with difficulty restrained an explosion of merriment, lest it should offend her majesty, Laurie tapped, and was graciously received.

"Sit down and rest while I put these things away; then I want to consult you about a very serious matter," said Amy, when she had shown her splendor, and driven Polly into a corner. "That bird is the trial of my life," she continued, removing the pink mountain from her head while Laurie seated himself astride of a chair. "Yesterday, when Aunt was asleep, and I was trying to be as still as a mouse, Polly began to squall and flap about in his cage, so I went to let him out, and found a big spider there. I poked it out, and it ran under the bookcase. Polly marched straight after it, stooped down and peeped under the bookcase, saying in his funny way, with a cock of his eye, 'Come out and take a walk, my dear,' I *couldn't* help laughing, which made Poll swear, and Aunt woke up and scolded us both."

"Did the spider accept the old fellow's invitation?" asked Laurie, yawning.

"Yes, out it came, and away ran Polly, frightened to death, and scrambled up on Aunt's chair, calling out, 'Catch her! Catch her! Catch her!' as I chased the spider."

"That's a lie! Oh lor!" cried the parrot, pecking at Laurie's toes.

"I'd wring your neck if you were mine, you old torment," cried Laurie, shaking his fist at the bird, who put his head on one side and gravely croaked: "Allyluyer! Bless your buttons, dear!"

"Now I'm ready," said Amy, shutting the wardrobe and taking a paper out of her pocket. "I want you to read that, please, and tell me if it is legal and right. I felt that I ought to do it, for life is uncertain, and I don't want any ill feeling over my tomb."

Laurie bit his lips, and turning a little from the pensive speaker, read the following document, with praiseworthy gravity considering the spelling:

148

MY LAST WILL AND TESTIMENT

I, Amy Curtis March, being in my sane mind, do give and bequeethe all my earthly property—viz. to wit:—namely

To my father, my best pictures, sketches, maps, and works of art, including frames. Also my $100, to do what he likes with.

To my mother, all my clothes, except the blue apron with pockets—also my likeness, and my medal, with much love.

To my dear sister Margaret, I give my turkquoise ring (if I get it), also my green box with the doves on it, also my piece of real lace for her neck, and my sketch of her as a memorial of her "little girl."

To Jo I leave my breastpin, the one mended with sealing wax, also my bronze inkstand—she lost the cover—and my most precious plaster rabbit, because I am sorry I burned up her story.

To Beth (if she lives after me) I give my dolls and the little bureau, my fan, my linen collars and my new slippers if she can wear them being thin when she gets well. And I herewith also leave her my regret that I ever made fun of old Joanna.

To my friend and neighbor Theodore Laurence I bequeethe my paper marshay portfolio, my clay model of a horse though he did say it hadn't any neck. Also in return for his great kindness in the hour of affliction any one of my artistic works he likes, Notre Dame is the best.

To our venerable benefactor Mr. Laurence I leave my purple box with a looking glass in the cover which will be nice for his pens and remind him of the departed girl who thanks him for his favors to her family, specially Beth.

I wish my favorite playmate Kitty Bryant to have the blue silk apron and my gold-bead ring with a kiss.

To Hannah I give the bandbox she wanted and all the patchwork I leave hoping she "will remember me, when it you see."

And now having disposed of my most valuable property I hope all will be satisfied and not blame the dead. I forgive everyone, and trust we may all meet when the trump shall sound. Amen.

To this will and testiment I set my hand and seal on this 20th day of Nov. Anni Domino 1861.

AMY CURTIS MARCH

Witnesses: { ESTELLE VALNOR
             { THEODORE LAURENCE

The last name was written in pencil, and Amy explained that he was to rewrite it in ink, and seal it up for her properly.

"What put it into your head? Did anyone tell you about Beth's giving away her things?" asked Laurie soberly.

"What about Beth?"

"I'm sorry I spoke, but as I did, I'll tell you. She felt so ill one day that she told Jo she wanted to give her piano to Meg, her cats to you, and the poor old doll to Jo, who would love it for her sake. She was sorry she had so little to give, and left locks of hair to the rest of us, and her best love to Grandpa. *She* never thought of a will."

Amy's face was full of trouble. "Don't people put sort of postscripts to their wills, sometimes?"

"Yes, 'codicils,' they call them."

"Put one in mine then—that I wish *all* my curls cut off, and given round to my friends. I forgot it, but I want it done, though it will spoil my looks."

Laurie added it, smiling at Amy's last and greatest sacrifice.

CONFIDENTIAL

I don't think I have any words in which to tell the meeting of the mother and daughters. Such hours are beautiful to live, but very hard to describe, so I will leave it to the imagination of my readers, merely saying that the house was full of genuine happiness.

Hannah had "dished up" an astonishing breakfast for the traveler, finding it impossible to vent her excitement in any other way; and Meg and Jo fed their mother like dutiful young storks while they listened to her whispered account of Father's state, Mr. Brooke's promise to stay and nurse him, and the unspeakable comfort Laurie's hopeful face had given her when she arrived worn-out with fatigue, anxiety, and cold.

What a strange, yet pleasant day that was! So brilliant and gay without, for all the world seemed abroad to welcome the first snow; so quiet and reposeful within, for everyone slept, spent with watching, and a Sabbath stillness reigned through the house while nodding Hannah mounted guard at the door. With a blissful sense of burdens lifted off, Meg and Jo closed their weary eyes and lay at rest, like storm-beaten boats safe at anchor in a quiet harbor. Mrs. March would not leave Beth's side, but rested in the big chair, waking often to look at, touch, and brood over her child, like a miser over some recovered treasure.

Laurie, meanwhile, posted off to comfort Amy, and told his story so well that Aunt March actually "sniffed" herself, and never once said "I told you so." Amy dried her tears quickly, calmly restrained her impatience to see her mother, and never even thought of the turquoise ring when the old lady heartily agreed in Laurie's opinion that she behaved "like a capital little woman." Even Polly seemed impressed, for he called her "good girl," blessed her buttons, and begged her to "come and take a walk, dear," in his most affable tone. She would very gladly have gone out to enjoy the bright wintry weather but, discovering that Laurie was dropping with sleep in spite of manful efforts to conceal the fact, she persuaded him to rest on the sofa while she wrote a note to her mother. When she returned, he was stretched out, with both arms under his head, sound asleep. Aunt March had pulled down the curtains, and sat doing nothing in an unusual fit of benignity.

After a while, they began to think he was not going to wake till night, and I'm not sure that he would had he not been effectually roused by Amy's cry of joy at sight of her mother. There probably were a good many happy little girls in and about the city that day, but it is my private opinion that Amy was the happiest of all when she sat in her mother's lap and told her trials, receiving consolation and compensation in the shape of approving smiles and fond caresses.

Mrs. March saw something on the lifted hand that made her smile. She said nothing, but Amy understood the look and after a minute's pause she added gravely: "I wanted to speak to you about this, but I forgot it. Aunt gave me the ring today. She called me to her and kissed me, and put it on my finger, and said I was a credit to her, and she'd like to keep me always. She gave me that funny guard to keep the turquoise on, as it's too big. I'd like to wear them, Mother. Can I?"

"They are very pretty, but I think you're rather too young for such ornaments, Amy," said Mrs. March, looking at the plump little hand with the band of sky-blue stones on the forefinger, and the quaint guard formed of two tiny golden hands clasped together.

"I'll try not to be vain," said Amy. "I don't think I like it only because it's so pretty. I want to wear it as the girl in the story wore her bracelet, to remind me of something."

"Do you mean Aunt March?" asked her mother, laughing.

"No, to remind me not to be selfish." Amy looked so earnest and sincere about it that her mother stopped laughing, and listened respectfully to the little plan.

"I've thought a great deal lately about my 'bundle of naughties,' and being selfish is the largest one in it; so I'm going to try hard to cure it, if I can. Beth isn't selfish, and that's the reason everyone loves her and feels so bad at the thought of losing her. People wouldn't feel half so bad about me if I was sick, and I don't deserve to have them! But I'd like to be loved and missed by a great many friends, so I'm going to try and be like Beth all I can. I'm apt to forget my resolutions; but if I had something always about me to remind me, I guess I should do better. May I try this way?"

"Yes. Wear your ring, dear, and do your best."

That evening while Meg was writing to her father to report the traveler's safe arrival, Jo slipped upstairs into Beth's room, and finding her mother in her usual place, stood a minute twisting her fingers in her hair with a worried gesture and an undecided look.

"What is it, dearie?" asked Mrs. March.

"I want to tell you something, Mother."

"About Meg?"

"How quickly you guessed! Yes, it's about her, and though it's a little thing, it fidgets me."

"Beth is asleep. Speak low, and tell me all about it."

"Last summer Meg left a pair of gloves over at the Laurences', and only one was returned. We forgot all about it till Teddy told me that Mr. Brooke had it. He kept it in his waistcoat pocket, and once it fell out, and Teddy joked him about it, and Mr. Brooke owned that he liked Meg, but didn't dare say so, she was so young and he so poor. Now isn't it a *dread*ful state of things?"

"Do you think Meg cares for him?"

"Mercy me! I don't know anything about love and such nonsense!" cried Jo, with a funny mixture of interest and contempt. "In novels, the girls show it by starting and blushing, fainting away, growing thin, and acting like fools. Now Meg does not do anything of the sort. She eats and drinks and sleeps like a sensible creature; she looks straight in my face when I talk about that man, and only blushes a little bit when Teddy jokes about lovers."

"Then you fancy that Meg is *not* interested in John?"

"Who?" cried Jo, staring.

"Mr. Brooke. I call him John now. We fell into the way of doing so at the hospital, and he likes it."

"Oh dear! I know you'll take his part. He's been good to Father, and you won't send him away, but let Meg marry him, if she wants to." And Jo pulled her hair again with a wrathful tweak.

"My dear, don't get angry about it, and I will tell you how it happened. John went with me at Mr. Laurence's request, and was so devoted to poor Father that we couldn't help getting fond of him. He was perfectly open and honorable about Meg, for he told us he loved her, but would earn a comfortable home before he asked her to marry him. He only wanted our leave to love her and work for her, and the right to make her love him if he could. He is a truly excellent young man, and we could not refuse to listen to him; but I will not consent to Meg's engaging herself so young."

"Of course not, it would be idiotic! I just wish I could marry Meg myself, and keep her safe in the family."

This odd arrangement made Mrs. March smile, but she said gravely:

"Jo, I confide in you, and don't wish you to say anything to Meg yet. When John comes back, and I see them together, I can judge better of her feelings toward him."

"She'll see his in those handsome eyes that she talks about, and then it will be all up with her. She's got such a soft heart it will melt like butter in the sun if anyone looks sentimentally at her. She read the short reports he sent more than she did your letters, and likes brown eyes, and doesn't think John an ugly name, and she'll go and fall in love, and there's an end of peace and fun, and cozy times together. Oh dear me! Why weren't we all boys? Then there wouldn't be any bother." Mrs. March sighed, and Jo looked up with an air of relief. "You don't like it, Mother? I'm glad of it. Let's send him about his business, and not tell Meg a word of it, but all be happy together as we always have been."

"I did wrong to sigh, Jo. It is natural and right you should all go to homes of your own, in time; but I am sorry that this happened so soon, for Meg is only seventeen. Your father and I have agreed that she shall not bind herself in any way, nor be married, before twenty. If she and John love one another, they can wait, and test their love by doing so."

"I'm disappointed about Meg, for I'd planned to have her marry Teddy by and by. Wouldn't it be nice?" asked Jo.

"I'm afraid Laurie is hardly grown-up enough for Meg, and altogether too much of a weathercock, just now, for anyone to depend on. Don't make plans, Jo, but let time and their own hearts mate your friends."

"Well, I won't; but I hate to see things going all crisscross and getting snarled up. I wish wearing flatirons on our heads would keep us from growing up. But buds will be roses, and kittens, cats—more's the pity!"

"What's that about flatirons and cats?" asked Meg as she crept into the room with the finished letter in her hand.

"Only one of my stupid speeches. I'm going to bed. Come, Peggy," said Jo, unfolding herself like an animated puzzle.

"Quite right, and beautifully written. Please add that I send my love to John," said Mrs. March as she glanced over the letter and gave it back.

"Do you call him John?" asked Meg smiling.

"Yes. He has been like a son to us, and we are very fond of him," replied Mrs. March, returning the look with a keen one.

"I'm glad of that, he is so lonely. Good night, Mother dear. It is so inexpressibly comfortable to have you here," was Meg's quiet answer.

The kiss her mother gave her was a very tender one, and as she went away Mrs. March said, with a mixture of satisfaction and regret:

"She does not love John yet, but will soon learn to."

LAURIE MAKES MISCHIEF, AND JO MAKES PEACE

Laurie no sooner suspected a mystery than he set himself to find it out, and led Jo a trying life of it. He wheedled, bribed, ridiculed, threatened, and scolded; affected indifference, that he might surprise the truth from her; declared he knew, then that he didn't care; and at last, by dint of perseverance, he satisfied himself that it concerned Meg and Mr. Brooke. Feeling indignant that he was not taken into his tutor's confidence, he set his wits to work to devise some proper retaliation for the slight.

Meg meanwhile had apparently forgotten the matter, and was absorbed in preparations for her father's return; but all of a sudden a change seemed to come over her, and for a day or two she was quite unlike herself. She started when spoken to, blushed when looked at, was very quiet, and sat over her sewing with a timid, troubled look on her face.

"She feels it in the air—love, I mean—and she's going very fast. She's got most of the symptoms—is twittery and cross, doesn't eat, lies awake, and mopes in corners. I caught her singing that song he gave her, and once she said 'John,' as you do, and then turned as red as a poppy. Whatever shall we do?" said Jo.

"Nothing but wait. Let her alone, be kind and patient, and Father's coming will settle everything," replied her mother.

"Here's a note to you, Meg, all sealed up," said Jo next day as she distributed the contents of the little post office.

Mrs. March and Jo were deep in their own affairs when a sound from Meg made them look up to see her staring at her note with a frightened face.

"My child, what is it?" cried her mother, running to her while Jo tried to take the paper which had done the mischief.

"It's all a mistake—he didn't send it. O Jo, how could you do it?" And Meg hid her face in her hands, crying as if her heart was quite broken.

"Me! I've done nothing! What's she talking about?" cried Jo, bewildered.

Meg's mild eyes kindled with anger as she pulled a crumpled note from her pocket and threw it at Jo, saying reproachfully: "You wrote it, and that bad boy helped you. How could you be so rude, so mean and cruel to us both?"

Jo hardly heard her, for she and her mother were reading the note, which was written in a peculiar hand.

"My Dearest Margaret,

"I can no longer restrain my passion, and must know my fate before I return. I dare not tell your parents yet, but I think they would consent if they knew that we adored one another. Mr. Laurence will help me to some good place, and then, my sweet girl, you will make me happy. I implore you to say nothing to your family yet, but to send one word of hope through Laurie to

"Your devoted JOHN"

"Oh, the little villain! That's the way he meant to pay me for keeping my word to Mother. I'll give him a hearty scolding, and bring him over to beg pardon," cried Jo, burning to execute immediate justice. But her mother held her back.

"Stop, Jo, you must clear yourself first. You have played so many pranks that I am afraid you have had a hand in this."

"On my word, Mother, I haven't! I never saw that note before, and don't know anything about it, as true as I live!" said Jo, so earnestly that they believed her. "If I *had* taken a part in it I'd have done it better than this, and have written a sensible note. I should think you'd have known Mr. Brooke wouldn't write such stuff as that," she added scornfully.

"It's like his writing," faltered Meg.

"O Meg, you didn't answer it?" cried Mrs. March quickly.

"Yes, I did!" and Meg hid her face again.

"Margaret, tell me the whole story," commanded Mrs. March.

"I received the first letter from Laurie, who didn't look as if he knew anything about it," began Meg, without looking up. "I was worried at first, and meant to tell you; then I remembered how you liked Mr. Brooke, so I thought you wouldn't mind if I kept my little secret for a few days."

"What did you say to him?" asked Mrs. March.

"I only said I was too young to do anything about it yet; that I didn't wish to have secrets from you, and he must speak to Father. I was very grateful for his kindness, and would be his friend, but nothing more, for a long while."

Mrs. March smiled as if well pleased, and Jo clapped her hands, exclaiming with a laugh: "You are almost equal to Caroline Percy, who was a pattern of prudence! Tell on, Meg. What did he say to that?"

"He writes in a different way entirely, telling me that he never sent any love letter at all, and is very sorry that my roguish sister Jo should take such liberties with our names. It's very kind and respectful, but think how dreadful for me!"

Meg leaned against her mother looking the image of despair, and Jo tramped about the room calling Laurie names. All of a sudden she stopped, caught up the two notes, and after looking at them closely, said decidedly:

"I don't believe Brooke ever saw either of these letters. Teddy wrote both, and keeps yours to crow over me with, because I wouldn't tell him my secret."

"Don't have any secrets, Jo. Tell it to Mother, and keep out of trouble, as I should have done," said Meg warningly.

"Bless you, child! Mother told me."

"That will do, Jo. I'll comfort Meg while you go and get Laurie. I shall sift the matter to the bottom, and put a stop to such pranks at once."

Away ran Jo, and Mrs. March gently told Meg Mr. Brooke's real feelings. "Now, dear, what are your own? Do you love him enough to wait till he can make a home for you, or will you keep yourself quite free for the present?"

"I've been so scared and worried I don't want to have anything to do with lovers for a long while—perhaps never," answered Meg petulantly. "If John *doesn't* know anything about this nonsense, don't tell him, and make Jo and Laurie hold their tongues. I won't be deceived and plagued and made a fool of—it's a shame!"

Seeing that Meg's usually gentle temper was roused and her pride hurt by this mischievous joke, Mrs. March soothed her by promises of entire silence, and great discretion for the future. The instant Laurie's step was heard in the hall, Meg fled into the study, and Mrs. March received the culprit alone. Jo had not told him why he was wanted, fearing he wouldn't come, but he knew the minute he saw Mrs. March's face, and stood twirling his hat with a guilty air which convicted him at once. Jo was dismissed, but chose to march up and down the hall like a sentinel, having some fear that the prisoner might bolt. The sound of voices in the parlor rose and fell for half an hour, but what happened during that interview the girls never knew.

When they were called in, Laurie was standing by their mother, with such a penitent face that Jo forgave him on the spot but did not think it wise to betray the fact. Meg received his humble apology, and was much comforted by the assurance that Brooke knew nothing of the joke.

"I'll never tell him to my dying day—wild horses shan't drag it out of me; so you'll forgive me, Meg, and I'll do anything to show how out-and-out sorry I am."

"I'll try, but it was a very ungentlemanly thing to do. I didn't think you could be so sly and malicious, Laurie," replied Meg.

"It was altogether abominable, and I don't deserve to be spoken to for a month—but you will, though, won't you?" And Laurie folded his hands together with such an imploring gesture as he spoke in his irresistibly persuasive tone that it was impossible to frown upon him, in spite of his scandalous behavior. Meg pardoned him, and Mrs. March's grave face relaxed.

Everyone thought the matter ended and the little cloud blown over; but the mischief was done, for though others forgot it, Meg remembered. She never alluded to a certain person, but she thought of him a good deal, dreamed dreams more than ever; and once Jo, rummaging her sister's desk for stamps, found a bit of paper scribbled over with the words "Mrs. John Brooke," whereat she groaned tragically and cast it into the fire, feeling that Laurie's prank had hastened the evil day for her.

ℙLEASANT MEADOWS

Like sunshine after storm were the peaceful weeks which followed. The invalids improved rapidly, and Mr. March began to talk of returning early in the new year. Beth was soon able to lie on the study sofa all day, amusing herself with the well-beloved cats at first, and in time with doll's sewing, which had fallen sadly behindhand. Her once active limbs were so stiff and feeble that Jo took her a daily airing about the house in her strong arms. Meg cheerfully blackened and burned her white hands cooking delicate messes for "the dear," while Amy, a loyal slave of the ring, celebrated her return by giving away as many of her treasures as she could prevail on her sisters to accept.

As Christmas approached, the usual mysteries began to haunt the house, and Jo frequently convulsed the family by proposing utterly impossible or magnificently absurd ceremonies in honor of this unusually merry Christmas. Laurie was equally impracticable, and would have had bonfires, skyrockets, and triumphal arches if he had had his own way. After many skirmishes and snubbings, the ambitious pair were considered effectually quenched and went about with forlorn faces, which were rather belied by explosions of laughter when the two got together.

Several days of unusually mild weather fitly ushered in a splendid Christmas Day. Everybody and everything seemed bound to produce a grand success. To begin with, Mr. March wrote that he would soon be with them; then Beth felt uncommonly well that morning and, being dressed in her mother's gift—a soft crimson merino wrapper—was borne in triumph to the window to behold the offering of Jo and Laurie. The Unquenchables had done their best to be worthy of the name, for, like elves, they had worked by night, and conjured up a comical surprise. Out in the garden stood a stately snow maiden crowned with holly, bearing a basket of fruit and flowers in one hand, a great roll of new music in the other, a perfect rainbow of an afghan round her chilly shoulders, and a Christmas carol issuing from her lips on a pink paper streamer:

THE JUNGFRAU TO BETH

God bless you, dear Queen Bess!
    May nothing you dismay,
But health and peace and happiness
    Be yours this Christmas Day.

Here's fruit to feed our busy bee,
    And flowers for her nose;
Here's music for her pianee,
    An Afghan for her toes.

A portrait of Joanna, see,
    By Raphael No. 2,
Who labored with great industry
    To make it fair and true.

Accept a ribbon red, I beg,
    For Madam Purrer's tail;
And ice cream made by lovely Peg—
    A Mont Blanc in a pail.

Their dearest love my makers laid
    Within my breast of snow:
Accept it, and the Alpine maid,
    From Laurie and from Jo.

How Beth laughed when she saw it, how Laurie ran up and down to bring in the gifts, and what ridiculous speeches Jo made as she presented them!

"I'm so full of happiness that if Father was only here, I couldn't hold one drop more," said Beth.

"So am I," added Jo, slapping the pocket wherein reposed the long-desired *Undine and Sintram.*

"I'm sure I am," echoed Amy, poring over the engraved copy of the Madonna and Child her mother had given her.

"Of course I am!" cried Meg, smoothing the silvery folds of her first silk dress, for Mr. Laurence had insisted on giving it.

159

"How can *I* be otherwise?" said Mrs. March gratefully as her eyes went from her husband's letter to Beth's smiling face.

Half an hour after everyone had said they were so happy they could only hold one drop more, the drop came. Laurie opened the parlor door, and popped his head in very quietly. He might just as well have turned a somersault and uttered an Indian war whoop; for his face was so full of suppressed excitement and his voice so treacherously joyful that everyone jumped up, though he only said, in a queer, breathless voice, "Here's another Christmas present for the March family."

Before the words were well out of his mouth, he was whisked away somehow, and in his place appeared a tall man, muffled up to the eyes, leaning on the arm of another tall man, who tried to say something and couldn't. Of course there was a general stampede. Mr. March became invisible in the embrace of four pairs of loving arms; Jo disgraced herself by nearly fainting away; Mr. Brooke kissed Meg entirely by mistake, as he somewhat incoherently explained; and Amy, the dignified, tumbled over a stool and, never stopping to get up, hugged and cried over her father's boots in the most touching manner. Mrs. March was the first to recover herself, and held up her hand with a warning "Hush! Remember Beth!"

But it was too late. The study door flew open, the little red wrapper appeared on the threshold—joy put strength into the feeble limbs—and Beth ran straight into her father's arms. Never mind what happened just after that, for the full hearts overflowed, washing away the bitterness of the past and leaving only the sweetness of the present.

It was not at all romantic, but a hearty laugh set everybody straight again, for Hannah was discovered behind the door sobbing over the fat turkey, which she had forgotten to put down when she rushed up from the kitchen. As the laugh subsided Mrs. March began to thank Mr. Brooke for his faithful care of her husband, at which Mr. Brooke suddenly remembered that Mr. March needed rest and, seizing Laurie, he precipitately retired. Then the two invalids were ordered to repose, which they did by both sitting in one big chair, and talking hard.

Mr. March told how he had longed to surprise them, and how when the fine weather came, he had been allowed by his doctor to take advantage of it; how devoted Brooke had been, and how he was altogether a most estimable and upright young man. Why Mr. March paused a minute just there, and after a glance at Meg, who was violently poking the fire, looked at his wife with an inquiring lift of his eyebrows, I leave you to imagine; also why Mrs. March gently nodded her head, and asked, rather abruptly, if he wouldn't like something to eat. Jo saw and understood the look, and she stalked grimly away to get wine and beef tea, muttering to herself as she slammed the door, "I hate estimable young men with brown eyes!"

There never *was* such a Christmas dinner as they had that day. The fat turkey was a sight to behold when Hannah sent him up stuffed, browned, and decorated; so was the plum pudding, which quite melted in one's mouth; likewise the jellies, in which Amy reveled like a fly in a honey pot. Everything turned out well, which was a mercy, Hannah said:

"For my mind was that flustered, mum, that it's a merrycle I didn't roast the pudding, and stuff the turkey with raisins, let alone bilin' of it in a cloth."

Mr. Laurence and his grandson dined with them, also Mr. Brooke—at whom Jo glowered darkly, to Laurie's infinite amusement. Two easy chairs stood side by side at the head of the table, in which sat Beth and her father, feasting modestly on chicken and a little fruit. They drank healths, told stories, sang songs, "reminisced," as the old folks say, and had a thoroughly good time. The guests departed early, and as twilight gathered the happy family sat together round the fire.

"Just a year ago we were groaning over the dismal Christmas we expected to have. Do you remember?" asked Jo, breaking a short pause which had followed a long conversation about many things.

"Rather a pleasant year on the whole!" said Meg, smiling at the fire.

"I think it's been a pretty hard one," observed Amy.

"I'm glad it's over, because we've got you back," whispered Beth, who sat on her father's knee.

"Rather a rough road for you to travel, my little pilgrims, especially the latter part of it. But you have got on bravely, and I think the burdens are in a fair way to tumble off very soon," said Mr. March, looking with fatherly satisfaction at the four young faces gathered round him.

"How do you know? Did mother tell you?" asked Jo.

"Not much. Straws show which way the wind blows, and I've made several discoveries today."

"Oh, tell us what they are!" cried Meg, who sat beside him.

"Here is one," and taking up the hand which lay on the arm of his chair, he pointed to the roughened forefinger, a burn on the back, and two or three little hard spots on the palm. "I remember a time when this hand was white and smooth, and your first care was to keep it so. It was very pretty then, but to me it is much prettier now—for in these seeming blemishes I read a little history. A burnt offering has been made of vanity; this hardened palm has earned something better than blisters; and I'm sure the sewing done by these pricked fingers will last a long time, so much goodwill went into the stitches. Meg, my dear, I value the womanly skill which keeps home happy more than white hands or fashionable accomplishments. I'm proud to shake this good, industrious little hand, and hope I shall not soon be asked to give it away."

"What about Jo? Please say something nice, for she has tried so hard, and been so very, very good to me," said Beth in her father's ear.

He laughed, and looked across at the tall girl who sat opposite.

"In spite of the curly crop, I don't see the 'son Jo' whom I left a year ago," said Mr. March. "I see a young lady who pins her collar straight, laces her boots neatly, and neither whistles, talks slang, nor lies on the rug as she used to do. Her face is rather thin and pale just now, with watching and anxiety; but I like to look at it, for it has grown gentler, and her voice is lower; she doesn't bounce, but moves quietly, and takes care of a certain little person in a motherly way which delights me. I rather miss my wild girl; but if I get a strong, helpful, tenderhearted woman in her place, I shall feel quite satisfied. I don't know whether the shearing sobered our black sheep, but I do know that in all Washington I couldn't find anything beautiful enough to be bought with the five and twenty dollars which my good girl sent me."

Jo's keen eyes were rather dim for a minute, and her thin face grew rosy in the firelight.

"Now Beth," said Amy.

"There's so little of her I'm afraid to say much, for fear she will slip away altogether, though she is not so shy as she used to be," began their father cheerfully. But recollecting how nearly he *had* lost her, he held her close, saying tenderly, "I've got you safe, my Beth, and I'll keep you so, please God."

After a minute's silence, he looked down at Amy, who sat on the cricket at his feet, and said, with a caress of the shining hair: "I observed that Amy took drumsticks at dinner, ran errands for her mother all the afternoon, gave Meg her place tonight, and has waited on everyone with patience and good humor. I also observe that she does not fret much nor look in the glass, and has not even mentioned a very pretty ring which she wears; so I conclude that she has learned to think of other people more and of herself less, and has decided to try and mold her character as carefully as she molds her little clay figures. I am glad of this, for though I should be very proud of a graceful statue made by her, I shall be infinitely prouder of a lovable daughter with a talent for making life beautiful to herself and others."

"What are you thinking of, Beth?" asked Jo, when Amy had thanked her father and told about her ring.

"I read in *Pilgrim's Progress* today how, after many troubles, Christian and Hopeful came to a pleasant green meadow where lilies bloomed all the year round, and there they rested happily, as we do now, before they went on to their journey's end," answered Beth, adding as she slipped out of her father's arms and went slowly to the instrument: "It's singing time now, and I want to be in my old place. I'll try to sing the song of the shepherd boy which the Pilgrims heard. I made the music for Father, because he likes the verses."

So, sitting at the dear little piano, Beth softly touched the keys, and in the sweet voice they had thought never to hear again sang to her own

163

accompaniment the quaint hymn, which was a singularly fitting song for her:

> "He that is down need fear no fall,
>   He that is low no pride;
> He that is humble ever shall
>   Have God to be his guide.
>
> "I am content with what I have,
>   Little be it or much;
> And, Lord! contentment still I crave
>   Because Thou savest such.
>
> "Fullness to them a burden is
>   That go on pilgrimage;
> Here little, and hereafter bliss,
>   Is best from age to age!"

AUNT MARCH SETTLES THE QUESTION

Like bees swarming after their queen, mother and daughters hovered about Mr. March the next day, neglecting everything to look at, wait upon, and listen to the new invalid, who was in a fair way to be killed by kindness. As he sat propped up in a big chair by Beth's sofa, with the other three close by, nothing seemed needed to complete their happiness. But something *was* needed and the elder ones felt it, though none confessed the fact. Mr. and Mrs. March looked at one another with an anxious expression as their eyes followed Meg. Jo had sudden fits of sobriety, and was seen to shake her fist at Mr. Brooke's umbrella, which had been left in the hall; Meg was absent-minded, started when the bell rang, and colored when John's name was mentioned; Amy said everyone seemed waiting for something, and couldn't settle down, which was queer, since Father was safe at home; and Beth innocently wondered why their neighbors didn't run over as usual.

Laurie went by in the afternoon, and seeing Meg at the window, seemed suddenly possessed with a melodramatic fit, for he fell down upon one knee in the snow, beat his breast, tore his hair, and clasped his hands imploringly, as if begging some boon; and when Meg told him to behave himself and go away, he wrung imaginary tears out of his handkerchief, and staggered round the corner as if in utter despair.

"What does the goose mean?" said Meg.

"He's showing you how your John will go on by and by. Touching, isn't it?" answered Jo scornfully.

"Don't say *my John*, it isn't proper or true." But Meg's voice lingered over the words as if they sounded pleasant to her. "Please don't plague me, Jo. I've told you I don't care *much* about him, but we are all to be friendly, and go on as before."

"We can't, for something *has* been said, and Laurie's mischief has spoiled you for me. I see it, and so does Mother; you are not like your old self a bit, and seem ever so far away from me. I don't mean to plague you, and will bear it like a man, but I do wish it was all settled. I hate to wait, so if you mean ever to do it, make haste and have it over quickly," said Jo pettishly.

"*I* can't say or do anything till he speaks, and he won't, because Father said I was too young," began Meg, bending over her work.

"If he did speak, you wouldn't know what to say, but would cry or blush, or let him have his own way, instead of giving a good, decided No."

"I'm not so silly and weak as you think. I know just what I should say, for I've planned it all, so I needn't be taken unawares. There's no knowing what may happen, and I wished to be prepared."

"Would you mind telling me what you'd say?" asked Jo more respectfully.

"Not at all. You are sixteen now, quite old enough to be my confidante, and my experience will be useful to you by and by, perhaps, in your own affairs of this sort."

"Don't mean to have any. It's fun to watch other people philander, but I should feel like a fool doing it myself," said Jo.

"I think not, if you liked anyone very much, and he liked you."

"I thought you were going to tell your speech to that man," said Jo.

"Oh, I should merely say, quite calmly and decidedly, 'Thank you, Mr. Brooke, you are very kind, but I agree with Father that I am too young to enter into any engagement at present; so please say no more, but let us be friends as we were.'"

"Hum! That's stiff and cool enough. I don't believe you'll ever say it, and I know he won't be satisfied if you do. If he goes on like the rejected lovers in books, you'll give in rather than hurt his feelings."

"No I won't. I shall tell him I've made up my mind, and shall walk out of the room with dignity."

Meg rose as she spoke, and was just going to rehearse the dignified exit when a step in the hall made her fly into her seat and begin to sew as if her life depended on finishing that particular seam in a given time. Jo smothered a laugh at the sudden change, and when someone gave a modest tap, opened the door with a grim aspect which was anything but hospitable.

"Good afternoon. I came to get my umbrella—that is, to see how your father finds himself today," said Mr. Brooke.

"It's very well, he's in the rack, I'll get him, and tell it you are here." And having jumbled her father and the umbrella well together in her reply, Jo slipped out of the room. But the instant she vanished, Meg began to sidle toward the door, murmuring: "Mother will like to see you. Pray sit down, I'll call her."

"Don't go—are you afraid of me, Margaret?" And Mr. Brooke looked so hurt that Meg thought she must have done something very rude. She blushed up to the little curls on her forehead, for he had never called her Margaret before. Anxious to appear friendly and at her ease, she put out her hand with a confiding gesture and said gratefully: "How can I be afraid when you have been so kind to Father? I only wish I could thank you for it."

"Shall I tell you how?" asked Mr. Brooke, holding the small hand fast in both his own and looking down at Meg with so much love in the brown eyes that her heart began to flutter.

"Oh no, please don't—I'd rather not," she said, trying to withdraw her hand, and looking frightened in spite of her denial.

"I won't trouble you. I only want to know if you care for me a little, Meg. I love you so much, dear."

This was the moment for the calm, proper speech, but Meg didn't make it; she forgot every word of it, hung her head, and answered, "I don't know," so softly that John had to stoop down to catch the foolish little reply. He seemed to think it was worth the trouble, for he smiled to himself as if quite satisfied, pressed the plump hand gratefully, and said, in his most persuasive tone: "Will you try and find out? I want to know so much, for I can't go to work with any heart until I learn whether I am to have my reward in the end or not."

"I'm too young," faltered Meg.

"I'll wait, and in the meantime you could be learning to like me. Would it be a very hard lesson, dear?"

"Not if I chose to learn it, but——"

"Please choose to learn, Meg. I love to teach, and this is easier than German," broke in John, getting possession of the other hand.

His tone was properly beseeching; but, stealing a shy look at him, Meg saw that his eyes were merry as well as tender, and that he wore the satisfied smile of one who had no doubt of his success. The love of power, which sleeps in the bosoms of the best of little women, woke up all of a sudden and took possession of her. She felt excited and strange and, withdrawing her hands, said petulantly: "I *don't* choose. Please go away and let me be!"

Poor Mr. Brooke looked as if his lovely castle in the air was tumbling about his ears, for he had never seen Meg in such a mood before, and it rather bewildered him. "Do you really mean that?" he asked anxiously.

"Yes, I do. I don't want to be worried about such things. Father says I needn't; it's too soon and I'd rather not."

"Mayn't I hope you'll change your mind by and by? I'll wait, and say nothing till you have had more time. Don't play with me, Meg. I didn't think that of you."

"Don't think of me at all. I'd rather you wouldn't," said Meg, taking a naughty satisfaction in trying her lover's patience and her own power.

He was grave and pale now; he just stood looking at her so wistfully, so tenderly, that she found her heart relenting in spite of her. What would have happened next I cannot say if Aunt March had not come hobbling in at this interesting minute. The old lady couldn't resist her longing to see her nephew, for she had met Laurie as she took her airing, and hearing of Mr. March's arrival, drove straight out to see him. The family were all busy in the back part of the house, and she had made her way quietly in, hoping to surprise them. She did surprise two of them so much that Meg started as if she had seen a ghost, and Mr. Brooke vanished into the study.

"Bless me, what's all this?" cried the old lady, with a rap of her cane.

"It's Father's friend. I'm *so* surprised to see you!" stammered Meg, feeling that she was in for a lecture now.

"That's evident," returned Aunt March, sitting down. "But what is Father's friend saying to make you look like a peony? There's mischief going on, and I insist upon knowing what it is," with another rap.

"We were merely talking. Mr. Brooke came for his umbrella," began Meg, wishing that Mr. Brooke and the umbrella were safely out of the house.

"Brooke? That boy's tutor? Ah! I understand now. I know all about it. Jo blundered into a wrong message in one of your father's letters, and I made her tell me. You haven't gone and accepted him, child?" cried Aunt March.

"Hush! He'll hear. Shan't I call Mother?"

"Not yet. I've something to say to you, and I must free my mind at once. Tell me, do you mean to marry this Cook? If you do, not one penny of my money ever goes to you. Remember that, and be a sensible girl."

Now Aunt March possessed in perfection the art of rousing the spirit of opposition in the gentlest people, and enjoyed doing it. If Aunt March had begged Meg to accept John Brooke, she would probably have declared she couldn't think of it; but as she was peremptorily ordered *not* to like him, she immediately made up her mind that she would. Inclination as well as perversity made the decision easy, and being already much excited, Meg opposed the old lady with unusual spirit.

"I shall marry whom I please, Aunt March, and you can leave your money to anyone you like," she said.

"Highty-tighty! Is that the way you take my advice, miss? You'll be sorry for it by and by, when you've tried love in a cottage and found it a failure."

"It can't be a worse one than some people find in big houses."

Aunt March put on her glasses and took a look at the girl, for she did not know her in this new mood. Meg hardly knew herself, she felt so brave and independent—so glad to defend John, and assert her right to love him, if she liked. Aunt March saw that she had begun wrong, and after a little pause made a fresh start, saying, as mildly as she could:

"Now, Meg, my dear, be reasonable and take my advice. I mean it kindly, and don't want you to spoil your whole life by making a mistake at the beginning. You ought to marry well, and help your family. It's your duty to make a rich match."

"Father and Mother don't think so. They like John, though he *is* poor."

"Your parents, my dear, have no more worldly wisdom than two babies."

"I'm glad of it," cried Meg stoutly.

Aunt March took no notice, but went on with her lecture. "This Rook is poor, and hasn't got any rich relations, has he?"

"No but he has many warm friends."

"You can't live on friends. Try it, and see how cool they'll grow. He hasn't any business, has he?"

"Not yet. Mr. Laurence is going to help him."

"That won't last long. James Laurence is a crotchety old fellow, and not to be depended on. So you intend to marry a man without money, position, or business, and go on working harder than you do now, when you might be comfortable all your days by minding me and doing better? I thought you had more sense, Meg."

"I couldn't do better if I waited half my life! John is good and wise; he's got heaps of talent; he's willing to work, and sure to get on, he's so energetic and brave. Everyone likes and respects him, and I'm proud to think he cares for me, though I'm so poor and young and silly."

"He knows *you* have got rich relations, child. That's the secret of his liking, I suspect."

"Aunt March, how dare you say such a thing? John is above such meanness, and I won't listen to you a minute if you talk so," cried Meg indignantly, forgetting everything but the injustice of the old lady's suspicions. "My John wouldn't marry for money any more than I would. We are willing to work, and we mean to wait. I'm not afraid of being poor, for I've been happy so far, and I know I shall be with him, because he loves me, and I——"

Meg stopped there, remembering all of a sudden that she hadn't made up her mind; that she had told "her John" to go away; and that he might be overhearing her inconsistent remarks.

Aunt March was very angry, for she had set her heart on having her pretty niece make a fine match, and something in the girl's happy young face made the lonely old woman feel both sad and sour.

"Well, I wash my hands of the whole affair! You are a willful child, and you've lost more than you know by this piece of folly. No, I won't stop. I'm disappointed in you, and haven't spirits to see your father now. Don't expect anything from me when you are married; your Mr. Book's friends must take care of you. I'm done with you forever."

And Aunt March drove off in high dudgeon. She seemed to take all the girl's courage with her; for when left alone Meg stood a moment, undecided whether to laugh or cry. Before she could make up her mind, she was taken possession of by Mr. Brooke, who said, all in one breath:

"I couldn't help hearing, Meg. Thank you for defending me, and Aunt March for proving that you *do* care for me a little bit."

"I didn't know how much till she abused you," began Meg.

"And I needn't go away, but may stay and be happy, may I, dear?"

Here was another fine chance to make the crushing speech and the stately exit, but Meg never thought of doing either, and disgraced herself forever in Jo's eyes by meekly whispering, "Yes, John," and hiding her face on Mr. Brooke's waistcoat.

Fifteen minutes after Aunt March's departure, Jo came softly downstairs, paused an instant at the parlor door, and, hearing no sound within, nodded and smiled with a satisfied expression, saying to herself: "She has sent him away as we planned, and that affair is settled. I'll go and hear the fun, and have a good laugh over it."

But poor Jo never got her laugh, for she was transfixed upon the threshold by a spectacle which held her there, staring with her mouth nearly as wide-open as her eyes. Going in to exult over a fallen enemy, and to praise a strong-minded sister for the banishment of an objectionable lover, it certainly *was* a shock to behold the aforesaid enemy serenely sitting on the sofa with the strong-minded sister enthroned upon his knee, and wearing an expression of the most abject submission. Jo gave a sort of gasp, as if a cold shower bath had suddenly fallen upon her. At the odd sound, the lovers turned and saw her. Meg jumped up looking both proud and shy, but "that man," as Jo called him, actually laughed, and said coolly as he kissed the astonished newcomer, "Sister Jo, congratulate us!"

That was adding insult to injury—it was altogether too much—and, making some wild demonstration with her hands, Jo vanished without a word. Rushing upstairs, she startled the invalids by exclaiming tragically as she burst into the room: "Oh, *do* somebody go down quick. John Brooke is acting dreadfully, and Meg likes it!"

Mr. and Mrs. March left the room with speed and, casting herself upon the bed, Jo cried and scolded tempestuously as she told the awful news to Beth and Amy. The little girls, however, considered it a most agreeable and interesting event, and Jo got little comfort from them, so she went up to her refuge in the garret, and confided her troubles to the rats.

Nobody ever knew what went on in the parlor that afternoon; but a great deal of talking was done, and quiet Mr. Brooke astonished his friends by the eloquence and spirit with which he pleaded his suit, told his plans, and persuaded them to arrange everything just as he wanted it. The tea bell rang before he had finished describing the paradise which he meant to earn for Meg, and he proudly took her in to supper, both looking so happy that Jo hadn't the heart to be jealous or dismal. Amy was very much impressed by John's devotion and Meg's dignity, Beth beamed at them from a distance, while Mr. and Mrs. March surveyed the young couple with such tender satisfaction that it was perfectly evident Aunt March was right in calling them as unworldly as a pair of babies. No one ate much, but everyone looked very happy.

"You can't say nothing pleasant ever happens now, can you, Meg?" said Amy.

"No, I'm sure I can't. How much has happened since I said that! It seems a year ago," answered Meg.

"The joys come close upon the sorrows this time, and I rather think the changes have begun," said Mrs. March. "In most families there comes, now and then, a year full of events; this has been such a one, but it ends well, after all."

"Hope the next will end better," muttered Jo, who found it very hard to see Meg absorbed in a stranger before her face.

"I hope the third year from this *will* end better. I mean it shall if I live to work out my plans," said Mr. Brooke, smiling at Meg as if everything had become possible to him now.

"Doesn't it seem very long to wait?" asked Amy.

"I've got so much to learn before I shall be ready it seems a short time to me," answered Meg, with a sweet gravity in her face never seen there before.

"You have only to wait. *I* am to do the work," said John, beginning his labors by picking up Meg's napkin with an expression which caused Jo to shake her head, and then say to herself, with an air of relief, as the front door banged:

"Here comes Laurie. Now we shall have a little sensible conversation."

But Jo was mistaken; for Laurie came prancing in bearing a great bridal-looking bouquet for "Mrs. John Brooke," and evidently laboring under the delusion that the whole affair had been brought about by his excellent management.

"I knew Brooke would have it all his own way, he always does; for when he makes up his mind to accomplish anything, it's done, though the sky falls," said Laurie.

"Much obliged for that recommendation. I take it as a good omen for the future, and invite you to my wedding on the spot," answered Mr. Brooke.

"I'll come if I'm at the ends of the earth; for the sight of Jo's face alone on that occasion would be worth a long journey. You don't look festive, ma'am. What's the matter?" asked Laurie, following her into a corner of the parlor, whither all had adjourned to greet Mr. Laurence.

"I don't approve of the match, but I've made up my mind to bear it, and shall not say a word against it," said Jo solemnly. "You can't know how hard it is for me to give up Meg."

"You don't give her up. You only go halves," said Laurie consolingly.

"It never can be the same again. I've lost my dearest friend," sighed Jo.

"You've got me, anyhow. I'm not good for much, I know, but I'll stand by you, Jo, all the days of my life, upon my word I will!" And Laurie meant what he said.

"I know you will, and I'm ever so much obliged. You are always a great comfort to me, Teddy," returned Jo gratefully.

"Well, now, don't be dismal, there's a good fellow. It's all right, you see. Meg is happy, Brooke will fly round and get settled immediately, Grandpa will attend to him, and it will be very jolly to see Meg in her own little house. We'll have capital times after she is gone, for I shall be through college before long, and then we'll go abroad, or some nice trip or other. Wouldn't that console you?"

"I rather think it would, but there's no knowing what may happen in three years," said Jo thoughtfully.

"That's true. Don't you wish you could take a look forward and see where we shall all be then? I do," returned Laurie.

"I think not, for I might see something sad; and everyone looks so happy now I don't believe they could be much improved." And Jo's eyes went slowly round the room, brightening as they looked, for the prospect was a pleasant one.

Father and Mother sat together, quietly reliving the first chapter of the romance which for them began some twenty years ago. Amy was drawing the lovers, who sat apart in a beautiful world of their own, the light of which touched their faces with a grace the little artist could not copy. Beth lay on her sofa talking cheerily with her old friend, who held her little hand as if he felt that it possessed the power to lead him along the peaceful way she walked. Jo lounged in her favorite low seat, with the grave, quiet look which best became her; and Laurie, leaning on the back of her chair, smiled with his friendliest aspect, and nodded at her in the long glass which reflected them both.

So grouped, the curtain falls upon Meg, Jo, Beth, and Amy.

PART 2

GOSSIP

In order that we may start afresh, and go to Meg's wedding with free minds, it will be well to begin with a little gossip about the Marches. The three years that have passed have brought but few changes to the quiet family. The war is over, and Mr. March safely at home, busy with his books and the small parish which found in him a minister by nature as by grace—a quiet, studious man, rich in the wisdom that is better than learning, the charity which calls all mankind "brother," the piety that blossoms into character, making it august and lovely. To outsiders, the five energetic women seemed to rule the house, and so they did in many things; but the quiet scholar sitting among his books was still the head of the family, the household conscience, anchor, and comforter; for to him the busy, anxious women always turned in troublous times.

Mrs. March is as brisk and cheery, though rather grayer, than when we saw her last, and just now so absorbed in Meg's affairs that the hospitals and homes, still full of wounded "boys" and soldiers' widows, decidedly miss the motherly missionary's visits. John Brooke did his duty manfully for a year, got wounded, was sent home, and not allowed to return. He received no stars or bars, but he deserved them, for he cheerfully risked all he had, and life and love are very precious when both are in full bloom. Perfectly resigned to his discharge, he devoted himself to getting well, preparing for business, and earning a home for Meg. With the good sense and sturdy independence that characterized him, he refused Mr. Laurence's more generous offers, and accepted the place of bookkeeper, feeling better satisfied to begin with an honestly earned salary than by running any risks with borrowed money.

Meg had spent the time in working as well as waiting, growing womanly in character, wise in housewifely arts, and prettier than ever; for love is a great beautifier. She had her girlish ambitions and hopes, and felt some disappointment at the humble way in which the new life must begin. Ned Moffat had just married Sallie Gardiner, and Meg couldn't help contrasting their fine house and carriage, many gifts, and splendid outfit with her own, and secretly wishing she could have the same. But somehow envy and discontent soon vanished when she thought of all the patient love and labor John had put into the little home awaiting her; and when they sat together in the twilight talking over their small plans, the future always grew so beautiful and bright that she forgot Sallie's splendor, and felt herself the richest, happiest girl in Christendom.

Jo never went back to Aunt March, for the old lady took such a fancy to Amy that she bribed her with the offer of drawing lessons from one of the best teachers going, and for the sake of this advantage Amy would have served a far harder mistress. So she gave her mornings to duty, her afternoons to pleasure, and prospered finely. Jo, meantime, devoted herself to literature and Beth, who remained delicate long after the fever was a thing of the past. Not an invalid exactly, but never again the rosy, healthy creature she had been; yet always hopeful, happy, and serene, busy with the quiet duties she loved, everyone's friend, and an angel in the house.

As long as the *Spread Eagle* paid her a dollar a column for her "rubbish," as she called it, Jo felt herself a woman of means, and spun her little romances diligently. But great plans fermented in her busy brain and ambitious mind, and the old tin kitchen in the garret held a slowly increasing pile of blotted manuscript which was one day to place the name of March upon the roll of fame.

Laurie, having dutifully gone to college to please his grandfather, was now getting through it in the easiest possible manner to please himself. A universal favorite, thanks to money, manners, much talent, and the kindest heart that ever got its owner into scrapes by trying to get other people out of them, he stood in great danger of being spoiled, and probably would have been, like many another promising boy, if he had not possessed a talisman against evil in the memory of the kind old man who was bound up in his success, the motherly friend who watched over him as if he were her son, and last, but not least by any means, the knowledge that four innocent girls loved, admired, and believed in him with all their hearts.

Being only "a glorious human boy," of course he frolicked and flirted, grew dandified, aquatic, sentimental, or gymnastic as college fashions ordained; hazed and was hazed, talked slang, and more than once came perilously near suspension and expulsion. But as high spirits and the love of fun were the causes of these pranks, he always managed to save himself by frank confession, honorable atonement, or the irresistible power of persuasion which he possessed in perfection. The "men of my class" were heroes in the eyes of the girls, who never wearied of the exploits of "our fellows," and were frequently allowed to bask in the smiles of these great creatures when Laurie brought them home with him.

Amy especially enjoyed this high honor, and became quite a belle among them; for her ladyship early felt and learned to use the gift of fascination with which she was endowed. Meg was too much absorbed in her private and particular John to care for any other lords of creation, and Beth too shy to do more than peep at them and wonder how Amy dared to order them about so. But Jo felt quite in her element, and found it very difficult to refrain from imitating the gentlemanly attitudes, phrases, and feats which seemed more natural to her than the decorums prescribed for young ladies. They all liked Jo immensely, but never fell in love with her, though very few escaped without paying the tribute of a sentimental sigh or two at Amy's shrine. And speaking of sentiment brings us very naturally to the Dovecote.

That was the name of the little brown house which Mr. Brooke had prepared for Meg's first home. Laurie had christened it, saying it was highly appropriate to the gentle lovers, who "went on together like a pair of turtledoves, with first a bill and then a coo." It was a tiny house, with a little garden behind, and a lawn about as big as a pocket handkerchief in front. Here Meg meant to have a fountain, shrubbery, and a profusion of lovely flowers; though just at present the fountain was represented by a weather-beaten urn very like a dilapidated slop bowl; the shrubbery consisted of several young larches undecided whether to live or die; and the profusion of flowers was merely hinted by regiments of sticks to show where seeds were planted. But inside, it was altogether charming, and the happy bride saw no fault from garret to cellar. To be sure, the hall was so narrow it was fortunate that they had no piano, for one never could have been got in whole; the dining room was so small that six people were a tight fit; and the kitchen stairs seemed built for the express purpose of precipitating both servants and china pell-mell into the coalbin. But once get used to these slight blemishes and nothing could be more complete, for good sense and good taste had presided over the furnishings, and the result was highly satisfactory. There were no marble-topped tables, long mirrors, or lace curtains in the little parlor, but simple furniture, plenty of books, a fine picture or two, a stand of flowers in the bay window, and, scattered all about, the pretty gifts which came from friendly hands. Everything was done at last, even to Amy's arranging different-colored soaps to match the different-colored rooms, and Beth's setting the table for the first meal.

"Are you satisfied? Does it seem like home, and do you feel as if you should be happy here?" asked Mrs. March as she and her daughter went through the new kingdom arm-in-arm.

"Yes, Mother, perfectly satisfied, thanks to you all, and so happy that I can't talk about it," answered Meg.

"If she only had a servant or two it would be all right," said Amy, coming out of the parlor.

"Mother and I have talked it over, and I have made up my mind to try her way first. There will be so little to do that, with Lotty to run my errands and help me here and there, I shall only have enough work to keep me from getting lazy or homesick," answered Meg tranquilly.

"Sallie Moffat has four," began Amy.

"If Meg had four the house wouldn't hold them, and master and missis would have to camp in the garden," broke in Jo, who was giving the last polish to the door handles.

"Sallie isn't a poor man's wife, and many maids are in keeping with her fine establishment. Meg and John begin humbly, but I have a feeling that there will be quite as much happiness in the little house as in the big one. It's a great mistake for young girls like Meg to leave themselves nothing to do but dress, give orders, and gossip. When I was first married, I used to long for my new clothes to wear out or get torn, so that I might have the pleasure of mending them; for I got heartily sick of doing fancywork and tending my pocket handkerchief."

"Why didn't you go into the kitchen and make messes, as Sallie says she does to amuse herself?" said Meg.

"I did, after a while—not to 'mess,' but to learn of Hannah how things should be done, that my servants need *not* laugh at me. It was play then, but there came a time when I was truly grateful that I not only possessed the will but the power to cook wholesome food for my little girls, and help myself when I could no longer afford to hire help. You begin at the other end, Meg dear; but the lessons you learn now will be of use to you by and by, when John is a richer man, for the mistress of a house, however splendid, should know how work ought to be done if she wishes to be well and honestly served."

"Yes, Mother, I'm sure of that," said Meg, listening respectfully to the little lecture. "Do you know I like this room most of all in my baby house," added Meg as they went upstairs and she looked into her well-stored linen closet.

Beth was there, laying the snowy piles smoothly on the shelves, and exulting over the goodly array. All three laughed as Meg spoke, for that linen closet was a joke. You see, after having said that if Meg married "that Brooke" she shouldn't have a cent of her money, Aunt March was rather in a quandary when time had appeased her wrath and made her repent her vow. She never broke her word, and was much exercised in her mind how to get round it, and at last devised a plan whereby she could satisfy herself. Mrs. Carrol, Florence's mamma, was ordered to buy, have made, and marked a generous supply of house and table linen, and send it as *her* present. But the secret leaked out, and was greatly enjoyed by the family; for Aunt March insisted that she could give nothing but the old-fashioned pearls long promised to the first bride.

"That's a housewifely taste which I am glad to see. I had a young friend who set up housekeeping with six sheets, but she had finger bowls for company, and that satisfied her," said Mrs. March, patting the damask tablecloths.

"I haven't a single finger bowl, but this is a 'setout' that will last me all my days, Hannah says." And Meg looked quite contented, as well she might.

"Toodles is coming," cried Jo from below, and they all went down to meet Laurie, whose weekly visit was an important event in their quiet lives.

A tall, broad-shouldered young fellow with a cropped head, a felt basin of a hat, and a flyaway coat came tramping down the road at a great pace, walked over the low fence without stopping to open the gate, straight up to Mrs. March, with both hands out, and a hearty "Here I am, Mother! Yes, it's all right." The last words were in answer to the look the elder lady gave him, a kindly questioning look, which the handsome eyes met so frankly that the little ceremony closed, as usual, with a motherly kiss.

"Bless you, Beth! What a refreshing spectacle you are, Jo. Amy, you are getting altogether too handsome for a single lady."

As Laurie spoke, he pulled Beth's hair ribbon, stared at Jo's big pinafore, and fell into an attitude of mock rapture before Amy, then shook hands all round, and everyone began to talk.

"Where is John?" asked Meg anxiously.

"Stopped to get the license for tomorrow, ma'am."

"Which side won the last match, Teddy?" inquired Jo, who persisted in feeling an interest in manly sports despite her nineteen years.

"Ours, of course. Wish you'd been there to see."

"How is the lovely Miss Randal?" asked Amy.

"More cruel than ever. Don't you see how I'm pining away?" And Laurie gave his broad chest a sounding slap and heaved a melodramatic sigh.

"I wonder if you will ever grow up, Laurie," said Meg in a matronly tone.

"I'm doing my best, ma'am, but can't get much higher, I'm afraid, as six feet is about all men can do in these degenerate days," responded the young gentleman, whose head was about level with the little chandelier. "I suppose it would be profanation to eat anything in this spick-and-span new bower, so, as I'm tremendously hungry, I propose an adjournment."

"Mother and I are going to wait for John. There are some last things to settle," said Meg, bustling away.

"Beth and I are going over to Kitty Bryant's to get more flowers for tomorrow," added Amy.

"Come, Jo, don't desert a fellow. I'm in such a state of exhaustion I can't get home without help."

"Now, Teddy, I want to talk seriously to you about tomorrow," began Jo as they strolled away together. "You *must* promise to behave well, and not cut up any pranks, and spoil our plans."

"Not a prank."

"And don't say funny things when we ought to be sober."

"I never do. You are the one for that."

"And I implore you not to look at me during the ceremony. I shall certainly laugh if you do."

"You won't see me. You'll be crying so hard that the thick fog round you will obscure the prospect. I say, Jo, how is Grandpa this week—pretty amiable?"

"Very. Why, have you got into a scrape, and want to know how he'll take it?" asked Jo rather sharply.

"Now, Jo, do you think I'd look your mother in the face and say 'All right' if it wasn't?"

"No, I don't."

"Then don't go and be suspicious. I only want some money," said Laurie, appeased by her hearty tone.

"You spend a great deal, Teddy."

"Bless you, I don't spend it; it spends itself, somehow, and is gone before I know it."

"I don't see the use of your having seventeen waistcoats, endless neckties, and a new hat every time you come home. I thought you'd got over the dandy period, but every now and then it breaks out in a new spot. Just now it's the fashion to be hideous—to make your head look like a scrubbing brush, wear a strait jacket, and clumping, square-toed boots. If it was cheap ugliness, I'd say nothing, but it costs as much as the other, and I don't get any satisfaction out of it."

Laurie threw back his head and laughed so heartily at this attack that the felt basin fell off, and Jo walked on it, which insult only afforded him an opportunity for expatiating on the advantages of a rough-and-ready costume as he folded up the maltreated hat and stuffed it into his pocket.

"Don't lecture any more, there's a good soul! I have enough all through the week, and like to enjoy myself when I come home."

"I'll leave you in peace if you'll only let your hair grow. I'm not aristocratic, but I do object to being seen with a person who looks like a young prize fighter," observed Jo severely.

"This unassuming style promotes study; that's why we adopt it," returned Laurie, who certainly could not be accused of vanity, having voluntarily sacrificed a handsome curly crop to the demand for quarter-of-an-inch-long stubble.

"By the way, Jo, I think that little Parker is really getting desperate about Amy. He talks of her constantly, writes poetry, and moons about in a most suspicious manner. He'd better nip his little passion in the bud, hadn't he?"

"Of course he had. We don't want any more marrying in this family for years to come. Mercy on us, what *are* the children thinking of?" And Jo looked as much scandalized as if Amy and little Parker were not yet in their teens.

"It's a fast age, and I don't know what we are coming to, ma'am. You are a mere infant, but you'll go next, Jo, and we'll be left lamenting," said Laurie, shaking his head over the degeneracy of the times.

"Don't be alarmed. I'm not one of the agreeable sort. Nobody will want me, and it's a mercy, for there should always be one old maid in a family."

"You won't give anyone a chance," said Laurie, with a sidelong glance, and a little more color than before in his sunburned face. "You won't show the soft side of your character, and if a fellow gets a peep at it by

183

accident, and can't help showing that he likes it, you treat him as Mrs. Gummidge did her sweetheart—throw cold water over him—and get so thorny no one dares touch or look at you."

"I don't like that sort of thing. I'm too busy to be worried with nonsense, and I think it's dreadful to break up families so. Now don't say any more about it. Meg's wedding has turned all our heads, and we talk of nothing but lovers and such absurdities. I don't wish to get cross, so let's change the subject."

Whatever his feelings might have been, Laurie found a vent for them in a long low whistle, and the fearful prediction, as they parted at the gate: "Mark my words, Jo, you'll go next."

THE FIRST WEDDING

The June roses over the porch were awake bright and early on that morning, rejoicing with all their hearts in the cloudless sunshine, like friendly little neighbors, as they were. Quite flushed with excitement were their ruddy faces as they swung in the wind whispering to one another what they had seen; for some peeped in at the dining-room windows, where the feast was spread, some climbed up to nod and smile at the sisters as they dressed the bride, others waved a welcome to those who came and went on various errands in garden, porch, and hall, and all, from the rosiest full-blown flower to the palest baby bud, offered their tribute of beauty and fragrance to the gentle mistress who had loved and tended them so long.

Meg looked very like a rose herself; for all that was best and sweetest in heart and soul seemed to bloom into her face that day, making it fair and tender. Neither silk, lace, nor orange flowers would she have. "I don't want to look strange or fixed-up today," she said. "I don't want a fashionable wedding, but only those about me whom I love, and to them I wish to look and be my familiar self."

So she made her wedding gown herself, sewing into it the tender hopes and innocent romances of a girlish heart. Her sisters braided up her pretty hair, and the only ornaments she wore were the lilies of the valley which "her John" liked best of all the flowers that grew.

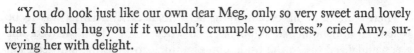

"You *do* look just like our own dear Meg, only so very sweet and lovely that I should hug you if it wouldn't crumple your dress," cried Amy, surveying her with delight.

"Then I am satisfied. But please hug and kiss me, every one, and don't mind my dress. I want a great many crumples of this sort put into it today." And Meg opened her arms to her sisters.

"Now I'm going to tie John's cravat for him, and then to stay a few minutes with Father quietly in the study." And Meg ran down to perform these little ceremonies, and then to follow her mother wherever she went, conscious that in spite of the smiles on the motherly face, there was a secret sorrow hid in the motherly heart at the flight of the first bird from the nest.

As the younger girls stand together, giving the last touches to their simple toilet, it may be a good time to tell of a few changes three years have wrought in their appearance, for all are looking their best just now.

Jo's angles are much softened; she has learned to carry herself with ease, if not grace. The curly crop has lengthened into a thick coil, more becoming to the small head atop of the tall figure. There is a fresh color in her brown cheeks, a soft shine in her eyes, and only gentle words fall from her sharp tongue today.

Beth has grown slender, pale, and more quiet than ever; the beautiful, kind eyes are larger, and in them lies an expression that saddens one, although it is not sad itself. It is the shadow of pain which touches the young face with such pathetic patience, but Beth seldom complains, and always speaks hopefully of "being better soon."

Amy is with truth considered "the flower of the family," for at sixteen she has the air and bearing of a full-grown woman—not beautiful, but possessed of that indescribable charm called grace. One saw it in the lines of her figure, the make and motion of her hands, the flow of her dress, the droop of her hair. Amy's nose still afflicted her, for it never *would* grow Grecian; so did her mouth, being too wide. These offending features gave character to her whole face, but she never could see it, and consoled herself with her wonderfully fair complexion, keen blue eyes, and curls more golden and abundant than ever.

All three wore suits of thin silver-gray (their best gowns for the summer), with blush roses in hair and bosom; and all three looked just what they were—fresh-faced, happy-hearted girls pausing a moment in their busy lives to read with wistful eyes the sweetest chapter in the romance of womanhood.

There were to be no ceremonious performances, everything was to be as natural and homelike as possible; so when Aunt March arrived, she was scandalized to see the bride come running to welcome and lead her in, to find the bridegroom fastening up a garland that had fallen down, and to catch a glimpse of the paternal minister marching upstairs with a grave countenance, and a wine bottle under each arm.

"Upon my word, here's a state of things!" cried the old lady, taking the seat of honor prepared for her and settling the folds of her lavender moiré. "You oughtn't to be seen till the last minute, child."

"I'm not a show, Aunty, and no one is coming to stare at me, to criticize my dress, or count the cost of my luncheon. I'm too happy to care what anyone says or thinks, and I'm going to have my little wedding just as I like it. John dear, here's your hammer." And away went Meg to help "that man" in his highly improper employment.

Mr. Brooke didn't even say "Thank you," but as he stooped for the unromantic tool, he kissed his little bride behind the folding door with a look that made Aunt March whisk out her pocket handkerchief, with a sudden dew in her sharp old eyes.

A crash, a cry, and a laugh from Laurie, accompanied by the indecorous exclamation "Jupiter Ammon! Jo's upset the cake again!" caused a momentary flurry, which was hardly over when a flock of cousins arrived, and "the party came in," as Beth used to say when a child.

"Don't let that young giant come near me. He worries me worse than mosquitoes," whispered the old lady to Amy as the rooms filled and Laurie's black head towered above the rest.

"He has promised to be very good today, and he *can* be perfectly elegant if he likes," returned Amy, gliding away to warn Hercules to beware of the dragon, which warning caused him to haunt the old lady with a devotion that nearly distracted her.

There was no bridal procession, but a sudden silence fell upon the room, as Mr. March and the young pair took their places under the green arch. Mother and sisters gathered close, as if loath to give Meg up; the fatherly voice broke more than once, which only seemed to make the service more beautiful and solemn; the bridegroom's hand trembled visibly, and no one heard his replies; but Meg looked straight up in her husband's eyes, and said "I will!" with such tender trust in her own face and voice that her mother's heart rejoiced, and Aunt March sniffed audibly.

Jo did *not* cry, though she was very near it once, and was only saved from a demonstration by the consciousness that Laurie was staring fixedly at her with a comical mixture of merriment and emotion in his wicked black eyes. Beth kept her face hidden on her mother's shoulder, but Amy stood like a graceful statue, with a most becoming ray of sunshine touching her white forehead and the flower in her hair.

It wasn't at all the thing, I'm afraid, but the minute she was fairly married, Meg cried, "The first kiss for Marmee!" and gave it with her heart on her lips. During the next fifteen minutes she looked more like a rose than ever, for everyone availed themselves of their privileges to the fullest extent, from Mr. Laurence to old Hannah, who, adorned with a headdress fearfully and wonderfully made, fell upon her in the hall, crying, with a sob and a chuckle, "Bless you, dearie, a hundred times! The cake ain't hurt a mite, and everything looks lovely."

Everybody cleared up after that, and said something brilliant, or tried to, which did just as well, for laughter is ready when hearts are light. There was no display of gifts, for they were already in the little house, nor was there an elaborate breakfast, but a plentiful lunch of cake and fruit, dressed with flowers. Mr. Laurence and Aunt March shrugged and smiled at one another when water, lemonade, and coffee were found to be the only sorts of nectar which the three Hebes carried round. No one said anything, however, till Laurie, who insisted on serving the bride, appeared before her with a loaded salver in his hand and a puzzled expression on his face.

"Has Jo smashed all the bottles by accident?" he whispered. "Or am I merely laboring under a delusion that I saw some lying about loose this morning?"

"No. Your grandfather kindly offered us his best, and Aunt March actually sent some, but Father put away a little for Beth, and dispatched the rest to the Soldiers' Home. You know he thinks that wine should be used only in illness, and Mother says that neither she nor her daughters will ever offer it to any young man under her roof."

After lunch, people strolled about by twos and threes through house and garden, enjoying the sunshine without and within. Meg and John happened to be standing together in the middle of the grass plot when Laurie was seized with an inspiration which put the finishing touch to this unfashionable wedding.

"All the married people take hands and dance round the new-made husband and wife, as the Germans do, while we bachelors and spinsters prance in couples outside!" cried Laurie, promenading down the path with Amy with such infectious spirit and skill that everyone else followed their example without a murmur. Mr. and Mrs. March, Aunt and Uncle Carrol, began it; others rapidly joined in; even Sallie Moffat, after a moment's hesitation, threw her train over her arm and whisked Ned into the ring. But the crowning joke was Mr. Laurence and Aunt March; for when the stately old gentleman chasséd solemnly up to the old lady, she just tucked her cane under her arm and hopped briskly away to join hands with the rest and dance about the bridal pair. Want of breath brought the impromptu ball to a close, and then people began to go.

"I wish you well, my dear, I heartily wish you well; but I think you'll be sorry for it," said Aunt March to Meg, adding to the bridegroom as he led her to the carriage: "You've got a treasure, young man. See that you deserve it."

"That is the prettiest wedding I've been to for an age, Ned, and I don't see why, for there wasn't a bit of style about it," observed Mrs. Moffat to her husband as they drove away.

"Laurie my lad, if you ever want to indulge in this sort of thing, get one of those little girls to help you and I shall be perfectly satisfied," said Mr. Laurence.

"I'll do my best to gratify you, sir," was Laurie's unusually dutiful reply as he carefully unpinned the posy Jo had put in his buttonhole.

The little house was not far away, and the only bridal journey Meg had was the quiet walk with John from the old home to the new. When she came down, looking like a pretty Quakeress in her dove-colored suit and straw bonnet tied with white, they all gathered about her to say good-by as tenderly as if she had been going to make the grand tour.

"Don't feel that I am separated from you, Marmee dear, or that I love you any the less for loving John so much," she said, clinging to her mother, with full eyes, for a moment. "I shall come every day, Father, and expect to keep my old place in all your hearts, though I *am* married. Beth is going to be with me a great deal, and the other girls will drop in now and then to laugh at my housekeeping struggles. Thank you all for my happy wedding day. Good-by, good-by!"

They stood watching her, with faces full of love and hope and tender pride, as she walked away leaning on her husband's arm, with her hands full of flowers and the June sunshine brightening her happy face—and so Meg's married life began.

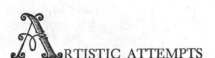

RTISTIC ATTEMPTS

It takes people a long time to learn the difference between talent and genius, especially ambitious young men and women. Amy was learning this distinction through much tribulation; for, mistaking enthusiasm for inspiration, she attempted every branch of art with youthful audacity. For a long time there was a lull in the "mud-pie" business, and she devoted herself to the finest pen-and-ink drawing, in which she showed such taste and skill that her graceful handiwork proved both pleasant and profitable. But overstrained eyes soon caused pen and ink to be laid aside for a bold attempt at poker sketching. While this attack lasted, the family lived in constant fear of a conflagration; for the odor of burning wood pervaded the house at all hours, smoke issued from attic and shed with alarming frequency, red-hot pokers lay about promiscuously, and Hannah never went to bed without a pail of water and the dinner bell at her door, in case of fire. Raphael's face was found boldly executed on the underside of the molding board and Bacchus on the head of a beer barrel, a chanting cherub adorned the cover of the sugar bucket, and attempts to portray Romeo and Juliet supplied kindlings for some time.

From fire to oil was a natural transition for burned fingers, and Amy fell to painting with undiminished ardor. An artist friend fitted her out with his cast-off palettes, brushes, and colors, and she daubed away, producing pastoral and marine views such as were never seen on land or sea. Her monstrosities in the way of cattle would have taken prizes at an agricultural fair; and the perilous pitching of her vessels would have produced seasickness in the most nautical observer, if the utter disregard to all known rules of shipbuilding and rigging had not convulsed him with laughter at the first glance. Swarthy boys and dark-eyed Madonnas, staring at you from one corner of the studio, suggested Murillo; oily-brown shadows of faces, with a lurid streak in the wrong place, meant Rembrandt; buxom ladies and dropsical infants, Rubens; and Turner appeared in tempests of blue thunder, orange lightning, brown rain, and purple clouds, with a tomato-colored splash in the middle which might be the sun or a buoy, a sailor's shirt or a king's robe, as the spectator pleased.

189

Charcoal portraits came next, and the entire family hung in a row, looking as wild and crocky as if just evoked from a coalbin. Softened into crayon sketches, they did better; for the likenesses were good, and Amy's hair, Jo's nose, Meg's mouth, and Laurie's eyes were pronounced "wonderfully fine." A return to clay and plaster followed, and ghostly casts of her acquaintances haunted corners of the house, or tumbled off closet shelves onto people's heads. Her efforts in this line, however, were brought to an abrupt close by an untoward accident which quenched her ardor. Other models failing her for a time, she undertook to cast her own pretty foot, and the family were one day alarmed by an unearthly bumping and screaming, and running to the rescue, found the young enthusiast hopping wildly about the shed with her foot held fast in a panful of plaster, which had hardened with unexpected rapidity. With much difficulty and some danger she was dug out; for Jo was so overcome with laughter while she excavated that her knife went too far, cut the poor foot, and left a lasting memorial of one artistic attempt, at least.

After this Amy subsided till a mania for sketching from nature set her to haunting river, field, and wood for picturesque studies, and sighing for ruins to copy. She caught endless colds sitting on damp grass to book "a delicious bit" composed of a stone, a stump, one mushroom, and a broken mullein stalk, or "a heavenly mass of clouds" that looked like a choice display of feather beds when done. She sacrificed her complexion floating on the river in the midsummer sun to study light and shade, and got a wrinkle over her nose trying after "points of sight," or whatever the squint-and-string performance is called.

If "genius is eternal patience," as Michelangelo affirms, Amy certainly had some claim to the divine attribute, for she persevered in spite of all obstacles, failures, and discouragements, firmly believing that in time she should do something worthy to be called "high art."

She was learning, doing, and enjoying other things meanwhile, for she had resolved to be an attractive and accomplished woman, even if she never became a great artist. Here she succeeded better; for she was one of those happily created beings who please without effort, make friends everywhere, and take life so gracefully and easily that less fortunate souls are tempted to believe that such are born under a lucky star. Everybody liked her, for among her good gifts was tact. She had an instinctive sense of what was pleasing and proper, always said the right thing to the right person, did just what suited the time and place, and was so self-possessed that her sisters used to say, "If Amy went to Court without any rehearsal beforehand, she'd know exactly what to do."

One of her weaknesses was a desire to move in "our best society," without being quite sure what the *best* really was. Money, position, fashionable accomplishments, and elegant manners were most desirable things in her eyes, and she liked to associate with those who possessed them, often mistaking the false for the true, and admiring what was not admirable. Never forgetting that by birth she was a gentlewoman, she cultivated her aristocratic tastes and feelings, so that when the opportunity came she might be ready to take the place from which poverty now excluded her. "My lady," as her friends called her, sincerely desired to be a genuine lady, and was so at heart, but had yet to learn that money cannot buy refinement of nature, that rank does not always confer nobility, and that true breeding makes itself felt in spite of external drawbacks.

"I want to ask a favor of you, Mamma," Amy said, coming in with an important air one day.

"Well, little girl, what is it?" replied her mother.

"Our drawing class breaks up next week, and before the girls separate for the summer, I want to ask them out here for a day. They are wild to see the river, sketch the broken bridge, and copy some of the things they admire in my book. They have been very kind to me in many ways. They are all rich and know I am poor, yet they never made any difference."

"Why should they?" And Mrs. March put the question with what the girls called her "Maria Theresa air."

"You know as well as I that it *does* make a difference with nearly everyone, so don't ruffle up like a dear, motherly hen when your chickens get pecked by smarter birds; the ugly duckling turned out a swan, you know."

Mrs. March laughed, and smoothed down her maternal pride as she asked, "Well, my swan, what is your plan?"

"I should like to ask the girls out to lunch next week, to take them a drive to the places they want to see, a row on the river, perhaps, and make a little artistic fete for them."

"That looks feasible. What do you want for lunch? Cake, sandwiches, fruit, and coffee will be all that is necessary, I suppose?"

"Oh dear no! We must have cold tongue and chicken, French chocolate and ice cream, besides. The girls are used to such things, and I want my lunch to be proper and elegant, though I *do* work for my living."

"How many young ladies are there?" asked her mother, beginning to look sober.

"Twelve or fourteen, but I dare say they won't all come."

"Bless me, child, you will have to charter an omnibus to carry them about."

"Why, Mother, how *can* you think of such a thing? Not more than six or eight will probably come, so I shall hire a beach wagon, and borrow Mr. Laurence's cherry bounce" (Hannah's pronunciation of charabanc).

"All this will be expensive, Amy."

"Not very. I've calculated the cost, and I'll pay for it myself."

"Don't you think, dear, that as these girls are used to such things, and the best we can do will be nothing new, that some simpler plan would be pleasanter to them, as a change, if nothing more, and much better for us than buying or borrowing what we don't need, and attempting a style not in keeping with our circumstances?"

"If I can't have it as I like, I don't care to have it at all. I know that I can carry it out perfectly well if you and the girls will help a little; and I don't see why I can't if I'm willing to pay for it," said Amy.

Mrs. March knew that experience was an excellent teacher, and when it was possible she left her children to learn alone the lessons which she would gladly have made easier if they had not objected to taking advice as much as they did salts and senna.

"Very well, Amy. If your heart is set upon it, and you see your way through without too great an outlay of money, time, and temper, I'll say no more. Talk it over with the girls, and whichever way you decide, I'll do my best to help you."

"Thanks, Mother. You are always so kind." And away went Amy to lay her plan before her sisters.

Meg agreed at once, and promised her aid, gladly offering anything she possessed, from her little house itself to her very best salt spoons. But Jo frowned upon the whole project, and would have nothing to do with it at first.

"Why in the world should you spend your money, worry your family, and turn the house upside down for a parcel of girls who don't care a sixpence for you? I thought you had too much pride and sense to truckle to any mortal woman just because she wears French boots and rides in a coupé," said Jo.

"I *don't* truckle, and I hate being patronized as much as you do!" returned Amy indignantly. "The girls do care for me, and I for them, and there's a great deal of kindness and sense and talent among them, in spite of what you call fashionable nonsense. You don't care to make people like you, to go into good society, and cultivate your manners and tastes. I do, and I mean to make the most of every chance that comes. You can go through the world with your elbows out and your nose in the air and call it independence, if you like. That's not my way."

When Amy whetted her tongue and freed her mind she usually got the best of it, for she seldom failed to have common sense on her side, while Jo carried her love of liberty and hate of conventionalities to such an unlimited extent that she naturally found herself worsted in an argument. Amy's definition of Jo's idea of independence was such a good hit that both burst out laughing, and the discussion took a more amiable turn. Much against her will, Jo at length consented to sacrifice a day to Mrs. Grundy and help her sister through what she regarded as "a nonsensical business."

The invitations were sent, nearly all accepted, and the following Monday was set apart for the grand event. Hannah was out of humor because her week's work was deranged, and prophesied that "ef the washin' and ironin' warn't done reg'lar nothin' would go well anywheres." This hitch in the mainspring of the domestic machinery had a bad effect upon the whole concern; but Amy's motto was "Nil desperandum," and having made up her mind what to do, she proceeded to do it in spite of all obstacles. To begin with, Hannah's cooking didn't turn out well: the chicken was tough, the tongue too salt, and the chocolate wouldn't froth properly. Then the cake and ice cost more than Amy expected, so did the wagon, and various other expenses, which seemed trifling at the outset, counted up rather alarmingly afterward. Beth got cold and took to her bed, Meg had an unusual number of callers to keep her at home, and Jo was in such a divided state of mind that her breakages, accidents, and mistakes were uncommonly numerous, serious, and trying.

"If it hadn't been for Mother I never should have got through," Amy gratefully remembered when "the best joke of the season" was entirely forgotten by everybody else.

If it was not fair on Monday, the young ladies were to come on Tuesday—an arrangement which aggravated Jo and Hannah to the last degree. On Monday morning the weather was in that undecided state which is more exasperating than a steady pour. It drizzled a little, shone a little, blew a little, and didn't make up its mind till it was too late for anyone else to make up theirs. Amy was up at dawn, hustling people out of their beds and through their breakfasts, that the house might be got in order. The parlor struck her as looking uncommonly shabby; but without stopping to sigh for what she had not, she skillfully made the best of what she had, arranging chairs over the worn places in the carpet, covering stains on the walls with pictures framed in ivy, and filling up empty corners with homemade statuary, which gave an artistic air to the room, as did the lovely vases of flowers Jo scattered about.

The lunch looked charming; and as she surveyed it she sincerely hoped it would taste well, and that the borrowed glass, china, and silver would get safely home again. The carriages were promised, Meg and mother were all ready to do the honors, Beth was able to help Hannah behind the scenes, Jo had engaged to be as lively and amiable as an absent mind, an aching head, and a very decided disapproval of everybody and everything would allow, and as she wearily dressed, Amy cheered herself with anticipations of the happy moment when, lunch safely over, she should drive away with her friends for an afternoon of artistic delights; for the "cherry bounce" and the broken bridge were her strong points.

Then came two hours of suspense, during which she vibrated from parlor to porch while public opinion varied like the weathercock. A smart shower at eleven had evidently quenched the enthusiasm of the young ladies who were to arrive at twelve, for nobody came, and at two the exhausted family sat down in a blaze of sunshine to consume the perishable portions of the feast, that nothing might be lost.

"No doubt about the weather today. They will certainly come, so we must fly round and be ready for them," said Amy as the sun woke her next morning. She spoke briskly, but in her secret soul she wished she had said nothing about Tuesday, for her interest, like her cake, was getting a little stale.

"I can't get any lobsters, so you will have to do without salad today," said Mr. March, coming in half an hour later.

"Use the chicken, then. The toughness won't matter in a salad," advised his wife.

"Hannah left it on the kitchen table a minute and the kittens got at it. I'm very sorry, Amy," added Beth.

"Then I *must* have a lobster, for tongue alone won't do," said Amy decidedly.

"Shall I rush into town and demand one?" asked Jo, with the magnanimity of a martyr.

"You'd come bringing it home under your arm, without any paper, just to try me. I'll go myself," answered Amy.

Shrouded in a thick veil and armed with a genteel traveling basket, she departed, feeling that a cool drive would soothe her ruffled spirit, and fit her for the labors of the day. After some delay, the object of her desire was procured, likewise a bottle of dressing, to prevent further loss of time at home, and off she drove again, well pleased with her own forethought.

As the omnibus contained only one other passenger, a sleepy old lady, Amy pocketed her veil, and beguiled the tedium of the way by trying to find out where all her money had gone to. So busy was she with her card full of refractory figures that she did not observe a newcomer who entered without stopping the vehicle till a masculine voice said, "Good morning, Miss March," and looking up, she beheld one of Laurie's most elegant college friends. Fervently hoping that he would get out before she did, Amy utterly ignored the basket at her feet and returned the young man's greeting with her usual suavity and spirit.

They got on excellently; for Amy's chief care was soon set at rest by learning that the gentleman would leave first, and she was chatting away in a peculiarly lofty strain when the old lady got out. In stumbling to the door, she upset the basket, and—oh, horror!—the lobster, in all its vulgar size and brilliancy, was revealed to the highborn eyes of a Tudor.

"By Jove, she's forgotten her dinner!" cried the unconscious youth, poking the scarlet monster into its place with his cane, and preparing to hand out the basket after the old lady.

"Please don't—it's—it's mine," murmured Amy, with a face nearly as red as her fish.

"Oh, really, I beg pardon. It's an uncommonly fine one, isn't it?" said Tudor, with great presence of mind.

Amy recovered herself in a breath, set her basket boldly on the seat, and said, laughing: "Don't you wish you were to have some of the salad he's to make, and to see the charming young ladies who are to eat it?"

Now that was tact, for two of the ruling foibles of the masculine mind were touched: the lobster was instantly surrounded by a halo of pleasing reminiscences, and curiosity about "the charming young ladies" diverted his mind from the comical mishap.

"I suppose he'll laugh and joke over it with Laurie, but I shan't see them, that's a comfort," thought Amy as Tudor bowed and departed.

She did not mention this meeting at home, but went through with the preparations, which now seemed more irksome than before, and at twelve o'clock all was ready again. Feeling that the neighbors were interested in her movements, she wished to efface the memory of yesterday's failure by a grand success today, so she ordered the "cherry bounce" and drove away in state to meet and escort her guests to the banquet.

"There's the rumble, they're coming! I'll go into the porch to meet them. It looks hospitable, and I want the poor child to have a good time after all her trouble," said Mrs. March, suiting the action to the word. But after one glance she retired, with an indescribable expression, for looking quite lost in the big carriage sat Amy and one young lady.

"Run, Beth, and help Hannah clear half the things off the table. It will be too absurd to put a luncheon for twelve before a single girl," cried Jo, hurrying away to the lower regions.

In came Amy, quite calm, and delightfully cordial to the one guest who had kept her promise. The rest of the family, being of a dramatic turn, played their parts equally well, and Miss Eliott found them a most hilarious set; for it was impossible to entirely control the merriment which possessed them. The remodeled lunch being gaily partaken of, the studio and garden visited, and art discussed with enthusiasm, Amy ordered a buggy (alas for the elegant cherry bounce!) and drove her friend quietly about the neighborhood till sunset, when "the party went out." As she came walking in, looking very tired but as composed as ever, she observed that every vestige of the unfortunate fete had disappeared, except a suspicious pucker about the corners of Jo's mouth.

"You've had a lovely afternoon for your drive, dear," said her mother, as respectfully as if the whole twelve had come.

"Miss Eliott is a very sweet girl, and seemed to enjoy herself, I thought," observed Beth, with unusual warmth.

"Could you spare me some of your cake? I really need some, I have so much company, and I can't make such delicious stuff as yours," asked Meg soberly.

"Take it all. I'm the only one here who likes sweet things, and it will mold before I can dispose of it," answered Amy.

"It's a pity Laurie isn't here to help us," began Jo as they sat down to ice cream and salad for the second time in two days.

A warning look from her mother checked any further remarks, and the whole family ate in heroic silence till Mr. March mildly observed, "Salad was one of the favorite dishes of the ancients, and Evelyn——" Here a general explosion of laughter cut short the "history of sallets," to the great surprise of the learned gentleman.

"Bundle everything into a basket and send it to the Hummels. Germans like messes. I'm sick of the sight of this, and there's no reason you should all die of a surfeit because I've been a fool," cried Amy, wiping her eyes.

"I thought I *should* have died when I saw you two girls rattling about in the what-you-call-it, like two little kernels in a very big nutshell, and Mother waiting in state to receive the throng," sighed Jo, quite spent with laughter.

"I'm very sorry you were disappointed, dear, but we all did our best to satisfy you," said Mrs. March.

"I *am* satisfied. I've done what I undertook, and it's not my fault that it failed. I comfort myself with that," said Amy, with a little quaver in her voice. "I thank you all very much for helping me, and I'll thank you still more if you won't allude to it for a month, at least."

No one did for several months, but the word "fete" always produced a general smile, and Laurie's birthday gift to Amy was a tiny coral lobster in the shape of a charm for her watch guard.

LITERARY LESSONS

Fortune suddenly smiled upon Jo, and dropped a good-luck penny in her path. Not a golden penny, exactly, but I doubt if half a million would have given more real happiness than did the little sum that came to her in this wise.

Every few weeks she would shut herself up in her room, put on her scribbling suit, and "fall into a vortex," as she expressed it, writing away at her novel with all her heart and soul, for till that was finished she could find no peace. Her "scribbling suit" consisted of a black woolen pinafore on which she could wipe her pen at will, and a cap of the same material, adorned with a cheerful red bow, into which she bundled her hair when the decks were cleared for action. This cap was a beacon to the inquiring eyes of her family, who during these periods kept their distance, merely popping in their heads semioccasionally to ask with interest, "Does genius burn, Jo?" They did not always venture even to ask this question, but took an observation of the cap and judged accordingly. If this expressive article of dress was drawn low upon the forehead, it was a sign that hard work was going on; in exciting moments it was pushed rakishly askew; and when despair seized the author it was plucked wholly off, and cast upon the floor. At such times the intruder silently withdrew, and not until the red bow was seen gaily erect upon the gifted brow did anyone dare address Jo.

She did not think herself a genius by any means; but when the writing fit came on, she gave herself up to it with entire abandon, and led a blissful life, unconscious of want, care, or bad weather while she sat safe and happy in an imaginary world full of friends almost as real and dear to her as any in the flesh. Sleep forsook her eyes, meals stood untasted, day and night were all too short to enjoy the happiness which blessed her only at such times, and made these hours worth living, even if they bore no other fruit. The divine afflatus usually lasted a week or two, and then she emerged from her "vortex" hungry, sleepy, cross, or despondent.

She was just recovering from one of these attacks when she was prevailed upon to escort Miss Crocker to a lecture, and in return for her virtue was rewarded with a new idea. It was a People's Course, the lecture on the Pyramids, and Jo rather wondered at the choice of such a subject for such an audience, but took it for granted that some great social evil would be remedied or some great want supplied by unfolding the glories of the Pharaohs to an audience whose thoughts were busy with the price of coal and flour, and whose lives were spent in trying to solve harder riddles than that of the Sphinx.

They were early, and while Miss Crocker set the heel of her stocking

Jo amused herself by examining the faces of the people who occupied the seat with them. On her left were two matrons with massive foreheads, and bonnets to match, discussing Woman's Rights and making tatting. Beyond sat a pair of humble lovers artlessly holding each other by the hand, a somber spinster eating peppermints out of a paper bag, and an old gentleman taking his preparatory nap behind a yellow bandanna. On her right, her only neighbor was a studious-looking lad absorbed in a newspaper.

It was a pictorial sheet, and Jo examined the work of art nearest her, idly wondering what unfortuitous concatenation of circumstances needed the melodramatic illustration of an Indian in full war costume tumbling over a precipice with a wolf at his throat while two infuriated young gentlemen, with unnaturally small feet and big eyes, were stabbing each other close by, and a disheveled female was flying away in the background with her mouth wide-open. Pausing to turn a page, the lad saw her looking, and with boyish good nature offered half his paper, saying bluntly:

"Want to read it? That's a first-rate story."

Jo accepted it with a smile, for she had never outgrown her liking for lads, and soon found herself involved in the usual labyrinth of love, mystery, and murder, for the story belonged to that class of light literature in which the passions have a holiday, and when the author's invention fails, a grand catastrophe clears the stage of one half the dramatis personae, leaving the other half to exult over their downfall.

"Prime, isn't it?" asked the boy as her eye went down the last paragraph of her portion.

"I think you and I could do as well as that if we tried," returned Jo, amused at his admiration of the trash.

"I should think I was a pretty lucky chap if I could. She makes a good living out of such stories, they say," and he pointed to the name of Mrs. S. L. A. N. G. Northbury under the title of the tale.

"Do you know her?" asked Jo, with sudden interest.

"No, but I read all her pieces, and I know a fellow who works in the office where this paper is printed."

"Do you say she makes a good living out of stories like this?" And Jo looked more respectfully at the agitated group and thickly sprinkled exclamation points that adorned the page.

"Guess she does! She knows just what folks like, and gets paid well for writing it."

Here the lecture began, but Jo heard very little of it, for while Professor Sands was prosing away about Belzoni, Cheops, scarabei, and hieroglyphics, she was covertly taking down the address of the paper, and boldly resolving to try for the hundred-dollar prize offered in its columns for a sensational story. By the time the lecture ended and the audience awoke, she had built up a splendid fortune for herself (not the first founded upon paper), and was already deep in the concoction of her story, being unable to decide whether the duel should come before the elopement or after the murder.

She said nothing of her plan at home, but fell to work next day, much to the disquiet of her mother, who always looked a little anxious when "genius took to burning." Jo had never tried this style before, contenting herself with very mild romances for the *Spread Eagle*. Her theatrical experience and miscellaneous reading were of service now, for they gave her some idea of dramatic effect, and supplied plot, language, and costumes. Her story was as full of desperation and despair as her limited acquaintance with those uncomfortable emotions enabled her to make it and, having located it in Lisbon, she wound up with an earthquake, as a striking and appropriate denouement. The manuscript was privately dispatched, accompanied by a note modestly saying that if the tale didn't get the prize, which the writer hardly dared expect, she would be very glad to receive any sum it might be considered worth.

Six weeks is a long time to wait, and a still longer time for a girl to keep a secret. But Jo did both, and was just beginning to give up all hope of ever seeing her manuscript again when a letter arrived which almost took her breath away; for on opening it, a check for a hundred dollars fell into her lap. For a minute she stared at it as if it had been a snake, then she read her letter and began to cry. If the amiable gentleman who wrote that kindly note could have known what intense happiness he was giving a fellow creature, I think he would devote his leisure hours, if he has any, to that amusement; for Jo valued the letter more than the money, because it was encouraging, and after years of effort it was so pleasant to find that she had learned to do something, though it was only to write a sensation story.

A prouder young woman was seldom seen than she when, having composed herself, she electrified the family by appearing before them with the letter in one hand, the check in the other, announcing that she had won the prize. Of course there was a great jubilee, and when the story came everyone read and praised it; though after her father had told her that the language was good, the romance fresh and hearty, and the tragedy quite thrilling, he shook his head, and said in his unworldly way:

"You can do better than this, Jo. Aim at the highest, and never mind the money."

"I think the money is the best part of it. What *will* you do with such a fortune?" asked Amy.

"Send Beth and Mother to the seaside for a month or two," answered Jo promptly.

"Oh, how splendid! No, I can't do it, dear, it would be so selfish," cried Beth, who had clapped her thin hands, and taken a long breath, as if pining for fresh ocean-breezes, then stopped herself and motioned away the check which her sister waved before her.

"Ah, but you shall go, I've set my heart on it. That's what I tried for, and that's why I succeeded. I never get on when I think of myself alone, so it will help me to work for you, don't you see? Besides, Marmee needs the change, and she won't leave you, so you *must* go. Won't it be fun to see you come home plump and rosy again? Hurrah for Dr. Jo, who always cures her patients!"

To the seaside they went, after much discussion; and though Beth didn't come home as plump and rosy as could be desired, she was much better, while Mrs. March declared she felt ten years younger. So Jo was satisfied with the investment of her prize money, and fell to work with a cheery spirit, bent on earning more of those delightful checks. She did earn several that year, and began to feel herself a power in the house; for by the magic of a pen, her "rubbish" turned into comforts for them all. "The Duke's Daughter" paid the butcher's bill, "A Phantom Hand" put down a new carpet, and "The Curse of the Coventrys" proved the blessing of the Marches in the way of groceries and gowns.

Little notice was taken of her stories, but they found a market, and encouraged by this fact, she resolved to make a bold stroke for fame and fortune. Having copied her novel for the fourth time, read it to all her confidential friends, and submitted it with fear and trembling to three publishers, she at last disposed of it, on condition that she would cut it down one third, and omit all the parts which she particularly admired.

"Now I must either bundle it back into my tin kitchen to mold, pay for printing it myself, or chop it up to suit purchasers and get what I can for it. Fame is a very good thing to have in the house, but cash is more convenient, so I wish to take the sense of the meeting on this important subject," said Jo, calling a family council.

"Don't spoil your book, my girl, for there is more in it than you know, and the idea is well worked out. Let it wait and ripen," was her father's advice.

"It seems to me that Jo will profit more by making the trial than by waiting," said Mrs. March. "Criticism is the best test of such work, for it will show her both unsuspected merits and faults, and help her to do better next time. We are too partial, but the praise and blame of outsiders will prove useful, even if she gets but little money."

"Yes," said Jo, knitting her brows, "that's just it. I've been fussing over the thing so long I really don't know whether it's good, bad, or indifferent. It will be a great help to have cool, impartial persons take a look at it and tell me what they think of it."

"I wouldn't leave out a word of it. You'll spoil it if you do, for the interest of the story is more in the minds than in the actions of the people, and it will be all a muddle if you don't explain as you go on," said Meg.

"But Mr. Allen says, 'Leave out the explanations, make it brief and dramatic, and let the characters tell the story,'" interrupted Jo, turning to the publisher's note.

"Do as he tells you. He knows what will sell, and we don't. Make a good, popular book, and get as much money as you can. By and by, when you've got a name, you can afford to digress, and have philosophical and metaphysical people in your novels," said Amy.

"Well," said Jo, laughing, "if my people *are* 'philosophical and metaphysical,' it isn't my fault, for I know nothing about such things, except what I hear Father say sometimes. If I've got some of his wise ideas jumbled up with my romance, so much the better for me. Now, Beth, what do you say?"

"I should so like to see it printed *soon*," was all Beth said, and smiled in saying it; but there was an unconscious emphasis on the last word, and a wistful look in the eyes that never lost their childlike candor, which chilled Jo's heart for a minute with a foreboding fear, and decided her to make her little venture "soon."

So, with Spartan firmness, the young authoress laid her firstborn on her table and chopped it up as ruthlessly as any ogre. In the hope of pleasing everyone, she took everyone's advice, and like the old man and his donkey in the fable, suited nobody. Her father liked the metaphysical streak which had unconsciously got into it; so that was allowed to remain, though she had her doubts about it. Her mother thought that there was a trifle too much description; out, therefore, it nearly all came, and with it many necessary links in the story. Meg admired the tragedy, so Jo piled up the agony to suit her, while Amy objected to the fun and, with the best intentions, Jo quenched the sprightly scenes which relieved the somber character of the story. Then, to complete the ruin, she cut it down one-third, and confidingly sent the poor little romance, like a picked robin, out into the big, busy world to try its fate.

Well, it was printed, and she got three hundred dollars for it; likewise plenty of praise and blame, both so much greater than she expected that she was thrown into a state of bewilderment from which it took her some time to recover.

"You said, Mother, that criticism would help me, but how can it when it's so contradictory that I don't know whether I've written a promising book or broken all the Ten Commandments?" cried poor Jo, turning over a heap of notices the perusal of which filled her with pride and joy one minute, wrath and dire dismay the next. "This man says 'An exquisite book, full of truth, beauty, and earnestness; all is sweet, pure, and healthy,' the next, 'The theory of the book is bad, full of morbid fancies, spiritualistic ideas, and unnatural characters.' Now, as I had no theory of any kind, don't believe in spiritualism, and copied my characters from life, I don't see how this critic *can* be right. Another says, 'It's one of the best American novels which has appeared for years' (I know better than that), and the next asserts that 'though it is original, and written with great force and feeling, it is a dangerous book.' 'Tisn't! Some make fun of it, some overpraise, and nearly all insist that I had a deep theory to expound, when I only wrote it for the pleasure and the money. I wish I'd printed it whole or not at all, for I do hate to be so misjudged."

Her family and friends administered comfort and commendation liberally; yet it was a hard time for sensitive, high-spirited Jo, who meant so well and had apparently done so ill. But it did her good, for those whose opinion had real value gave her the criticism which is an author's best education; and when the first soreness was over, she could laugh at her poor little book yet believe in it still, and feel herself the wiser and stronger for the buffeting she had received.

"Not being a genius, like Keats, it won't kill me," she said stoutly. "And I've got the joke on my side, after all; for the parts that were taken straight out of real life are denounced as impossible and absurd, and the scenes that I made up out of my own silly head are pronounced 'charmingly natural, tender, and true.' So I'll comfort myself with that, and when I'm ready, I'll up again and take another."

DOMESTIC EXPERIENCES

Like most other young matrons, Meg began her married life with the determination to be a model housekeeper. John should find home a paradise; he should always see a smiling face, should fare sumptuously every day, and never know the loss of a button. She brought so much love, energy, and cheerfulness to the work that she could not but succeed. Her paradise was not a tranquil one; for the little woman fussed, was overanxious to please, and bustled about like a true Martha, cumbered with many cares. She was too tired sometimes even to smile; John grew dyspeptic after a course of dainty dishes, and ungratefully demanded plain fare. As for buttons, she soon learned to wonder where they went, to shake her head over the carelessness of men, and to threaten to make him sew them on himself and then see if *his* work would stand impatient tugs and clumsy fingers any better than hers.

They were very happy, even after they discovered that they couldn't live on love alone. John did not find Meg's beauty diminished though she beamed at him from behind the familiar coffeepot; nor did Meg miss any of the romance from the daily parting when her husband followed up his kiss with the tender inquiry, "Shall I send home veal or mutton for dinner, darling?" The little house ceased to be a glorified bower, but it became a home, and the young couple soon felt that it was a change for the better. At first they played keep-house, and frolicked over it like children; then John took steadily to business, feeling the cares of the head of a family upon his shoulders, and Meg laid by her cambric wrappers, put on a big apron, and fell to work, as before said, with more energy than discretion.

While the cooking mania lasted she went through Mrs. Cornelius's *Receipt Book* as if it were a mathematical exercise, working out the problems with patience and care. Sometimes her family were invited in to help eat up a too bounteous feast of successes, or Lotty would be privately dispatched with a batch of failures which were to be concealed from all eyes in the convenient stomachs of the little Hummels. An evening with John over the account books usually produced a temporary lull in the culinary enthusiasm, and a frugal fit would ensue, during which the poor man was put through a course of bread pudding, hash, and warmed-over coffee which tried his soul, although he bore it with praiseworthy fortitude. Before the golden mean was found, however, Meg added to her domestic possessions what young couples seldom get on long without—a family jar.

Fired with a housewifely wish to see her storeroom stocked with home-made preserves, she undertook to put up her own currant jelly. John was requested to order home a dozen or so of little pots and an extra quantity of sugar, for their own currants were ripe. As John firmly believed that "my wife" was equal to anything, and took a natural pride in her skill, he resolved that she should be gratified, and their only crop of fruit laid by in a most pleasing form for winter use. Home came four dozen delightful little pots, half a barrel of sugar, and a small boy to pick the currants for her. With her pretty hair tucked into a little cap, arms bared to the elbow, and a checked apron which had a coquettish look in spite of the bib, the young housewife fell to work, feeling no doubts about her success; for hadn't she seen Hannah do it hundreds of times? The array of pots rather amazed her at first, but John was so fond of jelly, and the nice little jars would look so well on the top shelf, that Meg resolved to fill them all, and spent a long day picking, boiling, straining, and fussing over her jelly. She did her best; she racked her brain to remember what Hannah did that she had left undone; she reboiled, resugared, and restrained, but that dreadful stuff wouldn't jell.

She longed to run home, bib and all, and ask Mother to lend a hand, but John and she had agreed that they would never annoy anyone with their private worries, experiments, or quarrels. They had laughed over that last word as if the idea it suggested was a most preposterous one; but they had held to their resolve, and whenever they could get on without help they did so, and no one interfered, for Mrs. March had advised the plan. So Meg wrestled alone with the refractory sweetmeats all that hot summer day, and at five o'clock sat down in her topsy-turvy kitchen, wrung her bedaubed hands, lifted up her voice, and wept.

Now in the first flush of the new life she had often said: "My husband shall always feel free to bring a friend home whenever he likes. I shall always be prepared; there shall be no flurry, no scolding, but a neat house, a cheerful wife, and a good dinner. John dear, never stop to ask my leave, invite whom you please, and be sure of a welcome from me."

How charming that was, to be sure! John quite glowed with pride to hear her say it, and felt what a blessed thing it was to have a superior wife. But although they had had company from time to time, it never happened to be unexpected, and Meg had never had an opportunity to distinguish herself till now.

If John had not forgotten all about the jelly, it really would have been unpardonable in him to choose that day, of all the days in the year, to bring a friend home to dinner unexpectedly. Congratulating himself that a handsome repast had been ordered that morning, feeling sure that it would be ready to the minute, and indulging in pleasant anticipations of the charming effect it would produce when his pretty wife came running out to meet him, he escorted his friend to his mansion with the irrepressible satisfaction of a young host and husband.

It is a world of disappointments, as John discovered when he reached the Dovecote. The front door usually stood hospitably open; now it was not only shut, but locked, and yesterday's mud still adorned the steps. The parlor windows were closed and curtained, no picture of the pretty wife sewing on the piazza, in white with a distracting little bow in her hair, or a bright-eyed hostess smiling a shy welcome as she greeted her guest. Nothing of the sort, for not a soul appeared but a sanguinary-looking boy asleep under the currant bushes.

"I'm afraid something has happened. Step into the garden, Scott, while I look up Mrs. Brooke," said John, alarmed at the silence and solitude.

Round the house he hurried, led by a pungent smell of burned sugar, and Mr. Scott strolled after him, with a queer look on his face. He paused discreetly at a distance when Brooke disappeared, but he could both see and hear and, being a bachelor, enjoyed the prospect mightily.

In the kitchen reigned confusion and despair; one edition of jelly was trickled from pot to pot, another lay upon the floor, and a third was burning gaily on the stove. Lotty, with Teutonic phlegm, was calmly eating bread and currant wine, for the jelly was still in a hopelessly liquid state, while Mrs. Brooke, with her apron over her head, sat sobbing dismally.

"My dearest girl, what is the matter?" cried John, rushing in with awful visions of scalded hands, sudden news of affliction, and with secret consternation at the thought of the guest in the garden.

"O John, I *am* so tired and hot and cross and worried! I've been at it till I'm all worn out. Do come and help me or I *shall* die!" And the exhausted housewife cast herself upon his breast, giving him a sweet welcome in every sense of the word, for her pinafore had been baptized at the same time as the floor.

"What worries you, dear? Has anything dreadful happened?" asked the anxious John, tenderly kissing the crown of the little cap, which was all askew.

"Yes," sobbed Meg despairingly.

"Tell me quick, then. Don't cry. I can bear anything better than that. Out with it, love."

"The—the jelly won't jell and I don't know what to do!"

John Brooke laughed then as he never dared to laugh afterward, and the derisive Scott smiled involuntarily as he heard the hearty peal, which put the finishing stroke to poor Meg's woe.

"Is that all? Fling it out of window, and don't bother any more about it. I'll buy you quarts if you want it, but for heaven's sake don't have hysterics, for I've brought Jack Scott home to dinner, and——"

John got no further, for Meg cast him off, and clasped her hands with a tragic gesture as she fell into a chair, exclaiming in a tone of mingled indignation, reproach, and dismay:

"A man to dinner, and everything in a mess! John Brooke, how *could* you do such a thing?"

"Hush, he's in the garden! I forgot the confounded jelly, but it can't be helped now," said John.

"You ought to have sent word, or told me this morning, and you ought to have remembered how busy I was," continued Meg petulantly; for even turtledoves will peck when ruffled.

"I didn't know it this morning, and there was no time to send word, for I met him on the way out. I never thought of asking leave when you have always told me to do as I liked. I never tried it before, and hang me if I ever do again!"

"I should hope not! Take him away at once. I can't see him, and there isn't any dinner."

"Well, I like that! Where's the beef and vegetables I sent home, and the pudding you promised?" cried John.

"I hadn't time to cook anything. I meant to dine at Mother's. I'm sorry, but I was *so* busy." And Meg's tears began again.

John was a mild man, but he was human; and after a long day's work to come home tired, hungry, and hopeful to find a chaotic house, an empty table, and a cross wife was not exactly conducive to repose of mind or manner. He restrained himself, however, and the little squall would have blown over but for one unlucky word.

"It's a scrape, I acknowledge, but if you will lend a hand, we'll pull through and have a good time yet. Don't cry, dear, but just exert yourself a bit, and knock us up something to eat. We're both as hungry as hunters, so we shan't mind what it is. Give us the cold meat, and bread and cheese. We won't ask for jelly."

He meant it for a good-natured joke, but that one word sealed his fate. Meg thought it was *too* cruel to hint about her sad failure, and the last atom of patience vanished as he spoke.

"You must get yourself out of the scrape as you can. I'm too used-up to 'exert' myself for anyone. It's like a man to propose a bone and vulgar bread and cheese for company. I won't have anything of the sort in my house. Take that Scott up to Mother's, and tell him I'm away, sick, dead —anything. I won't see him, and you two can laugh at me and my jelly as much as you like. You won't have anything else here." And having delivered her defiance all in one breath, Meg precipitately left the field to bemoan herself in her own room.

What those two creatures did in her absence she never knew, but Mr. Scott was not taken "up to Mother's," and when Meg descended after they had strolled away together, she found traces of a promiscuous lunch which filled her with horror. Lotty reported that they had eaten "a much, and greatly laughed, and the master bid her throw away all the sweet stuff, and hide the pots." Meg longed to go and tell Mother, but a sense of shame at her own shortcomings, of loyalty to John, who might "be cruel," but nobody should know it, restrained her, and after a summary clearing-up, she dressed herself prettily and sat down to wait for John to come and be forgiven.

Unfortunately, John didn't come, not seeing the matter in that light. He had carried it off as a good joke with Scott, excused his little wife as well as he could, and played the host so hospitably that his friend enjoyed the impromptu dinner, and promised to come again. But John was angry, though he did not show it; he felt that Meg had got him into a scrape and then deserted him in his hour of need. It wasn't fair to tell a man to bring folks home any time, with perfect freedom, and when he took you at your word, to flare up and blame him, and leave him in the lurch, to be laughed at or pitied. No, by George, it wasn't! And Meg must know it. He had fumed inwardly during the feast, but when the flurry was over and he strolled home after seeing Scott off, a milder mood came over him. "Poor little thing! It was hard on her when she tried so heartily to please me. She was wrong, of course, but then she is young. I must be patient and teach her." He hoped she had not gone home—he hated gossip and interference. For a minute he was ruffled again at the mere thought of it; and then the fear that Meg would cry herself sick softened his heart, and sent him on at a quicker pace, resolving to be calm and kind, but firm, quite firm, and show her where she had failed in her duty to her spouse.

Meg likewise resolved to be "calm and kind, but firm," and show *him* his duty. She longed to run to meet him, and beg pardon, and be kissed and comforted, as she was sure of being; but of course she did nothing of the sort, and when she saw John coming, began to hum quite naturally as she rocked and sewed like a lady of leisure in her best parlor. John was a little disappointed not to find a tender Niobe, but feeling that his dignity demanded the first apology, he made none, only came leisurely in, and laid himself upon the sofa with the singularly relevant remark:

"We are going to have a new moon, my dear."

"I've no objection" was Meg's equally soothing remark.

A few other topics of general interest were introduced by Mr. Brooke and wet-blanketed by Mrs. Brooke, and conversation languished. John went to one window, unfolded his paper, and wrapped himself in it, figuratively speaking. Meg went to the other window and sewed as if new rosettes for her slippers were among the necessaries of life. Neither spoke, both looked quite "calm and firm," and both felt desperately uncomfortable.

"Oh dear," thought Meg, "married life is very trying, and does need infinite patience, as well as love, as Mother says." The word "Mother" suggested other maternal counsels, given long ago, and received with unbelieving protests.

"John is a good man, but he has his faults, and you must learn to see and bear with them, remembering your own. He is very decided, but never will be obstinate if you reason kindly, not oppose impatiently. He is very accurate, and particular about the truth—a good trait, though you call him 'fussy.' Never deceive him by look or word, Meg, and he will give you the confidence you deserve, the support you need. He has a temper not like ours—one flash, and then all over—but the white, still anger that is seldom stirred, but once kindled, is hard to quench. Be careful, very careful, not to wake this anger against yourself, for peace and happiness depend on keeping his respect. Watch yourself, be the first to ask pardon if you both err, and guard against the little piques, misunderstandings, and hasty words that often pave the way for bitter sorrow and regret."

These words came back to Meg as she sat sewing in the sunset, especially the last. This was the first serious disagreement. Her own hasty speeches sounded both silly and unkind as she recalled them, her own anger looked childish now, and thoughts of poor John coming home to such a scene quite melted her heart. She glanced at him with tears in her eyes, but he did not see them. She put down her work and got up, thinking "I *will* be the first to say 'Forgive me,'" but he did not seem to hear her. She went very slowly across the room, for pride was hard to swallow, and stood by him, but he did not turn his head. For a minute she felt as if she really couldn't do it. Then came the thought, "This is the beginning. I'll do my part, and have nothing to reproach myself with," and stooping down, she softly kissed her husband on the forehead. Of course that settled it; the penitent kiss was better than a world of words, and John had her on his knee in a minute, saying tenderly: "It was too bad to laugh at the poor little jelly pots. Forgive me, dear, I never will again!"

But he did, oh bless you yes, hundreds of times, and so did Meg, both declaring that it was the sweetest jelly they ever made; for family peace was preserved in that little family jar.

After this, Meg had Mr. Scott to dinner by special invitation, and served him up a pleasant feast without a cooked wife for the first course; on which occasion she was so gay and gracious, and made everything go off so charmingly, that Mr. Scott told John he was a happy fellow, and shook his head over the hardships of bachelorhood all the way home.

In the autumn, new trials and experiences came to Meg. Sallie Moffat renewed her friendship, was always running out for a dish of gossip at the little house, or inviting "that poor dear" to come in and spend the day at the big house. It was pleasant, for in dull weather Meg often felt lonely. All were busy at home, John absent till night, and nothing to do but sew, or read, or potter about. So it naturally fell out that Meg got into the way of gadding and gossiping with her friend. Seeing Sallie's pretty things made her long for such, and pity herself because she had not got them. Sallie was very kind, and often offered her the coveted trifles; but Meg declined them, knowing that John wouldn't like it—and then this foolish little woman went and did what John disliked infinitely worse.

She knew her husband's income, and she loved to feel that he trusted her not only with his happiness, but with what some men seem to value more—his money. She knew where it was, was free to take what she liked, and all he asked was that she should keep account of every penny, pay bills once a month, and remember that she was a poor man's wife. Till now, she had done well, been prudent and exact, kept her little account books neatly, and showed them to him monthly without fear. But that autumn the serpent got into Meg's paradise and tempted her, like many a modern Eve, not with apples, but with dress. Meg didn't like to be pitied and made to feel poor. It irritated her, but she was ashamed to confess it, and now and then she tried to console herself by buying something pretty, so that Sallie needn't think she had to economize. She always felt wicked after it, for the pretty things were seldom necessaries, but then they cost so little it wasn't worth worrying about; so the trifles increased unconsciously, and in the shopping excursions she was no longer a passive looker-on.

But the trifles cost more than one would imagine, and when she cast up her accounts at the end of the month, the sum total rather scared her. John was busy that month, and left the bills to her; the next month he was absent; but the third he had a grand quarterly settling-up, and Meg never forgot it. A few days before she had done a dreadful thing, and it weighed upon her conscience. Sallie had been buying silks, and Meg longed for a new one—just a handsome light one for parties, her black silk was so common. Aunt March usually gave the sisters a present of twenty-five dollars apiece at New Year's. That was only a month to wait, and here was a lovely violet silk going at a bargain, and she had the money, if she only dared to take it. John always said what was his was hers; but would he think it right to spend not only the prospective five and twenty, but another five and twenty out of the household fund? That was the question. Sallie had offered to loan the money, and with the best intentions in life, had tempted Meg beyond her strength. In an evil moment the shopman held up the lovely, shimmering folds, and said, "A bargain, I assure you, ma'am." She answered, "I'll take it," and it was cut off and paid for, and Sallie had exulted, and she had laughed as if it were a thing of no consequence, and driven away feeling as if she had stolen something and the police were after her.

When she got home, she tried to assuage the pangs of remorse by spreading forth the lovely silk; but it looked less silvery now, didn't become her, after all, and the words "fifty dollars" seemed stamped like a pattern down each breadth. She put it away, but it haunted her—not delightfully, as a new dress should, but dreadfully, like the ghost of a folly that was not easily laid. When John got out his books that night, Meg's heart sank, and for the first time in her married life she was afraid of her husband. The kind brown eyes looked as if they could be stern, and though he was unusually merry, she fancied he had found her out, but didn't mean to let her know it. The house bills were all paid, the books all in order. John had praised her, and was undoing the old pocketbook which they called the "bank" when Meg, knowing that it was quite empty, stopped his hand, saying nervously:

"You haven't seen my private expense book yet."

John never asked to see it, but she always insisted on his doing so, and used to enjoy his masculine amazement at the queer things women wanted, and made him guess what "piping" was, demand fiercely the meaning of a "hug-me-tight," or wonder how a little thing composed of three rosebuds, a bit of velvet, and a pair of strings could possibly be a bonnet, and cost five or six dollars. That night he looked as if he would like the fun of quizzing her figures and pretending to be horrified at her extravagance, as he often did, being particularly proud of his prudent wife.

The little book was brought slowly out, and laid down before him. Meg got behind his chair under pretense of smoothing the wrinkles out of his tired forehead, and standing there, she said, with her panic increasing with every word: "John dear, I'm ashamed to show you my book, for I've really been dreadfully extravagant lately. I go about so much I must have things, you know, and Sallie advised my getting it, so I did, and my New Year's money will partly pay for it. But I was sorry after I'd done it, for I knew you'd think it wrong."

John laughed, and drew her round beside him, saying good-humoredly: "Don't go and hide. I won't beat you if you *have* got a pair of killing boots. I'm rather proud of my wife's feet, and don't mind if she does pay eight or nine dollars for her boots, if they are good ones."

That had been one of her last "trifles," and John's eye had fallen on it as he spoke. "Oh, what *will* he say when he comes to that awful fifty dollars!" thought Meg, with a shiver.

"It's worse than boots, it's a silk dress," she said, with the calmness of desperation, for she wanted the worst over.

"Well, dear, what is the 'dem'd total,' as Mr. Mantalini says?"

That didn't sound like John, and she knew he was looking up at her with the straightforward look that she had always been ready to meet and answer with one as frank till now. She turned the page and her head at the same time, pointing to the sum which would have been bad enough without the fifty, but which was appalling to her with that added. For a minute the room was very still, then John said slowly, but she could feel it cost him an effort to express no displeasure: "Well, I don't know that fifty is much for a dress, with all the furbelows you have to have to finish it off these days."

"It isn't made or trimmed," sighed Meg faintly, for a sudden recollection of the cost still to be incurred quite overwhelmed her.

"Twenty-five yards of silk seems a good deal to cover one small woman, but I've no doubt my wife will look as fine as Ned Moffat's when she gets it on," said John dryly.

"I know you are angry, John, but I can't help it. I don't mean to waste your money, and I didn't think those little things would count up so. I can't resist them when I see Sallie buying all she wants, and pitying me because I don't. I try to be contented, but it is hard, and I'm tired of being poor."

The last words were spoken so low she thought he did not hear them, but he did, and they wounded him deeply, for he had denied himself many pleasures for Meg's sake. She could have bitten her tongue out the minute she had said it, for John pushed the books away, and got up saying, with a little quiver in his voice: "I was afraid of this. I do my best, Meg." If he had scolded her, or even shaken her, it would not have broken her heart like those few words. She ran to him and held him close, crying, with repentant tears:

"O John, my dear, kind, hard-working boy, I didn't mean it! It was so wicked, so untrue and ungrateful, how could I say it! Oh, how could I say it!"

He was very kind, forgave her readily, and did not utter one reproach; but Meg knew that she had done and said a thing which would not be forgotten soon, although he might never allude to it again. She had promised to love him for better, for worse, and then she, his wife, had reproached him with his poverty, after spending his earnings recklessly. It was dreadful, and the worst of it was John went on so quietly afterward, just as if nothing had happened, except that he stayed in town later, and worked at night when she had gone to cry herself to sleep. A week of remorse nearly made Meg sick, and the discovery that John had countermanded the order for his new greatcoat reduced her to a state of despair. He had simply said, in answer to her surprised inquiries as to the change, "I can't afford it, my dear."

Meg said no more, but a few minutes after he found her in the hall, with her face buried in the old greatcoat, crying as if her heart would break. They had a long talk that night, and Meg learned to love her husband better for his poverty, because it seemed to have made a man of him, given him the strength and courage to fight his own way, and taught him a tender patience with which to bear and comfort the natural longings and failures of those he loved.

Next day she put her pride in her pocket, went to Sallie, told the truth, and asked her to buy the silk as a favor. The good-natured Mrs. Moffat willingly did so, and had the delicacy not to make her a present of it immediately afterward. Then Meg ordered home the greatcoat, and when John arrived, she put it on and asked him how he liked her new silk gown. One can imagine what answer he made, how he received his present, and what a blissful state of things ensued. John came home early, Meg gadded no more, and that greatcoat was put on in the morning by a very happy husband and taken off at night by a most devoted little wife. So the year rolled round, and at midsummer there came to Meg a new experience—the deepest and tenderest of a woman's life.

Laurie came sneaking into the kitchen of the Dovecote one Saturday with an excited face, and was received with the clash of cymbals, for Hannah clapped her hands with a saucepan in one and the cover in the other.

"How's the little mamma? Where is everybody? Why didn't you tell me before I came home?" began Laurie in a loud whisper.

"Happy as a queen, the dear! Every soul of 'em is upstairs a-worshipin'. We didn't want no hurrycanes round. Now you go into the parlor, and I'll send 'em down to you." With which somewhat involved reply Hannah vanished, chuckling ecstatically.

Presently Jo appeared, proudly bearing a flannel bundle laid forth upon a large pillow. Jo's face was very sober, but her eyes twinkled, and there was an odd sound in her voice of repressed emotion of some sort.

"Shut your eyes and hold out your arms," she said invitingly.

Laurie backed precipitately into a corner, and put his hands behind him with an imploring gesture. "No thank you, I'd rather not. I shall drop it or smash it, as sure as fate."

"Then you shan't see your nevvy," said Jo decidedly, turning as if to go.

"I will, I will! Only you must be responsible for damages." And, obeying orders, Laurie heroically shut his eyes while something was put into his arms. A peal of laughter from Jo, Amy, Mrs. March, Hannah, and John caused him to open them the next minute, to find himself invested with two babies instead of one. No wonder they laughed, for the expression of his face was droll enough to convulse a Quaker as he stood and stared wildly from the unconscious innocents to the hilarious spectators with such dismay that Jo sat down on the floor and screamed.

"Twins, by Jupiter!" was all he said for a minute. Then, turning to the women with an appealing look that was comically piteous, he added: "Take 'em quick, somebody! I'm going to laugh, and I shall drop 'em."

John rescued his babies, and marched up and down with one on each arm while Laurie laughed till the tears ran down his cheeks.

"It's the best joke of the season, isn't it? I wouldn't have you told, for I set my heart on surprising you, and I flatter myself I've done it," said Jo.

"I never was more staggered in my life. Isn't it fun? Are they boys? What are you going to name them? Let's have another look. Hold me up, Jo, for upon my life it's one too many for me," returned Laurie, regarding the infants with the air of a big, benevolent Newfoundland looking at a pair of infantile kittens.

"Boy and girl. Aren't they beauties?" said the proud papa, beaming upon the little red squirmers as if they were unfledged angels.

"Most remarkable children I ever saw. Which is which?" And Laurie bent like a well sweep to examine the prodigies.

"Amy put a blue ribbon on the boy and a pink on the girl, French fashion, so you can always tell. Besides, one has blue eyes and one brown. Kiss them, Uncle Teddy," said wicked Jo.

"I'm afraid they mightn't like it," began Laurie, with unusual timidity in such matters.

"Of course they will. They are used to it now. Do it this minute, sir!" commanded Jo.

Laurie screwed up his face and obeyed with a gingerly peck at each little cheek that produced another laugh, and made the babies squeal.

"There, I knew they didn't like it! That's the boy. See him kick; he hits out with his fists like a good one. Now then, young Brooke, pitch into a man of your own size, will you?" cried Laurie, delighted with a poke in the face from a tiny fist flapping aimlessly about.

"He's to be named John Laurence, and the girl Margaret, after Mother and Grandmother. We shall call her Daisy, so as not to have two Megs, and I suppose the mannie will be Jack, unless we find a better name," said Amy.

"Name him Demijohn, and call him 'Demi' for short," said Laurie.

"Daisy and Demi—just the thing! I *knew* Teddy would do it," cried Jo, clapping her hands.

Teddy certainly had done it that time, for the babies were "Daisy" and "Demi" to the end of the chapter.

CALLS

"Come, Jo, it's time."

"For what?"

"You don't mean to say you have forgotten that you promised to make half a dozen calls with me today?"

"I've done a good many rash and foolish things in my life, but I don't think I ever was mad enough to say I'd make six calls in one day, when a single one upsets me for a week."

"Yes you did, it was a bargain between us. I was to finish the crayon of Beth for you, and you were to go properly with me and return our neighbors' visits."

"If it was fair—that was in the bond, and I stand to the letter of my bond, Shylock. There is a pile of clouds in the east; it's *not* fair, and I don't go."

"Now that's shirking. It's a lovely day, no prospect of rain, and you pride yourself on keeping promises. So be honorable, come and do your duty, and then be at peace for another six months."

At that minute Jo was particularly absorbed in dressmaking; for she was mantuamaker general to the family, and took especial credit to herself because she could use a needle as well as a pen. It was very provoking to be arrested in the act of a first trying-on and ordered out to make calls in her best array on a warm July day. She hated calls of the formal sort, and never made any till Amy compelled her with a bargain, bribe, or promise. In the present instance there was no escape, and she put away her work, and taking up her hat and gloves with an air of resignation, told Amy the victim was ready.

"Jo March, you are perverse enough to provoke a saint! You don't intend to make calls in that state, I hope," cried Amy, surveying her with amazement.

"Why not? I'm neat and cool and comfortable, quite proper for a dusty walk on a warm day. If people care more for my clothes than they do for me, I don't wish to see them. You can dress for both, and be as elegant as you please. It pays for you to be fine; it doesn't for me, and furbelows only worry me."

"Oh dear!" sighed Amy. "Now she's in a contrary fit, and will drive me distracted before I can get her properly ready. I'm sure it's no pleasure to me to go today, but it's a debt we owe society, and there's no one to pay it but you and me. I'll do anything for you, Jo, if you'll only dress yourself nicely and come and help me do the civil. You can talk so well, look so aristocratic in your best things, and behave so beautifully, if you try, that I'm proud of you. I'm afraid to go alone. Do come and take care of me."

"You're an artful little puss to flatter and wheedle your cross old sister in that way. The idea of my being aristocratic and well-bred, and your being afraid to go anywhere alone! I don't know which is the most absurd. Well, I'll go if I must, and do my best. You shall be commander of the expedition, and I'll obey blindly. Will that satisfy you?" said Jo.

"You're a perfect cherub! Now put on all your best things, and I'll tell you how to behave at each place so that you will make a good impression. I want people to like you, and they would if you'd only try to be a little more agreeable. Do your hair the pretty way, and put the pink rose in your bonnet; it's becoming, and you look too sober in your plain suit. Take your light gloves and the embroidered handkerchief. We'll stop at Meg's and borrow her white sunshade, and then you can have my dove-colored one."

While Amy dressed she issued orders, and Jo obeyed them—not without entering her protest, however, for she sighed as she rustled into her new organdie, frowned darkly at herself as she tied her bonnet strings in an irreproachable bow, wrestled viciously with pins as she put on her

collar, wrinkled up her features generally as she shook out the handkerchief whose embroidery was as irritating to her nose as the present mission was to her feelings; and when she had squeezed her hands into tight
gloves with three buttons and a tassel, as the last touch of elegance, she
turned to Amy with an imbecile expression of countenance, saying
meekly: "I'm perfectly miserable, but if you consider me presentable,
I die happy."

"You are highly satisfactory. Turn slowly round and let me get a careful view." Jo revolved, and Amy gave a touch here and there, then fell
back, with her head on one side, observing graciously: "Yes, you'll do.
Hold back your shoulders, and carry your hands easily, no matter if your
gloves do pinch. Is the point of my mantle in the middle, and have I
looped my dress evenly? I like to show my boots, for my feet are pretty,
though my nose isn't."

"You are a thing of beauty and a joy forever," said Jo, looking through
her hand with the air of a connoisseur at the blue feather against the
gold hair. "Am I to drag my best dress through the dust, or loop it up,
please, ma'am?"

"Hold it up when you walk, but drop it in the house. The sweeping
style suits you best, and you must learn to trail your skirts gracefully. You
haven't half buttoned one cuff; do it at once. You'll never look finished
if you are not careful about the little details, for they make up the pleasing whole."

Jo sighed, and proceeded to burst the buttons off her glove in doing up
her cuff; but at last both were ready, and sailed away looking as "pretty
as picters," Hannah said as she hung out of the upper window to watch
them.

"Now, Jo dear, the Chesters consider themselves very elegant people,
so I want you to put on your best deportment. Don't make any of your
abrupt remarks, or do anything odd, will you? Just be calm, cool, and
quiet—that's safe and ladylike, and you can easily do it for fifteen minutes," said Amy as they approached the first place, having borrowed the
white parasol and been inspected by Meg, with a baby on each arm.

"Let me see. 'Calm, cool, and quiet'—yes, I think I can promise that.
I've played the part of a prim young lady on the stage, so be easy in your
mind, my child."

Amy looked relieved, but naughty Jo took her at her word; for during
the first call she sat with every limb gracefully composed, every fold correctly draped, calm as a summer sea, cool as a snowbank, and as silent

as a sphinx. In vain Mrs. Chester alluded to her "charming novel," and the Misses Chester introduced parties, picnics, the opera, and the fashions; each and all were answered by a smile, a bow, and a demure "Yes" or "No" with the chill on. In vain Amy telegraphed the word "Talk," and administered covert pokes with her foot. Jo sat as if blandly unconscious of it all, with deportment like Maud's face, "icily regular, splendidly null."

"What a haughty, uninteresting creature that oldest Miss March is!" was the unfortunately audible remark of one of the ladies as the door closed upon their guests. Jo laughed noiselessly all through the hall, but Amy looked disgusted at the failure of her instructions, and very naturally laid the blame upon Jo.

"How could you mistake me so? I merely meant you to be properly dignified and composed, and you made yourself a perfect stock and stone. Try to be sociable at the Lambs', gossip as other girls do, and be interested in dress and flirtations and whatever nonsense comes up. They move in the best society, are valuable persons for us to know, and I wouldn't fail to make a good impression there for anything."

"I'll be agreeable. I'll gossip and giggle, and have horrors and raptures over any trifle you like. I rather enjoy this, and now I'll imitate what is called 'a charming girl.' I can do it, for I have May Chester as a model, and I'll improve upon her. See if the Lambs don't say 'What a lively, nice creature that Jo March is!' "

Amy felt anxious, as well she might, for when Jo turned freakish there was no knowing where she would stop. Amy's face was a study when she saw her sister skim into the next drawing room, kiss all the young ladies with effusion, beam graciously upon the young gentlemen, and join in the chat with a spirit which amazed the beholder. Amy was taken possession of by Mrs. Lamb, with whom she was a favorite, and forced to hear a long account of Lucretia's last attack, while three delightful young gentlemen hovered near, waiting for a pause when they might rush in and rescue her. So situated, she was powerless to check Jo, who seemed possessed by a spirit of mischief, and talked away as volubly as the old lady. A knot of heads gathered about her, and Amy strained her ears to hear what was going on; for broken sentences filled her with alarm, round eyes and uplifted hands tormented her with curiosity, and frequent peals of laughter made her wild to share the fun. One may imagine her suffering on overhearing fragments of this sort of conversation:

"She rides splendidly—who taught her?"

"No one. She used to practice mounting, holding the reins, and sitting straight on an old saddle in a tree. Now she rides anything, for she doesn't know what fear is, and the stableman lets her have horses cheap because she trains them to carry ladies so well. She has such a passion for it I often tell her if everything else fails she can be a horsebreaker, and get her living so."

At this awful speech Amy contained herself with difficulty, for the impression was being given that she was rather a fast young lady, which was her especial aversion. But what could she do? For the old lady was in the middle of her story, and long before it was done Jo was off again, making more droll revelations.

"Yes, Amy was in despair that day, for all the good beasts were gone, and of three left one was lame, one blind, and the other so balky that you had to put dirt in his mouth before he would start. Nice animal for a pleasure party, wasn't it?"

"Which did she choose?" asked one of the laughing gentlemen, who enjoyed the subject.

"None of them. She heard of a young horse at the farmhouse over the river, and though a lady had never ridden him, she resolved to try, because he was handsome and spirited. Her struggles were really pathetic; there was no one to bring the horse to the saddle, so she took the saddle to the horse. My dear creature, she actually rowed it over the river, put it on her head, and marched up to the barn, to the utter amazement of the old man!"

"Did she ride the horse?"

"Of course she did, and had a capital time. I expected to see her brought home in fragments, but she managed him perfectly, and was the life of the party."

"Well, I call that plucky!" And young Mr. Lamb turned an approving glance upon Amy, wondering what his mother could be saying to make the girl look so red and uncomfortable.

She was still redder and more uncomfortable a moment after, when a sudden turn in the conversation introduced the subject of dress. One of the young ladies asked Jo where she got the pretty drab hat she wore to the picnic and stupid Jo, instead of mentioning the place where it was bought two years ago, must needs answer, with unnecessary frankness:

"Oh, Amy painted it. You can't buy those soft shades, so we paint ours any color we like. It's a great comfort to have an artistic sister."

"Isn't that an original idea!" cried Miss Lamb, who found Jo great fun.

"That's nothing compared to some of her brilliant performances. There's nothing the child can't do. Why, she wanted a pair of blue boots for Sallie's party, so she just painted her soiled white ones the loveliest shade of sky-blue you ever saw, and they looked exactly like satin," added Jo, with an air of pride in her sister's accomplishments that exasperated Amy till she felt that it would be a relief to throw her cardcase at her.

"We read a story of yours the other day, and enjoyed it very much," observed the elder Miss Lamb, wishing to compliment the literary lady, who did not look the character just then, it must be confessed.

Any mention of her "works" always had a bad effect upon Jo, who either grew rigid and looked offended, or changed the subject with a brusque remark, as now.

"Sorry you could find nothing better to read. I write that rubbish because it sells, and ordinary people like it. Are you going to New York this winter?"

As Miss Lamb had "enjoyed" the story, this speech was not exactly grateful or complimentary. The minute it was made Jo saw her mistake, but fearing to make the matter worse, suddenly remembered that it was for her to make the first move toward departure, and did so with an abruptness that left three people with half-finished sentences in their mouths.

"Amy, we *must* go. *Good*-by, dear. *Do* come and see us, we are *pining* for a visit. I don't dare to ask *you*, Mr. Lamb, but if you *should* come, I don't think I shall have the heart to send you away."

Jo said this with such a droll imitation of May Chester's gushing style that Amy got out of the room as rapidly as possible, feeling a strong desire to laugh and cry at the same time.

"Didn't I do that well?" asked Jo with a satisfied air as they walked away.

"Nothing could have been worse," was Amy's crushing reply. "What possessed you to tell those stories about my saddle, and the hats and boots, and all the rest of it?"

"Why, it's funny, and amuses people. They know we're poor, so it's no use pretending that we have grooms, buy three or four hats a season, and have things as easy and fine as they do."

"You needn't go and tell them all our little shifts, and expose our poverty in that perfectly unnecessary way. You haven't a bit of proper pride, and never will learn when to hold your tongue and when to speak," said Amy despairingly.

Poor Jo looked abashed. "How shall I behave here?" she asked as they approached the third mansion.

"Just as you please. I wash my hands of you" was Amy's short answer.

"Then I'll enjoy myself. The boys are at home, and we'll have a comfortable time. Goodness knows I need a little change, for elegance has a bad effect upon my constitution," returned Jo gruffly, being disturbed by her failures to suit.

An enthusiastic welcome from three big boys and several pretty children speedily soothed her ruffled feelings, and leaving Amy to entertain the hostess and Mr. Tudor, who happened to be calling likewise, Jo devoted herself to the young folks, and found the change refreshing. She listened to college stories with deep interest, caressed pointers and poodles without a murmur. And when one lad proposed a visit to his turtle tank, she went with an alacrity which caused Mamma to smile upon her as that motherly lady settled the cap which was left in a ruinous condition by filial hugs, bearlike but affectionate, and dearer to her than the most faultless coiffure from the hands of an inspired Frenchwoman.

Leaving her sister to her own devices, Amy proceeded to enjoy herself to her heart's content. Mr. Tudor's uncle had married an English lady who was third cousin to a living lord, and Amy regarded the whole family with great respect; for in spite of her American birth and breeding she possessed that reverence for titles which haunts the best of us—that unacknowledged loyalty to the early faith in kings which still has something to do with the love the young country bears the old, like that of a big son for an imperious little mother who held him while she could, and let him go with a farewell scolding when he rebelled. But even the satisfaction of talking with a distant connection of the British nobility did not render Amy forgetful of time, and when the proper number of minutes had passed, she reluctantly tore herself from this aristocratic society, and looked about for Jo fervently hoping that her incorrigible sister would not be found in any position which should bring disgrace upon the name of March.

It might have been worse, but Amy considered it bad; for Jo sat on the grass with an encampment of boys about her, and a dirty-footed dog reposing on the skirt of her state and festival dress, as she related one of Laurie's pranks to her admiring audience. One small child was poking turtles with Amy's cherished parasol, a second was eating gingerbread over Jo's best bonnet, and a third playing ball with her gloves. But all were enjoying themselves, and when Jo collected her damaged property to go, her escort accompanied her, begging her to come again, "It was such fun to hear about Laurie's larks."

"Capital boys, aren't they? I feel quite young and brisk again after that," said Jo, strolling along with her hands behind her, partly from habit, partly to conceal the bespattered parasol.

"Why do you always avoid Mr. Tudor?" asked Amy, wisely refraining from any comment upon Jo's dilapidated appearance.

"Don't like him. He puts on airs, snubs his sisters, worries his father, and doesn't speak respectfully of his mother. Laurie says he is fast, and I don't consider him a desirable acquaintance, so I let him alone."

"You might treat him civilly, at least. You gave him a cool nod, and just now you bowed and smiled in the politest way to Tommy Chamberlain, whose father keeps a grocery store. If you had just reversed the nod and the bow, it would have been right," said Amy reprovingly.

"No it wouldn't," returned perverse Jo. "I neither like, respect, nor admire Tudor, though his grandfather's uncle's nephew's niece *was* third cousin to a lord. Tommy is poor and bashful and good and very clever. I think well of him, and like to show that I do, for he *is* a gentleman in spite of the brown-paper parcels."

"It's no use trying to argue with you," began Amy.

"Not the least, my dear," interrupted Jo, "so let us look amiable, and drop a card here, as the Kings are evidently out, for which I'm deeply grateful."

The family cardcase having done its duty, the girls walked on, and Jo uttered another thanksgiving on reaching the fifth house and being told that the young ladies were engaged.

"Now let us go home, and never mind Aunt March today. We can run down there any time, and it's really a pity to trail through the dust in our best bibs and tuckers."

"Speak for yourself, if you please. Aunt likes to have us pay her the compliment of coming in style, and making a formal call. It's a little thing to do, but it gives her pleasure, and I don't believe it will hurt your things half so much as letting dirty dogs and clumping boys spoil them."

"What a good girl you are, Amy!" said Jo, with a repentant glance from her own damaged costume to that of her sister, which was fresh and spotless still. "I wish it was as easy for me to do little things to please people as it is for you. I think of them, but it takes too much time to do them, so I wait for a chance to confer a great favor, and let the small ones slip; but they tell best in the end, I fancy."

Amy smiled, and was mollified at once, saying with a maternal air: "Women should learn to be agreeable, particularly poor ones, for they have no other way of repaying the kindnesses they receive. If you'd remember that, and practice it, you'd be better liked than I am, because there is more of you."

"I'm a crotchety old thing, and always shall be, but I'm willing to own that you are right—only it's easier for me to risk my life for a person than to be pleasant to him when I don't feel like it. It's a great misfortune to have such strong likes and dislikes, isn't it?"

"It's a greater not to be able to hide them. I don't mind saying that I don't approve of Tudor any more than you do, but I'm not called upon to tell him so; neither are you, and there is no use in making yourself disagreeable because he is."

"But I think girls ought to show when they disapprove of young men, and how can they do it except by their manners? Preaching does not do any good, as I know to my sorrow since I've had Teddy to manage; but there are many little ways in which I can influence him without a word, and I say we *ought* to do it to others if we can."

"Teddy is a remarkable boy, and can't be taken as a sample of other boys," said Amy. "If we were belles, or women of wealth and position, we might do something, perhaps; but for us to frown at one set of young gentlemen because we don't approve of them, and smile upon another set because we do, wouldn't have a particle of effect, and we should only be considered odd and puritanical."

"So we are to countenance things and people which we detest merely because we are not belles and millionaires, are we? That's a nice sort of morality."

"I can't argue about it, I only know that it's the way of the world, and people who set themselves against it only get laughed at for their pains. I don't like reformers, and I hope you will never try to be one."

"I do like them, and I shall be one if I can; for in spite of the laughing, the world would never get on without them. We can't agree about that, for you belong to the old set and I to the new. You will get on best, but I shall have the liveliest time of it."

"Well, compose yourself now, and don't worry Aunt with your new ideas."

"I'll try not to, but I'm always possessed to burst out with some particularly blunt speech or revolutionary sentiment before her. It's my doom, and I can't help it."

They found Aunt Carrol with the old lady, both absorbed in some very interesting subject; but they dropped it as the girls came in, with a conscious look which betrayed that they had been talking about their nieces. Jo was not in a good humor, and the perverse fit returned; but Amy, who had virtuously done her duty, kept her temper, and pleased everybody, was in a most angelic frame of mind. This amiable spirit was felt at once, and both aunts "my-deared" her affectionately, looking what they afterward said emphatically, "That child improves every day."

"Are you going to help about the fair, dear?" asked Mrs. Carrol as Amy sat down beside her with the confiding air elderly people like so well in the young.

"Yes, Aunt. Mrs. Chester asked me if I would, and I offered to tend a table, as I have nothing but my time to give."

"I'm not," put in Jo decidedly. "I hate to be patronized, and the Chesters think it's a great favor to allow us to help with their highly connected fair. I wonder you consented, Amy; they only want you to work."

"I am willing to work. It's for the freedmen as well as the Chesters, and I think it very kind of them to let me share the labor and the fun. Patronage does not trouble me when it is well meant."

"Quite right and proper. I like your grateful spirit, my dear. It's a pleasure to help people who appreciate our efforts—some do not, and that is trying," observed Aunt March, looking over her spectacles at Jo, who sat apart, rocking herself, with a somewhat morose expression.

If Jo had only known what a great happiness was wavering in the balance for one of them, she would have turned dovelike in a minute; but unfortunately we don't have windows in our breasts, and cannot see what goes on in the minds of our friends. Better for us that we cannot as a general thing, but now and then it would be such a comfort, such a saving of time and temper. By her next speech Jo deprived herself of several years of pleasure, and received a timely lesson in the art of holding her tongue.

"I don't like favors, they oppress and make me feel like a slave. I'd rather do everything for myself, and be perfectly independent."

"Ahem!" coughed Aunt Carrol softly, with a look at Aunt March.

"I told you so," said Aunt March, with a decided nod to Aunt Carrol.

Mercifully unconscious of what she had done, Jo sat with her nose in the air and a revolutionary aspect which was anything but inviting.

"Do you speak French, dear?" asked Mrs. Carrol, laying her hand on Amy's.

"Pretty well, thanks to Aunt March, who lets Esther talk to me as often as I like," replied Amy.

"How are you about languages?" asked Mrs. Carrol of Jo.

"Don't know a word. I'm very stupid about studying anything. Can't bear French, it's such a slippery, silly sort of language," was the brusque reply.

Another look passed between the ladies, and Aunt March said to Amy: "You are quite strong and well now, dear, I believe? Eyes don't trouble you any more, do they?"

"Not at all, thank you, ma'am. I'm very well, and mean to do great things next winter, so that I may be ready for Rome whenever that joyful time arrives."

"Good girl. You deserve to go, and I'm sure you will someday," said Aunt March, with an approving pat on the head as Amy picked up her ball for her.

> "Crosspatch, draw the latch,
> Sit by the fire and spin,"

squalled Polly, bending down from his perch on the back of her chair to peep into Jo's face with such a comical air of impertinent inquiry that it was impossible to help laughing.

"Most observing bird," said the old lady.

"Come and take a walk, my dear?" cried Polly, hopping toward the china closet, with a look suggestive of lump sugar.

"Thank you, I will. Come, Amy." And Jo brought the visit to an end, feeling more strongly than ever that calls did have a bad effect upon her constitution. She shook hands in a gentlemanly manner, but Amy kissed both aunts, and the girls departed leaving behind them the impression of shadow and sunshine, which impression caused Aunt March to say as they vanished: "You'd better do it, Mary. I'll supply the money," and Aunt Carrol to reply decidedly, "I certainly will, if her father and mother consent."

CONSEQUENCES

Mrs. Chester's fair was so very elegant and select that it was considered a great honor by the young ladies of the neighborhood to be invited to take a table. Amy was asked, but Jo was not, which was fortunate for all parties, as her elbows were decidedly akimbo at this period of her life. The "haughty, uninteresting creature" was let severely alone; but Amy's talent and taste were duly complimented by the offer of the art table, and she exerted herself to prepare and secure appropriate and valuable contributions to it.

Everything went on smoothly till the day before the fair opened; then there occurred one of the little skirmishes which it is almost impossible to avoid when some five and twenty women, old and young, with all their private piques and prejudices, try to work together.

May Chester was rather jealous of Amy because the latter was a greater favorite than herself, and just at this time several trifling circumstances occurred to increase the feeling. Amy's dainty pen-and-ink work entirely eclipsed May's painted vases—that was one thorn; then the all-conquering Tudor had danced four times with Amy at a late party, and only once with May—that was thorn number two. But the chief grievance that rankled in her soul, and gave her an excuse for her unfriendly conduct, was a rumor which some obliging gossip had whispered to her that the March girls had made fun of her at the Lambs'. All the blame of this should have fallen upon Jo, for her naughty imitation had been too lifelike to escape detection, and the frolicsome Lambs had permitted the joke to escape. No hint of this had reached the culprits, however, and Amy's dismay can be imagined when, the very evening before the fair, as she was putting the last touches to her pretty table Mrs. Chester, who of course resented the supposed ridicule of her daughter, said, in a bland tone but with a cold look:

"I find, dear, that there is some feeling among the young ladies about giving this table to anyone but my girls. As this is the most prominent and some say the most attractive table of all, and they are the chief getters-up of the fair it is thought best for them to take this place. I'm sorry, but I know you are too interested in the cause to mind a little personal disappointment, and you shall have another table if you like."

Mrs. Chester had fancied beforehand that it would be easy to deliver this little speech; but when the time came, she found it rather difficult to utter it naturally with Amy's unsuspicious eyes looking straight at her, full of surprise and trouble.

Amy felt that there was something behind this, but could not guess what, and said quietly, feeling hurt, and showing that she did, "Perhaps you had rather I took no table at all?"

"Now, my dear, don't have any ill feeling, I beg. It's merely a matter of expediency, you see; my girls will naturally take the lead, and this table is considered their proper place. I think it very appropriate to you, and feel very grateful for your efforts to make it so pretty; but we must give up our private wishes, of course, and I will see that you have a good place elsewhere. Wouldn't you like the flower table? The little girls undertook it, but they are discouraged. You could make a charming thing of it, and the flower table is always attractive, you know."

"Especially to gentlemen," added May, with a look which enlightened Amy as to one cause of her sudden fall from favor. She colored angrily, but took no other notice of that girlish sarcasm, and answered, with unexpected amiability:

"It shall be as you please, Mrs. Chester. I'll give up my place here at once, and attend to the flowers, if you like."

"You can put your own things on your own table, if you prefer," began May, feeling a little conscience-stricken as she looked at the pretty racks, the painted shells, and quaint illuminations Amy had so carefully made and so gracefully arranged. She meant it kindly, but Amy mistook her meaning, and said quickly: "Oh, certainly, if they are in your way." And sweeping her contributions into her apron pell-mell, she walked off feeling that herself and her works of art had been insulted past forgiveness.

"Now she's mad. Oh dear, I wish I hadn't asked you to speak, Mamma," said May, looking disconsolately at the empty spaces on her table.

"Girls' quarrels are soon over," returned her mother, feeling a trifle ashamed of her own part in this one, as well she might.

The little girls hailed Amy and her treasures with delight, which cordial reception somewhat soothed her perturbed spirit, and she fell to work, determined to succeed florally if she could not artistically. But everything seemed against her. It was late, and she was tired; everyone was too busy with their own affairs to help her; and the little girls were only hindrances. The evergreen arch wouldn't stay firm after she got it up, but wiggled and threatened to tumble down on her head when the hanging baskets were filled; her best tile got a splash of water which left a sepia tear on the Cupid's cheek; she bruised her hands with hammering, and got cold working in a draught, which last affliction filled her with apprehensions for the morrow.

There was great indignation at home when she told her story that evening. Her mother said it was a shame, but told her she had done right; Beth declared she wouldn't go to the fair at all; and Jo demanded why she didn't take all her pretty things and leave those mean people to get on without her.

"Because they are mean is no reason why I should be. I hate such things, and though I think I've a right to be hurt, I don't intend to show it. They will feel that more than angry speeches or huffy actions, won't they, Marmee?"

"That's the right spirit, my dear. A kiss for a blow is always best, though it's not very easy to give it sometimes," said her mother.

In spite of various very natural temptations to resent and retaliate,

Amy adhered to her resolution all the next day, bent on conquering her enemy by kindness. She began well, thanks to a silent reminder that came to her unexpectedly, but most opportunely. As she arranged her table that morning while the little girls were in an anteroom filling the baskets, she took up her pet production—a little book the antique cover of which her father had found among his treasures, and in which, on leaves of vellum, she had beautifully illuminated different texts. As she turned the pages, rich in dainty devices, with very pardonable pride, her eye fell upon one verse that made her stop and think. Framed in a brilliant scrollwork of scarlet, blue, and gold, with little spirits of goodwill helping one another up and down among the thorns and flowers, were the words "Thou shalt love thy neighbor as thyself."

"I ought, but I don't," thought Amy as her eye went from the bright page to May's discontented face behind the big vases that could not hide the vacancies her pretty work had once filled. Her conscience preached her a little sermon from that text, then and there, and she did what many of us do not always do—took the sermon to heart, and straightway put it in practice.

A group of girls were standing about May's table, admiring the pretty things and talking over the change of saleswomen. They dropped their voices, but Amy knew they were speaking of her, hearing one side of the story and judging accordingly. It was not pleasant, but a better spirit had come over her, and presently a chance offered for proving it. She heard May say sorrowfully: "It's too bad, for there is no time to make other things, and I don't want to fill up with odds and ends. The table was just complete then. Now it's spoiled."

"I dare say she'd put them back if you asked her," suggested someone.

"How could I after all the fuss?" began May, but she did not finish, for Amy's voice came across the hall, saying pleasantly:

"You may have them and welcome without asking, if you want them. I was just thinking I'd offer to put them back, for they belong to your table rather than mine. Here they are. Please take them, and forgive me if I was hasty in carrying them away last night."

As she spoke, Amy returned her contribution, with a nod and a smile, and hurried away again, feeling that it was easier to do a friendly thing than it was to stay and be thanked for it.

It was a very long day, and a hard one to Amy as she sat behind her table, often quite alone, for the little girls deserted very soon. Few cared to buy flowers in summer, and her bouquets began to droop long before night. The art table was the most attractive in the room; there was a crowd about it all day long, and the tenders were constantly flying to and fro with important faces and rattling money boxes. Amy often looked wistfully across, longing to be there, where she felt at home and happy, instead of in a corner with nothing to do.

She did not go home till night, and then she looked so pale and quiet that they knew the day had been a hard one, though she made no complaint, and did not even tell what she had done. Her mother gave her an extra-cordial cup of tea, Beth helped her dress and made a charming little wreath for her hair, while Jo astonished her family by getting herself up with unusual care, and hinting darkly that the tables were about to be turned.

"Don't do anything rude, pray, Jo. I won't have any fuss made, so let it all pass, and behave yourself," begged Amy as she departed early, hoping to find a reinforcement of flowers to refresh her poor little table.

"I merely intend to make myself entrancingly agreeable to everyone I know, and to keep them in your corner as long as possible. Teddy and his boys will lend a hand, and we'll have a good time yet," returned Jo, leaning over the gate to watch for Laurie. Presently the familiar tramp was heard in the dusk, and she ran out to meet him.

"Is that my boy?"

"As sure as this is my girl!" And Laurie tucked her hand under his arm with the air of a man whose every wish was gratified.

"O Teddy, such doings!" And Jo told Amy's wrongs with sisterly zeal.

"A flock of our fellows are going to drive over by and by, and I'll be hanged if I don't make them buy every flower she's got, and camp down before her table afterward," said Laurie.

"The flowers are not at all nice, Amy says, and the fresh ones may not arrive in time. I don't wish to be unjust or suspicious, but I shouldn't wonder if they never came at all. When people do one mean thing they are very likely to do another," observed Jo in a disgusted tone.

"Didn't Hayes give you the best out of our gardens? I told him to."

"I didn't know that. He forgot, I suppose, and as your grandpa was poorly, I didn't like to worry him by asking."

"Now, Jo, how could you think there was any need of asking! They are just as much yours as mine. Don't we always go halves in everything?" began Laurie in the tone that always made Jo turn thorny.

"Gracious, I hope not! Half of some of your things wouldn't suit me at all. But we mustn't stand philandering here. I've got to help Amy, so you

232

go and make yourself splendid; and if you'll be so very kind as to let Hayes take a few nice flowers up to the Hall, I'll bless you forever."

"Couldn't you do it now?" asked Laurie, so suggestively that Jo shut the gate in his face with inhospitable haste, and called through the bars:

"Go away, Teddy. I'm busy."

Thanks to the conspirators, the tables *were* turned that night; for Hayes sent up a wilderness of flowers, with a lovely basket, arranged in his best manner, for a centerpiece. Then the March family turned out en

masse, and Jo exerted herself to some purpose, for people not only came, but stayed, laughing at her nonsense, admiring Amy's taste, and apparently enjoying themselves very much. Laurie and his friends gallantly threw themselves into the breach, bought up the bouquets, encamped before the table, and made that corner the liveliest spot in the room. Amy was in her element now, and out of gratitude, if nothing more, was as sprightly and gracious as possible—coming to the conclusion, about that time, that virtue *was* its own reward after all.

Jo behaved herself with exemplary propriety; and when Amy was happily surrounded by her guard of honor, Jo circulated about the hall, picking up various bits of gossip which enlightened her upon the subject of the Chester change of base. She reproached herself for her share of the ill feeling, and resolved to exonerate Amy as soon as possible; she also discovered what Amy had done about the things in the morning, and considered her a model of magnanimity. As she passed the art table, she glanced over it for her sister's things, but saw no signs of them. "Tucked away out of sight, I dare say," thought Jo.

"Good evening, Miss Jo. How does Amy get on?" asked May—with a conciliatory air, for she wanted to show that she also could be generous.

"She has sold everything she had that was worth selling, and now she is enjoying herself. The flower table is always attractive, you know, 'especially to gentlemen.'"

Jo *couldn't* resist giving that little slap, but May took it so meekly she regretted it a minute after, and fell to praising the great vases, which still remained unsold.

"Is Amy's illumination anywhere about? I took a fancy to buy that for Father," said Jo.

"Everything of Amy's sold long ago. I took care that the right people saw them, and they made a nice little sum of money for us," returned May, who had overcome sundry small temptations, as well as Amy, that day.

Much gratified, Jo rushed back to tell the good news, and Amy looked both touched and surprised by the report of May's words and manner.

"Now, gentlemen, I want you to go and do your duty by the other tables as generously as you have by mine—especially the art table," she said, ordering out "Teddy's Own," as the girls called the college friends.

"'Charge, Chester, charge!' is the motto for that table; but do your duty like men, and you'll get your money's worth of *art* in every sense of the word," said the irrepressible Jo as the devoted phalanx prepared to take the field.

"Buy the vases," whispered Amy to Laurie, as a final heaping of coals of fire on her enemy's head.

To May's great delight, Mr. Laurence not only bought the vases, but pervaded the hall with one under each arm. The other gentlemen speculated with equal rashness in all sorts of frail trifles, and wandered helplessly about afterward burdened with wax flowers, painted fans, filigree portfolios, and other useful and appropriate purchases.

Aunt Carrol was there, heard the story, looked pleased, and said some-

234

thing to Mrs. March in a corner which made the latter lady beam with satisfaction, and watch Amy with a face full of mingled pride and anxiety, though she did not betray the cause of her pleasure till several days later.

The fair was pronounced a success, and when May bade Amy good night, she did not "gush" as usual, but gave her an affectionate kiss, and a look which said "Forgive and forget." That satisfied Amy, and when she got home she found the vases paraded on the parlor chimney piece, with a great bouquet in each. "The reward of merit for a magnanimous March," as Laurie announced with a flourish.

"You've a deal more principle and generosity and nobleness of character than I ever gave you credit for, Amy. You've behaved sweetly, and I respect you with all my heart," said Jo warmly as they brushed their hair together late that night.

"Yes, we all do, and love her for being so ready to forgive. It must have been dreadfully hard, after working so long, and setting your heart on selling your own pretty things. I don't believe I could have done it as kindly as you did," added Beth from her pillow.

"Why, girls, you needn't praise me so. I only did as I'd be done by. You laugh at me when I say I want to be a lady, but I mean a true gentlewoman in mind and manners, and I try to do it as far as I know how. I can't explain exactly, but I want to be above the little meannesses and follies and faults that spoil so many women. I'm far from it now, but I do my best, and hope in time to be what Mother is."

Amy spoke earnestly, and Jo said, with a cordial hug: "I understand now what you mean, and I'll never laugh at you again. You are getting on faster than you think, and I'll take lessons of you in true politeness, for you've learned the secret, I believe. Try away, dearie. You'll get your reward someday, and no one will be more delighted than I shall."

A week later Amy did get her reward, and poor Jo found it hard to be delighted. A letter came from Aunt Carrol, and Mrs. March's face was illuminated to such a degree when she read it that Jo and Beth, who were with her, demanded what the glad tidings were.

"Aunt Carrol is going abroad next month, and wants——"

"Me to go with her!" burst in Jo, flying out of her chair in an uncontrollable rapture.

"No, dear, not you. It's Amy."

"O Mother! She's too young; it's my turn first. I've wanted it so long —it would do me so much good, and be so altogether splendid—I *must* go."

"I'm afraid it's impossible, Jo. Aunt says Amy, decidedly, and it is not for us to dictate when she offers such a favor."

"It's always so. Amy has all the fun and I have all the work. It isn't fair, oh, it isn't fair," cried Jo passionately.

"I'm afraid it is partly your own fault, dear. When Aunt spoke to me the other day, she regretted your blunt manners and too independent spirit, and here she writes, as if quoting something you had said, 'I planned at first to ask Jo, but as "favors burden her," and she "hates French," I think I won't venture to invite her. Amy is more docile, will make a good companion for Flo, and receive gratefully any help the trip may give her.'"

"Oh, my tongue, my abominable tongue! Why can't I learn to keep it quiet?" groaned Jo, remembering words which had been her undoing.

When she had heard the explanation of the quoted phrases, Mrs. March said sorrowfully: "I wish you could have gone, but there is no hope of it this time; so try to bear it cheerfully, and don't sadden Amy's pleasure by reproaches or regrets."

"I'll try," said Jo, winking hard. "I'll take a leaf out of her book, and try not only to seem glad, but to be so, and not grudge her one minute of happiness; but it won't be easy, for it is a dreadful disappointment."

"Jo, dear, I'm very selfish, but I couldn't spare you, and I'm glad you are not going quite yet," whispered Beth, embracing her with such a clinging touch and loving face that Jo felt comforted in spite of the sharp regret that made her want to box her own ears, and humbly beg Aunt Carrol to burden her with this favor and see how gratefully she would bear it.

By the time Amy came in, Jo was able to take her part in the family jubilation—not quite as heartily as usual, perhaps, but without repinings at Amy's good fortune. The young lady herself received the news as tidings of great joy, went about in a solemn sort of rapture, and began to sort her colors and pack her pencils that evening, leaving such trifles as clothes, money, and passports to those less absorbed in visions of art.

"It isn't a mere pleasure trip to me, girls," she said impressively as she scraped her best palette. "It will decide my career; for if I have any genius, I shall find it out in Rome, and will do something to prove it."

"Suppose you haven't?" said Jo, sewing away, with red eyes, at the new collars which were to be handed over to Amy.

"Then I shall come home and teach drawing for my living," replied the aspirant for fame with philosophic composure; but she made a wry face at the prospect, and scratched away at her palette as if bent on vigorous measures before she gave up her hopes.

"No you won't. You hate hard work, and you'll marry some rich man, and come home to sit in the lap of luxury all your days," said Jo.

"Your predictions sometimes come to pass, but I don't believe that one will. I'm sure I wish it would, for if I can't be an artist myself, I should like to be able to help those who are," said Amy.

"Hum!" said Jo, with a sigh. "If you wish it you'll have it, for your wishes are always granted—mine never."

"Would you like to go?" asked Amy.

"Rather!"

"Well, in a year or two I'll send for you, and we'll dig in the Forum for relics, and carry out all the plans we've made so many times."

"Thank you. I'll remind you of your promise when that joyful day comes, if it ever does," returned Jo, accepting the vague but magnificent offer as gratefully as she could.

There was not much time for preparation, and the house was in a ferment till Amy was off. Jo bore up very well till the last flutter of blue ribbon vanished, when she retired to her refuge, the garret, and cried till she couldn't cry any more. Amy likewise bore up stoutly till the steamer sailed; then, just as the gangway was about to be withdrawn, it suddenly came over her that a whole ocean was soon to roll between her and those who loved her best, and she clung to Laurie, the last lingerer, saying with a sob: "Oh, take care of them for me, and if anything should happen——"

"I will, dear, I will; and if anything happens, I'll come and comfort you," whispered Laurie, little dreaming that he would be called upon to keep his word.

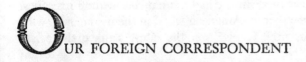

UR FOREIGN CORRESPONDENT

London

Dearest People,

Here I really sit at a front window of the Bath Hotel, Piccadilly. It's not a fashionable place, but Uncle stopped here years ago, and won't go anywhere else; however, we don't mean to stay long, so it's no great matter. Oh, I can't begin to tell you how I enjoy it all! I never can, so I'll only give you bits out of my notebook, for I've done nothing but sketch and scribble since I started. I sent a line from Halifax, when I felt pretty miserable, but after that I got on delightfully, seldom ill, on deck all day, with plenty of pleasant people to amuse me. Everyone was very kind to me, especially the officers. Don't laugh, Jo. Gentlemen really are very necessary aboard ship, to hold onto, or to wait upon one.

It was all heavenly, but I was glad to see the Irish coast, and found it very lovely, so green and sunny, with brown cabins here and there, ruins on some of the hills, and gentlemen's country seats in the valleys, with deer feeding in the parks.

We only stopped at Liverpool a few hours. It's a dirty, noisy place, and I was glad to leave it. Uncle rushed out and bought a pair of dogskin gloves, some ugly, thick shoes, and an umbrella, and got shaved à la mutton chop, the first thing. Then he flattered himself that he looked like a true Briton; but the first time he had the mud cleaned off his shoes, the little bootblack knew that an American stood in them, and said, with a grin, "There yer har, sir. I've give 'em the latest Yankee shine." It amused Uncle immensely.

The trip was like riding through a long picture gallery full of lovely landscapes. The farmhouses were my delight, with thatched roofs, ivy up to the eaves, latticed windows, and stout women with rosy children at the doors. The very cattle looked more tranquil than ours as they stood knee-deep in clover, and the hens had a contented cluck, as if they never got nervous, like Yankee biddies. Such perfect color I never saw—the grass so green, sky so blue, grain so yellow, wood so dark—I was in a rapture all the way. So was Flo, and we kept bouncing from one side to the other, trying to see everything while we were whisking along at the rate of sixty miles an hour. Aunt was tired and went to sleep, but Uncle read his guidebook, and wouldn't be astonished at anything. This is the way we went on: Amy, flying up—"Oh, that must be Kenilworth, that gray place among the trees!" Flo, darting to my window—"How sweet! We must go there sometime, won't we, Papa?" Uncle, calmly admiring his boots —"No, my dear, not unless you want beer. That's a brewery."

A pause—then Flo cried out, "Bless me, there's a gallows and a man going up." "Where, where?" shrieks Amy, staring out at two tall posts with a crossbeam and some dangling chains. "A colliery," remarks Uncle, with a twinkle of the eye. "Here's a lovely flock of lambs all lying down," says Amy. "See, Papa, aren't they pretty!" added Flo sentimentally. "Geese, young ladies," returns Uncle, in a tone that keeps us quiet till Flo settles down to enjoy *The Flirtations of Captain Cavendish*, and I have the scenery all to myself.

Of course it rained when we got to London, and there was nothing to be seen but fog and umbrellas. We rested, unpacked, and shopped a little between showers. Aunt Mary got me some new things, for I came off in such a hurry I wasn't half ready. A white hat and blue feather, a muslin dress to match, and the loveliest mantle you ever saw. Shopping in Regent Street is perfectly splendid; things seem so cheap—nice ribbons only sixpence a yard. I laid in a stock, but shall get my gloves in Paris. Doesn't that sound sort of elegant and rich?

Today was fair, and we went to Hyde Park, close by, for we are more aristocratic than we look. The Duke of Devonshire lives near. I often see his footmen lounging at the back gate, and the Duke of Wellington's house is not far off. Such sights as I saw, my dear! It was as good as *Punch*, for there were fat dowagers rolling about in their red-and-yellow coaches, with gorgeous Jeameses in silk stockings and velvet coats up behind, and powdered coachmen in front. Smart maids, with the rosiest children I ever saw; handsome girls, looking half asleep; dandies in queer English hats and lavender kids lounging about, and tall soldiers in short red jackets and muffin caps stuck on one side, looking so funny I longed to sketch them.

In the P.M. to Westminster Abbey, but don't expect me to describe it, that's impossible—so I'll only say it was sublime! This evening we are going to see Fechter, which will be an appropriate end to the happiest day of my life.

Midnight

It's very late, but I can't let my letter go in the morning without telling you what happened last evening. Who do you think came in as we were at tea? Laurie's English friends, Fred and Frank Vaughn! I was so surprised, for I shouldn't have known them but for the cards. Both are tall fellows, with whiskers, Fred handsome in the English style, and Frank much better, for he only limps slightly, and uses no crutches. They had heard from Laurie where we were to be. They went to the theater with us, and we did have *such* a good time, for Frank devoted himself to Flo and Fred and I talked over past, present, and future fun as if we had known each other all our days. Tell Beth Frank asked for her, and was sorry to hear of her ill-health. Fred laughed when I spoke of Jo, and sent his "respectful compliments to the big hat." Neither of them had forgotten Camp Laurence, or the fun we had there. What ages ago it seems, doesn't it?

I long to see you all, and in spite of my nonsense am, as ever, your loving

Amy

Paris

Dear Girls,

In my last I told you about our London visit—how kind the Vaughns were, and what pleasant parties they made for us. I enjoyed the trips to Hampton Court and the Kensington Museum more than anything else —for at Hampton I saw Raphael's cartoons, and at the Museum, rooms full of pictures by Turner, Lawrence, Reynolds, Hogarth, and the other great creatures. We "did" London to our hearts' content, thanks to Fred and Frank, and were sorry to go away; for though English people are slow to take you in, when they once make up their minds to do it they cannot be outdone in hospitality, I think. The Vaughns hope to meet us in Rome next winter, and I shall be dreadfully disappointed if they don't, for Grace and I are great friends, and the boys very nice fellows—especially Fred.

Well, we were hardly settled here when he turned up again, saying he had come for a holiday, and was going to Switzerland. Aunt looked sober at first, but he was so cool about it she couldn't say a word; and now we get on nicely, and are very glad he came, for he speaks French like a native and I don't know what we should do without him. Uncle doesn't know ten words, and insists on talking English very loud, as if that would make people understand him. Aunt's pronunciation is old-fashioned, and Flo and I, though we flattered ourselves that we knew a good deal, find we don't, and are very grateful to have Fred do the *parley-vooing*, as Uncle calls it.

The Palais Royal is a heavenly place—so full of *bijouterie* and lovely things that I'm nearly distracted because I can't buy them. Fred wanted to get me some, but of course I didn't allow it. Then the Bois and the Champs Elysées are *très magnifiques*. I've seen the imperial family several times—the Emperor an ugly, hard-looking man, the Empress pale and pretty, but dressed in bad taste, I thought—purple dress, green hat, and yellow gloves. Little Nap is a handsome boy, who sits chatting to his tutor and kisses his hand to the people as he passes in his four-horse barouche with postilions in red-satin jackets, and a mounted guard before and behind.

Next week we are off to Germany and Switzerland, and as we shall travel fast, I shall only be able to give you hasty letters. I keep my diary, and try to "remember correctly and describe clearly all that I see and admire," as Father advised. It is good practice for me, and, with my sketchbook, will give you a better idea of my tour than these scribbles.

Adieu. I embrace you tenderly.

Votre Amie

Heidelberg

My dear Mamma,

Having a quiet hour before we leave for Berne, I'll try to tell you what has happened, for some of it is very important, as you will see.

The sail up the Rhine was perfect, and I just sat and enjoyed it with all my might. Get Father's old guidebooks and read about it. I haven't words beautiful enough to describe it. At Coblenz we had a lovely time, for some students from Bonn with whom Fred got acquainted on the boat gave us a serenade. It was a moonlight night, and about one o'clock Flo and I were waked by the most delicious music under our windows. We flew up, and hid behind the curtains; but sly peeps showed us Fred and the students singing away down below. It was the most romantic thing I ever saw—the river, the bridge, the boats, the great fortress opposite, moonlight everywhere, and music fit to melt a heart of stone.

When they were done we threw down some flowers, and saw them scramble for them, kiss their hands to the invisible ladies, and go laughing away—to smoke and drink beer, I suppose. Next morning Fred showed me one of the crumpled flowers in his vest pocket, and looked very sentimental. I laughed at him, and said I didn't throw it, but Flo, which seemed to disgust him, for he tossed it out of the window and turned sensible again. I'm afraid I'm going to have trouble with that boy. It begins to look like it.

The baths at Nassau were very gay, so was Baden-Baden, where Fred lost some money, and I scolded him. He needs someone to look after him when Frank is not with him. Kate said once she hoped he'd marry soon, and I quite agree with her that it would be well for him.

Now comes the serious part—for it happened here, and Fred is just gone. He has been so kind and jolly that we all got quite fond of him. I never thought of anything but a traveling friendship till the serenade night. Since then I've begun to feel that the moonlight walks, balcony talks, and daily adventures were something more to him than fun. I haven't flirted, Mother, truly, but remembered what you said to me, and have done my very best. I can't help it if people like me. I don't try to make them, and it worries me if I don't care for them, though Jo says I haven't got any heart. Now I know Mother will shake her head, and the girls say, "Oh, the mercenary little wretch!" but I've made up my mind, and if Fred asks me, I shall accept him, though I'm not madly in love. I like him, and we get on comfortably together. He is handsome, young, clever enough, and very rich—ever so much richer than the Laurences. I don't think his family would object, and I should be very happy, for they are all kind, well-bred, generous people, and they like me. Fred, as the eldest twin, will have the estate, I suppose, and such a splendid one as it is! A city house in a fashionable street, not so showy as our big houses, but twice as comfortable, and full of solid luxury such as English people believe in. I like it, for it's genuine. I've seen the plate, the family jewels, the old servants, and pictures of the country place, with its park, great house, lovely grounds, and fine horses. Oh, it would be all I should ask! And I'd rather have it than any title such as girls snap up so readily, and find nothing behind. I may be mercenary, but I hate poverty, and don't mean to bear it a minute longer than I can help. One of us *must* marry well. Meg didn't, Jo won't, Beth can't yet, so I shall, and make everything cozy all round.

I wouldn't marry a man I hated or despised. You may be sure of that. And though Fred is not my model hero, he does very well, and in time I should get fond enough of him if he was very fond of me, and let me do just as I liked. So I've been turning the matter over in my mind the last week, for it was impossible to help seeing that Fred liked me. Well, last evening we went up to the castle about sunset—at least all of us but Fred, who was to meet us there after going to the poste restante for letters. We had a charming time poking about the ruins, the vaults where the monster tun is, and the beautiful gardens made by the Elector long ago for his English wife. I liked the great terrace best, for the view was divine; so while the rest went to see the rooms inside, I sat there trying to sketch the gray stone lion's head on the wall, with scarlet woodbine sprays hanging round it. I felt as if I'd got into a romance, sitting there watching the Neckar rolling through the valley, listening to the music of the Austrian band below, and waiting for my lover, like a real storybook girl. I had a feeling that something was going to happen, and I was ready for it. I didn't feel blushy or quaky, but quite cool, and only a little excited.

By and by I heard Fred's voice, and then he came hurrying through the great arch to find me. He looked so troubled that I forgot all about myself, and asked what the matter was. He said he'd just got a letter begging him to come home, for Frank was very ill; so he was going at once, in the night train, and only had time to say good-by. I was very sorry for him, and disappointed for myself, but only for a minute, because he said as he shook hands—and said it in a way that I could not mistake—"I shall come back. You won't forget me, Amy?"

I didn't promise, but I looked at him, and he seemed satisfied, and there was no time for anything but messages and good-bys, for he was off in an hour, and we all miss him very much. I know he wanted to speak, but I think from something he once hinted that he had promised his father not to do anything of the sort yet awhile, for he is a rash boy, and the old gentleman dreads a foreign daughter-in-law. We shall soon meet in Rome, and then, if I don't change my mind, I'll say "Yes, thank you" when he says "Will you, please?"

Of course this is all *very private*, but I wished you to know what was going on. Don't be anxious about me. Remember I am your "prudent Amy," and be sure I will do nothing rashly. Send me as much advice as you like. I'll use it if I can. I wish I could see you for a good talk, Marmee. Love and trust me.

Ever your
Amy

TENDER TROUBLES

"Jo, I'm anxious about Beth."

"Why, Mother, she has seemed unusually well since the babies came."

"It's not her health that troubles me now, it's her spirits. I'm sure there is something on her mind, and I want you to discover what it is."

"What makes you think so, Mother?"

"She sits alone a good deal, and doesn't talk to her father as much as she used. I found her crying over the babies the other day. This isn't like Beth, and it worries me."

"Have you asked her about it?"

"I have tried once or twice, but she either evaded my questions or looked so distressed that I stopped. I never force my children's confidence, and I seldom have to wait for it long."

After sewing thoughtfully for a minute, Jo said:

"I think she is growing up, and so begins to dream dreams, and have hopes and fears and fidgets, without knowing why, or being able to explain them. Why, Mother, Beth's eighteen, but we treat her like a child, forgetting she's a woman."

"So she is. Dear heart, how fast you do grow up."

"Can't be helped, Marmee, so you must resign yourself to all sorts of worries, and let your birds hop out of the nest, one by one. I promise never to hop very far, if that's any comfort to you."

"It's a great comfort, Jo. I always feel strong when you are at home, now Meg is gone. Beth is too feeble and Amy too young to depend upon, but when the tug comes, you are always ready."

"Why, you know I don't mind hard jobs much, and there must always be one scrub in a family. I feel in my element when all the carpets are to be taken up, or half the family fall sick at once. Amy is distinguishing herself abroad, but if anything is amiss at home, I'm your man."

"I leave Beth to your hands, then, for she will open her tender little heart to her Jo sooner than to anyone else. Be very kind, and don't let her think anyone watches or talks about her. If she only would get quite strong and cheerful again, I shouldn't have a wish in the world."

"Happy woman! I've got heaps."

"My dear, what are they?"

"I'll settle Bethy's troubles, and then I'll tell you mine. They are not very wearing, so they'll keep."

While apparently absorbed in her own affairs, Jo watched Beth, and, after many conflicting conjectures, finally settled upon one which seemed to explain the change in her. A slight incident gave Jo the clue to the mystery, she thought, and a lively fancy and a loving heart did the rest. She was affecting to write busily one Saturday afternoon when she and Beth were alone together; yet as she scribbled she kept her eye on her sister, who seemed unusually quiet. Sitting at the window, Beth leaned her head upon her hand in a dejected attitude while her eyes rested on the dull, autumnal landscape. Suddenly someone passed below whistling like an operatic blackbird, and a voice called out:

"All serene! Coming in tonight."

Beth started, leaned forward, smiled and nodded, watched the passerby till his quick tramp died away, then said softly, "How strong and well and happy that dear boy looks."

"Hum!" said Jo, still intent upon her sister's face; for the bright color faded as quickly as it came, the smile vanished, and presently a tear lay shining on the window ledge. Jo saw Beth's hand go quietly to her eyes more than once, and in her half-averted face read a tender sorrow that made her own eyes fill. Fearing to betray herself, she slipped away, murmuring something about needing more paper.

"Mercy on me, Beth loves Laurie!" she said, sitting down in her own room, pale with the shock of the discovery which she believed she had just made. "I never dreamed of such a thing. What *will* Mother say? I wonder if he——" There Jo stopped, and turned scarlet with a sudden thought. "If he shouldn't love back again, how dreadful it would be. He must, I'll make him!" And she shook her head threateningly at the picture of the mischievous-looking boy laughing at her from the wall. "Oh dear, we *are* growing up with a vengeance. Here's Meg married and a mamma, Amy flourishing away at Paris, and Beth in love. I'm the only one that has sense enough to keep out of mischief." Jo thought intently for a minute, with her eyes fixed on the picture; then she smoothed out her wrinkled forehead and said, with a decided nod at the face opposite:

"No thank you, sir. You're very charming, but you've no more stability than a weathercock; so you needn't write touching notes, and smile in that insinuating way, for it won't do a bit of good, and I won't have it."

Then she sighed, and fell into a reverie from which she did not wake till the early twilight sent her down to take new observations which only confirmed her suspicion. Though Laurie flirted with Amy and joked with Jo, his manner to Beth had always been peculiarly kind and gentle, but so was everybody's; therefore no one thought of imagining that he cared more for her than for the others. Indeed, a general impression had prevailed in the family of late that "our boy" was getting fonder than ever of Jo, who, however, wouldn't hear a word upon the subject, and scolded violently if anyone dared to suggest it.

When Laurie first went to college, he fell in love about once a month; but these small flames were as brief as ardent, did no damage, and much amused Jo, who took great interest in the alternations of hope, despair, and resignation which were confided to her in their weekly conferences. But there came a time when Laurie ceased to worship at many shrines, hinted darkly at one all-absorbing passion, and indulged occasionally in Byronic fits of gloom. Then he avoided the tender subject altogether, wrote philosophical notes to Jo, turned studious, and gave out that he was going to "dig," intending to graduate in a blaze of glory. This suited the young lady better than twilight confidences, tender pressures of the hand, and eloquent glances of the eye; for with Jo, brain developed earlier than heart, and she preferred imaginary heroes to real ones, because when tired of them the former could be shut up in the tin kitchen till called for, and the latter were less manageable.

Things were in this state when the grand discovery was made, and Jo watched Laurie that night as she had never done before. If she had not got the new idea into her head, she would have seen nothing unusual in the fact that Beth was very quiet, and Laurie very kind to her. But having given the rein to her lively fancy, it galloped away with her at a great pace. As usual, Beth lay on the sofa and Laurie sat in a low chair close by, amusing her with all sorts of gossip; for she depended on her weekly "spin," and he never disappointed her. But that evening, Jo fancied that Beth's eyes rested on the lively, dark face beside her with peculiar pleasure. She also fancied, having set her heart upon seeing it, that she saw a certain increase of gentleness in Laurie's manner, that he dropped his voice now and then, laughed less than usual, was a little absent-minded, and settled the afghan over Beth's feet with an assiduity that was really almost tender.

"Who knows? Stranger things have happened," thought Jo as she fussed about the room. "She will make quite an angel of him, and he will make life delightfully easy and pleasant for the dear, if they only love each other. I don't see how he can help it, and I do believe he would if the rest of us were out of the way."

As everyone *was* out of the way but herself, Jo began to feel that she ought to dispose of herself with all speed. But where should she go? And burning to lay herself upon the shrine of sisterly devotion, she sat down to settle that point.

Now the old sofa was a regular patriarch of a sofa—long, broad, well-cushioned, and low; a trifle shabby, as well it might be, for the girls had slept and sprawled on it as babies, fished over the back, ridden on the arms, and had menageries under it as children, and rested tired heads, dreamed dreams, and listened to tender talk on it as young women. They all loved it, for it was a family refuge, and one corner had always been Jo's favorite lounging place. Among the many pillows that adorned the venerable couch was one hard, round, covered with prickly horsehair, and furnished with a knobby button at each end; this repulsive pillow was her especial property, being used as a weapon of defense, a barricade, or a stern preventive of too much slumber.

Laurie knew this pillow well, and had cause to regard it with deep aversion, having been unmercifully pummeled with it in former days when romping was allowed, and now frequently debarred by it from taking the seat he most coveted, next to Jo in the sofa corner. If "the sausage," as they called it, stood on end, it was a sign that he might approach and repose; but if it lay flat across the sofa, woe to the man, woman, or child who dared disturb it! That evening Jo forgot to barricade her corner, and had not been in her seat five minutes before a massive form appeared beside her, and with both arms spread over the sofa back, both long legs stretched out before him, Laurie exclaimed, with a sigh of satisfaction:

"Now *this* is filling at the price."

"No slang," snapped Jo, slamming down the pillow. But it was too late, there was no room for it, and, coasting onto the floor, it disappeared in a most mysterious manner.

"Come, Jo, don't be thorny. After studying himself to a skeleton all the week, a fellow deserves petting, and ought to get it."

"Beth will pet you. I'm busy."

"No, she's not to be bothered with me, but you like that sort of thing, unless you've suddenly lost your taste for it. Have you? Do you hate your boy, and want to fire pillows at him?"

Anything more wheedlesome than that touching appeal was seldom heard, but Jo quenched "her boy" by the stern query: "How many bouquets have you sent Miss Randal this week?"

"Not one, upon my word. She's engaged. Now then."

"I'm glad of it. That's one of your foolish extravagances—sending flowers and things to girls for whom you don't care two pins," continued Jo reprovingly.

"Sensible girls for whom I do care whole papers of pins won't let me send them 'flowers and things,' so what can I do? My feelings must have a *went*."

"Mother doesn't approve of flirting, even in fun, and you do flirt desperately, Teddy."

"I'd give anything if I could answer 'So do you.' As I can't, I'll merely say that I don't see any harm in that pleasant little game, if all parties understand that it's only play."

"Well, it does look pleasant, but I can't learn how it's done. I've tried, because one feels awkward in company not to do as everybody else is doing, but I don't seem to get on," said Jo.

"Take lessons of Amy. She has a regular talent for it."

"Yes, she does it very prettily, and never seems to go too far. I suppose it's natural to some people to please without trying, and others to always say and do the wrong thing in the wrong place."

"I'm glad you can't flirt. It's really refreshing to see a sensible, straightforward girl who can be jolly and kind without making a fool of herself. Between ourselves, Jo, some of the girls I know really do go on at such a rate I'm ashamed of them. Bless your innocent soul! If you could be in my place for a month you'd see things that would astonish you a trifle. Upon my word, when I see one of those harum-scarum girls, I always want to say with our friend Cock Robin:

" 'Out upon you, fie upon you,
Bold-faced jig!' "

It was impossible to help laughing at the funny conflict between Laurie's chivalrous reluctance to speak ill of womankind and his very natural dislike of the unfeminine folly of which fashionable society showed him many samples. Jo knew that "young Laurence" was regarded as a most eligible party by worldly mammas, was much smiled upon by their daughters, and flattered enough by ladies of all ages to make a coxcomb of him; so she watched him rather jealously, fearing he would be spoiled. Returning suddenly to her admonitory tone, she said, dropping her voice: "If you *must* have a 'went,' Teddy, go and devote yourself to one of the 'pretty modest girls' whom you do respect, and not waste your time with the silly ones."

"You really advise it?" And Laurie looked at her with an odd mixture of anxiety and merriment in his face.

"Yes, I do, but you'd better wait till you are through college, on the whole, and be fitting yourself for the place meantime. You're not half good enough for—well, whoever the girl may be." And Jo looked a little queer likewise, for a name had almost escaped her.

"That I'm not!" acquiesced Laurie, with an expression of humility quite new to him as he dropped his eyes, and absently wound Jo's apron tassel round his finger.

"Mercy on us, this will never do," thought Jo, adding aloud: "Go and sing to me. I'm dying for some music, and always like yours."

"I'd rather stay here, thank you."

"Well, you can't, there isn't room. Go and make yourself useful, since you are too big to be ornamental. I thought you hated to be tied to a woman's apron string?" retorted Jo, quoting certain rebellious words of his own.

"Ah, that depends on who wears the apron!" And Laurie gave an audacious tweak at the tassel.

"Are you going?" demanded Jo, diving for the pillow.

He fled at once, and the minute it was well "Up with the bonnets of bonnie Dundee," she slipped away, to return no more till the young gentleman had departed in high dudgeon.

Jo lay long awake that night, and was just dropping off when the sound of a stifled sob made her fly to Beth's bedside with the anxious inquiry: "What is it, dear?"

"I thought you were asleep," sobbed Beth.

"Is it the old pain, my precious?"

"No, it's a new one, but I can bear it."

"Tell me all about it, and let me cure it as I often did the other."

"You can't, there is no cure." There Beth's voice gave way, and clinging to her sister, she cried so despairingly that Jo was frightened.

"Where is it? Shall I call Mother?"

Beth did not answer the first question, but in the dark one hand went involuntarily to her heart, as if the pain were there; with the other she held Jo fast, whispering eagerly: "No, no, don't call her, don't tell her. I shall be better soon. Lie down here and 'poor' my head. I'll be quiet and go to sleep, indeed I will."

Jo obeyed, but as her hand went softly to and fro across Beth's hot forehead and wet eyelids, her heart was very full, and she longed to speak. But young as she was, Jo had learned that hearts, like flowers, cannot be rudely handled, but must open naturally; so, though she believed she knew the cause of Beth's new pain, she only said, in her tenderest tone:

"Does anything trouble you, dearie?"

"Yes, Jo," after a long pause.

"Wouldn't it comfort you to tell me what it is?"

"Not now, not yet."

"Then I won't ask, but remember, Beth, that Mother and Jo are always glad to hear and help you, if they can."

"I know it. I'll tell you by and by."

"Is the pain better now?"

"Oh yes, much better. You are so comfortable, Jo!"

"Go to sleep, dear. I'll stay with you."

So cheek to cheek they fell asleep, and on the morrow Beth seemed quite herself again. But Jo had made up her mind, and after pondering over a project for some days, she confided it to her mother. "You asked me the other day what my wishes were. I'll tell you one of them, Marmee," she began as they sat alone together. "I want to go away somewhere this winter for a change."

"Why, Jo?" And her mother looked up quickly.

With her eyes on her work, Jo answered soberly: "I want something new. I feel restless, and anxious to be seeing, doing, and learning more than I am. I brood too much over my own small affairs, and need stirring up, so as I can be spared this winter, I'd like to hop a little way, and try my wings."

"Where will you hop?"

"To New York. I had a bright idea yesterday, and this is it. You know Mrs. Kirke wrote to you for some respectable young person to teach her children and sew. It's rather hard to find just the thing, but I think I should suit if I tried."

"My dear, go out to service in that great boardinghouse!" And Mrs. March looked surprised, but not displeased.

"It's not exactly going out to service, for Mrs. Kirke is your friend—the kindest soul that ever lived—and would make things pleasant for me, I know. Her family is separate from the rest, and no one knows me there. Don't care if they do. It's honest work, and I'm not ashamed of it."

"Nor I—but your writing?"

"All the better for the change. I shall see and hear new things, get new ideas, and even if I haven't much time there, I shall bring home quantities of material for my rubbish."

"I have no doubt of it, but are these your only reasons for this sudden fancy?"

"No, Mother."

"May I know the others?"

Jo looked up and Jo looked down, then said slowly, with sudden color in her cheeks: "It may be vain and wrong to say it, but—I'm afraid—Laurie is getting too fond of me."

"Then you don't care for him in the way it is evident he begins to care for you?"

"Mercy no! I love the dear boy, as I always have, and am immensely proud of him; but as for anything more, it's out of the question."

"I'm glad of that, Jo."

"Why, please?"

"Because, dear, I don't think you are suited to one another. As friends you are very happy, and your frequent quarrels soon blow over; but I fear you would both rebel if you were mated for life. You are too much alike and too fond of freedom, not to mention hot tempers and strong wills, to get on happily together in a relation which needs infinite patience and forbearance, as well as love."

"That's just the feeling I had, though I couldn't express it. I'm glad you think he is only beginning to care for me. It would trouble me sadly to make him unhappy, for I couldn't fall in love with the dear old fellow merely out of gratitude, could I?"

"You are sure of his feeling for you?"

The color deepened in Jo's cheeks as she answered, with the look of mingled pleasure, pride, and pain which young girls wear when speaking of first lovers: "I'm afraid it is so, Mother. He hasn't said anything, but he looks a great deal. I think I had better go away before it comes to anything."

"I agree with you, and if it can be managed you shall go."

Jo looked relieved, and after a pause said, smiling: "How Mrs. Moffat would wonder at your want of management if she knew, and how she will rejoice that Annie still may hope."

251

"Ah, Jo, mothers may differ in their management, but the hope is the same in all—the desire to see their children happy. Meg is so, and I am content with her success. You I leave to enjoy your liberty till you tire of it, for only then will you find that there is something sweeter. Amy is my chief care now, but her good sense will help her. For Beth, I indulge no hopes except that she may be well. By the way, she seems brighter this last day or two. Have you spoken to her?"

"Yes. She owned she had a trouble, and promised to tell me by and by. I said no more, for I think I know it." And Jo told her little story.

Mrs. March shook her head, and did not take so romantic a view of the case, but looked grave and repeated her opinion that, for Laurie's sake, Jo should go away for a time.

"Let us say nothing about it to him till the plan is settled; then I'll run away before he can collect his wits and be tragical. Beth must think I'm going to please myself, as I am, for I can't talk about Laurie to her; but she can pet and comfort him after I'm gone, and so cure him of this romantic notion. He's been through so many little trials of the sort he's used to it, and will soon get over his lovelornity."

Jo spoke hopefully, but could not rid herself of the foreboding fear that this "little trial" would be harder than the others, and that Laurie would not get over his "lovelornity" as easily as heretofore.

The plan was talked over in a family council, and agreed upon; for Mrs. Kirke gladly accepted Jo, and promised to make a pleasant home for her. The teaching would render her independent, and such leisure as she got might be made profitable by writing, while the new scenes and society would be both useful and agreeable. Jo liked the prospect and was eager to be gone, for the home nest was growing too narrow for her restless nature and adventurous spirit. When all was settled, with fear and trembling she told Laurie, but to her surprise he took it very quietly. He had been graver than usual of late, but very pleasant, and when jokingly accused of turning over a new leaf, he answered soberly, "So I am, and I mean this one shall stay turned."

Jo was very much relieved that one of his virtuous fits should come on just then, and made her preparations with a lightened heart—for Beth seemed more cheerful—and hoped she was doing the best for all.

"One thing I leave to your especial care," she said, the night before she left.

"You mean your papers?" asked Beth.

"No, my boy. Be very good to him, won't you?"

"Of course I will, but I can't fill your place, and he'll miss you sadly."

"It won't hurt him. So remember, I leave him in your charge, to plague, pet, and keep in order."

"I'll do my best, for your sake," promised Beth, wondering why Jo looked at her so queerly.

When Laurie said "Good-by," he whispered significantly:

"It won't do a bit of good, Jo. My eye is on you, so mind what you do, or I'll come and bring you home."

JO'S JOURNAL

New York, November

Dear Marmee and Beth,

I'm going to write you a regular volume, for I've got heaps to tell, though I'm not a fine young lady traveling on the Continent. When I lost sight of Father's dear old face, I felt a trifle blue, and might have shed a briny drop or two if an Irish lady with four small children, all crying more or less, hadn't diverted my mind; for I amused myself by dropping gingerbread nuts over the seat every time they opened their mouths to roar.

Soon the sun came out, and taking it as a good omen, I cleared up likewise, and enjoyed my journey with all my heart.

Mrs. Kirke welcomed me so kindly I felt at home at once, even in that big house full of strangers. She gave me a funny little sky parlor—all she had—but there is a stove in it, and a nice table in a sunny window, so I can sit here and write whenever I like. A fine view and a church tower opposite atone for the many stairs, and I took a fancy to my den on the spot. The nursery, where I am to teach and sew, is a pleasant room next Mrs. Kirke's private parlor, and the two little girls are pretty children—rather spoiled, I fancy, but they took to me after telling them "The Seven Bad Pigs," and I've no doubt I shall make a model governess. I am to have my meals with the children if I prefer it to the great table, and for the present I do, for I *am* bashful, though no one will believe it.

"Now, my dear, make yourself at home," said Mrs. K. in her motherly way. "I'm on the drive from morning to night, as you may suppose with such a family; but a great anxiety will be off my mind if I know the children are safe with you. My rooms are always open to you, and your own shall be as comfortable as I can make it. There are some pleasant people in the house if you feel sociable, and your evenings are always free. Come to me if anything goes wrong, and be as happy as you can. There's the tea bell. I must run and change my cap." And off she bustled, leaving me to settle myself in my new nest.

As I went downstairs soon after, I saw something I liked. The flights are very long in this tall house, and as I stood waiting at the head of the third one for a little servant girl to lumber up, I saw a gentleman come along behind her, take the heavy hod of coal out of her hand, carry it all the way up, put it down at a door near by, and walk away, saying, with a kind nod and a foreign accent: "It goes better so. The little back is too young to haf such heaviness."

Wasn't it good of him? I like such things, for as Father says, trifles show character. When I mentioned it to Mrs. K., that evening, she laughed, and said: "That must have been Professor Bhaer. He's always doing things of that sort."

Mrs. K. told me he was from Berlin, very learned and good, but poor as a church mouse, and gives lessons to support himself and two little orphan nephews whom he is educating here according to the wishes of his sister, who married an American. Not a very romantic story, but it interested me, and I was glad to hear that Mrs. K. lends him her parlor for some of his scholars. There is a glass door between it and the nursery, and I mean to peep at him, and then I'll tell you how he looks. He's almost forty, so it's no harm, Marmee.

After tea and a go-to-bed romp with the little girls, I attacked the big workbasket, and had a quiet evening with my new friend. I shall keep a journal-letter, and send it once a week, so good night, and more to-morrow.

Tuesday Eve

Had a lively time in my seminary this morning, for the children acted like Sancho, and at one time I really thought I should shake them all round. Some good angel inspired me to try gymnastics, and I kept it up till they were glad to sit down and keep still. After luncheon, the girl took them out for a walk, and I went to my needlework, like little Mabel, "with a willing mind." I was thanking my stars that I'd learned to make nice buttonholes when the parlor door opened and shut, and someone began to hum *"Kennst du das Land,"* like a big bumblebee. It was dreadfully improper, I know, but I couldn't resist the temptation, and lifting one end of the curtain before the glass door, I peeped in. Professor Bhaer was there, and while he arranged his books I took a good look at him. A regular German—rather stout, with brown hair tumbled all over his head, a bushy beard, good nose, the kindest eyes I ever saw, and a splendid big voice that does one's ears good after our sharp or slipshod American gabble. His clothes were rusty, his hands were large, and he hadn't a really handsome feature in his face, except his beautiful teeth; yet I liked him, for he had a fine head, his linen was very nice, and he looked like a gentleman, though two buttons were off his coat and there was a patch on one shoe. He looked sober in spite of his humming till he went to the window to turn the hyacinth bulbs toward the sun, and stroke the cat, who received him like an old friend. Then he smiled, and when a tap came at the door, called out in a loud, brisk tone: *"Herein!"*

I was just going to run when I caught sight of a morsel of a child carrying a big book, and stopped to see what was going on.

"Me wants my Bhaer," said the mite, slamming down her book and running to meet him.

"Thou shalt haf thy Bhaer. Come, then, and take a goot hug from him, my Tina," said the Professor, catching her up with a laugh, and holding her so high over his head that she had to stoop her little face to kiss him.

"Now me mus tuddy my lessin," went on the funny little thing. So he put her up at the table, opened the great dictionary she had brought, and gave her a paper and pencil, and she scribbled away, turning a leaf now and then, and passing her little fat finger down the page as if finding a word so soberly that I nearly betrayed myself by a laugh, while Mr. Bhaer stood stroking her pretty hair with a fatherly look that made me think she must be his own, though she looked more French than German.

Another knock and the appearance of two young ladies sent me back to my work, and there I virtuously remained through all the noise and gabbling that went on next door. One of the girls kept laughing affectedly, and saying, "Now, Professor," in a coquettish tone, and the other pronounced her German with an accent that must have made it hard for him to keep sober.

Both seemed to try his patience sorely, for more than once I heard him say emphatically, "No, no, it is *not* so. You haf not attend to what I say," and once there was a loud rap, as if he struck the table with his book, followed by the despairing exclamation. "*Prut!* It all goes bad this day."

Poor man, I pitied him, and when the girls were gone, took just one more peep, to see if he survived it. He seemed to have thrown himself back in his chair, tired out, and sat there with his eyes shut till the clock struck two, when he jumped up, put his books in his pocket as if ready for another lesson, and, taking little Tina, who had fallen asleep on the sofa, in his arms, he carried her quietly away. I fancy he has a hard life of it.

Mrs. Kirke asked me if I wouldn't go down to the five-o'clock dinner, and, feeling a little bit homesick, I thought I would, just to see what sort of people are under the same roof with me. So I made myself respectable, and tried to slip in behind Mrs. Kirke; but as she is short and I'm tall, my efforts at concealment were rather a failure. She gave me a seat by her, and after my face cooled off, I plucked up courage and looked about me. The long table was full, and everyone intent on getting their dinner. There was the usual assortment of young men absorbed in themselves, young couples absorbed in each other, married ladies in their babies, and old gentlemen in politics. I don't think I shall care to have much to do with any of them except one sweet-faced maiden lady, who looks as if she had something in her.

Cast away at the very bottom of the table was the Professor, shouting answers to the questions of a very inquisitive deaf old gentleman on one side, and talking philosophy with a Frenchman on the other. If Amy had been here, she'd have turned her back on him forever, because, sad to relate, he had a great appetite, and shoveled in his dinner in a manner which would have horrified "her ladyship." I didn't mind, for I like to "see folks eat with a relish," as Hannah says, and the poor man must have needed a deal of food after teaching idiots all day.

As I went upstairs after dinner, two of the young men were settling their hats before the hall mirror, and I heard one say low to the other:

"Who's the new party?"

"Governess, or something of that sort."

"What the deuce is she at our table for?"

"Friend of the old lady's."

"Handsome head, but no style."

"Not a bit of it. Give us a light and come on."

I felt angry at first, and then I didn't care, for a governess is as good as a clerk, and I've got sense, if I haven't style, which is more than some people have, judging from the remarks of the elegant beings who clattered away smoking like bad chimneys. I hate ordinary people!

Thursday

Yesterday was a quiet day, spent in teaching, sewing, and writing in my little room, which is very cozy, with a light and a fire. I picked up a few bits of news, and was introduced to the Professor. It seems that Tina is the child of the Frenchwoman who does the fine ironing in the laundry here. The little thing has lost her heart to Mr. Bhaer, and follows him about the house like a dog whenever he is at home, which delights him, as he is very fond of children, though a "bacheldore." Kitty and Minnie Kirke likewise regard him with affection, and tell all sorts of stories about the plays he invents, the presents he brings, and the splendid tales he tells. The young men quiz him, it seems, call him Old Fritz, Lager Beer, Ursa Major, and make all manner of jokes on his name. But he enjoys it like a boy, Mrs. K. says, and takes it so good-naturedly that they all like him, in spite of his foreign ways.

The maiden lady is a Miss Norton—rich, cultivated, and kind. She spoke to me at dinner today (for I went to table again, it's such fun to watch people), and asked me to come and see her at her room. She has fine books and pictures, knows interesting persons, and seems friendly; so I shall make myself agreeable, for I *do* want to get into good society, only it isn't the same sort that Amy likes.

I was in our parlor last evening when Mr. Bhaer came in with some newspapers for Mrs. Kirke. She wasn't there, but Minnie, who is a little old woman, introduced me very prettily: "This is Mamma's friend, Miss March."

"Yes, and she's jolly and we like her lots," added Kitty, who is an enfant terrible.

We both bowed, and then we laughed, for the prim introduction and the blunt addition were rather a comical contrast.

"Ah, yes, I hear these naughty ones go to vex you, Mees Marsch. If so again, call at me and I come," he said, with a threatening frown that delighted the little wretches.

I promised I would, and he departed; but it seems as if I was doomed to see a good deal of him, for today as I passed his door on my way out by accident I knocked against it with my umbrella. It flew open, and there he stood in his dressing gown, with a big blue sock in one hand and a darning needle in the other. He didn't seem at all ashamed of it, for when I explained and hurried on, he waved his hand, sock and all, saying in his loud, cheerful way: "You haf a fine day to make your walk. *Bon voyage, mademoiselle.*"

I laughed all the way downstairs, but it was a little pathetic also to think of the poor man having to mend his own clothes.

Saturday

Nothing has happened to write about, except a call on Miss Norton, who has a room full of lovely things, and who was very charming, for she showed me all her treasures, and asked me if I would sometimes go with her to lectures and concerts as her escort—if I enjoyed them. She put it as a favor, but I'm sure Mrs. Kirke has told her about us, and she does it out of kindness to me. I'm as proud as Lucifer, but such favors from such people don't burden me, and I accepted gratefully.

When I got back to the nursery there was such an uproar in the parlor that I looked in; and there was Mr. Bhaer down on his hands and knees, with Tina on his back, Kitty leading him with a jump rope, and Minnie feeding two small boys with seedcakes as they roared and ramped in cages built of chairs.

"We are playing *nargerie*," explained Kitty.

"Dis is mine effalunt!" added Tina, holding on by the Professor's hair.

"Mamma always allows us to do what we like Saturday afternoons, when Franz and Emil come, doesn't she, Mr. Bhaer?" said Minnie.

The "effalunt" sat up, looking as much in earnest as any of them, and said soberly to me:

"I gif you my wort it is so. If we make too large a noise you shall say 'Hush!' to us, and we go more softly."

I promised to do so, but left the door open, and enjoyed the fun as much as they did—for a more glorious frolic I never witnessed. They played tag and soldiers, danced and sang, and when it began to grow dark they all piled onto the sofa about the Professor while he told fairy stories. I wish Americans were as simple and natural as Germans, don't you?

I'm so fond of writing I should go spinning on forever if motives of economy didn't stop me; for though I've used thin paper and written fine, I tremble to think of the stamps this long letter will need. Pray forward Amy's as soon as you can spare them. My small news will sound very flat after her splendors, but you will like them, I know. Is Teddy studying so hard that he can't find time to write to his friends? Take good care of him for me, Beth, and tell me all about the babies, and give heaps of love to everyone.

From your faithful

Jo

P.S. On reading over my letter it strikes me as rather Bhaery, but I am always interested in odd people, and I really had nothing else to write about. Bless you!

December

My precious Betsey,

As this is to be a scribble-scrabble letter, I direct it to you, for it may amuse you, and give you some idea of my goings-on; for though quiet, they are rather amusing, for which oh be joyful! After what Amy would call Herculaneum efforts in the way of mental and moral agriculture, my young ideas begin to shoot and my little twigs to bend as I could wish. They are not so interesting to me as Tina and the boys, but I do my duty by them, and they are fond of me. Franz and Emil are jolly little lads, quite after my own heart, for the mixture of German and American spirit in them produces a constant state of effervescence. Saturday afternoons are riotous times, whether spent in the house or out; for on pleasant days they all go to walk, like a seminary, with the Professor and myself to keep order, and then such fun!

We are very good friends now, and I've begun to take lessons. I really couldn't help it, and it all came about in such a droll way that I must tell you. To begin at the beginning, Mrs. Kirke called to me one day as I passed Mr. Bhaer's room, where she was rummaging: "Did you ever see such a den, my dear? Just come and help me put these books to rights, for I've turned everything upside down trying to discover what he has done with the six new handkerchiefs I gave him not long ago."

I went in, and while we worked I looked about me, for it was a "den," to be sure. Books and papers everywhere; a broken meerschaum and an old flute over the mantelpiece as if done with; a ragged bird, without any tail, chirped on one window seat and a box of white mice adorned the other; half-finished boats and bits of string lay among the manuscripts; dirty little boots stood drying before the fire; and traces of the dearly beloved boys, for whom he makes a slave of himself, were to be seen all over the room. After a grand rummage three of the missing articles were found—one over the bird cage, one covered with ink, and a third burned brown, having been used as a holder.

"Such a man!" laughed good-natured Mrs. K. as she put the relics in the ragbag. I suppose the others are torn up to rig ships, bandage cut fingers, or make kite tails. It's dreadful, but I can't scold him—he's so absent-minded and good-natured he lets those boys ride over him rough-shod. I agreed to do his washing and mending, but he forgets to give out his things and I forget to look them over, so he comes to a sad pass sometimes."

"Let me mend them," said I. "I don't mind it, and he needn't know. I'd like to—he's so kind to me about bringing my letters and lending books."

So I have got his things in order, and knit heels into two pairs of the socks—for they were boggled out of shape with his queer darns. Nothing was said, and I hoped he wouldn't find it out, but one day last week he caught me at it. Hearing the lessons he gives to others has interested and amused me so much that I took a fancy to learn, for Tina runs in and out leaving the door open, and I can hear. I had been sitting near this door, finishing off the last sock and trying to understand what he said to a new scholar who is as stupid as I am. The girl had gone, and I thought he had also, it was so still, and I was busily gabbling over a verb when a little crow made me look up, and there was Mr. Bhaer looking and laughing quietly while he made signs to Tina not to betray him.

"So!" he said as I stopped and stared like a goose. "You peep at me, I peep at you, and that is not bad; but see, I am not pleasanting when I say, haf you a wish for German?"

"Yes, but you are too busy. I am too stupid to learn," I blundered out, as red as a peony.

"*Prut!* We will make the time, and we fail not to find the sense. At efening I shall gif a little lesson with much gladness; for look you, Mees Marsch, I haf this debt to pay," and he pointed to my work. 'Yes,' they say to one another, these so kind ladies, 'he is a stupid old fellow. He will see not what we do, he will never opserve that his sock heels go not in holes any more, he will think his buttons grow out new when they fall, and believe that strings make theirselves.' Ah, but I haf an eye, and I see much. I haf a heart, and I feel the thanks for this. Come, a little lesson then and now, or no more good fairy works for me and mine."

Of course I couldn't say anything after that, and as it really is a splendid opportunity, I made the bargain, and we began. I took four lessons, and then I stuck fast in a grammatical bog. The Professor was very patient with me, but it must have been torment to him, and now and then he'd look at me with such an expression of mild despair that it was a toss-up with me whether to laugh or cry. I tried both ways; and when it came to a sniff of utter mortification and woe, he just threw the grammar on to the floor and marched out of the room. I felt myself disgraced and deserted forever, but didn't blame him a particle, and was scrambling my papers together, meaning to rush upstairs and shake myself hard, when in he came as brisk and beaming as if I'd covered myself with glory.

"Now we shall try a new way. You and I will read these pleasant little *Märchen* together, and dig no more in that dry book, that goes in the corner for making us trouble."

He spoke so kindly, and opened Hans Andersen's fairy tales so invitingly before me, that I was more ashamed than ever, and went at my lesson in a neck-or-nothing style that seemed to amuse him immensely. I forgot my bashfulness, and pegged away (no other word will express it) with all my might, tumbling over long words, pronouncing according to the inspiration of the minute, and doing my very best. When I finished reading my first page and stopped for breath, he clapped his hands and cried out, in his hearty way: "*Das ist gut!* Now we go well! My turn. I do him in German. Gif me your ear." And away he went, rumbling out the words with his strong voice and a relish which was good to see as well as hear. Fortunately the story was "The Constant Tin Soldier," which is droll, you know, so I could laugh—and I did—though I didn't understand half he read, for I couldn't help it, he was so earnest, I so excited, and the whole thing so comical.

After that we got on better, and now I read my lessons pretty well; for this way of studying suits me, and I can see that the grammar gets tucked into the tales and poetry as one gives pills in jelly. I like it very much, and he doesn't seem tired of it yet—which is very good of him, isn't it? I mean to give him something on Christmas, for I dare not offer money.

January

A Happy New Year to you all, my dearest family, which of course includes Mr. L., and a young man by the name of Teddy. I can't tell you how much I enjoyed your Christmas bundle, for I didn't get it till night, and had given up hoping. Your letter came in the morning, but you said nothing about a parcel, meaning it for a surprise; so I was disappointed, for I'd had a "kind of feeling" that you wouldn't forget me. I felt a little low in my mind as I sat up in my room after tea, and when the big, muddy, battered-looking bundle was brought to me, I just hugged it and pranced. It was so *homey* and refreshing that I sat down on the floor and read and looked and ate and laughed and cried, in my usual absurd way. The things were just what I wanted, and all the better for being made instead of bought. Beth's new "ink bib" was capital, and Hannah's box of hard gingerbread will be a treasure. I'll be sure and wear the nice flannels you sent, Marmee, and read carefully the books Father has marked. Thank you all, heaps and heaps!

Speaking of books reminds me that I'm getting rich in that line, for on New Year's Day Mr. Bhaer gave me a fine Shakespeare. It is one he values much, and I've often admired it, set up in the place of honor with his German Bible, Plato, Homer, and Milton; so you may imagine how I felt when he brought it down and showed me my name in it, from my "friend Friedrich Bhaer."

"You say often you wish a library. Here I gif you one, for between these lids (he meant covers) is many books in one. Read him well, and he will help you much; for the study of character in this book will help you to read it in the world and paint it with your pen."

I thanked him as well as I could, and talk now about "my library" as if I had a hundred books. I never knew how much there was in Shakespeare before, but then I never had a Bhaer to explain it to me. Now *don't* laugh at his horrid name; it isn't pronounced either Bear or Beer, as people *will* say it, but something between the two, as only Germans can give it. I'm glad you both like what I tell you about him, and hope you will know him some day. Mother would admire his warm heart, Father his wise head. I admire both, and feel rich in my new "friend Friedrich Bhaer."

Not having much money, or knowing what he'd like, I got several little things, and put them about the room where he would find them unexpectedly. They were useful, pretty, or funny: a new standish on his table, a little vase for his flowers—he always has one, or a bit of green in a glass, to keep him fresh, he says—and a holder for his blower, so that he needn't burn up what Amy calls *mouchoirs*. I made it like those Beth invented—a big butterfly with a fat body, and black and yellow wings, worsted feelers, and bead eyes. It took his fancy immensely, and he put it on his mantelpiece as an article of virtu, so it was rather a failure after all. Poor as he is, he didn't forget a servant or a child in the house and not a soul here, from the French laundrywoman to Miss Norton, forgot him. I was so glad of that.

They got up a masquerade and had a gay time New Year's Eve. I didn't mean to go down, having no dress, but at the last minute Mrs. Kirke remembered some old brocades, and Miss Norton lent me lace and feathers, so I dressed up as Mrs. Malaprop and sailed in with a mask on. No one knew me, for I disguised my voice, and no one dreamed the silent, haughty Miss March (for they think I am very stiff and cool, most of them, and so I am to whippersnappers) could dance and dress, and burst out into a "nice derangement of epitaphs, like an allegory on the banks of the Nile." I enjoyed it very much, and when we unmasked, it was fun to see them stare at me. I heard one of the young men tell another that he knew I'd been an actress; in fact, he thought he remembered seeing me at one of the minor theaters. Meg will relish that joke. Mr. Bhaer was Nick Bottom, and Tina was Titania—a perfect little fairy in his arms. To see them dance was "quite a landscape," to use a Teddyism.

I had a very happy New Year, after all, and when I thought it over in my room, I felt as if I was getting on a little in spite of my many failures; for I'm cheerful all the time now, work with a will, and take more interest in other people than I used to, which is satisfactory. Bless you all! Ever your loving

Jo

 FRIEND

Though very happy in the social atmosphere about her, and very busy with the daily work that earned her bread and made it sweeter for the effort, Jo still found time for literary labors. The purpose which now took possession of her was a natural one to a poor and ambitious girl, but the means she took to gain her end were not the best. She saw that money conferred power. Money and power, therefore, she resolved to have—not to be used for herself alone, but for those whom she loved more than self. The dream of filling home with comforts, giving Beth everything she wanted, from strawberries in winter to an organ in her bedroom, going abroad herself, and always having *more* than enough, so that she might indulge in the luxury of charity, had been for years Jo's most cherished castle in the air. The prize-story experience had seemed to open a way which might, after long traveling and much uphill work, lead to this delightful château en Espagne. But the novel disaster quenched her courage for a time, for public opinion is a giant which has frightened stouter-hearted Jacks on bigger beanstalks than hers.

She took to writing sensation stories, for in those dark ages even all-perfect America read rubbish. She told no one, but concocted a "thrilling tale," and boldly carried it herself to Mr. Dashwood, editor of the *Weekly Volcano*. She had never read *Sartor Resartus*, but she had a womanly instinct that clothes possess an influence more powerful over many than the worth of character or the magic of manners. So she dressed herself in her best, and trying to persuade herself that she was neither excited nor nervous, bravely climbed two pairs of dark and dirty stairs to find herself in a disorderly room, a cloud of cigar smoke, and the presence of three gentlemen sitting with their heels rather higher than their hats, which articles of dress none of them took the trouble to remove on her appearance. Somewhat daunted by this reception, Jo hesitated on the threshold, murmuring in much embarrassment:

"Excuse me, I was looking for the *Weekly Volcano* office. I wished to see Mr. Dashwood."

Down went the highest pair of heels, up rose the smokiest gentleman, and, carefully cherishing his cigar between his fingers, he advanced with a nod, and a countenance expressive of nothing but sleep. Feeling that she must get through the matter somehow, Jo produced her manuscript and, blushing redder and redder with each sentence, blundered out fragments of the little speech carefully prepared for the occasion.

"A friend of mine desired me to offer—a story—just as an experiment —would like your opinion—be glad to write more if this suits."

While she blushed and blundered, Mr. Dashwood had taken the manuscript and was turning over the leaves with a pair of rather dirty fingers, and casting critical glances up and down the neat pages.

"Not a first attempt, I take it?"—observing that pages were numbered, covered only on one side, and not tied up with a ribbon, sure sign of a novice.

"No, sir. She has had some experience, and got a prize for a tale in the *Blarneystone Banner*."

"Oh, did she?" And Mr. Dashwood gave Jo a quick look, which seemed to take note of everything she had on, from the bow in her bonnet to the buttons on her boots. "Well, you can leave it, if you like. We've more of this sort of thing on hand than we know what to do with at present, but I'll run my eye over it, and give you an answer next week."

Now Jo did *not* like to leave it, for Mr. Dashwood didn't suit her at all; but under the circumstances there was nothing for her to do but bow and walk away—looking particularly tall and dignified, as she was apt to do when nettled or abashed. Just then she was both; for it was perfectly evident, from the knowing glances exchanged among the gentlemen, that her little fiction of "my friend" was considered a good joke and a laugh, produced by some inaudible remark of the editor as he closed the door, completed her discomfiture. Half-resolving never to return, she went home and worked off her irritation by stitching pinafores vigorously, and in an hour or two was cool enough to laugh over the scene, and long for next week.

When she went again, Mr. Dashwood was alone, whereat she rejoiced. Mr. Dashwood was much wider awake than before, which was agreeable, and Mr. Dashwood was not too deeply absorbed in a cigar to remember his manners. So the second interview was much more comfortable than the first.

"We'll take this" (editors never say "I") "if you don't object to a few alterations. It's too long, but omitting the passages I've marked will make it just the right length," he said in a businesslike tone.

Jo hardly knew her own MS. again, so crumpled and underscored were its pages and paragraphs; but, feeling as a tender parent might on being asked to cut off her baby's legs in order that it might fit into a new cradle, she looked at the marked passages, and was surprised to find that all the moral reflections—which she had carefully put in as ballast for much romance—had been stricken out.

"But, sir, I thought every story should have some sort of a moral, so I took care to have a few of my sinners repent."

Mr. Dashwood's editorial gravity relaxed into a smile, for Jo had forgotten her "friend," and spoken as only an author could.

"People want to be amused, not preached at, you know. Morals don't sell nowadays."

"You think it would do with these alterations, then?"

"Yes. It's a new plot, and pretty well worked up—language good, and so on," was Mr. Dashwood's affable reply.

"What do you—that is, what compensation——" began Jo.

"Oh yes. Well, we give from twenty-five to thirty for things of this sort. Pay when it comes out," returned Mr. Dashwood, as if that point had escaped him. Such trifles often do escape the editorial mind, it is said.

"Very well, you can have it," said Jo, handing back the story with a satisfied air; for after the dollar-a-column work, even twenty-five dollars seemed good pay.

"Shall I tell my friend you will take another if she has one better than this?" asked Jo, unconscious of her little slip of the tongue, and emboldened by her success.

"Well, we'll look at it, can't promise to take it. Tell her to make it short and spicy, and never mind the moral. What name would your friend like to put to it?"—in a careless tone.

"None at all, if you please. She doesn't wish her name to appear, and has no nom de plume," said Jo, blushing in spite of herself.

"Just as she likes, of course. The tale will be out next week. Will you call for the money, or shall I send it?" asked Mr. Dashwood, who felt a natural desire to know who his new contributor might be.

"I'll call. Good morning, sir."

Following Mr. Dashwood's directions, and making Mrs. Northbury her model, Jo rashly took a plunge into the frothy sea of sensational literature, but, thanks to the life preserver thrown her by a friend, she came up again not much worse for her ducking. Like most young scribblers, she went abroad for her characters and scenery; and banditti, counts, gypsies, nuns, and duchesses appeared upon her stage, and played their parts with as much accuracy and spirit as could be expected. Her readers were not particular about such trifles as grammar, punctuation, and probability, and Mr. Dashwood graciously permitted her to fill his columns at the lowest prices, not thinking it necessary to tell her that the real cause of his hospitality was the fact that one of his hacks, on being offered higher wages, had basely left him in the lurch.

She soon became interested in her work, for her emaciated purse grew stout, and the little hoard she was making to take Beth to the mountains next summer grew slowly but surely as the weeks passed. One thing disturbed her satisfaction, and that was that she did not tell them at home. She had a feeling that Father and Mother would not approve, and preferred to have her own way first and beg pardon afterward. It was easy to keep her secret, for no name appeared with her stories. Mr. Dashwood had of course found it out very soon, but promised to be dumb, and for a wonder, kept his word. She thought it would do her no harm, for she sincerely meant to write nothing of which she should be ashamed, and quieted all pricks of conscience by anticipations of the happy minute when she should show her earnings and laugh over her well-kept secret.

But Mr. Dashwood rejected any but thrilling tales; and as thrills could not be produced except by harrowing up the souls of the readers, history and romance, land and sea, science and art, police records and lunatic asylums, had to be ransacked for the purpose. Jo soon found that her innocent experience had given her but few glimpses of the tragic world which underlies society, so, regarding it in a business light, she set about supplying her deficiencies with characteristic energy. Eager to find material for stories, and bent on making them original in plot if not masterly in execution, she searched newspapers for accidents, incidents, and crimes; she excited the suspicions of public librarians by asking for works on poisons; she studied faces in the street, and characters, good, bad, and indifferent, all about her; she delved in the dust of ancient times for facts or fictions so old that they were as good as new, and introduced herself to folly, sin, and misery as well as her limited opportunities allowed. She thought she was prospering finely, but, unconsciously, she was beginning to desecrate some of the womanliest attributes of a woman's character. She was living in bad society; and, imaginary though it was, its influence affected her.

She was beginning to feel rather than see this, for much describing of other people's passions and feelings set her to studying and speculating about her own—a morbid amusement in which healthy young minds do not voluntarily indulge. Wrongdoing always brings its own punishment, and when Jo most needed hers, she got it.

I don't know whether the study of Shakespeare helped her to read character, or the natural instinct of a woman for what was honest, brave, and strong; but while endowing her imaginary heroes with every perfection under the sun, Jo was discovering a live hero who interested her in spite of many human imperfections. Mr. Bhaer, in one of their conversations, had advised her to study simple, true, and lovely characters wherever she found them, as good training for a writer. Jo took him at his word, for she coolly turned round and studied him—a proceeding which would have much surprised him had he known it, for the worthy Professor was very humble.

Why everybody liked him was what puzzled Jo at first. He was neither rich nor great, young nor handsome, in no respect what is called fascinating, imposing, or brilliant; and yet he was as attractive as a genial fire, and people seemed to gather about him as naturally as about a warm hearth. He was poor, yet always appeared to be giving something away; a stranger, yet everyone was his friend; no longer young, but as happy-hearted as a boy; plain and peculiar, yet his face looked beautiful to many, and his oddities were freely forgiven for his sake. Jo often watched him, trying to discover the charm, and at last decided that it was benevolence which worked the miracle. If he had any sorrow, it sat "with its head under its wing," and he turned only his sunny side to the world. There were lines on his forehead, but Time seemed to have touched him gently, remembering how kind he was to others. The pleasant curves about his mouth were the memorials of many friendly words and cheery laughs, his eyes were never cold or hard, and his big hand had a warm, strong grasp that was more expressive than words.

His very clothes seemed to partake of the hospitable nature of the wearer. They looked as if they were at ease, and liked to make him comfortable; his capacious waistcoat was suggestive of a large heart underneath; his rusty coat had a social air, and the baggy pockets plainly proved that little hands often went in empty and came out full; his very boots were benevolent, and his collar never stiff and raspy like other people's.

"That's it!" said Jo to herself when she at length discovered that genuine goodwill toward one's fellow men could beautify and dignify even a stout German teacher who shoveled in his dinner, darned his own socks, and was burdened with the name of Bhaer.

Jo valued goodness highly, but she also possessed a most feminine respect for intellect, and a little discovery which she made about the Professor added much to her regard for him. He never spoke of himself, and no one ever knew that in his native city he had been a man much honored and esteemed for learning and integrity till a countryman came to see him, and in a conversation with Miss Norton divulged the pleasing fact. From her Jo learned it, and liked it all the better because Mr. Bhaer had never told it. She felt proud to know that he was an honored professor in Berlin, though only a poor language master in America, and his homely, hard-working life was much beautified by the spice of romance which this discovery gave it.

Another and better gift than intellect was shown her in a most unexpected manner. Miss Norton had the entrée into literary society, which Jo would have had no chance of seeing but for her. The solitary woman felt an interest in the ambitious girl, and kindly conferred many favors of this sort on both Jo and the Professor. She took them with her one night to a select symposium held in honor of several celebrities.

Jo went prepared to bow down and adore the mighty ones whom she had worshiped with youthful enthusiasm afar off. But her reverence for genius received a severe shock that night, and it took her some time to recover from the discovery that the great creatures were only men and women after all. Imagine her dismay, on stealing a glance of timid admiration at the poet whose lines suggested an ethereal being fed on "spirit, fire, and dew," to behold him devouring his supper with an ardor which flushed his intellectual countenance. Turning as from a fallen idol, she made other discoveries which rapidly dispelled her romantic illusions. The great novelist vibrated between two decanters with the regularity of a pendulum; the famous divine flirted openly with one of the Madame de Staëls of the age, who looked daggers at another Corinne, who was amiably satirizing her after outmaneuvering her in efforts to absorb the profound philosopher. The scientific celebrities, forgetting their mollusks and glacial periods, gossiped about art while devoting themselves to oysters and ices; the young musician who was charming the city like a second Orpheus talked horses.

Before the evening was half over, Jo felt so completely *désillusionnée* that she sat down in a corner to recover herself. Mr. Bhaer soon joined her, looking rather out of his element, and presently several of the philosophers, each mounted on his hobby, came ambling up to hold an intellectual tournament in the recess. The conversation was miles beyond Jo's comprehension, but she enjoyed it, though Kant and Hegel were unknown gods, the "subjective" and "objective" unintelligible terms, and the only thing "evolved from her inner consciousness" was a bad headache after it was all over. It dawned upon her gradually that the world was being picked to pieces, and put together on new and, according to the talkers, on infinitely better principles than before; that religion was in a fair way to be reasoned into nothingness, and intellect was to be the only God. Jo knew nothing about philosophy or metaphysics of any sort, but a curious excitement, half pleasurable, half painful, came over her as she listened with a sense of being turned adrift into time and space, like a young balloon out on a holiday.

She looked round to see how the Professor liked it, and found him looking at her with the grimmest expression she had ever seen him wear. He shook his head, and beckoned her to come away; but she was fascinated just then by the freedom of speculative philosophy, and kept her seat, trying to find out what the wise gentlemen intended to rely upon after they had annihilated all the old beliefs.

Now Mr. Bhaer was a diffident man, and slow to offer his own opinions —not because they were unsettled, but too sincere and earnest to be lightly spoken. As he glanced from Jo to several other young people attracted by the brilliancy of the philosophic pyrotechnics, he knit his brows, and longed to speak, fearing that some inflammable young soul would be led astray by the rockets, to find when the display was over that they had only an empty stick or a scorched hand.

He bore it as long as he could; but when he was appealed to for an opinion, he blazed up with honest indignation, and defended religion with all the eloquence of truth—an eloquence which made his broken English musical, and his plain face beautiful. He had a hard fight, for the wise men argued well; but he didn't know when he was beaten, and stood to his colors like a man. Somehow, as he talked the world got right again to Jo; the old beliefs seemed better than the new; God was not a blind force, and immortality was not a pretty fable, but a blessed fact.

She felt as if she had solid ground under her feet again, and when Mr. Bhaer paused, outtalked but not one whit convinced, Jo wanted to clap her hands and thank him.

She did neither, but she remembered this scene, and gave the Professor her heartiest respect, for she knew it cost him an effort to speak out then and there because his conscience would not let him be silent. She began to see that character is a better possession than money, rank, intellect, or beauty, and to feel that if greatness is what a wise man has defined it to be, "truth, reverence, and goodwill," then her friend Friedrich Bhaer was not only good, but great. This belief strengthened daily. She valued his esteem, she coveted his respect, she wanted to be worthy of his friendship, and just when the wish was sincerest, she came near losing everything. It all grew out of a cocked hat; for one evening the Professor came in to give Jo her lesson with a paper soldier cap on his head, which Tina had put there and he had forgotten to take off.

"It's evident he doesn't look in his glass before coming down," thought Jo with a smile as he said "Goot efening," and sat soberly down, quite unconscious of the ludicrous contrast between his subject and his headgear, for he was going to read her *The Death of Wallenstein.*"

She said nothing at first, for she liked to hear him laugh out his big hearty laugh when anything funny happened, so she left him to discover it for himself, and presently forgot all about it; for to hear a German read Schiller is rather an absorbing occupation. After the reading came the lesson, which was a lively one, for Jo was in a gay mood that night, and the cocked hat kept her eyes dancing with merriment. The Professor didn't know what to make of her, and stopped at last to ask, with an air of mild surprise that was irresistible:

"Mees Marsch, for what do you laugh in your master's face? Haf you no respect for me, that you go on so bad?"

"How can I be respectful, sir, when you forget to take your hat off?"

Lifting his hand to his head, the absent-minded Professor gravely felt and removed the little cocked hat, looked at it a minute, and then threw back his head and laughed like a merry bass viol.

"Ah! I see him now. It is that imp Tina who makes me a fool with my cap. Well, it is nothing. But see you, if this lesson goes not well, you too shall wear him." But the lesson did not go at all for a few minutes, because Mr. Bhaer caught sight of a picture on the hat, and unfolding it, said with an air of great disgust: "I wish these papers did not come in the house. They are not for children to see, nor young people to read.

It is not well, and I haf no patience with those who make this harm."

Jo glanced at the sheet and saw a pleasing illustration composed of a lunatic, a corpse, a villain, and a viper. She did not like it, but the impulse that made her turn it over was not of displeasure, but fear, because for a minute she fancied the paper was the *Volcano*. It was not, however, and her panic subsided as she remembered that even if it had been, and one of her own tales in it, there would have been no name to betray her. She had betrayed herself, however, by a look and a blush, for though an absent man, the Professor saw a good deal more than people fancied. He knew that Jo wrote, and had met her down among the newspaper offices more than once; but as she never spoke of it, he asked no questions, in spite of a strong desire to see her work. Now it occurred to him that she was doing what she was ashamed to own, and it troubled him. He did not say to himself, "It is none of my business, I've no right to say anything," as many people would have done. He only remembered that she was young and poor, a girl far away from mother's love and father's care; and he was moved to help her with an impulse as quick and natural as that which would prompt him to put out his hand to save a baby from a puddle. All this flashed through his mind in a minute, but not a trace of it appeared in his face, and by the time the paper was turned and Jo's needle threaded, he was ready to say quite naturally, but very gravely:

"Yes, you are right to put it from you. I do not like to think that good young girls should see such things. They are made pleasant to some, but I would more rather give my boys gunpowder to play with than this bad trash."

"All may not be bad, only silly, you know; and if there is a demand for it, I don't see any harm in supplying it. Many very respectable people make an honest living out of what are called sensation stories," said Jo.

"There is a demand for whisky, but I think you and I do not care to sell it. If the respectable people knew what harm they did, they would not feel that the living *was* honest. They haf no right to put poison in the sugarplum and let the small ones eat it. No, they should think a little, and sweep mud in the street before they do this thing."

Mr. Bhaer spoke warmly, and walked to the fire, crumpling the paper in his hands. Jo sat still, looking as if the fire had come to her, for her cheeks burned long after the cocked hat had turned to smoke and gone harmlessly up the chimney.

"I should like much to send all the rest after him," muttered the Professor, coming back with a relieved air.

Jo thought what a blaze her pile of papers upstairs would make, and her hard-earned money lay rather heavily on her conscience at that minute. Then she thought consolingly to herself: "Mine are not like that. They are only silly, never bad, so I won't be worried," and taking up her book, she said: "Shall we go on, sir? I'll be very good and proper now."

"I shall hope so," was all he said, but he meant more than she imagined, and the grave, kind look he gave her made her feel as if the words *Weekly Volcano* were printed in large type on her forehead.

As soon as she went to her room, she got out her papers and carefully reread every one of her stories. Being a little shortsighted, Mr. Bhaer sometimes used eyeglasses, and Jo had tried them once, smiling to see how they magnified the fine print of her book. Now she seemed to have got on the Professor's mental or moral spectacles also, for the faults of these poor stories glared at her dreadfully, and filled her with dismay.

"They *are* trash, and will soon be worse than trash if I go on, for each is more sensational than the last. I've gone blindly on, hurting myself and other people, for the sake of money. I know it's so, for I can't read this stuff in sober earnest without being horribly ashamed of it, and what *should* I do if they were seen at home, or Mr. Bhaer got hold of them?"

Jo turned hot at the bare idea, and stuffed the whole bundle into her stove, nearly setting the chimney afire with the blaze.

"Yes, that's the best place for such inflammable nonsense. I'd better burn the house down, I suppose, than let other people blow themselves up with my gunpowder," she thought as she watched "The Demon of the Jura" whisk away, a little black cinder with fiery eyes. But when nothing remained of all her three months' work except a heap of ashes and the money in her lap, Jo looked sober as she sat on the floor wondering what she ought to do about her wages. "I think I haven't done much harm *yet*, and may keep this to pay for my time," she said, after a long meditation, adding impatiently: "I almost wish I hadn't any conscience, it's so inconvenient. If I didn't care about doing right, and didn't feel uncomfortable when doing wrong, I should get on capitally. I can't help wishing sometimes that Father and Mother hadn't been so particular about such things."

Jo wrote no more sensational stories, deciding that the money did not pay for her share of the sensation; but, going to the other extreme, as is the way with people of her stamp, she took a course of Mrs. Sherwood, Miss Edgeworth, and Hannah More, and then produced a tale which might have been more properly called an essay or a sermon, so intensely moral was it. She had her doubts about it from the beginning; for her lively fancy and girlish romance felt as ill at ease in the new style as she would have done masquerading in the stiff and cumbrous costume of the last century. She sent this didactic gem to several markets, but it found no purchaser, and she was inclined to agree with Mr. Dashwood that morals didn't sell.

Then she tried a child's story, which she could easily have disposed of if she had not been mercenary enough to demand filthy lucre for it. The only person who offered enough to make it worth while to try juvenile literature was a worthy gentleman who felt it his mission to convert all the world to his particular belief. But much as she liked to write for children, Jo could not consent to depict all her naughty boys as being eaten by bears or tossed by mad bulls because they did not go to a particular Sabbath school, nor all the good infants who did go as rewarded by every kind of bliss, from gilded gingerbread to escorts of angels when they departed this life with psalms or sermons on their lisping tongues. So nothing came of these trials, and Jo corked up her inkstand and said, in a fit of very wholesome humility:

"I don't know anything. I'll wait till I do before I try again, and meantime 'sweep mud in the street' if I can't do better; that's honest, at least."

While these internal revolutions were going on, her external life had been as busy and uneventful as usual, and if she sometimes looked serious or a little sad, no one observed it but Professor Bhaer. He did it so quietly that Jo never knew he was watching to see if she would accept and profit by his reproof. But she stood the test, and he was satisfied; for though no words passed between them, he knew that she had given up writing. Not only did he guess it by the fact that the second finger of her right hand was no longer inky, but she spent her evenings downstairs now, was met no more among newspaper offices, and studied with a dogged patience which assured him that she was bent on occupying her mind with something useful, if not pleasant.

He helped her in many ways, proving himself a true friend, and Jo was happy; for while her pen lay idle she was learning other lessons beside German, and laying a foundation for the sensation story of her own life. It was a pleasant winter and a long one, for she did not leave Mrs. Kirke till June. Everyone seemed sorry when the time came; the children were inconsolable, and Mr. Bhaer's hair stuck straight up all over his head, for he always rumpled it wildly when disturbed in mind.

"Going home? Ah, you are happy that you haf a home to go in," he said when she told him, and sat silently pulling his beard in the corner while she held a little levee on that last evening.

She was going early, so she bade them all good-by overnight, and when his turn came, she said warmly:

"Now, sir, you won't forget to come and see us if you ever travel our way, will you? I'll never forgive you if you do, for I want them all to know my friend."

"Do you? Shall I come?" he asked, looking down at her with an eager expression which she did not see.

"Yes, come next month. Laurie graduates then, and you'd enjoy Commencement as something new."

"That is your best friend of whom you speak?"

"Yes, my boy Teddy. I'm very proud of him, and should like you to see him."

Jo looked up then, quite unconscious of anything but her own pleasure in the prospect of showing them to one another. Something in Mr. Bhaer's face suddenly recalled the fact that she might find Laurie more than a "best friend" and, simply because she particularly wished not to look as if anything was the matter, she involuntarily began to blush; and the more she tried not to, the redder she grew. If it had not been for Tina on her knee, she didn't know what would have become of her. Fortunately, the child was moved to hug her, so she managed to hide her face an instant, hoping the Professor did not see it. But he did, and his own changed again from that momentary anxiety to its usual expression as he said cordially:

"I fear I shall not make the time for that, but I wish the friend much success, and you all happiness. Gott bless you!" And with that, he shook hands warmly, shouldered Tina, and went away. But after the boys were abed, he sat long before his fire, with the tired look on his face, and the "Heimweh," or homesickness, lying heavy at his heart. Once, when he remembered Jo as she sat with the little child in her lap and that new softness in her face, he leaned his head on his hands a minute, and then roamed about the room as if in search of something he could not find.

"It is not for me. I must not hope it now," he said to himself, with a sigh that was almost a groan. Then, as if reproaching himself for the longing that he could not repress, he went and kissed the two tousled heads on the pillow, took down his seldom-used meerschaum, and opened his Plato. He did his best, and did it manfully; but I don't think he found that a pair of rampant boys, a pipe, or even the divine Plato, were satisfactory substitutes for wife and child and home.

Early as it was, he was at the station next morning to see Jo off, and thanks to him, she began her solitary journey with the pleasant memory of a familiar face smiling its farewell, a bunch of violets to keep her company, and, best of all, the happy thought: "Well, the winter's gone, and I've written no books, earned no fortune; but I've made a friend worth having and I'll try to keep him all my life."

HEARTACHE

Whatever his motive might have been, Laurie studied to some purpose that year, for he graduated with honor, and gave the Latin oration with the grace of a Phillips and the eloquence of a Demosthenes, so his friends said. They were all there, his grandfather—oh, so proud!—Mr. and Mrs. March, John and Meg, Jo and Beth, and all exulted over him with the sincere admiration which boys make light of at the time, but fail to win from the world by any after-triumphs.

"I've got to stay for this confounded supper, but I shall be home early tomorrow. You'll come and meet me as usual, girls?" Laurie said as he put the sisters into the carriage after the joys of the day were over. He said "girls," but he meant Jo, for she was the only one who kept up the old custom. She had not the heart to refuse her splendid, successful boy anything, and answered warmly:

"I'll come, Teddy, rain or shine, and march before you playing 'Hail the conquering hero comes' on a jew's-harp." Laurie thanked her with a look that made her think, in a sudden panic: "Oh dearie me! I know he'll say something, and then what shall I do?"

Evening meditation and morning work somewhat allayed her fears, and having decided that she wouldn't be vain enough to think people were going to propose when she had given them every reason to know what her answer would be, she set forth at the appointed time. A call at Meg's, and a refreshing sniff and sip at Daisy and Demijohn, still further fortified her for the tête-à-tête, but when she saw a stalwart figure looming in the distance, she had a strong desire to turn about and run away.

"Where's the jew's-harp, Jo?" cried Laurie as soon as he was within speaking distance.

"I forgot it." And Jo took heart again, for that salutation could not be called loverlike.

She always used to take his arm on these occasions; now she did not, and he made no complaint, which was a bad sign, but talked on rapidly about all sorts of faraway subjects till they turned from the road into the little path that led homeward through the grove. Then he walked more slowly, suddenly lost his fine flow of language, and now and then a dreadful pause occurred. To rescue the conversation from one of the wells of silence into which it kept falling, Jo said hastily:

"Now you must have a good long holiday!"

"I intend to."

Something in his resolute tone made Jo look up quickly to find him looking down at her with an expression that assured her the dreaded moment had come, and made her put out her hand with an imploring "No, Teddy, please don't!"

"I will, and you *must* hear me. It's no use, Jo. We've got to have it out, and the sooner the better for both of us," he answered, getting flushed and excited all at once.

"Say what you like then. I'll listen," said Jo, with a desperate sort of patience.

Laurie was a young lover, but he was in earnest, and meant to "have it out" if he died in the attempt; so he plunged into the subject with characteristic impetuosity, saying in a voice that *would* get choky now and then, in spite of manful efforts to keep it steady:

"I've loved you ever since I've known you, Jo—couldn't help it, you've been so good to me. I've tried to show it, but you wouldn't let me. Now I'm going to make you hear, and give me an answer, for I *can't* go on so any longer."

"I wanted to save you this! I thought you'd understand——" began Jo, finding it a great deal harder than she expected.

"I know you did, but girls are so queer you never know what they mean. They say No when they mean Yes, and drive a man out of his wits for the fun of it," returned Laurie.

"I don't. I never wanted to make you care for me so, and I went away to keep you from it if I could."

"I thought so. It was like you, but it was no use. I only loved you all the more, and I worked hard to please you, and I gave up billiards and everything you didn't like, and waited and never complained, for I hoped you'd love me, though I'm not half good enough——" Here there was a choke that couldn't be controlled, so he decapitated buttercups while he cleared his "confounded throat."

"Yes you are. You're a great deal too good for me, and I'm grateful to you, and so proud and fond of you I don't see why I can't love you as you want me to. I've tried, but I can't change the feeling."

"Really, truly, Jo?"

He stopped short, and caught both her hands as he put his question with a look that she did not soon forget.

"Really, truly, dear."

They were in the grove now, close by the stile; and when the last words fell reluctantly from Jo's lips, Laurie dropped her hands and turned as if to go on, but for once in his life that fence was too much for him, so he just laid his head down on the mossy post, and stood so still that Jo was frightened.

"O Teddy, I'm sorry, so desperately sorry I could kill myself if it would do any good! I wish you wouldn't take it so hard. I can't help it, you know it's impossible for people to make themselves love other people if they don't," cried Jo, inelegantly but remorsefully.

"They do sometimes," said a muffled voice from the post.

"I don't believe it's the right sort of love, and I'd rather not try it," was the decided answer.

There was a long pause while a blackbird sang blithely on the willow by the river, and the tall grass rustled in the wind. Presently Jo said very soberly as she sat down on the step of the stile: "Laurie, I want to tell you something."

He started as if he had been shot, threw up his head, and cried out, in a fierce tone:

"*Don't* tell me that, Jo. I can't bear it now!"

"Tell what?" she asked, wondering at his violence.

"That you love that old man."

"What old man?"

"That devilish Professor you were always writing about. If you say you love him, I know I shall do something desperate."

Jo wanted to laugh, but restrained herself, and said warmly: "Don't swear, Teddy! He isn't old, nor anything bad, but good and kind, and the best friend I've got, next to you. Pray don't fly into a passion. I haven't the least idea of loving him, or anybody else."

278

"But you will after a while, and then what will become of me?"

"You'll love someone else too, like a sensible boy, and forget all this trouble."

"I *can't* love anyone else, and I'll never forget you, Jo, never, never!" —with a stamp to emphasize his passionate words.

"What *shall* I do with him?" sighed Jo, finding that emotions were more unmanageable than she expected. "You haven't heard what I wanted to tell you. Sit down and listen."

Seeing a ray of hope in that last speech, Laurie threw himself down on the grass at her feet, leaned his arm on the lower step of the stile, and looked up at her with an expectant face. Now that arrangement was not conducive to calm speech or clear thought on Jo's part; for how *could* she say hard things to her boy while he watched her with eyes full of love and longing, and lashes still wet with the bitter drop or two her hardness of heart had wrung from him? She gently turned his head away.

"I agree with Mother that you and I are not suited to each other, because our quick tempers and strong wills would probably make us very miserable if we were so foolish as to——" Jo paused a little over the last word, but Laurie uttered it with a rapturous expression:

"Marry.—No we shouldn't! If you loved me, Jo, I should be a perfect saint, for you could make me anything you like."

"No, I can't. I've tried it and failed, and I won't risk our happiness by such a serious experiment. We'll be good friends all our lives, but we won't go and do anything rash."

"Yes we will, if we get the chance," muttered Laurie rebelliously.

"Now do be reasonable, and take a sensible view of the case," implored Jo, almost at her wit's end.

"I won't be reasonable. I don't want to take what you call 'a sensible view.' It won't help me, and it only makes you harder. I don't believe you've got any heart."

"I wish I hadn't!"

There was a little quiver in Jo's voice, and thinking it a good omen, Laurie turned round, bringing all his persuasive powers to bear as he said in the wheedlesome tone that had never been so dangerously wheedlesome before:

"Don't disappoint us, dear! Everyone expects it. Grandpa has set his heart upon it, your people like it, and I can't get on without you. Say you will, and let's be happy. Do, do!"

Not until months afterward did Jo understand how she had the strength of mind to hold fast to the resolution she had made when she decided that she did not love her boy, and never could. It was very hard to do, but she did it, knowing that delay was both useless and cruel.

"I can't say Yes truly, so I won't say it at all. You'll see that I'm right, by and by, and thank me for it."

"I'll be hanged if I do!" And Laurie bounced up off the grass, burning with indignation at the bare idea.

"Yes you will!" persisted Jo. "You'll get over this after a while, and find some lovely, accomplished girl who will adore you, and make a fine mistress for your fine house. I shouldn't. I'm homely and awkward and odd and old, and you'd be ashamed of me, and we should quarrel—we can't help it even now, you see—and I shouldn't like elegant society and you would, and you'd hate my scribbling and I couldn't get on without it, and we should be unhappy, and wish we hadn't done it, and everything would be horrid!"

"Anything more?" asked Laurie.

"Nothing more, except that I don't believe I shall ever marry. I'm happy as I am, and love my liberty too well to be in any hurry to give it up for any mortal man."

"I know better!" broke in Laurie. "You think so now, but there'll come a time when you *will* care for somebody, and you'll love him tremendously, and live and die for him. I know you will, it's your way, and I shall have to stand by and see it."

"Yes, I *will* live and die for him, if he ever comes and makes me love him in spite of myself, and you must do the best you can!" cried Jo, losing patience with poor Teddy. "I've done my best, but you *won't* be reasonable. I shall always be fond of you, very fond indeed, as a friend, but I'll never marry you, and the sooner you believe it the better for both of us—so now!"

Laurie looked at her a minute as if he did not quite know what to do with himself, then turned sharply away, saying in a desperate sort of tone, "You'll be sorry someday, Jo."

"Oh, where are you going?" she cried, for his face frightened her.

"To the devil!" was the consoling answer.

For a minute Jo's heart stood still as he swung himself down the bank toward the river; but it takes much folly, sin, or misery to send a young man to a violent death, and Laurie was not one of the weak sort who are conquered by a single failure. Some blind instinct led him to fling hat and coat into his boat and row away with all his might. Jo drew a long

breath and unclasped her hands as she watched the poor fellow trying to outstrip the trouble which he carried in his heart.

"That will do him good, and he'll come home in such a tender, penitent state of mind that I shan't dare to see him," she said, adding as she went slowly home feeling as if she had murdered some innocent thing and buried it under the leaves: "Now I must go and prepare Mr. Laurence to be very kind to my poor boy. Oh dear! How can girls like to have lovers and refuse them? I think it's dreadful."

Being sure that no one could do it so well as herself, she went straight to Mr. Laurence, told the hard story bravely through, and then broke down, crying so dismally over her own insensibility that the kind old gentleman, though sorely disappointed, did not utter a reproach. He shook his head sadly, and resolved to carry his boy out of harm's way; for Young Impetuosity's parting words to Jo disturbed him more than he would confess.

When Laurie came home, dead-tired but quite composed, his grandfather met him as if he knew nothing, and kept up the delusion very successfully for an hour or two. But when they sat together in the twilight, the time they used to enjoy so much, it was hard work for the old man to ramble on as usual, and harder still for the young one to listen to praises of the last year's success, which to him now seemed love's labor lost. He bore it as long as he could, then went to his piano and began to play. The windows were open, and Jo for once understood music better than her sister, for he played the "Sonata Pathétique," and played it as he never did before.

"That's very fine, I dare say, but it's sad enough to make one cry. Give us something gayer, lad," said Mr. Laurence, whose kind old heart was full of sympathy.

Laurie dashed into a livelier strain, and would have got through bravely if, in a momentary lull, Mrs. March's voice had not been heard calling: "Jo, dear, come in. I want you."

Just what Laurie longed to say, with a different meaning! As he listened, he lost his place, the music ended with a broken chord, and the musician sat silent in the dark.

"I can't stand this," muttered the old gentleman. Up he got, groped his way to the piano, laid a kind hand on either of the broad shoulders, and said, as gently as a woman, "I know, my boy, I know."

Laurie asked sharply, "Who told you?"

"Jo herself."

"Then there's an end of it!" And he shook off his grandfather's hands with an impatient motion.

"Not quite. I want to say one thing, and then there shall be an end of it," returned Mr. Laurence, with unusual mildness. "You won't care to stay at home just now, perhaps?"

"I don't intend to run away from a girl. Jo can't prevent my seeing her, and I shall stay and do it as long as I like."

"Not if you are the gentleman I think you. I'm disappointed, but the girl can't help it, and the only thing left for you to do is to go away for a time. Where will you go?"

"Anywhere. I don't care what becomes of me."

"Take it like a man, and don't do anything rash, for God's sake. Why not go abroad, as you planned, and forget it?"

"I can't."

"But you've been wild to go, and I promised you should when you got through college."

"Ah, but I didn't mean to go alone!" And Laurie walked fast through the room, with an expression which it was well his grandfather did not see.

"I don't ask you to go alone. There's someone ready and glad to go with you—anywhere in the world."

"Who, sir?" stopping to listen.

"Myself."

Laurie came back as quickly as he went: "I'm a selfish brute, but—you know—Grandfather——"

"Lord help me, yes, I do know, for I've been through it all before, once in my own young days, and then with your father. Now, my dear boy, just sit quietly down and hear my plan. It's all settled, and can be carried out at once."

"Well, sir, what is it?" And Laurie sat down without a sign of interest in face or voice.

"There is business in London that needs looking after. I meant you should attend to it, but I can do it better myself, and things here will get on very well with Brooke to manage them."

"But you hate traveling, sir. I can't ask it of you at your age," began Laurie.

The old gentleman, stifling a natural regret at the thought of the home comforts he would leave behind him, said stoutly: "Bless your soul, I'm not superannuated yet. I quite enjoy the idea. It will do me good, and my old bones won't suffer, for traveling nowadays is almost as easy as sitting in a chair. I don't mean to be a marplot or a burden. I don't intend to gad about with you, but leave you free to go where you like while I amuse myself in my own way. I've friends in London and Paris, and should like to visit them; meantime you can go to Italy, Germany, Switzerland, where you will, and enjoy pictures, music, scenery, and adventures to your heart's content."

Now Laurie felt just then that his heart was entirely broken, and the world a howling wilderness; but at the sound of certain words which the old gentleman artfully introduced into his closing sentence, the broken heart gave an unexpected leap, and a green oasis or two suddenly appeared in the howling wilderness. He sighed, and said in a spiritless tone:

"Just as you like, sir. It doesn't matter where I go or what I do."

"It does to me, remember that, my lad. I give you entire liberty, but I trust you to make an honest use of it. Promise me that, Laurie."

"Anything you like, sir."

"Good," thought the old gentleman. "You don't care now, but there'll come a time when that promise will keep you out of mischief, or I'm much mistaken."

Being an energetic individual, Mr. Laurence struck while the iron was hot, and before the blighted being recovered spirit enough to rebel, they were off.

When the parting came he affected high spirits, to conceal certain inconvenient emotions. This gaiety did not impose upon anybody, but they tried to look as if it did, for his sake, and he got on very well till Mrs. March kissed him, with a whisper full of motherly solicitude; then, feeling that he was going very fast, he hastily embraced them all around and ran downstairs as if for his life. Jo followed a minute after to wave her hand to him if he looked round. He did look round, came back, put his arms about her as she stood on the step above him, and looked up at her with a face that made his short appeal both eloquent and pathetic.

"O Jo, can't you?"

"Teddy dear, I wish I could!"

That was all, except a little pause; then Laurie straightened himself up, said, "It's all right, never mind," and went away without another word. Ah, but it wasn't all right, and Jo *did* mind; for while the curly head lay on her arm a minute after her hard answer, she felt as if she had stabbed her dearest friend, and when he left her without a look behind him, she knew that the boy Laurie never would come again.

BETH'S SECRET

When Jo came home that spring, she had been struck with the change in Beth. No one spoke of it or seemed aware of it, for it had come too gradually to startle those who saw her daily; but to eyes sharpened by absence it was very plain, and a heavy weight fell on Jo's heart as she saw her sister's face. It was no paler and but little thinner than in the autumn; yet there was a strange, transparent look about it, as if the mortal was being slowly refined away and the immortal shining through the frail flesh with an indescribably pathetic beauty. Soon the first impression lost much of its power, for Beth seemed happy, and presently, in other cares, Jo for a time forgot her fear.

But when Laurie was gone, and peace prevailed again, the vague anxiety returned and haunted her. When she showed her savings and proposed the mountain trip, Beth had thanked her heartily, but begged not to go so far away from home. Another little visit to the seashore would suit her better, and as Grandma could not be prevailed upon to leave the babies, Jo took Beth down to the quiet place.

It was not a fashionable place, but even among the pleasant people there the girls made few friends, preferring to live for one another. Beth was too shy to enjoy society, and Jo too wrapped up in her to care for anyone else; so they were all in all to each other.

Jo felt as if a veil had fallen between her heart and Beth's, but when she put out her hand to lift it up, there seemed something sacred in the silence, and she waited for Beth to speak. She wondered, and was thankful also, that her parents did not seem to see what she saw. She wondered still more if her sister really guessed the hard truth, and what thoughts were passing through her mind during the long hours when she lay on the warm rocks with her head in Jo's lap while the winds blew healthfully over her, and the sea made music at her feet.

One day Beth told her. Jo thought she was asleep, she lay so still, and sat looking at her with wistful eyes, trying to see signs of hope in the faint color on Beth's cheeks. But she could not find enough to satisfy her, for the cheeks were very thin, and the hands seemed too feeble to hold even the rosy little shells they had been gathering. It came to her then more bitterly than ever that Beth was slowly drifting away from her, and her arms instinctively tightened their hold upon the dearest treasure she possessed. For a minute her eyes were too dim for seeing, and when they cleared, Beth was looking up at her so tenderly that there was hardly any need for her to say: "Jo, dear, I'm glad you know it. I've tried to tell you, but I couldn't."

There was no answer except her sister's cheek against her own, not even tears, for when most deeply moved, Jo did not cry. She was the weaker then, and Beth tried to comfort and sustain her with her arms about her and the soothing words she whispered in her ear.

"I've known it for a good while, dear, and, now I'm used to it, it isn't hard to think of or to bear. Try to see it so, and don't be troubled about me, because it's best, indeed it is."

"Is this what made you so unhappy in the autumn, Beth?" asked Jo.

"Yes, I gave up hoping then, but I didn't like to own it. I tried to think it was a sick fancy. But when I saw you all so well and strong, and full of happy plans, it was hard to feel that I could never be like you, and then I was miserable, Jo."

"O Beth, and you didn't tell me, didn't let me comfort and help you! How could you shut me out, and bear it all alone?" Jo's voice was full of tender reproach.

"Perhaps it was wrong, but I tried to do right. I wasn't sure, no one said anything, and I hoped I was mistaken. It would have been selfish to frighten you all when Marmee was so anxious about Meg, and Amy away, and you so happy with Laurie—at least, I thought so then."

"And I thought that you loved him, Beth, and I went away because I couldn't," cried Jo, glad to say all the truth.

Beth looked so amazed at the idea that Jo smiled in spite of her pain, and added softly: "Then you didn't, dearie?"

"Why, Jo, how could I when he was so fond of you?" asked Beth, as innocently as a child. "I do love him dearly, but he never could be anything to me but my brother. I hope he truly will be, sometime."

"Not through me," said Jo decidedly. "Amy is left for him, and they would suit excellently, but I have no heart for such things now. I don't care what becomes of anybody but you, Beth. You *must* get well."

"I want to, oh, so much! I try, but every day I lose a little, and feel more sure that I shall never gain it back. It's like the tide, Jo—when it turns it goes slowly, but it can't be stopped."

"It *shall* be stopped. Your tide must not turn so soon, nineteen is too young. Beth, I can't let you go. I'll work and pray and fight against it. God won't be so cruel as to take you from me," cried poor Jo rebelliously.

Beth did not rebuke Jo with saintly speeches, only loved her better for her passionate affection. She could not say "I'm glad to go," for life was very sweet to her; she could only sob out "I try to be willing" while she held fast to Jo.

By and by Beth said, with recovered serenity, "You'll tell them this when we go home?"

"I think they will see it without words," sighed Jo.

"Perhaps not. I've heard that the people who love best are often blindest to such things. If they don't see it, you will tell them for me. I don't want any secrets, and it's kinder to prepare them. Meg has John and the babies to comfort her, but you must stand by Father and Mother, won't you, Jo?"

"If I can, but, Beth, I don't give up yet. I'm going to believe that it *is* a sick fancy, and not let you think it's true," said Jo, trying to speak cheerfully.

Beth lay a minute thinking, and then said in her quiet way:

"I don't know how to express myself, and shouldn't try to anyone but you, because I can't speak out except to my Jo. I only mean to say that I have a feeling that it never was intended I should live long. I'm not like the rest of you. I never made any plans about what I'd do when I grew up; I never thought of being married, as you all did. I never wanted to go away, and the hard part now is the leaving you all. I'm not afraid, but it seems as if I should be homesick for you even in Heaven."

Jo could not speak, and for several minutes there was no sound but the sigh of the wind and the lapping of the tide. A white-winged gull flew by. A little gray-coated sand bird came tripping over the beach, "peeping" softly to itself, as if enjoying the sun and sea; it came quite close to Beth, looked at her with a friendly eye, and sat upon a warm stone dressing its wet feathers, quite at home. Beth smiled, and felt comforted, for the tiny thing seemed to offer its small friendship and remind her that a pleasant world was still to be enjoyed.

"Dear little bird! See, Jo, how tame it is. I like peeps better than the gulls. They are not so wild and handsome, but they seem happy, confiding little things. I used to call them my birds last summer, and mother said they reminded her of me—busy, quaker-colored creatures, always near the shore, and always chirping that contented little song of theirs. You are the gull, Jo, strong and wild, fond of the storm and the wind, flying far out to sea, and happy all alone. Meg is the turtledove, and Amy is like the lark she writes about, trying to get up among the clouds, but always dropping down into its nest again. Dear little girl! She's so ambitious, but her heart is good and tender, and no matter how high she flies, she never will forget home. I hope I shall see her again."

"She is coming in the spring, and I'm going to have you well and rosy by that time," began Jo, feeling that of all the changes in Beth, the talking change was the greatest, for she thought aloud in a way quite unlike bashful Beth.

"Jo, dear, don't hope any more. It won't do any good, I'm sure of that. We won't be miserable, but enjoy being together while we wait. We'll have happy times, for I don't suffer much, and I think the tide will go out easily, if you help me."

Jo leaned down to kiss the tranquil face, and with that silent kiss she dedicated herself soul and body to Beth.

She was right. There was no need of any words when they got home, for Father and Mother saw plainly now what they had prayed to be saved from seeing. Tired with her short journey, Beth went at once to bed, saying how glad she was to be at home; and when Jo went down, she found that she would be spared the hard task of telling Beth's secret. Her father stood leaning his head on the mantelpiece and did not turn as she came in, but her mother stretched out her arms as if for help, and Jo went to comfort her without a word.

NEW IMPRESSIONS

At three o'clock in the afternoon, all the fashionable world at Nice may be seen on the Promenade des Anglais—a charming place; for the wide walk, bordered with palms, flowers, and tropical shrubs, is bounded on one side by the sea, on the other by the grand drive lined with hotels and villas, while beyond lie orange orchards and the hills. Many nations are represented, many languages spoken, many costumes worn, and on a sunny day the spectacle is as gay and brilliant as a carnival. Haughty English, lively French, sober Germans, handsome Spaniards, meek Jews, free-and-easy Americans, all drive, sit, or saunter here, chatting over the news, and criticizing the latest celebrity who has arrived—Ristori or Dickens, Victor Emmanuel or the Queen of the Sandwich Islands. The equipages are as varied as the company, and attract as much attention.

Along this walk, on Christmas Day a tall young man walked slowly, with his hands behind him and a somewhat absent expression of countenance. He looked like an Italian, was dressed like an Englishman, and had the independent air of an American—a combination which caused sundry pairs of feminine eyes to look approvingly after him, and sundry dandies in black-velvet suits, with rose-colored neckties, buff gloves, and orange flowers in their buttonholes, to shrug their shoulders, and then envy him his inches. There were plenty of pretty faces to admire, but the young man took little notice of them. The quick trot of ponies' feet made him look up as one of the little carriages, containing a single lady, came rapidly down the street. The lady was young, blonde, and dressed in blue. He stared a minute, then his whole face woke up, and waving his hat like a boy, he hurried forward to meet her.

"O Laurie, is it really you? I thought you'd never come!" cried Amy, dropping the reins and holding out both hands.

"I was detained by the way, but I promised to spend Christmas with you, and here I am."

"How is your grandfather? When did you come? Where are you staying?"

"Very well—last night—at the Chauvain. I called at your hotel, but you were all out."

"I have so much to say I don't know where to begin! Get in, and we can talk at our ease. I was going for a drive, and longing for company. Flo's saving up for tonight."

"What happens then, a ball?"

"A Christmas party at our hotel. There are many Americans there, and they give it in honor of the day. You'll go with us, of course?"

"Thank you. Where now?" asked Laurie, leaning back and folding his arms, a proceeding which suited Amy, who preferred to drive.

"I'm going to the banker's first, for letters, and then to Castle Hill. The view is so lovely, and I like to feed the peacocks. Have you ever been there?"

"Often, years ago, but I don't mind having a look at it."

"Now tell me all about yourself. The last I heard of you your grandfather wrote that he expected you from Berlin."

"Yes, I spent a month there, and then joined him in Paris, where he

288

has settled for the winter. He has friends there, and finds plenty to amuse him, so I go and come and we get on capitally."

"That's a sociable arrangement," said Amy.

"Why, you see he hates to travel, and I hate to keep still, so we each suit ourselves and there is no trouble. I am often with him, and he enjoys my adventures, while I like to feel that someone is glad to see me when I get back from my wanderings."

Amy watched him, and felt a new sort of shyness steal over her; for he was changed, and she could not find the merry-faced boy she left in the moody-looking man beside her. He was handsomer than ever, and greatly improved, she thought; but now that the flush of pleasure at meeting her was over, he looked tired and spiritless—not sick, nor exactly unhappy, but older and graver than a year or two of prosperous life should have made him.

"*Que pensez-vous?*" she said, airing her French, which had improved in quantity, if not in quality, since she came abroad.

"That mademoiselle has made good use of her time, and the result is charming," replied Laurie, bowing with his hand on his heart, and an admiring look.

She blushed with pleasure, but somehow the compliment did not satisfy her like the blunt praises he used to give her at home, when he promenaded round her on festival occasions and told her she was "altogether jolly."

"If that's the way he's going to grow up, I wish he'd stay a boy," she thought.

At Avigdor's she found the precious home letters and, giving the reins to Laurie, read them luxuriously as they wound up the shady road between green hedges where tea roses bloomed as freshly as in June.

"Beth is very poorly, Mother says. I often think I ought to go home, but they all say 'stay,' so I do, for I shall never have another chance like this," said Amy, looking sober over one page.

"I think you are right there. You could do nothing at home, and it is a great comfort to them to know that you are well and happy, and enjoying so much, my dear."

He drew a little nearer and looked more like his old self as he said that, and the fear that sometimes weighed on Amy's heart was lightened, for the look, the act, the brotherly "my dear," seemed to assure her that if any trouble did come, she would not be alone in a strange land. Presently she laughed, and showed him a small sketch of Jo in her scribbling suit, with the bow rampantly erect upon her cap, and issuing from her mouth the words "Genius burns!" Laurie smiled, took it, put it in his vest pocket, "To keep it from blowing away."

"This will be a regularly merry Christmas to me, with presents in the morning, you and letters in the afternoon, and a party at night," said Amy as they alighted among the ruins of the old fort, and a flock of splendid peacocks came trooping about them, tamely waiting to be fed. While Amy stood laughing on the bank above him as she scattered crumbs to the brilliant birds, Laurie looked at her as she had looked at him, with a natural curiosity to see what changes time and absence had wrought. He found nothing to perplex or disappoint, much to admire and approve; for she was as sprightly and graceful as ever, with the addition of that indescribable something in dress and bearing which we call elegance. Always mature for her age, she had gained a certain aplomb in both carriage and conversation which made her seem more of a woman of the world than she was; but her old petulance now and then showed itself, her strong will still held its own, and her native frankness was unspoiled by foreign polish.

Laurie did not read all this while he watched her feed the peacocks, but he saw enough to satisfy and interest him, and carried away a pretty little picture of a bright-faced girl standing in the sunshine, which brought out the soft hue of her dress, the fresh color of her cheeks, the golden gloss of her hair.

As they came up onto the stone plateau that crowns the hill, Amy waved her hand as if welcoming him to her favorite haunt, and said, pointing here and there: "Do you remember the Cathedral and the Corso, and the lovely road to Villa Franca, Schubert's Tower, just below, and, best of all, that speck far out to sea which they say is Corsica?"

"I remember. It's not much changed," he answered without enthusiasm.

"What Jo would give for a sight of that famous speck!" said Amy.

"Yes," was all he said, but he turned and strained his eyes to see the island.

"Take a good look at it for her sake, and then come and tell me what you have been doing with yourself all this while," said Amy, seating herself, ready for a good talk.

But she did not get it, for though he joined her, and answered all her questions freely, she could only learn that he had roved about the Continent and been to Greece. So after idling away an hour they drove home again, and having paid his respects to Mrs. Carrol, Laurie left them, promising to return in the evening.

It must be recorded of Amy that she deliberately "prinked" that night. She had seen her old friend in a new light, not as "our boy," but as a handsome and agreeable man, and she was conscious of a very natural desire to find favor in his sight. Amy knew her good points, and made the most of them, with the taste and skill which is a fortune to a poor and pretty woman. Tarlatan and tulle were cheap at Nice, so she enveloped herself in them on such occasions and, following the sensible English fashion of simple dress for young girls, got up charming little toilets with fresh flowers, a few trinkets, and all manner of dainty devices which were both inexpensive and effective.

"I do want him to think I look well, and tell them so at home," said Amy to herself as she put on Flo's old white-silk ball dress, and covered it with a cloud of fresh illusion, out of which her white shoulders and golden head emerged with a most artistic effect. Her hair she had the sense to let alone, after gathering up the thick waves and curls into a

Hebelike knot at the back of her head. Having no ornaments fine enough for this important occasion, Amy looped her fleecy skirts with rosy clusters of azalea, and framed the white shoulders in delicate green vines. Remembering the painted boots, she surveyed her white satin slippers with girlish satisfaction, and chasséd down the room admiring her aristocratic feet all by herself.

"My new fan just matches my flowers, my gloves fit to a charm, and the real lace on aunt's *mouchoir* gives an air to my whole dress. If I only had a classical nose and mouth I should be perfectly happy," she said, surveying herself with a critical eye, and a candle in each hand.

In spite of this affliction, she looked unusually gay and graceful as she glided away. She seldom ran—it did not suit her style, she thought, for, being tall, the stately and Junoesque was more appropriate than the sportive or piquant. She walked up and down the long saloon while waiting for Laurie, and once arranged herself under the chandelier, which had a good effect upon her hair; then she thought better of it, and went away to the other end of the room, as if ashamed of the girlish desire to have the first view a propitious one. It so happened that she could not have done a better thing, for Laurie came in so quietly she did not hear him, and as she stood at the distant window with her head half turned and one hand gathering up her dress, the slender white figure against the red curtains was as effective as a well-placed statue.

"Good evening, Diana!" said Laurie, with the look of satisfaction she liked to see in his eyes when they rested on her.

"Good evening, Apollo!" she answered, smiling back at him, for he too looked unusually debonair.

"Here are your flowers. I arranged them myself, remembering that you didn't like what Hannah calls a 'sot bookay,'" said Laurie, handing her a delicate nosegay in a holder that she had long coveted as she daily passed it in Cardiglia's window.

"How kind you are!" she exclaimed gratefully. "If I'd known you were coming I'd have had something ready for you today, though not as pretty as this, I'm afraid."

"Thank you. It isn't what it should be, but you have improved it," he added as she snapped the silver bracelet on her wrist.

"Please don't."

"I thought you liked that sort of thing?"

"Not from you. It doesn't sound natural and I like your old bluntness better."

"I'm glad of it," he answered, with a look of relief, then buttoned her gloves for her, and asked if his tie was straight just as he used to do when they went to parties together at home.

The company assembled in the long salle à manger that evening was such as one sees nowhere but on the Continent. The hospitable Americans had invited every acquaintance they had in Nice, and having no prejudice against titles, secured a few to add luster to their Christmas ball.

A Russian prince condescended to sit in a corner for an hour and talk with a massive lady dressed like Hamlet's mother in black velvet, with a pearl bridle under her chin. A Polish count, aged eighteen, devoted himself to the ladies, who pronounced him "a fascinating dear," and a German Serene Something, having come for the supper alone, roamed vaguely about seeking what he might devour. Of course there were many light-footed and shrill-voiced American girls, handsome, lifeless-looking English ditto, and a few plain but piquant French demoiselles; likewise the usual set of traveling young gentlemen, who disported themselves gaily while mammas of all nations lined the walls, and smiled upon them benignly when they danced with their daughters.

Any young girl can imagine Amy's state of mind when she "took the stage" that night leaning on Laurie's arm. She knew she looked well, she loved to dance, she felt that her foot was on her native heath in a ballroom, and enjoyed the delightful sense of power which comes when young girls first discover the new and lovely kingdom they are born to rule by virtue of beauty, youth, and womanhood. With the first burst of the band, Amy's color rose, her eyes began to sparkle, and her feet to tap the floor impatiently; for she danced well, and wanted Laurie to know it. Therefore the shock she received can better be imagined than described when he said, in a perfectly tranquil tone: "Do you care to dance?"

"One usually does at a ball." Her amazed look and quick answer caused Laurie to repair his error as fast as possible. "I meant the first dance. May I have the honor?"

"I can give you one if I put off the Count. He dances divinely, but he will excuse me, as you are an old friend," said Amy, hoping that the name would show Laurie that she was not to be trifled with.

"Nice little boy, but rather a short Pole to support

> "'A daughter of the gods,
>   Divinely tall and most divinely fair,'"

was all the satisfaction she got, however.

The set in which they found themselves was composed of English, and Amy was compelled to walk decorously through a cotillion feeling all the while as if she could dance the tarantella with a relish. Laurie resigned her to the "nice little boy," and went to do his duty to Flo without securing Amy for the joys to come, which reprehensible want of forethought was properly punished, for she immediately engaged herself till supper, meaning to relent if he then gave any signs of penitence. She showed him her ball book with demure satisfaction when he strolled, instead of rushing, up to claim her for the next, a glorious polka redowa; but his polite regrets didn't impose upon her, and when she gallopaded away with the Count, she saw Laurie sit down by her aunt with an actual expression of relief.

That was unpardonable, and Amy took no more notice of him for a long while except a word now and then when she came to her chaperon between the dances for a necessary pin or a moment's rest. Her anger had a good effect, however, for she hid it under a smiling face, and seemed unusually blithe and brilliant. Laurie's eyes followed her with pleasure, for she neither romped nor sauntered, but danced with spirit and grace, making the delightsome pastime what it should be. He very naturally fell to studying her from this new point of view, and before the evening was half over had decided that "little Amy" was going "to make a very charming woman."

It was a lively scene, for soon the spirit of the social season took possession of everyone, and Christmas merriment made all faces shine, hearts happy, and heels light. The musicians fiddled, tooted, and banged as if they enjoyed it; everybody danced who could, and those who couldn't admired their neighbors with uncommon warmth.

Amy and her Pole distinguished themselves by graceful agility, and Laurie found himself involuntarily keeping time to the rhythmic rise and fall of the white slippers as they flew by as indefatigably as if winged. When little Vladimir finally relinquished her, with assurances that he was "desolated to leave so early," she was ready to rest and see how her recreant knight had borne his punishment.

It had been successful. Laurie had a waked-up look as he rose to give her his seat, and when he hurried away to bring her some supper, she said to herself, with a satisfied smile: "Ah, I thought that would do him good!"

"What do you call this stuff?" he asked, touching a fold of her dress that had blown over his knee.

"Illusion."

"Good name for it. It's very pretty—new thing, isn't it?"

"It's as old as the hills. You have seen it on dozens of girls, and you never found out that it was pretty till now—*stupid!*"

"I never saw it on you before, which accounts for the mistake, you see."

"None of that, it is forbidden. I'd rather take coffee than compliments just now. No, don't lounge, it makes me nervous."

Laurie sat bolt upright, and meekly took her empty plate, feeling an odd sort of pleasure in having "little Amy" order him about.

"Where did you learn all this sort of thing?" he asked.

"As 'this sort of thing' is rather a vague expression, would you kindly explain?" returned Amy, knowing perfectly well what he meant.

"Well—the general air, the style, the self-possession, the—the—illusion—you know," laughed Laurie, helping himself out of his quandary with the new word.

Amy was gratified, but of course didn't show it, and demurely answered: "Foreign life polishes one in spite of oneself. I study as well as play, and as for this"—with a little gesture toward her dress—"why, tulle is cheap, posies to be had for nothing, and I am used to making the most of my poor little things."

Amy rather regretted that last sentence, fearing it wasn't in good taste; but Laurie liked her the better for it, and found himself both admiring and respecting the brave patience that made the most of opportunity, and the cheerful spirit that covered poverty with flowers. He filled up her book with his own name and devoted himself to her for the rest of the evening in the most delightful manner. The impulse that wrought this agreeable change was the result of one of the new impressions which both of them were unconsciously giving and receiving.

ON THE SHELF

In France the young girls have a dull time of it till they are married, when "*Vive la liberté*" becomes their motto. In America, as everyone knows, girls early sign the declaration of independence, and enjoy their freedom with republican zest; but the young matrons usually abdicate with the first heir to the throne, and go into a seclusion almost as close as a French nunnery, though by no means as quiet. Whether they like it or not, they are virtually put upon the shelf as soon as the wedding excitement is over. Not being a belle or even a fashionable lady, Meg did not experience this affliction till her babies were a year old, for in her little world primitive customs prevailed, and she found herself more admired and beloved than ever.

As she was a womanly little woman, the maternal instinct was very strong, and she was entirely absorbed in her children, to the utter exclusion of everything and everybody else. Day and night she brooded over them with tireless devotion and anxiety, leaving John to the tender mercies of the help, for an Irish lady now presided over the kitchen department. Being a domestic man, John decidedly missed the wifely attentions he had been accustomed to receive; but as he adored his babies, he cheerfully relinquished his comfort for a time, supposing, with masculine ignorance, that peace would soon be restored. But three months passed, and there was no return of repose. Meg looked worn and nervous, the babies absorbed every minute of her time, the house was neglected, and Kitty, the cook, who took life "aisy," kept him on short commons. When he went out in the morning he was bewildered by small commissions for the captive mamma; if he came gaily in at night, eager to embrace his family, he was quenched by a "Hush! They are just asleep after worrying all day." If he proposed a little amusement at home, "No, it would disturb the babies." If he hinted at a lecture or concert, he was answered with a reproachful look and a decided "Leave my children for pleasure—never!" His sleep was broken by infant wails and visions of a phantom figure pacing noiselessly to and fro in the watches of the night; his meals were interrupted by the frequent flight of the presiding genius, who deserted him half helped if a muffled chirp sounded from the nest above.

He bore it very patiently for six months, and when no signs of amendment appeared, he did what other paternal exiles do—tried to get a little comfort elsewhere. Scott had married and gone to housekeeping not far off, and John fell into the way of running over for an hour or two of an evening when his own parlor was empty, and his own wife singing lullabies that seemed to have no end. Mrs. Scott was a lively, pretty girl with nothing to do but be agreeable, and she performed her mission most successfully. The parlor was always bright and attractive, the chessboard ready, the piano in tune, plenty of gay gossip, and a nice little supper set forth in tempting style.

John would have preferred his own fireside if it had not been so lonely, but as it was, he gratefully took the next best thing, and enjoyed his neighbor's society. Meg rather approved of the new arrangement at first, and found it a relief to know that John was having a good time instead of dozing in the parlor, or tramping about the house and waking the children. But by and by, when the teething worry was over, and the idols went to sleep at proper hours, leaving Mamma time to rest, she began to miss John, and find her workbasket dull company when he was not sitting opposite in his old dressing gown, comfortably scorching his slippers on the fender. She would not ask him to stay at home, but felt injured because he did not know that she wanted him without being told, entirely forgetting the many evenings he had waited for her in vain. She was nervous and worn-out with watching and worry, and in that unreasonable frame of mind which the best of mothers occasionally experience when domestic cares oppress them.

"Yes," she would say, looking in the glass, "I'm getting old and ugly. John doesn't find me interesting any longer, so he leaves his faded wife and goes to see his pretty neighbor, who has no incumbrances. Well, the babies love me. They don't care if I am thin and pale, and haven't time to crimp my hair; they are my comfort, and someday John will see what I've gladly sacrificed for them, won't he, my precious?"

To which pathetic appeal Daisy would answer with a coo, or Demi with a crow, and Meg would put by her lamentations for a maternal revel which soothed her solitude for the time being. But the pain increased as politics absorbed John, who was always running over to discuss interesting points with Scott, quite unconscious that Meg missed him. Not a word did she say, however, till her mother found her in tears one day and insisted on knowing what the matter was.

"I wouldn't tell anyone except you, Mother, but I really do need advice, for if John goes on so much longer I might as well be widowed."

"Goes on how, my dear?" asked her mother anxiously.

"He's away all day, and at night, when I want to see him, he is continually going over to the Scotts'. It isn't fair that I should have the hardest work, and never any amusement. Men are very selfish, even the best of them."

"So are women. Don't blame John till you see where you are wrong yourself."

"But it can't be right for him to neglect me."

"Don't you neglect him?"

"Why, Mother, I thought you'd take my part!"

"So I do, as far as sympathizing goes, but I think the fault is yours, Meg."

"I don't see how."

"Let me show you. Did John ever neglect you, as you call it, while you made it a point to give him your society of an evening, his only leisure time?"

"No, but I can't do it now, with two babies to tend."

"I think you could, dear, and I think you ought. May I speak quite freely, and will you remember that it's Mother who blames as well as Mother who sympathizes?"

"Indeed I will! Speak to me as if I were little Meg again. I often feel as if I needed teaching more than ever since these babies look to me for everything."

Meg drew her low chair beside her mother's and, with a little interruption in either lap, the two women rocked and talked lovingly together.

"You have only made the mistake that most young wives make—forgotten your duty to your husband in your love for your children. A very natural and forgivable mistake, Meg, but one that had better be remedied before you take to different ways; for children should draw you nearer than ever, not separate you, as if they were all yours and John had nothing to do but support them. I've seen it for some weeks, but have not spoken, feeling sure it would come right in time."

"I'm afraid it won't. If I ask him to stay, he'll think I'm jealous, and I wouldn't insult him by such an idea. He doesn't see that I want him, and I don't know how to tell him without words."

"Make it so pleasant he won't want to go away. My dear, he's longing for his little home but it isn't home without you, and you are always in the nursery."

"Oughtn't I to be there?"

"Not all the time. Too much confinement makes you nervous, and then you are unfitted for everything. Besides, you owe something to John as well as to the babies. Don't neglect husband for children, don't shut him out of the nursery, but teach him how to help in it. His place is there as well as yours, and the children need him. Let him feel that he has his part to do and he will do it gladly and faithfully, and it will be better for you all."

"You really think so, Mother?"

"I know it, Meg, for I've tried it, and I seldom give advice unless I've proved its practicability. When you and Jo were little I went on just as you are, feeling as if I didn't do my duty unless I devoted myself wholly to you. Poor Father took to his books after I had refused all offers of help, and left me to try my experiment alone. I struggled along as well as I could, but Jo was too much for me. I nearly spoiled her by indulgence. Then Father came to the rescue, quietly managed everything, and made himself so helpful that I saw my mistake, and never have been able to get on without him since. That is the secret of our home happiness. We each do our part alone in many things, but at home we work together, always."

"It is so, Mother, and my great wish is to be to my husband and children what you have been to yours. Show me how. I'll do anything you say."

"You always were my docile daughter. Well, dear, if I were you, I'd let

John have more to do with management of Demi, for the boy needs training, and it's none too soon to begin. Then I'd do what I have often proposed, let Hannah come and help you; she is a capital nurse, and you may trust the precious babies to her while you do more housework. You need the exercise, Hannah would enjoy the rest, and John would find his wife again. Get out more. Keep cheerful as well as busy, for you are the sunshine-maker of the family, and if you get dismal there is no fair weather. Then I'd try to take an interest in whatever John likes—talk with him, let him read to you, exchange ideas, and help each other in that way. Don't shut yourself up in a bandbox because you are a woman, but understand what is going on, and educate yourself to take your part in the world's work, for it all affects you and yours."

"John is so sensible I'm afraid he will think I'm stupid if I ask questions about politics and things."

"I don't believe he would. Love covers a multitude of sins, and of whom could you ask more freely than of him? Try it, and see if he doesn't find your society far more agreeable than Mrs. Scott's suppers."

"I will. Poor John! I'm afraid I *have* neglected him sadly, but I thought I was right, and he never said anything."

"He tried not to be selfish, but he *has* felt rather forlorn, I fancy. This is just the time, Meg, when young married people are apt to grow apart, and the very time when they ought to be most together; for the first tenderness soon wears off unless care is taken to preserve it, and no time is so beautiful and precious to parents as the first years of the little lives given them to train. Don't let John be a stranger to the babies, for they will do more to keep him safe and happy in this world of trial and temptation than anything else, and through them you will learn to know and love one another as you should. Now, dear, good-by. Think over Mother's preachment, act upon it if it seems good, and God bless you all!"

Meg did think it over, found it good, and acted upon it, though the first attempt was not made exactly as she planned to have it. Of course the children tyrannized over her, and ruled the house as soon as they found out that kicking and squalling brought them whatever they wanted. Mamma was an abject slave to their caprices, but Papa was not so easily subjugated, and occasionally afflicted his tender spouse by an attempt at paternal discipline with his obstreperous son. For Demi inherited a trifle of his sire's firmness of character—we won't call it obstinacy—and when he made up his little mind to have or to do anything, all the king's horses and all the king's men could not change that pertinacious little mind. Mamma thought the dear too young to be taught to conquer his prejudices, but Papa believed that it never was too soon to learn obedience, so Master Demi early discovered that when he undertook to "wrastle" with "Parpar," he always got the worst of it; yet, like the Englishman, Baby respected the man who conquered him, and loved the father whose grave "No, no," was more impressive than all Mamma's love pats.

A few days after the talk with her mother, Meg resolved to try a social evening with John; so she ordered a nice supper, set the parlor in order, dressed herself prettily, and put the children to bed early, that nothing should interfere with her experiment. But unfortunately Demi's most unconquerable prejudice was against going to bed, and that night he decided to go on a rampage; so poor Meg sang and rocked, told stories and tried every sleep-provoking wile she could devise, but all in vain, the big eyes wouldn't shut; and long after Daisy had gone to bye-low, like the chubby little bunch of good nature she was, naughty Demi lay staring at the light with the most discouragingly wide-awake expression of countenance.

"Will Demi lie still like a good boy while Mamma runs down and gives poor Papa his tea?" asked Meg as the hall door softly closed, and the well-known step went tiptoeing into the dining room.

"Me has tea!" said Demi, preparing to join in the revel.

"No, but I'll save you some little cakies for breakfast if you'll go bye-bye like Daisy. Will you, lovey?"

"Iss!" And Demi shut his eyes tight, as if to catch sleep and hurry the desired day.

Taking advantage of the propitious moment, Meg slipped away and ran down to greet her husband with a smiling face, and the little blue bow in her hair which was his especial admiration. He saw it at once, and said, with pleased surprise:

"Why, little Mother, how gay we are tonight. Do you expect company?"

"Only you, dear. I'm tired of being a dowdy, so I dressed up as a change. You always make yourself nice for table, no matter how tired you are so why shouldn't I when I have the time?"

"I do it out of respect to you, my dear," said the old-fashioned John.

"Ditto, ditto, Mr. Brooke," laughed Meg.

"Well, it's altogether delightful, and like old times. This tastes right.

I drink your health, dear." And John sipped his tea with an air of reposeful rapture, which was of very short duration, however; for as he put down his cup the door handle rattled mysteriously, and a little voice was heard saying impatiently, "Opy doy. Me's tummin!"

"It's that naughty boy. I told him to go to sleep alone, and here he is downstairs, getting his death cold pattering over that canvas," said Meg, answering the call.

"Mornin' now," announced Demi in a joyful tone as he entered with his long nightgown gracefully festooned over his arm, and every curl bobbing gaily as he pranced about the table eying the "cakies" with loving glances.

"No, it isn't morning yet. You must go to bed, and not trouble poor Mamma. Then you can have the little cake with sugar on it."

"Me loves Parpar," said the artful one, preparing to climb the paternal knee and revel in forbidden joys. But John shook his head, and said to Meg: "If you told him to stay up there and go to sleep alone, make him do it, or he will never learn to mind you."

"Yes, of course. Come, Demi." And Meg led her son away, feeling a strong desire to spank the little marplot who hopped beside her, laboring under the delusion that the bribe was to be administered as soon as they reached the nursery.

Nor was he disappointed, for that shortsighted woman actually gave him a lump of sugar, tucked him into his bed, and forbade any more promenades till morning.

"Iss!" said Demi the perjured, blissfully sucking his sugar, and regarding his first attempt as eminently successful.

Meg returned, and supper was progressing pleasantly when the little ghost walked again, and exposed the maternal delinquencies by boldly demanding "More sudar, Marmar."

"Now this won't do," said John, hardening his heart against the engaging little sinner. "We shall never know any peace till that child learns to go to bed properly. You have made a slave of yourself long enough. Give him one lesson, and then there will be an end of it. Put him in his bed and leave him, Meg."

"He won't stay there. He never does unless I sit by him."

"I'll manage him. Demi, go upstairs and get into your bed, as Mamma bids you."

"S'ant!" replied the young rebel, helping himself to the coveted "cakie," and beginning to eat the same.

"You must never say that to Papa. I shall carry you if you don't go yourself."

"Go 'way. Me don't love Parpar." And Demi retired to his mother's skirts for protection.

But even that refuge proved unavailing, for he was delivered over to the enemy with a "Be gentle with him, John," which struck the culprit with dismay; for when Mamma deserted him, then the judgment day was at hand. Bereft of his cake, defrauded of his frolic, and borne away by a strong hand to that detested bed, poor Demi could not restrain his wrath, but openly defied Papa, and kicked and screamed lustily all the way upstairs. The minute he was put into bed on one side, he rolled out on the other, and made for the door, only to be ignominiously caught up by the tail of his little toga and put back again, which lively performance was kept up till the young man's strength gave out, when he devoted himself to roaring at the top of his voice. The vocal exercise usually conquered Meg, but John sat as unmoved as the post which is popularly believed to be deaf. No coaxing, no sugar, no lullaby, no story; even the light was put out, and only the red glow of the fire enlivened the "big dark" which Demi regarded with curiosity rather than fear. This new order of things disgusted him, and he howled dismally for "Marmar."

The plaintive wail which succeeded the passionate roar went to Meg's heart, and she ran up to say beseechingly: "Let me stay with him. He'll be good now, John."

"No, my dear, I've told him he must go to sleep, as you bid him, and he must, if I stay here all night."

"But he'll cry himself sick," pleaded Meg.

"No he won't. He's so tired he will soon drop off, and then the matter is settled, for he will understand that he has got to mind. Don't interfere. I'll manage him."

"He's my child, and I can't have his spirit broken by harshness."

"He's my child, and I won't have his temper spoiled by indulgence. Go down, my dear, and leave the boy to me."

When John spoke in that masterful tone, Meg always obeyed, and never regretted her docility.

"Please let me kiss him once, John?"

"Certainly. Demi, say good night to Mamma, and let her go and rest, for she is very tired with taking care of you all day."

Meg always insisted upon it that the kiss won the victory; for after it was given, Demi sobbed more quietly, and lay quite still.

"Poor little man, he's worn out with sleep and crying. I'll cover him up, and then go and set Meg's heart at rest," thought John, creeping to the bedside hoping to find his rebellious heir asleep.

But he wasn't, for the moment his father peeped at him, Demi's eyes opened, and he put up his arms, saying, with a penitent hiccough, "Me's dood now."

Sitting on the stairs outside, Meg wondered at the long silence which followed the uproar, and after imagining all sorts of impossible accidents, she slipped into the room to set her fears at rest. Demi lay fast asleep; not in his usual spread-eagle attitude, but in a subdued bunch cuddled close in the circle of his father's arm and holding his father's finger as if he felt that justice was tempered with mercy, and had gone to sleep a sadder and a wiser baby. So held, John had waited with womanly patience till the little hand relaxed its hold, and while waiting had fallen asleep, more tired by that tussle with his son than with his whole day's work.

As Meg stood watching the two faces on the pillow, she smiled to herself, and then slipped away again, saying, in a satisfied tone: "I never need fear that John will be too harsh with my babies. He *does* know how to manage them, and will be a great help, for Demi *is* getting too much for me."

When John came down at last expecting to find a pensive or reproachful wife, he was agreeably surprised to find Meg placidly trimming a bonnet, and to be greeted with the request to read something about the election, if he was not too tired. John saw in a minute that a revolution of some kind was going on, but wisely asked no questions, knowing that Meg was such a transparent little person she couldn't keep a secret to save her life, and therefore the clue would soon appear. He read a long debate with the most amiable readiness and then explained it in his most lucid manner, while Meg tried to look deeply interested, to ask intelligent questions, and keep her thoughts from wandering from the state of the nation to the state of her bonnet. In her secret soul, however, she decided that politics were as bad as mathematics, and that the mission of politicians seemed to be calling each other names; but she kept these feminine ideas to herself, and when John paused, shook her head, and said with what she thought diplomatic ambiguity:

"Well, I really don't see what we are coming to."

John laughed, and watched her for a minute as she poised a pretty little preparation of lace and flowers on her hand.

304

"She is trying to like politics for my sake, so I'll try and like millinery for hers, that's only fair," thought John the Just, adding aloud: "That's very pretty. Is it what you call a breakfast cap?"

"My dear man, it's a bonnet! My very best go-to-concert-and-theater bonnet."

"I beg your pardon. It was so small I naturally mistook it for one of the flyaway things you sometimes wear. How do you keep it on?"

"These bits of lace are fastened under the chin with a rosebud, so." And Meg illustrated by putting on the bonnet, and regarding him with an air of calm satisfaction that was irresistible.

"It's a love of a bonnet, but I prefer the face inside, for it looks young and happy again." And John kissed the smiling face, to the great detriment of the rosebud under the chin.

"I'm glad you like it, for I want you to take me to one of the new concerts some night. I really need some music to put me in tune. Will you, please?"

"Of course I will, with all my heart, or anywhere else you like. You have been shut up so long it will do you no end of good. What put it into your head, little Mother?"

"Well, I had a talk with Marmee the other day, and told her how nervous and cross and out of sorts I felt, and she said I needed change and less care. So Hannah is to help me with the children, and I'm to see to things about the house more, and now and then have a little fun, just to keep me from getting to be a fidgety, broken-down old woman before my time. It's only an experiment, John, and I want to try it for your sake as much as for mine, because I've neglected you shamefully lately, and I'm going to make home what it used to be, if I can. You don't object, I hope?"

Never mind what John said, or what a very narrow escape the little bonnet had from utter ruin; all that we have any business to know is that John did *not* appear to object, judging from the changes which gradually took place in the house and its inmates. It was not all paradise by any means, but everyone was better for the division-of-labor system; the children throve under the paternal rule, for accurate, steadfast John brought order and obedience into Babydom, while Meg recovered her spirits and composed her nerves by plenty of wholesome exercise, a little pleasure, and much confidential conversation with her sensible husband. Home grew homelike again, and John had no wish to leave it unless he took Meg with him. The Scotts came to the Brookes now, and everyone found the little house a cheerful place, full of happiness, content, and family love.

LAZY LAURENCE

Laurie went to Nice intending to stay a week, and remained a month. He was tired of wandering about alone, and Amy's familiar presence seemed to give a homelike charm to the foreign scenes in which she bore a part. He rather missed the "petting" he used to receive, and enjoyed a taste of it again; for no attentions, however flattering, from strangers were half so pleasant as the sisterly adoration of the girls at home. Amy never would pet him like the others, but she was very glad to see him now, and quite clung to him, feeling that he was the representative of the dear family for whom she longed more than she would confess. They naturally took comfort in each other's society, and were much together, riding, walking, dancing, or dawdling. But while apparently amusing themselves in the most careless fashion, they were half-consciously making discoveries and forming opinions about each other. Amy rose daily in the estimation of her friend, but he sank in hers, and each felt the truth before a word was spoken. Amy tried to please, and succeeded, for she was grateful for the many pleasures he gave her, and repaid him with the little services to which womanly women know how to lend an indescribable charm. Laurie made no effort of any kind, but just let himself drift along as comfortably as possible, trying to forget, and feeling that all women owed him a kind word because one had been cold to him.

"All the rest have gone to Monaco for the day. I preferred to stay at home and write letters. They are done now, and I am going to Valrosa to sketch. Will you come?" said Amy as she joined Laurie one lovely day when he lounged in as usual, about noon.

"Well, yes, but isn't it rather warm for such a long walk?" he answered slowly.

"I'm going to have the little carriage, and Baptiste can drive, so you'll have nothing to do but hold your umbrella and keep your gloves nice," returned Amy, with a sarcastic glance at the immaculate kids which were a weak point with Laurie.

"Then I'll go with pleasure." And he put out his hand for her sketch-book. But she tucked it under her arm with a sharp "Don't trouble your-self. It's no exertion to me, but *you* don't look equal to it."

Laurie lifted his eyebrows, and followed at a leisurely pace as she ran downstairs; but when they got into the carriage he took the reins himself, and left little Baptiste nothing to do but fall asleep on his perch.

The two never quarreled—Amy was too well-bred, and just now Laurie was too lazy; so in a minute he peeped under her hat brim with an inquir-ing air, she answered with a smile, and they went on together in the most amicable manner.

It was a lovely drive, along winding roads rich in the picturesque scenes that delight beauty-loving eyes. Valrosa well deserved its name, for in that climate of perpetual summer roses blossomed everywhere. They overhung the archway, thrust themselves between the bars of the great gate with a sweet welcome to passers-by, and lined the avenue wind-ing through lemon trees and feathery palms up to the villa on the hill.

"This is a regular honeymoon paradise, isn't it? Did you ever see such roses?" asked Amy, pausing on the terrace to enjoy the view.

"No, nor felt such thorns," returned Laurie, with his thumb in his mouth after a vain attempt to capture a solitary scarlet flower that grew just beyond his reach.

"Try lower down, and pick those that have no thorns," said Amy, gathering three of the tiny cream-colored ones that starred the wall be-hind her. She put them in his buttonhole as a peace offering, and he stood a minute looking down at them with a curious expression, for in the Italian part of his nature there was a touch of superstition, and he was just then in that state of half-sweet, half-bitter melancholy when im-aginative young men find significance in trifles, and food for romance everywhere. He had thought of Jo in reaching after the thorny red rose, for vivid flowers became her, and she had often worn ones like that from the greenhouse at home. The pale roses Amy gave him were the sort that the Italians lay in dead hands, never in bridal wreaths, and for a moment he wondered if the omen was for Jo or for himself; but the next instant his American common sense got the better of sentimentality, and he laughed a heartier laugh than Amy had heard since he came.

"It's good advice. You'd better take it and save your fingers," she said, thinking her speech amused him.

"Thank you, I will," he answered in jest, and a few months later he did it in earnest.

"Laurie, when are you going to your grandfather?" she asked presently as she settled herself on a rustic seat.

"Very soon."

"You have said that a dozen times within the last three weeks. It's really dreadful!" And Amy looked severe.

"Not so bad as it seems, for I should only plague him if I went, so I might as well stay and plague you a little longer—you can bear it better; in fact, I think it agrees with you excellently."

Amy shook her head, and opened her sketchbook with an air of resignation, but she had made up her mind to lecture "that boy," and in a minute she began again.

"What are you doing just now?"

"Watching lizards."

"No, no. I mean what do you intend and wish to do?"

"Smoke a cigarette, if you'll allow me."

"How provoking you are! I don't approve of cigars, and I will only allow it on condition that you let me put you into my sketch. I need a figure."

"With all the pleasure in life. How will you have me—full-length or three-quarters, on my head or my heels? I should respectfully suggest a recumbent posture, then put yourself in also, and call it 'Dolce Far Niente.'"

"Stay as you are, and go to sleep if you like. *I* intend to work hard," said Amy, in her most energetic tone.

"What delightful enthusiasm!"

"What would Jo say if she saw you now?" asked Amy impatiently, hoping to stir him up by the mention of her still more energetic sister's name.

"As usual, 'Go away, Teddy. I'm busy!'" He laughed as he spoke, but the laugh was not natural, and a shade passed over his face, for the utterance of the familiar name touched the wound that was not healed yet. Both tone and shadow struck Amy, for she had seen and heard them before, and now she looked up in time to catch a new expression on Laurie's face—a hard, bitter look, full of pain, dissatisfaction, and regret. It was gone before she could study it, and the listless expression back again. She watched him for a moment with artistic pleasure, thinking how like an Italian he looked as he lay basking in the sun with uncovered head and eyes full of Southern dreaminess.

"You look like the effigy of a young knight asleep on his tomb," she said, carefully tracing the well-cut profile defined against the dark stone. "Wish I was!"

"That's a foolish wish, unless you have spoiled your life. You are so changed I sometimes think——" There Amy stopped, with a half-timid, half-wistful look more significant than her unfinished speech.

Laurie saw and understood the affectionate anxiety she hesitated to express, and looking straight into her eyes, said, just as he used to say it to her mother: "It's all right, ma'am."

That satisfied her and set at rest the doubts that had begun to worry her lately. It also touched her, and she showed that it did by the cordial tone in which she said: "I'm glad of that! I didn't think you'd been a very bad boy, but I fancied you might have wasted money at that wicked Baden-Baden, lost your heart to some charming Frenchwoman with a husband, or got into some of the scrapes that young men seem to consider a necessary part of a foreign tour. Don't stay out there in the sun. Come and lie on the grass here, and 'let us be friendly,' as Jo used to say when we got in the sofa corner and told secrets."

Laurie obediently threw himself down on the turf, and began to amuse himself by sticking daisies into the ribbons of Amy's hat that lay there. "I'm all ready for the secrets." And he glanced up with a decided expression of interest in his eyes.

"I've none to tell. You may begin."

"Haven't one to bless myself with. I thought perhaps you'd had some news from home."

"You have heard all that has come lately. Don't you hear often? I fancied Jo would send you volumes."

"She's very busy. I'm roving about so it's impossible to be regular, you know. When do you begin your great work of art, Raphaella?" he asked, changing the subject abruptly.

"Never," she answered, with a despondent but decided air. "Rome took all the vanity out of me; for after seeing the wonders there, I felt too insignificant to live, and gave up all my foolish hopes in despair."

"Why should you, with so much energy and talent?"

"That's just why—because talent isn't genius, and no amount of energy can make it so. I want to be great, or nothing. I won't be a commonplace dauber, so I don't intend to try any more."

"And what are you going to do with yourself now, if I may ask?"

"Polish up my other talents, and be an ornament to society, if I get the chance."

It was a characteristic speech, and sounded daring. Laurie smiled, but he liked the spirit with which she took up a new purpose when a long-cherished one died, and spent no time lamenting.

"Good! And here is where Fred Vaughn comes in, I fancy."

Amy preserved a discreet silence, but there was a conscious look in her downcast face that made Laurie sit up and say gravely: "Now I'm going to play brother, and ask questions. May I?"

"I don't promise to answer."

"Your face will, if your tongue won't. You aren't woman of the world enough yet to hide your feelings, my dear. I heard rumors about Fred and you last year, and it's my private opinion that if he had not been called home so suddenly and detained so long, something would have come of it—hey?"

"That's not for me to say," was Amy's prim reply, but her lips would smile, and there was a traitorous sparkle of the eye which betrayed that she knew her power and enjoyed the knowledge.

"You are not engaged, I hope?" And Laurie looked very elder-brotherly and grave all of a sudden.

"No."

"But you will be, if he comes back and goes properly down upon his knees, won't you?"

"Very likely."

"Then you are fond of old Fred?"

"I could be, if I tried."

"But you don't intend to try till the proper moment? Bless my soul, what unearthly prudence! He's a good fellow, Amy, but not the man I fancied you'd like."

"He is rich, a gentleman, and has delightful manners," began Amy, trying to be quite cool and dignified, but feeling a little ashamed of herself, in spite of the sincerity of her intentions.

"I understand. Queens of society can't get on without money, so you mean to make a good match, and start in that way? Quite right and proper, as the world goes, but it sounds odd from the lips of one of your mother's girls."

"True, nevertheless."

A short speech, but the quiet decision with which it was uttered contrasted curiously with the young speaker. Laurie felt this instinctively, and laid himself down again with a sense of disappointment which he could not explain. His look and silence, as well as a certain inward self-disapproval, ruffled Amy, and made her resolve to deliver her lecture without delay.

"I wish you'd do me the favor to rouse yourself a little," she said sharply.

"Do it for me, there's a dear girl."

"I could, if I tried." And she looked as if she would like doing it in the most summary style.

"Try, then, I give you leave," returned Laurie, who enjoyed having someone to tease after his long abstinence from his favorite pastime.

"You'd be angry in five minutes."

"I'm never angry with you. It takes two flints to make a fire. You are as cool and soft as snow."

"You don't know what I can do. Snow produces a glow and a tingle, if applied rightly. Your indifference is half affectation, and a good stirring up would prove it."

"Stir away. It won't hurt me and it may amuse you, as the big man said when his little wife beat him."

Being decidedly nettled herself, and longing to see him shake off the apathy that so altered him, Amy sharpened both tongue and pencil, and began: "Flo and I have got a new name for you. It's 'Lazy Laurence.' How do you like it?"

She thought it would annoy him, but he only folded his arms under his head with an imperturbable "That's not bad. Thank you, ladies."

"Do you want to know what I honestly think of you?"

"Pining to be told."

"Well, I despise you."

If she had even said "I hate you," in a petulant or coquettish tone, he would have laughed, and rather liked it; but the grave, almost sad, accent of her voice made him open his eyes, and ask quickly, "Why, if you please?"

"Because, with every chance for being good, useful, and happy, you are faulty, lazy, and miserable."

"Strong language, mademoiselle."

"If you like it, I'll go on."

"Pray do. It's quite interesting."

"I thought you'd find it so. Selfish people always like to talk about themselves."

"Am I selfish?" The question slipped out involuntarily and in a tone of surprise, for the one virtue on which he prided himself was generosity.

"Yes, very selfish," continued Amy in a calm, cool voice, twice as effective, just then, as an angry one. "I'll show you how, for I've studied you while we have been frolicking, and I'm not at all satisfied with you. Here you have been abroad nearly six months and done nothing but waste time and money and disappoint your friends."

"Isn't a fellow to have any pleasure after a four years' grind?"

"You don't look as if you'd had much; at any rate, you are none the better for it, as far as I can see. I said when we first met that you had improved. Now I take it all back, for I don't think you half so nice as when I left you at home. You have grown abominably lazy; you like gossip, and waste time on frivolous things; you are contented to be petted and admired by silly people instead of being loved and respected by wise ones. With money, talent, position, health, and beauty—ah, you like that, Old Vanity! but it's the truth, so I can't help saying it—with all these splendid things to use and enjoy, you can find nothing to do but dawdle, and instead of being the man you might and ought to be, you are only——" There she stopped, with a look that had both pain and pity in it.

"Saint Laurence on a gridiron," added Laurie, blandly finishing the sentence. But the lecture began to take effect, for there was a wide-awake sparkle in his eyes now, and a half-angry, half-injured expression replaced the former indifference.

"I supposed you'd take it so. You men tell us we are angels, and say we can make you what we will; but the instant we honestly try to do you good, you laugh at us, and won't listen, which proves how much your flattery is worth." Amy spoke bitterly, and turned her back on the exasperating martyr at her feet.

In a minute a hand came down over the page so that she could not draw, and Laurie's voice said, with a droll imitation of a penitent child:

"I will be good, oh, I will be good!"

But Amy did not laugh, for she was in earnest and, tapping on the outspread hand with her pencil, said soberly: "Aren't you ashamed of a hand like that? It's as soft and white as a woman's, and looks as if it never did anything but wear Jouvin's best gloves and pick flowers for ladies. You are not a dandy, thank Heaven! so I'm glad to see there are no diamonds or big seal rings on it, only the little old one Jo gave you so long ago. Dear soul, I wish she was here to help me!"

"So do I!"

The hand vanished as suddenly as it came, and there was energy enough in the echo of her wish to suit even Amy. She glanced down at him with a new thought in her mind; but he was lying with his hat half over his face, as if for shade, and his mustache hid his mouth. She only saw his chest rise and fall with a long breath that might have been a sigh, and the hand that wore the ring nestled down into the grass as if to hide something too precious or too tender to be spoken of. All in a minute various hints and trifles assumed shape and significance in Amy's mind, and told her what her sister never had confided to her. She remembered that Laurie never spoke voluntarily of Jo; she recalled the shadow on his face just now, the change in his character, and the wearing of the little old ring, which was no ornament to a handsome hand. Amy had fancied that perhaps a love trouble was at the bottom of the alteration, and now she was sure of it. Her keen eyes filled, and when she spoke again, it was in a voice that could be beautifully soft and kind when she chose to make it so.

"I know I have no right to talk so to you, Laurie, and if you weren't the sweetest-tempered fellow in the world, you'd be very angry with me. But we are all so fond and proud of you I couldn't bear to think they should be disappointed in you at home as I have been, though perhaps they would understand the change better than I do."

"I think they would" came from under the hat, in a grim tone quite as touching as a broken one.

"They ought to have told me, and not let me go blundering and scolding when I should have been more kind and patient than ever. I never did like that Miss Randal, and now I hate her!" said artful Amy, wishing to be sure of her facts this time.

"Hang Miss Randal!" And Laurie knocked the hat off his face with a look that left no doubt of his sentiments toward that young lady.

"I beg pardon, I thought——" And there she paused diplomatically.

"No you didn't. You knew perfectly well I never cared for anyone but Jo." Laurie said that in his old impetuous tone, and turned his face away.

"I did think so, but as they never said anything about it, and you came away, I supposed I was mistaken. And Jo wouldn't be kind to you? Why, I was sure she loved you dearly."

"She *was* kind, but not in the right way; and it's lucky for her she didn't love me if I'm the good-for-nothing fellow you think me. It's her fault, though, and you may tell her so."

The hard, bitter look came back again as he said that, and it troubled Amy, for she did not know what balm to apply.

"I was wrong, I didn't know. I'm very sorry I was so cross, but I can't help wishing you'd bear it better, Teddy dear."

"Don't—that's her name for me!" And Laurie put up his hand with a quick gesture to stop the words spoken in Jo's half-kind, half-reproachful tone. "Wait till you've tried it yourself," he added in a low voice.

"I'd take it manfully, and be respected if I couldn't be loved."

Now Laurie flattered himself that he *had* borne it remarkably well, making no moan, asking no sympathy, and taking his trouble away to live it down alone. Amy's lecture put the matter in a new light, and for the first time it did look weak and selfish to lose heart at the first failure, and shut himself up in moody indifference. He felt as if suddenly shaken out of a pensive dream, and found it impossible to go to sleep again. Presently he sat up, and asked slowly: "Do you think Jo would despise me as you do?"

"Yes, if she saw you now. She hates lazy people. Why don't you do something splendid, and *make* her love you?"

"I did my best, but it was no use."

"Graduating well, you mean? That was no more than you ought to have done for your grandfather's sake. It would have been shameful to fail after spending so much time and money when everyone knew you *could* do well."

"I did fail, say what you will, for Jo wouldn't love me."

"No you didn't, and you'll say so in the end, for it did you good, and proved that you could do something if you tried. If you'd only set about another task of some sort, you'd soon be your hearty, happy self again, and forget your trouble."

"That's impossible."

"Try it and see. You needn't shrug your shoulders, and think 'Much she knows about such things.' I don't pretend to be wise, but I *am* observing, and I see a great deal more than you'd imagine. I'm interested in other people's experiences and inconsistencies, and though I can't explain, I remember and use them for my own benefit. Love Jo all your days, if you choose, but don't let it spoil you, for it's wicked to throw away so many good gifts because you can't have the one you want. There, I won't lecture any more, for I know you'll wake up and be a man in spite of that hardhearted girl."

Neither spoke for several minutes. Laurie sat turning the little ring on his finger, and Amy put the last touches to the hasty sketch she had been working at while she talked. Presently she put it on his knee. "How do you like that?"

He looked and then he smiled, as he could not well help doing, for it was capitally done—the long, lazy figure on the grass, with listless face, half-shut eyes, and one hand holding a cigar, from which came the little wreath of smoke that encircled the dreamer's head.

"How well you draw!" he said with genuine surprise and pleasure at her skill. "Yes, that's me."

"As you are. This is as you were." And Amy laid another sketch beside the one he held.

It was not nearly so well done, but there was a life and spirit in it which atoned for many faults, and it recalled the past so vividly that a sudden change swept over the young man's face as he looked. Only a rough sketch of Laurie taming a horse; hat and coat were off, and every line of the active figure, resolute face, and commanding attitude was full of energy and meaning. The handsome brute, just subdued, stood arching his neck under the tightly drawn rein, with one foot impatiently pawing the ground and ears pricked up as if listening for the voice that had mastered him. In the ruffled mane, the rider's breezy hair and erect attitude, there was a suggestion of suddenly arrested motion, of strength, courage, and youthful buoyancy, that contrasted sharply with the supine grace of the "Dolce Far Niente" sketch. Laurie said nothing, but as his eye went from one to the other, Amy saw him flush as if he read and

315

accepted the little lesson she had given him. That satisfied her, and, without waiting for him to speak, she said in her sprightly way:

"Don't you remember the day you played Rarey with Puck, and we all looked on? Meg and Beth were frightened, but Jo clapped and pranced, and I sat on the fence and drew you. I found that sketch in my portfolio the other day, touched it up, and kept it to show you."

"Much obliged. You've improved immensely since then, and I congratulate you. May I venture to suggest in 'a honeymoon paradise' that five o'clock is the dinner hour at your hotel?"

Laurie rose as he spoke, returned the pictures with a smile and a bow, and looked at his watch, as if to remind her that even moral lectures should have an end. He tried to resume his former easy, indifferent air, but it *was* an affectation now, for the rousing had been more efficacious than he would confess. Amy felt the shade of coldness in his manner, and said to herself: "Now I've offended him. Well, if it does him good, I'm glad; if it makes him hate me, I'm sorry. But it's true, and I can't take back a word of it."

"Shall we see you this evening, *mon frère?*" asked Amy as they parted at her aunt's door.

"Unfortunately I have an engagement. *Au revoir, mademoiselle,*" and Laurie bent as if to kiss her hand in the foreign fashion, which became him better than many men. Something in his face made Amy say quickly and warmly:

"No, be yourself with me, Laurie, and part in the good old way. I'd rather have a hearty English handshake than all the sentimental salutations in France."

"Good-by, dear." And with these words, uttered in the tone she liked, Laurie left her, after a handshake almost painful in its heartiness. Next morning, instead of the usual call Amy received a note which made her smile at the beginning and sigh at the end:

My dear Mentor,

Please make my adieux to your aunt, and exult within yourself, for "Lazy Laurence" has gone to his grandpa, like the best of boys. A pleasant winter to you, and may the gods grant you a blissful honeymoon at Valrosa! I think Fred would be benefited by a rouser. Tell him so, with my congratulations.

Yours gratefully,
Telemachus

"Good boy! I'm glad he's gone," said Amy with an approving smile. The next minute her face fell as she glanced about the empty room, adding, with an involuntary sigh:

"Yes, I *am* glad, but how I shall miss him!"

THE VALLEY OF THE SHADOW

When the first bitterness was over, the family accepted the inevitable, and tried to bear it cheerfully, helping one another by the increased affection which comes to bind households tenderly together in times of trouble. They put away their grief, and each did his or her part toward making that last year a happy one. The pleasantest room in the house was set apart for Beth, and in it was gathered everything that she most loved—flowers, pictures, her piano, the little work table, and the beloved pussies. Father's best books found their way there, Mother's easy chair, Jo's desk, Amy's finest sketches; and every day Meg brought her babies on a loving pilgrimage, to make sunshine for Aunty Beth. John quietly set apart a little sum, that he might enjoy the pleasure of keeping the invalid supplied with the fruit she loved and longed for; old Hannah never wearied of concocting dainty dishes to tempt a capricious appetite, dropping tears as she worked; and from across the sea came little gifts and cheerful letters, seeming to bring breaths of warmth and fragrance from lands that know no winter.

Here, cherished like a household saint in its shrine, sat Beth, tranquil and busy as ever; for nothing could change the sweet, unselfish nature, and even while preparing to leave life she tried to make it happier for those who should remain behind. The feeble fingers were never idle. The first few months were very happy ones, and Beth often used to look round and say "How beautiful this is!" as they all sat together in her sunny room, the babies kicking and crowing on the floor, Mother and sisters working near, and Father reading from the wise old books which seemed rich in good and comfortable words, as applicable now as when written centuries ago.

It was well for all that this peaceful time was given them as preparation for the sad hours to come; for by and by Beth said the needle was "so heavy," and put it down forever. With the wreck of her frail body, Beth's soul grew strong; and though she said little, those about her felt that she was ready, saw that the first pilgrim called was likewise the fittest, and waited with her on the shore, trying to see the Shining Ones coming to receive her when she crossed the river.

Jo never left her for an hour since Beth had said "I feel stronger when you are here." She slept on a couch in the room, waking often to renew the fire, to feed, lift, or wait upon the patient creature who seldom asked for anything, and tried "not to be a trouble." All day she haunted the room, jealous of any other nurse, and prouder of being chosen then than of any honor her life ever brought her.

Often when she woke, Jo found Beth reading in her well-worn little book, heard her singing softly to beguile the sleepless night, or saw her lean her face upon her hands while slow tears dropped through the transparent fingers; and Jo would lie watching her, with thoughts too deep for tears, feeling that Beth, in her simple, unselfish way, was trying to wean herself from the dear old life, and fit herself for the life to come, by sacred words of comfort, quiet prayers, and the music she loved so well.

Seeing this did more for Jo than the wisest sermons, the saintliest hymns, the most fervent prayers that any voice could utter; for, with eyes made clear by many tears, and a heart softened by the tenderest sorrow, she recognized the beauty of her sister's life—uneventful, unambitious, yet full of the genuine virtues which "smell sweet, and blossom in the dust," the self-forgetfulness that makes the humblest on earth remembered soonest in Heaven, the true success which is possible to all.

One night, when Beth looked among the books upon her table to find something to make her forget the moral weariness that was almost as hard to bear as pain, as she turned the leaves of her old favorite *Pilgrim's Progress* she found a little paper scribbled over in Jo's hand. The name caught her eye, and the blurred look of the lines made her sure that tears had fallen on it.

"Poor Jo! She's fast asleep, so I won't wake her to ask leave; she shows me all her things, and I don't think she'll mind if I look at this," thought Beth, with a glance at her sister, who lay on the rug with the tongs beside her, ready to wake up the minute the log fell apart.

MY BETH

Sitting patient in the shadow
Till the blessed light shall come,

A serene and saintly presence
  Sanctifies our troubled home.
Earthly joys and hopes and sorrows
  Break like ripples on the strand
Of the deep and solemn river
  Where her willing feet now stand.

O my sister, passing from me
  Out of human care and strife,
Leave me, as a gift, those virtues
  Which have beautified your life.
Dear, bequeath me that great patience
  Which has power to sustain
A cheerful, uncomplaining spirit
  In its prison house of pain.

Give me, for I need it sorely,
  Of that courage, wise and sweet,
Which has made the path of duty
  Green beneath your willing feet.
Give me that unselfish nature
  That with charity divine
Can pardon wrong for love's dear sake—
  Meek heart, forgive me mine!

Thus our parting daily loseth
  Something of its bitter pain,
And while learning this hard lesson,
  My great loss becomes my gain.
For the touch of grief will render
  My wild nature more serene,
Give to life new aspirations,
  A new trust in the unseen.

Henceforth, safe across the river,
  I shall see forevermore
A beloved, household spirit
  Waiting for me on the shore.
Hope and faith, born of my sorrow,
  Guardian angels shall become,
And the sister gone before me
  By their hands shall lead me home.

Blurred and blotted, faulty and feeble, as the lines were, they brought a look of inexpressible comfort to Beth's face, for her one regret had been that she had done so little; and this seemed to assure her that her life had not been useless, that her death would not bring the despair she feared. As she sat with the paper folded between her hands, the charred log fell asunder. Jo started up, revived the blaze, and crept to the bedside, hoping Beth slept.

"Not asleep, but so happy, dear. See, I found this and read it. I knew you wouldn't care. Have I been all that to you, Jo?" she asked with wistful, humble earnestness.

"O Beth, so much, so much!" And Jo's head went down upon the pillow beside her sister's.

"Then I don't feel as if I'd wasted my life. I'm not so good as you make me, but I *have* tried to do right; and now, when it's too late to begin even to do better, it's such a comfort to know that someone loves me so much, and feels as if I'd helped them."

"More than anyone in the world, Beth. I used to think I couldn't let you go, but I'm learning to feel that I don't lose you, that you'll be more to me than ever, and death can't part us, though it seems to."

"I know it cannot, and I don't fear it any longer, for I'm sure I shall be your Beth still, to love and help you more than ever. You must take my place, Jo, and be everything to Father and Mother when I'm gone. They will turn to you, don't fail them. And if it's hard to work alone, remember that I don't forget you, and that you'll be happier in doing that than writing splendid books or seeing all the world; for love is the only thing that we can carry with us when we go, and it makes the end so easy."

"I'll try, Beth." And then and there Jo renounced her old ambition, pledged herself to a new and better one.

So the spring days came and went, the sky grew clearer, the earth greener, the flowers were up fair and early, and the birds came back in time to say good-by to Beth, who, like a tired but trustful child, clung to the hands that had led her all her life as Father and Mother guided her tenderly through the Valley of the Shadow, and gave her up to God. As Beth had hoped, the "tide went out easily," and in the dark hour before the dawn, on the bosom where she had drawn her first breath she quietly drew her last, with no farewell but one loving look, one little sigh.

When morning came, for the first time in many months the fire was out, Jo's place was empty, and the room was very still. But a bird sang blithely on a budding bough close by, the snowdrops blossomed freshly at the window, and the spring sunshine streamed in like a benediction over the placid face upon the pillow—a face so full of painless peace that those who loved it best smiled through their tears, and thanked God that Beth was well at last.

Learning to forget

Amy's lecture did Laurie good, though of course he did not own it till long afterward. Men seldom do, for when women are the advisers, the lords of creation don't take the advice till they have persuaded themselves that it is just what they intended to do; then they act upon it, and if it succeeds, they give the weaker vessel half the credit of it; if it fails, they generously give her the whole. Laurie went back to his grandfather, and was so dutifully devoted for several weeks that the old gentleman declared the climate of Nice had improved him wonderfully, and he had better try it again. There was nothing the young gentleman would have liked better, but elephants could not have dragged him back after the scolding he had received; pride forbade, and whenever the longing grew very strong, he fortified his resolution by repeating the words that had made the deepest impression—"I despise you." "Go and do something splendid that will *make* her love you."

Laurie turned the matter over in his mind so often that he soon brought himself to confess that he *had* been selfish and lazy; but then, when a man has a great sorrow, he should be indulged in all sorts of vagaries till he has lived it down. He felt that his blighted affections were quite dead now, and though he should never cease to be a faithful mourner, there was no occasion to wear his weeds ostentatiously. Jo *wouldn't* love him, but he might *make* her respect and admire him by doing something which should prove that a girl's No had not spoilt his life. He had always meant to do something, and Amy's advice was quite unnecessary.

As Goethe, when he had a joy or a grief, put it into a song, so Laurie resolved to embalm his love sorrow in music, and compose a Requiem which should harrow up Jo's soul and melt the heart of every hearer. Therefore the next time the old gentleman found him getting restless and moody and ordered him off, he went to Vienna, where he had musical friends, and fell to work with the firm determination to distinguish himself. But whether the sorrow was too vast to be embodied in music, or music too ethereal to uplift a mortal woe, he soon discovered that the Requiem was beyond him, just at present. It was evident that his mind was not in working order yet, and his ideas needed clarifying; for often in the middle of a plaintive strain he would find himself humming a dancing tune that vividly recalled the Christmas ball at Nice, and put an effectual stop to tragic composition for the time being.

Then he tried an opera, for nothing seemed impossible in the beginning; but here again unforeseen difficulties beset him. He wanted Jo for his heroine, and called upon his memory to supply him with tender recollections and romantic visions of his love. But memory turned traitor and, as if possessed by the perverse spirit of the girl, would only recall Jo's oddities, faults, and freaks, would only show her in the most unsentimental aspects—beating mats with her head tied up in a bandanna, barricading herself with the sofa pillow, or throwing cold water over his passion à la Gummidge—and an irresistible laugh spoiled the pensive picture he was endeavoring to paint. Jo wouldn't be put into the opera at any price, and he had to give her up with a "Bless that girl, what a torment she is!"

When he looked about him for another and a less intractable damsel to immortalize in melody, memory produced one with the most obliging readiness. This phantom wore many faces, but it always had golden hair, was enveloped in a diaphanous cloud, and floated airily before his mind's eye in a pleasing chaos of roses, peacocks, white ponies, and blue ribbons. He did not give the complacent wraith any name, but he took her for his heroine, and grew quite fond of her, as well he might; for he gifted her with every gift and grace under the sun, and escorted her unscathed through trials which would have annihilated any mortal woman.

Thanks to this inspiration, he got on swimmingly for a time, but gradually the work lost its charm, and he forgot to compose while he sat musing, pen in hand, or roamed about the gay city to get new ideas and refresh his mind. He did not do much, but he thought a great deal and was conscious of a change of some sort going on in spite of himself. "It's genius simmering, perhaps. I'll let it simmer, and see what comes of it," he said, with a secret suspicion all the while that it wasn't genius, but something far more common. Whatever it was, it simmered to some purpose, for he grew more and more discontented with his desultory life, began to long for some real and earnest work to go at, soul and body, and finally came to the wise conclusion that everyone who loved music was not a composer. Returning from one of Mozart's grand operas, splendidly performed at the Royal Theater, he looked over his own, played a few of the best parts, sat staring up at the busts of Mendelssohn, Beethoven, and Bach, who stared benignly back again; then suddenly he tore up his music sheets, one by one, and as the last fluttered out of his hand, he said soberly to himself: "She is right! Talent isn't genius, and you can't make it so. That music has taken the vanity out of me as Rome took it out of her, and I won't be a humbug any longer. Now what shall I do?"

That seemed a hard question to answer, and Laurie began to wish he had to work for his daily bread. Now, if ever, occurred an eligible opportunity for "going to the devil," as he once forcibly expressed it, for he had plenty of money and nothing to do. The poor fellow had temptations enough from without and from within, but he withstood them pretty well; for much as he valued liberty, he valued good faith and confidence more, so his promise to his grandfather, and his desire to be able to look honestly into the eyes of the women who loved him and say "All's well," kept him safe and steady.

Laurie thought that the task of forgetting his love for Jo would absorb all his powers for years, but to his great surprise he discovered it grew easier every day. He refused to believe it at first, got angry with himself, and couldn't understand it; but these hearts of ours are curious and contrary things, and time and nature work their will in spite of us. Laurie's heart *wouldn't* ache; the wound persisted in healing with a rapidity that astonished him, and instead of trying to forget, he found himself trying to remember. He had not foreseen this turn of affairs, and was not prepared for it. He was disgusted with himself, surprised at his own fickleness, and full of a queer mixture of disappointment and relief that he could recover from such a tremendous blow so soon. He carefully stirred up the embers of his lost love, but they refused to burst into a blaze. There was only a comfortable glow that warmed and did him good without putting him into a fever, and he was reluctantly obliged to confess that the boyish passion was slowly subsiding into a more tranquil sentiment, very tender, a little sad and resentful still, but that was sure to pass away in time, leaving a brotherly affection which would last unbroken to the end. As the word "brotherly" passed through his mind in one of these reveries, he smiled, and glanced up at the picture of Mozart that was before him: "Well, he was a great man, and when he couldn't have one sister he took the other, and was happy."

Laurie did not utter the words, but he thought them, and the next instant kissed the little old ring, saying to himself: "No, I won't! I haven't forgotten, I never can. I'll try again, and if that fails, why, then——"

Leaving his sentence unfinished, he seized pen and paper and wrote to Jo, telling her that he could not settle to anything while there was the least hope of her changing her mind. Couldn't she, wouldn't she, and let him come home and be happy? While waiting for an answer he did nothing, but he did it energetically, for he was in a fever of impatience. It came at last, and settled his mind effectually on one point, for Jo decidedly couldn't and wouldn't. She was wrapped up in Beth, and never wished to hear the word "love" again. Then she begged him to be happy with somebody else, but always to keep a little corner of his heart for his loving sister Jo. In a postscript she desired him not to tell Amy that

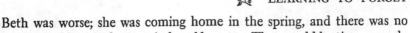

Beth was worse; she was coming home in the spring, and there was no need of saddening the remainder of her stay. That would be time enough, please God, but Laurie must write to her often, and not let her feel lonely, homesick, or anxious.

"So I will, at once. Poor little girl. It will be a sad going-home for her, I'm afraid." And Laurie opened his desk, as if writing to Amy had been the proper conclusion of the sentence left unfinished some weeks before.

But he did not write the letter that day, for as he rummaged out his best paper he came across something which changed his purpose. Tumbling about in one part of the desk among bills, passports, and business documents of various kinds were several of Jo's letters, and in another compartment were three notes from Amy, carefully tied up with one of her blue ribbons, and sweetly suggestive of the little dead roses put away inside. With a half-repentant, half-amused expression, Laurie gathered up all Jo's letters, smoothed, folded, and put them neatly into a small drawer of the desk, stood a minute turning the ring thoughtfully on his finger, then slowly drew it off, laid it with the letters, locked the drawer, and went out to hear High Mass at Saint Stefán's feeling as if there had been a funeral.

The letter went very soon, however, and was promptly answered, for Amy *was* homesick, and confessed it in the most delightfully confiding manner. The correspondence flourished famously, and letters flew to and fro with unfailing regularity all through the early spring. Laurie sold his busts, made allumettes of his opera, and went back to Paris hoping somebody would arrive before long. He wanted desperately to go to Nice, but would not till he was asked, and Amy would not ask him, for just then she was having little experiences of her own which made her rather wish to avoid the quizzical eyes of "our boy."

Fred Vaughn had returned, and put the question to which she had once decided to answer "Yes, thank you," but now she said "No, thank you," kindly but steadily; for when the time came, her courage failed her, and she found that something more than money and position was needed to satisfy the new longing that filled her heart so full of tender hopes and fears. The words "Fred is a good fellow, but not at all the man I fancied you'd ever like," and Laurie's face when he uttered them, kept returning to her as pertinaciously as her own did when she said in look, if not in words, "I shall marry for money." It troubled her to remember that now, she wished she could take it back, it sounded so unwomanly. She didn't want Laurie to think her a heartless, worldly creature; she didn't care to be a queen of society now half as much as she did to be a lovable woman; she was so glad he didn't hate her for the dreadful things she said, but took them so beautifully, and was kinder than ever. His letters were such a comfort, for the home letters were very irregular, and were not half so satisfactory as his when they did come. It was not only a pleasure but a duty to answer them, for the poor fellow was forlorn, and needed petting, since Jo persisted in being stonyhearted. So there was nothing to do but be very kind, and treat him like a brother.

If all brothers were treated as well as Laurie was at this period, they would be a much happier race of beings than they are. Amy never lectured now; she asked his opinion on all subjects; she was interested in everything he did, made charming little presents for him, and sent him two letters a week full of lively gossip, sisterly confidences, and captivating sketches of the lovely scenes about her. As few brothers are complimented by having their letters carried about in their sisters' pockets, read and reread diligently, cried over when short, kissed when long, and treasured carefully, we will not hint that Amy did any of these fond and foolish things. But she certainly did grow a little pale and pensive that spring, lost much of her relish for society, and went out sketching alone a good deal. She never had much to show when she came home, but was studying nature, I dare say, while she sat for hours, with her hands folded, on the terrace at Valrosa, or absently sketched any fancy that occurred to her—a stalwart knight carved on a tomb, a young man asleep in the grass, with his hat over his eyes, or a curly-haired girl in gorgeous array promenading down a ballroom on the arm of a tall gentleman, both faces being left a blur according to the last fashion in art, which was safe, but not altogether satisfactory.

Her aunt thought that she regretted her answer to Fred, and finding denials useless and explanations impossible, Amy left her to think what she liked, taking care that Laurie should know that Fred had gone to Egypt. That was all, but he understood it, and looked relieved as he said to himself, with a venerable air: "I was sure she would think better of it. Poor fellow! I've been through it all, and I can sympathize."

The letter telling that Beth was failing never reached Amy, and when the next found her, the grass was green above her sister. The sad news met her at Vevay, for the heat had driven them from Nice in May, and they had traveled slowly to Switzerland. She bore it very well, and quietly submitted to the family decree that she should not shorten her visit, since it was too late to say good-by to Beth. But her heart was very heavy;

she longed to be at home, and every day looked wistfully across the lake, waiting for Laurie to come and comfort her.

He did come very soon, for the same mail brought letters to them both, but he was in Germany, and it took some days to reach him. The moment he read it he packed his knapsack, bade adieu to his fellow pedestrians, and was off to keep his promise, with a heart full of joy and sorrow, hope and suspense.

He knew Vevay well, and as soon as the boat touched the little quay, he hurried along the shore to La Tour, where the Carrols were living *en pension.* The garçon was in despair that the whole family had gone to take a promenade on the lake—but no, the blonde mademoiselle might be in the château garden. If Monsieur would give himself the pain of sitting down, a flash of time should present her. But Monsieur could not wait even a "flash of time," and in the middle of the speech departed to find Mademoiselle himself.

A pleasant old garden on the borders of the lovely lake, with chestnuts rustling overhead, ivy climbing everywhere, and the black shadow of the tower falling far across the sunny water. At one corner of the wide, low wall was a seat, and here Amy often came to read or work, or console herself with the beauty all about her. She was sitting here that day, leaning her head on her hands, with a homesick heart and heavy eyes, thinking of Beth, and wondering why Laurie did not come. She did not hear him cross the courtyard beyond, nor see him pause in the archway that led from the subterranean path into the garden. He stood a minute, looking at her with new eyes, seeing what no one had ever seen before— the tender side of Amy's character. Everything about her mutely suggested love and sorrow—the blotted letters in her lap, the black ribbon that tied up her hair, the womanly pain and patience in her face; even the little ebony cross at her throat seemed pathetic to Laurie, for he had given it to her, and she wore it as her only ornament. If he had any doubts about the reception she would give him, they were set at rest the minute she looked up and saw him, for, dropping everything, she ran to him, exclaiming in a tone of unmistakable love and longing:

"O Laurie, Laurie, I knew you'd come to me!"

I think everything was said and settled then; for as they stood together quite silent for a moment, with the dark head bent down protectively over the light one, Amy felt that no one could comfort and sustain her so well as Laurie, and Laurie decided that Amy was the only woman in the world who could fill Jo's place, and make him happy. He did not tell her so, but she was not disappointed, for both felt the truth, were satisfied, and gladly left the rest to silence.

In a minute Amy went back to her place, and while she dried her tears Laurie gathered up the scattered papers, finding in the sight of sundry well-worn letters and suggestive sketches good omens for the future. As he sat down beside her, Amy felt shy again, and turned rosy-red at the recollection of her impulsive greeting.

"I couldn't help it. I felt so lonely and sad, and was so very glad to see you. It was such a surprise to look up and find you just as I was beginning to fear you wouldn't come."

"I came the minute I heard. I wish I could say something to comfort you for the loss of dear little Beth, but I can only feel, and——" He could not get any further, for he too turned bashful all of a sudden, and did not quite know what to say. He longed to lay Amy's head down on his shoulder and tell her to have a good cry, but he did not dare, so took her hand instead, and gave it a sympathetic squeeze that was better than words.

"You needn't say anything. This comforts me," she said softly. "Beth is well and happy, and I mustn't wish her back, but I dread the going-home, much as I long to see them all. We won't talk about it now, for it makes me cry, and I want to enjoy you while you stay. You needn't go right back, need you?"

"Not if you want me, dear."

"I do, so much. Aunt and Flo are very kind, but you seem like one of the family, and it would be so comfortable to have you for a little while."

Amy spoke and looked so like a homesick child whose heart was full that Laurie forgot his bashfulness all at once, and gave her just what she wanted—the petting she was used to and the cheerful conversation she needed.

"Poor little soul, you look as if you'd grieved yourself half-sick! I'm going to take care of you, so don't cry any more, but come and walk about with me," he said, in the half-caressing, half-commanding way that Amy liked, as he tied on her hat, drew her arm through his, and began to pace up and down the sunny walk under the new-leaved chestnuts. He felt more at ease upon his legs, and Amy found it very pleasant to have a strong arm to lean upon, a familiar face to smile at her, and a kind voice to talk delightfully for her alone.

The quaint old garden had sheltered many pairs of lovers, and seemed expressly made for them, so sunny and secluded was it, with nothing but the tower to overlook them and the wide lake to carry away the echo of their words as it rippled by below. For an hour this new pair walked and talked, or rested on the wall, enjoying the sweet influences which gave such a charm to time and place; and when an unromantic dinner bell warned them away, Amy felt as if she left her burden of loneliness and sorrow behind her in the château garden.

The moment Mrs. Carrol saw the girl's altered face, she was illuminated with a new idea, and exclaimed to herself:

"Now I understand it all—the child has been pining for young Laurence. Bless my heart, I never thought of such a thing!"

With praiseworthy discretion, the good lady said nothing and betrayed no sign of enlightenment, but cordially urged Laurie to stay, and begged Amy to enjoy his society, for it would do her more good than so much solitude. Amy was a model of docility, and as her aunt was a good deal occupied with Flo, she was left to entertain her friend, and did it with more than her usual success.

In spite of the new sorrow it was a very happy time, so happy that Laurie could not bear to disturb it by a word. It took him a little while to recover from his surprise at the rapid cure of his first and, as he had firmly believed, his last and only love. He consoled himself for the seeming disloyalty by the thought that Jo's sister was almost the same as Jo's self, and the conviction that it would have been impossible to love any other woman but Amy so soon and so well.

He had rather imagined that the denouement would take place in the château garden by moonlight, and in the most graceful and decorous manner; but it turned out exactly the reverse, for the matter was settled on the lake at noonday in a few blunt words. They had been floating about all the morning, from gloomy St. Gingolf to sunny Montreux, with the Alps of Savoy on one side, Mont St. Bernard and the Dent du Midi on the other, pretty Vevay in the valley, a cloudless blue sky overhead, and the bluer lake below, dotted with the picturesque boats that looked like white-winged gulls. Amy had been dabbling her hand in the water during the little pause that fell between them, and when she looked up, Laurie was leaning on his oars, with an expression in his eyes that made her say hastily, merely for the sake of saying something: "You must be tired. Rest a little, and let me row. It will do me good, for since you came I have been altogether lazy and luxurious."

"I'm not tired, but you may take an oar, if you like. There's room enough, though I have to sit nearly in the middle, else the boat won't trim," returned Laurie.

Feeling that she had not mended matters much, Amy took the offered third of a seat, shook her hair over her face, and accepted an oar. She rowed as well as she did many other things, and though she used both hands and Laurie but one, the oars kept time, and the boat went smoothly through the water.

"How well we pull together, don't we?" said Amy, who objected to silence just then.

"So well that I wish we might always pull in the same boat. Will you, Amy?"—very tenderly.

"Yes, Laurie"—very low.

Then they both stopped rowing, and unconsciously added a pretty little tableau of human love and happiness to the dissolving views reflected in the lake.

 LL ALONE

It was easy to promise self-abnegation when self was wrapped up in another and heart and soul were purified by a sweet example; but when the helpful voice was silent, the daily lesson over, the beloved presence gone, and nothing remained but loneliness and grief, then Jo found her promise very hard to keep. How could she "comfort Father and Mother" when her own heart ached with a ceaseless longing for her sister; how could she "make the house cheerful" when all its light and warmth and beauty seemed to have deserted it when Beth left the old home for the new; and where in all the world could she "find some useful, happy work to do" that would take the place of the loving service which had been its own reward? She tried in a blind, hopeless way to do her duty, secretly rebelling against it all the while, for it seemed unjust that her few joys should be lessened, her burdens made heavier, and life get harder and harder as she toiled along.

Poor Jo, these were dark days to her, for something like despair came over her when she thought of spending all her life in that quiet house, devoted to humdrum cares, a few small pleasures, and the duty that never seemed to grow any easier. "I can't do it. I wasn't meant for a life like this, and I know I shall break away and do something desperate if somebody don't come and help me," she said to herself when she fell into the moody, miserable state of mind which often comes when strong wills have to yield to the inevitable.

But someone did come and help her, though Jo did not recognize her good angels at once, because they wore familiar shapes, and used the simple spells best fitted to poor humanity. Often she started up at night thinking Beth called her, and when the sight of the little empty bed made her cry with the bitter cry of an unsubmissive sorrow—"O Beth, come back! Come back!"—she did not stretch out her yearning arms in vain; for, as quick to hear her sobbing as she had been to hear her sister's faintest whisper, her mother came to comfort her.

When aching heart was a little comforted, troubled mind likewise found help; for one day she went to the study, and, leaning over the good gray head lifted to welcome her with a tranquil smile, she said, very humbly: "Father, talk to me as you did to Beth. I need it more than she did, for I'm all wrong."

"My dear, nothing can comfort me like this," he answered, with a falter in his voice and both arms round her.

Then, sitting in Beth's little chair close beside him, Jo told her troubles—the resentful sorrow for her loss, the fruitless efforts that discouraged her, the want of faith that made life look so dark, and all the sad bewilderment which we call despair. She gave him entire confidence, he gave her the help she needed, and both found consolation in the act; for the time had come when they could talk together not only as father and daughter, but as man and woman, able and glad to serve each other with mutual sympathy as well as mutual love.

Other helps had Jo—humble, wholesome duties and delights that would not be denied their part in serving her, and which she slowly learned to see and value. Brooms and dishcloths never could be as distasteful as they once had been, for Beth had presided over both; and something of her housewifely spirit seemed to linger round the little mop and the old brush that were never thrown away. As she used them, Jo found herself humming the songs Beth used to hum, and giving the little touches here and there that kept everything fresh and cozy, which was the first step toward making home happy.

As they sat sewing together, Jo discovered how much improved her sister Meg was; how well she could talk, how much she knew about good, womanly impulses, thoughts, and feelings, how happy she was in husband and children, and how much they were all doing for each other.

"Marriage is an excellent thing, after all. I wonder if I should blossom out half as well as you have if I tried it?" said Jo as she constructed a kite for Demi.

"It's just what you need to bring out the tender, womanly half of your nature, Jo. You are like a chestnut burr, prickly outside, but silky-soft within, and a sweet kernel, if one can only get at it. Love will make you show your heart someday, and then the rough burr will fall off."

"Frost opens chestnut burrs, ma'am, and it takes a good shake to bring them down. Boys go nutting, and I don't care to be bagged by them," returned Jo, pasting away at the kite.

Meg laughed, for she was glad to see a glimmer of Jo's old spirit, but she felt it her duty to enforce her opinion by every argument in her power, and the sisterly chats were not wasted. Grief is the best opener for some hearts, and Jo's was nearly ready for the bag—a little more sunshine to ripen the nut, then not a boy's impatient shake, but a man's hand reached up to pick it gently from the burr, and find the kernel sound and sweet. If she had suspected this, she would have shut up tight, and been more prickly than ever; fortunately she wasn't thinking about herself, so when the time came, down she dropped.

Now if she had been the heroine of a moral story book, she ought at this period of her life to have become quite saintly, renounced the world, and gone about doing good in a mortified bonnet, with tracts in her pocket. But you see Jo wasn't a heroine; she was only a struggling human girl, and she just acted out her nature, being sad, cross, listless, or energetic, as the mood suggested. Jo had got so far, she was learning to do her duty, and to feel unhappy if she did not; but to do it cheerfully—ah, that was another thing! She had often said she wanted to do something splendid, no matter how hard; and now she had her wish, for what could be more beautiful than to devote her life to Father and Mother? And if difficulties were necessary to increase the splendor of the effort, what could be harder for a restless, ambitious girl than to give up her own hopes, plans, and desires, and cheerfully live for others?

"Why don't you write? That always used to make you happy," said her mother once when the desponding fit overshadowed Jo.

"I've no heart to write, and if I had, nobody cares for my things."

"We do. Write something for us, and never mind the rest of the world. Try it, dear. I'm sure it would do you good, and please us very much."

"Don't believe I can." But Jo got out her desk, and began to overhaul her half-finished manuscripts.

An hour afterward her mother peeped in, and there she was scratching away, with her black pinafore on, and an absorbed expression which caused Mrs. March to smile and slip away well pleased with the success of her suggestion. Jo never knew how it happened, but something got into that story that went straight to the hearts of those who read it; for when her family had laughed and cried over it, her father sent it, much against her will, to one of the popular magazines, and to her utter surprise it was not only paid for, but others requested. Letters from several persons whose praise was honor followed the appearance of the little story, newspapers copied it, and strangers as well as friends admired it. For a small thing it was a great success, and Jo was more astonished than when her novel was commended and condemned all at once.

"I don't understand it. What *can* there be in a simple little story like that to make people praise it so?" she said.

"There is truth in it, Jo, that's the secret. Humor and pathos make it alive, and you have found your style at last. You wrote with no thought of fame or money, and put your heart into it, my daughter; you have had the bitter, now comes the sweet. Do your best, and grow as happy as we are in your success."

"If there *is* anything good or true in what I write, it isn't mine. I owe it all to you and Mother and to Beth," said Jo, more touched by her father's words than by any amount of praise from the world.

When Amy and Laurie wrote of their engagement, Mrs. March feared that Jo would find it difficult to rejoice over it, but her fears were soon set at rest; for though Jo looked grave at first, she took it very quietly, and was full of hopes and plans for "the children" before she read the letter twice. It was a sort of written duet, wherein each glorified the other in loverlike fashion.

"You like it, Mother?" said Jo as they laid down the closely written sheets and looked at one another.

"Yes, I hoped it would be so, ever since Amy wrote that she had refused Fred. I felt sure then that something better than what you call the 'mercenary spirit' had come over her, and a hint here and there in her letters made me suspect that love and Laurie would win the day."

"How sharp you are, Marmee, and how silent! You never said a word to me."

"Mothers have need of sharp eyes and discreet tongues when they have girls to manage. I was half-afraid to put the idea into your head, lest you should write and congratulate them before the thing was settled."

"I'm not the scatterbrain I was. You may trust me, I'm sober and sensible enough for anyone's confidante now."

"So you are, dear, and I should have made you mine, only I fancied it might pain you to learn that your Teddy loved anyone else."

"Now, Mother, did you really think I could be so silly and selfish, after I'd refused his love when it was freshest, if not best?"

"I knew you were sincere then, Jo, but lately I have thought that if he came back and asked again, you might, perhaps, feel like giving another answer. Forgive me, dear, I can't help seeing that you are very lonely, so I fancied that your boy might fill the empty place if he tried now."

"No, Mother, it is better as it is, and I'm glad Amy has learned to love him. But you are right in one thing: I *am* lonely, and perhaps if Teddy had tried again, I might have said Yes, not because I love him any more, but because I care more to be loved than when he went away."

"I'm glad of that, Jo, for it shows that you are getting on. There are plenty to love you, so try to be satisfied with father and mother, sisters and brothers, friends and babies, till the best lover of all comes to give you your reward."

"Mothers are the *best* lovers in the world, but I don't mind whispering to Marmee that I'd like to try all kinds. It's very curious, but the more I try to satisfy myself with all sorts of natural affections, the more I seem to want. I'd no idea hearts could take in so many; mine is so elastic it never seems full now, and I used to be quite contented with my family. I don't understand it."

"I do!" And Mrs. March smiled her wise smile as Jo turned back the leaves to read what Amy said of Laurie.

"It is so beautiful to be loved as Laurie loves me. He isn't sentimental, doesn't say much about it, but I see and feel it in all he says and does, and it makes me so happy and so humble that I don't seem to be the same girl I was. I never knew how good and generous and tender he was till now, for he lets me read his heart, and I find it full of noble impulses and hopes and purposes, and am so proud to know it's mine. He says he feels as if he could 'make a prosperous voyage now' with me 'aboard as mate, and lots of love for ballast.' I pray he may, and try to be all he believes me, for I love my gallant captain with all my heart and soul and might, and never will desert him while God lets us be together. O Mother, I never knew how much like Heaven this world could be when two people love and live for one another!"

"And that's our cool, reserved, and worldly Amy! Truly, love does work miracles. How very, very happy they must be!"

By and by Jo roamed away upstairs, for it was rainy, and she could not walk. A restless spirit possessed her, and the old feeling came again, not bitter as it once was, but a sorrowfully patient wonder why one sister should have all she asked, the other nothing. It was not true; she knew that, and tried to put it away, but the natural craving for affection was strong, and Amy's happiness woke the hungry longing for someone to "love with heart and soul, and cling to while God let them be together."

Up in the garret, where Jo's unquiet wanderings ended, stood four little wooden chests in a row, each marked with its owner's name, and each filled with relics of the childhood and girlhood ended now for all. Jo glanced into them, and when she came to her own, leaned her chin on the edge and stared absently at the chaotic collection till a bundle of old exercise books caught her eye. She drew them out, turned them over, and relived that pleasant winter at kind Mrs. Kirke's. She had smiled at first, then she looked thoughtful, next sad, and when she came to a little message written in the Professor's hand, her lips began to tremble, the books slid out of her lap, and she sat looking at the friendly words as if they took a new meaning, and touched a tender spot in her heart.

"Wait for me, my friend. I may be a little late, but I shall surely come."

"Oh, if he only would! So kind, so good, so patient with me always, my dear old Fritz. I didn't value him half enough when I had him, but now how I should love to see him, for everyone seems going away from me, and I'm all alone."

And holding the little paper fast, as if it were a promise yet to be fulfilled, Jo laid her head down on a comfortable ragbag and cried, as if in opposition to the rain pattering on the roof.

SURPRISES

Jo was alone in the twilight, lying on the old sofa looking at the fire and thinking. It was her favorite way of spending the hour of dusk; no one disturbed her, and she used to lie there on Beth's little red pillow, planning stories, dreaming dreams, or thinking tender thoughts of the sister who never seemed far away. Her face looked tired, grave, and rather sad; for tomorrow was her birthday, and she was thinking how fast the years went by, how old she was getting, and how little she seemed to have accomplished. Almost twenty-five, and nothing to show for it. Jo was mistaken in that; there was a good deal to show, and by and by she saw and was grateful for it.

"An old maid, that's what I'm to be. A literary spinster, with a pen for a spouse, a family of stories for children, and twenty years hence a morsel of fame, perhaps—when, like poor Johnson, I'm old and can't enjoy it, solitary and can't share it, independent and don't need it. Well, I needn't be a sour saint nor a selfish sinner, and I dare say old maids are very comfortable when they get used to it, but——" And there Jo sighed, as if the prospect was not inviting.

Jo must have fallen asleep, for suddenly Laurie's ghost seemed to stand before her—a substantial, lifelike ghost leaning over her with the very look he used to wear when he felt a good deal and didn't like to show it. But, like Jenny in the ballad, "She could not think it he," and lay staring up at him in startled silence till he stooped and kissed her. Then she knew him, and flew up, crying joyfully:

"O my Teddy! O my Teddy!"

"Dear Jo, you are glad to see me, then?"

"Glad! My blessed boy, words can't express my gladness. Where's Amy?"

"Your mother has got her down at Meg's. We stopped there by the way, and there was no getting my wife out of their clutches."

"Your what?" cried Jo.

"Oh the dickens! Now I've done it." And he looked so guilty that Jo was down upon him like a flash.

"You've gone and got married!"

"Yes, please, but I never will again." And he went down on his knees, with a penitent clasping of hands, and a face full of mischief, mirth, and triumph.

"Actually married?"

"Very much so, thank you."

"Mercy on us! What dreadful thing will you do next?"

"A characteristic, but not exactly complimentary, congratulation," returned Laurie.

337

"What can you expect when you take one's breath away, creeping in like a burglar and letting cats out of bags like that? Get up, you ridiculous boy, and tell me all about it."

"Not a word unless you let me come in my old place, and promise not to barricade."

Jo laughed at that as she had not done for many a long day, and patted the sofa invitingly as she said in a cordial tone: "The old pillow is up garret, and we don't need it now, so come and 'fess, Teddy."

"How good it sounds to hear you say 'Teddy'! No one ever calls me that but you." And Laurie sat down, with an air of great content.

"What does Amy call you?"

"My lord."

"That's like her. Well, you look it." And Jo's eyes plainly betrayed that she found her boy comelier than ever.

The pillow was gone, but there *was* a barricade, nevertheless—a natural one, raised by time, absence, and change of heart. It was gone directly, however, for Laurie said, with a vain attempt at dignity: "Don't I look like a married man and the head of a family?"

"Not a bit, and you never will. You've grown bigger and bonnier, but you are the same scapegrace as ever."

"It's no use your going out in the cold to get Amy, for they are all coming up presently. I couldn't wait. I wanted to be the one to tell you the grand surprise, and have 'first skim,' as we used to say when we squabbled about the cream."

"Of course you did, and spoiled your story by beginning at the wrong end. Now start right, and tell me how it all happened. I'm pining to know."

"Well, I did it to please Amy," began Laurie, with a twinkle that made Jo exclaim:

"Fib number one. Amy did it to please you. Go on, and tell the truth, if you can, sir."

"Now she's beginning to marm it. Isn't it jolly to hear her?" said Laurie to the fire, and the fire glowed and sparkled as if it quite agreed. "It's all the same, you know, she and I being one. We planned to come home with the Carrols, a month or more ago, but they suddenly changed their minds and decided to pass another winter in Paris. But Grandpa wanted to come home. He went to please me, and I couldn't let him go alone, neither could I leave Amy; and Mrs. Carrol had got English notions about chaperons and such nonsense, and wouldn't let Amy come with us. So I just settled the difficulty by saying 'Let's be married, and then we can do as we like.'"

"How did you ever get Aunt to agree?"

"It was hard work, but between us we talked her over, for we had heaps of good reasons on our side. There wasn't time to write and ask leave, but you all liked it, had consented to it by and by, and it was only 'taking Time by the fetlock,' as my wife says."

"Aren't we proud of those two words, and don't we like to say them?" interrupted Jo, addressing the fire in her turn.

"A trifle, perhaps. She's such a captivating little woman I can't help being proud of her. Well, then, Uncle and Aunt were there to play propriety, we were so absorbed in one another we were of no mortal use apart, so we did it."

"When, where, how?" asked Jo.

"Six weeks ago, at the American consul's in Paris—a very quiet wedding, of course, for even in our happiness we didn't forget dear little Beth."

"Why didn't you let us know afterward?" asked Jo.

"We wanted to surprise you. We thought we were coming directly home at first; but the dear old gentleman, as soon as we were married, found he couldn't be ready under a month at least, and sent us off to spend our honeymoon wherever we liked. Amy had once called Valrosa a regular honeymoon home, so we went there, and were as happy as people are but once in their lives. My faith! Wasn't it love among the roses!

"Jo, dear, I want to say one thing, and then we'll put it by forever. As I told you in my letter when I wrote that Amy had been so kind to me, I never shall stop loving you; but the love is altered, and I have learned to see that it is better as it is. Amy and you change places in my heart, that's all. I think it was meant to be so, and would have come about naturally if I had waited, as you tried to make me; but I never could be patient, and so I got a heartache. I was a boy then, headstrong and violent, and it took a hard lesson to show me my mistake. For it *was* one, Jo, as you said, and I found it out, after making a fool of myself. Upon my word, I was so tumbled up in my mind at one time that I didn't know which I loved best, you or Amy, and tried to love both alike; but I couldn't, and when I saw her in Switzerland, everything seemed to clear up all at once. You both got into your right places, and I felt sure that it was well off with the old love before it was on with the new; that I could

339

honestly share my heart between sister Jo and wife Amy, and love them both dearly. Will you believe it, and go back to the happy old times when we first knew one another?"

"I'll believe it, with all my heart, but, Teddy, we never can be boy and girl again. The happy old times can't come back, and we mustn't expect it. We are man and woman now, with sober work to do, for playtime is over and we must give up frolicking. I'm sure you feel this. I see the change in you, and you'll find it in me. I shall miss my boy, but I shall love the man as much, and admire him more, because he means to be what I hoped he would. We can't be little playmates any longer, but we will be brother and sister, to love and help one another all our lives, won't we, Laurie?"

He did not say a word, but took the hand she offered him and laid his face down on it for a minute, feeling that out of the grave of a boyish passion there had risen a beautiful, strong friendship to bless them both. Presently Jo said cheerfully, for she didn't want the coming home to be a sad one: "I can't make it true that you children are really married, and going to set up housekeeping. Why, it seems only yesterday that I was buttoning Amy's pinafore, and pulling your hair when you teased. Mercy me, how time does fly!"

"As one of the children is older than yourself, you needn't talk so like a grandma. I flatter myself I'm a 'gentleman growed,' as Peggotty said of David, and when you see Amy, you'll find her rather a precocious infant."

"You may be a little older in years, but I'm ever so much older in feeling, Teddy. Women always are, and this last year has been such a hard one that I feel forty."

"Poor Jo! We left you to bear it alone while we went pleasuring. You *are* older; here's a line, and there's another; unless you smile, your eyes look sad. You've had a great deal to bear, all alone. What a selfish beast I've been!"

But Jo answered in a tone which she tried to make quite cheerful: "No, I had Father and Mother to help me, the dear babies to comfort me, and the thought that you and Amy were safe and happy, to make the troubles here easier to bear. I *am* lonely, sometimes, but I dare say it's good for me, and——"

"You never shall be again," broke in Laurie, putting his arm about her as if to fence out every human ill. "Amy and I can't get on without you, so you must come and teach 'the children' to keep house, and go halves in everything, just as we used to do, and all be blissfully happy and friendly together."

"If I shouldn't be in the way, it would be very pleasant. I begin to feel quite young already, for somehow all my troubles seemed to fly away when you came. You always were a comfort, Teddy." And Jo leaned her head on his shoulder, just as she did years ago when Beth lay ill, and Laurie told her to hold onto him.

He looked down at her, wondering if she remembered the time, but Jo was smiling to herself, as if in truth her troubles *had* all vanished at his coming. "You are the same Jo still, dropping tears about one minute and laughing the next. You look a little wicked now. What is it, Grandma?"

"I was wondering how you and Amy get on together."

"Like angels!"

"Yes, of course, at first. But which rules?"

"I don't mind telling you that she does now, at least I let her think so —it pleases her, you know. By and by we shall take turns, for marriage, they say, halves one's rights and doubles one's duties."

"You'll go on as you begin, and Amy will rule you all your life."

"Well, she does it so imperceptibly that I don't think I shall mind much. She is the sort of woman who knows how to rule well; in fact, I rather like it, for she winds one round her finger as softly and prettily as a skein of silk, and makes you feel as if she was doing you a favor all the while."

"That ever I should live to see you a henpecked husband and enjoying it!" cried Jo, with uplifted hands.

It was good to see Laurie smile with masculine scorn at that insinuation, as he replied, with his "high-and-mighty" air: "Amy is too well-bred for that, and I am not the sort of man to submit to it. My wife and I respect ourselves and one another too much ever to tyrannize or quarrel."

"I am sure of that. Amy and you never did quarrel as we used to. She is the sun and I the wind in the fable, and the sun managed the man best, you remember."

"She can blow him up as well as shine on him," laughed Laurie. "Such a lecture as I got at Nice! I give you my word it was a deal worse than any of your scoldings—a regular rouser. I'll tell you all about it sometime— *she* never will, because after telling me that she despised and was ashamed of me, she lost her heart to the despicable party and married the good-for-nothing."

341

"What baseness! Well, if she abuses you, come to me, and I'll defend you."

"I look as if I needed it, don't I?" said Laurie, getting up and striking an attitude which suddenly changed from the imposing to the rapturous as Amy's voice was heard calling:

"Where is she? Where's my dear old Jo?"

In trooped the whole family, and everyone was hugged and kissed all over again, and after several vain attempts, the three wanderers were set down to be looked at and exulted over. Mr. Laurence, hale and hearty as ever, was quite as much improved as the others by his foreign tour, for the crustiness seemed to be nearly gone, and the old-fashioned courtliness had received a polish which made it kindlier than ever. It was good to see him beam at "my children," as he called the young pair; it was better still to see Amy pay him the daughterly duty and affection which completely won his old heart; and best of all to watch Laurie revolve about the two as if never tired of enjoying the pretty picture they made.

Jo thought as she watched the pair: "How well they look together! I was right, and Laurie has found the beautiful, accomplished girl who will become his home better than clumsy old Jo, and be a pride, not a torment, to him." Mrs. March and her husband smiled and nodded at each other with happy faces, for they saw that their youngest had done well, not only in worldly things, but in the better wealth of love, confidence, and happiness.

For Amy's face was full of the soft brightness which betokens a peaceful heart, her voice had a new tenderness in it, and the cool, prim carriage was changed to a gentle dignity, both womanly and winning. No little affectations marred it, and the cordial sweetness of her manner was more charming than the new beauty or the old grace, for it stamped her at once with the unmistakable sign of the true gentlewoman she had hoped to become.

"Love has done much for our little girl," said her mother softly.

"She has had a good example before her all her life, my dear," Mr. March whispered back.

Daisy found it impossible to keep her eyes off her "pitty aunty," but attached herself like a lap dog to the wonderful chatelaine full of delightful charms. Demi paused to consider the new relationship before he compromised himself by the rash acceptance of a bribe, which took the tempting form of a family of wooden bears from Berne. A flank movement produced an unconditional surrender, however, for Laurie knew where to have him.

"Young man, when I first had the honor of making your acquaintance you hit me in the face. Now I demand the satisfaction of a gentleman." And with that the tall uncle proceeded to toss and tousle the small nephew in a way that damaged his philosophical dignity as much as it delighted his boyish soul.

Mercy on us, how they did talk! First one, then the other, then all burst out together, trying to tell the history of three years in half an hour. It was fortunate that tea was at hand to produce a lull and provide refreshment, for they would have been hoarse and faint if they had gone on much longer. Such a happy procession as filed away into the little dining room! Mr. March proudly escorted "Mrs. Laurence," Mrs. March as proudly leaned on the arm of "my son," the old gentleman took Jo, with a whispered "You must be my girl now," and a glance at the empty corner by the fire that made Jo whisper back, with trembling lips, "I'll try to fill her place, sir."

The twins pranced behind, feeling that the millennium was at hand, for everyone was so busy with the newcomers that they were left to revel at their own sweet will, and you may be sure they made the most of the opportunity. Didn't they steal sips of tea, stuff gingerbread ad libitum, get a hot biscuit apiece, and, as a crowning trespass, didn't they each whisk a captivating little tart into their tiny pockets, there to stick and crumble treacherously, teaching them that both human nature and pastry are frail? Burdened with the guilty consciousness of the sequestered tarts, and fearing that "Dodo's" sharp eyes would pierce the thin disguise of cambric and merino which hid their booty, the little sinners attached themselves to "Dranpa," who hadn't his spectacles on. Amy, who was handed about like refreshments, returned to the parlor on Father Laurence's arm; the others paired off as before, and this arrangement left Jo companionless. She stood a minute looking at the party vanishing above, and as Demi's short plaid legs toiled up the last stair, a sudden sense of loneliness came over her so strongly that she looked about her with dim eyes, as if to find something to lean upon, for even Teddy had deserted her. She had just managed to call up a smile when there came a knock at the porch door.

She opened it with hospitable haste, and started as if another ghost had come to surprise her; for there stood a tall bearded gentleman, beaming on her from the darkness like a midnight sun.

"O Mr. Bhaer, I *am* so glad to see you!" cried Jo, with a clutch, as if she feared the night would swallow him up before she could get him in.

"And I to see Miss Marsch—but no, you haf a party——" And the

Professor paused as the sound of voices and the tap of dancing feet came down to them.

"No we haven't, only the family. My sister and friends have just come home, and we are all very happy. Come in, and make one of us."

Though a very social man, I think Mr. Bhaer would have gone decorously away, and come again another day, but how could he when Jo shut the door behind him, and bereft him of his hat? Perhaps her face had something to do with it, for she forgot to hide her joy at seeing him, and showed it with a frankness that proved irresistible to the solitary man, whose welcome far exceeded his boldest hopes.

"If I shall not be Monsieur de Trop, I will so gladly see them all. You haf been ill, my friend?"

He put the question abruptly, for as Jo hung up his coat the light fell on her face, and he saw a change in it.

"Not ill, but tired and sorrowful. We have had trouble since I saw you last."

"Ah yes, I know. My heart was sore for you when I heard that!" And he shook hands again, with such a sympathetic face that Jo felt as if no comfort could equal the look of the kind eyes, the grasp of the big, warm hand.

"Father, Mother, this is my friend Professor Bhaer," she said, with a face and tone of such irrepressible pride and pleasure that she might as well have blown a trumpet and opened the door with a flourish.

If the stranger had had any doubts about his reception, they were set at rest in a minute by the cordial welcome he received. Everyone greeted him kindly—for Jo's sake at first, but very soon they liked him for his own. They could not help it, for he carried the talisman that opens all hearts, and these simple people warmed to him at once, feeling even the more friendly because he was poor; for poverty enriches those who live above it, and is a sure passport to truly hospitable spirits. Mr. Bhaer sat looking about him with the air of a traveler who knocks at a strange door and when it opens, finds himself at home. The children went to him like bees to a honey pot and, establishing themselves on each knee, proceeded to captivate him by rifling his pockets, pulling his beard, and investigating his watch, with juvenile audacity. The women telegraphed their approval to one another, and Mr. March, feeling that he had got a kindred spirit, opened his choicest stores for his guest's benefit, while silent John listened and enjoyed the talk but said not a word, and Mr. Laurence found it impossible to go to sleep.

If Jo had not been otherwise engaged, Laurie's behavior would have amused her; for a faint twinge, not of jealousy, but something like suspicion, caused that gentleman to stand aloof at first, and observe the newcomer with brotherly circumspection. But it did not last long. He got interested in spite of himself, and before he knew it was drawn into the circle; for Mr. Bhaer talked well in this genial atmosphere, and did himself justice. He seldom spoke to Laurie, but looked at him often, and a shadow would pass across his face, as if regretting his own lost youth, as he watched the young man in his prime. Then his eye would turn to Jo so wistfully that she would have surely answered the mute inquiry if she had seen it; but Jo had her own eyes to take care of and, feeling that they could not be trusted, she prudently kept them on the little sock she was knitting, like a model maiden aunt.

A stealthy glance now and then refreshed her like sips of fresh water after a dusty walk, for the sidelong peeps showed her several propitious omens. Mr. Bhaer's face had lost the absent-minded expression, and looked all alive with interest in the present moment, actually young and handsome, she thought. Then he seemed quite inspired, though the burial customs of the ancients, to which the conversation had strayed, might not be considered an exhilarating topic. Jo quite glowed with triumph when Teddy got quenched in an argument, and thought to herself as she watched her father's absorbed face, "How he would enjoy having such a man as my Professor to talk with every day!" Lastly, Mr. Bhaer was dressed in a new suit of black, which made him look more like a gentleman than ever. His bushy hair had been cut and smoothly brushed, but didn't stay in order long, for in exciting moments he rumpled it up in the droll way he used to do; and Jo liked it rampantly erect better than flat, because she thought it gave his fine forehead a Jovelike aspect. Poor Jo, how she did glorify that plain man as she sat knitting away so quietly, yet letting nothing escape her, not even the fact that Mr. Bhaer actually had gold sleeve buttons in his immaculate wristbands!

"Dear old fellow! He couldn't have got himself up with more care if he'd been going a-wooing," said Jo to herself, and then a sudden thought, born of the words, made her blush so dreadfully that she had to drop her ball, and go down after it to hide her face.

The maneuver did not succeed as well as she expected, however; for though just in the act of setting fire to a funeral pile, the Professor dropped his torch, metaphorically speaking, and made a dive after the

345

little blue ball. Of course they bumped their heads smartly together, saw stars, and both came up flushed and laughing, without the ball, to resume their seats wishing they had not left them. Nobody knew where the evening went to; for Hannah skillfully abstracted the babies at an early hour, nodding like two rosy poppies, and Mr. Laurence went home to rest. The others sat round the fire talking away utterly regardless of the lapse of time till Meg, whose maternal mind was impressed with a firm conviction that Daisy had tumbled out of bed, and Demi set his nightgown afire studying the structure of matches, made a move to go.

"We must have our sing in the good old way, for we are all together again once more," said Jo, feeling that a good shout would be a safe and pleasant vent for the jubilant emotions of her soul.

They were not *all* there. But no one found the words thoughtless or untrue; for Beth still seemed among them, a peaceful presence, invisible, but dearer than ever, since death could not break the household league that love made indissoluble.

"Play something, Amy. Let them hear how much you have improved," said Laurie.

But Amy whispered with full eyes as she twirled the faded stool: "Not tonight, dear. I can't show off tonight."

But she did show something better than brilliancy or skill; for she sang Beth's songs with a tender music in her voice which the best master could not have taught, and touched the listeners' hearts with a sweeter power than any other inspiration could have given her. The room was very still when the clear voice failed suddenly at the last line of Beth's favorite hymn. It was hard to say "Earth hath no sorrow that Heaven cannot heal," and Amy leaned against her husband, who stood behind her, feeling that her welcome home was not quite perfect without Beth's kiss.

"Now we must finish with Mignon's song, for Mr. Bhaer sings that," said Jo, before the pause grew painful. And Mr. Bhaer cleared his throat with a gratified "Hem!" as he stepped into the corner where Jo stood.

"You will sing with me? We go excellently well together."

A pleasing fiction, by the way, for Jo had no more idea of music than a grasshopper. But she would have consented if he had proposed to sing a whole opera, and warbled away blissfully regardless of time and tune. It didn't much matter; for Mr. Bhaer sang like a true German, heartily and well, and Jo soon subsided into a subdued hum, that she might listen to the mellow voice that seemed to sing for her alone. "Know'st thou the land where the citron blooms?" used to be the Professor's favorite line, for *"das Land"* meant Germany to him, but now he seemed to dwell with peculiar warmth and melody upon the words

> "There, oh there, might I with thee,
> O my beloved, go!"

and one listener was so thrilled by the tender invitation that she longed to say she did know the land, and would joyfully depart thither whenever he liked.

The song was considered a great success, and the singer retired covered with laurels. But a few minutes afterward he forgot his manners entirely, and stared at Amy putting on her bonnet; for she had been introduced simply as "my sister," and no one had called her by her new name since he came. He forgot himself still further when Laurie said, in his most gracious manner, at parting: "My wife and I are very glad to meet you, sir. Please remember that there is always a welcome waiting for you over the way."

Then the Professor thanked him so heartily and looked so suddenly illuminated with satisfaction that Laurie thought him the most delightfully demonstrative old fellow he ever met.

"I too shall go, but I shall gladly come again, if you will gif me leave, dear madame, for a little business in the city will keep me here some days."

He spoke to Mrs. March, but he looked at Jo, and the mother's voice gave as cordial an assent as did the daughter's eyes.

"I suspect that is a wise man," remarked Mr. March with placid satisfaction after the last guest had gone.

"I know he is a good one," added Mrs. March, with decided approval, as she wound up the clock.

"I thought you'd like him," was all Jo said as she slipped away to bed.

She wondered what the business was that brought Mr. Bhaer to the city, and finally decided that he had been appointed to some great honor somewhere, but had been too modest to mention the fact. If she had seen his face when, safe in his own room, he looked at the picture of a severe and rigid young lady with a good deal of hair who appeared to be gazing darkly into futurity, it might have thrown some light upon the subject, especially when he turned off the gas and kissed the picture in the dark.

MY LORD AND LADY

"Please, Madam Mother, could you lend me my wife for half an hour? The luggage has come, and I've been making hay of Amy's Paris finery trying to find some things I want," said Laurie, coming in the next day to find Mrs. Laurence sitting in her mother's lap, as if being made "the baby" again.

"Certainly. Go, dear. I forget that you have any home but this."

"I shouldn't have come over if I could have helped it, but can't get on without my little woman any more than a——"

"Weathercock can without wind," suggested Jo as he paused for a simile.

"Exactly, for Amy keeps me pointing due west most of the time, with only an occasional whiffle round to the south, and I haven't had an easterly spell since I was married. Don't know anything about the north, but am altogether salubrious and balmy, hey, my lady?"

"Lovely weather so far. I don't know how long it will last, but I'm not afraid of storms, for I'm learning how to sail my ship. Come home, dear, and I'll find your bootjack. I suppose that's what you are rummaging after among my things. Men are so helpless, Mother," said Amy, with a matronly air which delighted her husband.

"What are you going to do with yourselves after you get settled?" asked Jo.

"We have our plans. We don't mean to say much about them yet, because we are such very new brooms, but we don't intend to be idle. I'm going into business with a devotion that shall delight Grandfather, and prove to him that I'm not spoiled. I'm tired of dawdling, and mean to work like a man."

"And Amy, what is she going to do?" asked Mrs. March.

"After doing the civil all round, and airing our best bonnet, we shall astonish you by the elegant hospitalities of our mansion, the brilliant society we shall draw about us, and the beneficial influence we shall exert over the world at large. That's about it, isn't it, Madame Récamier?" asked Laurie, with a quizzical look at Amy.

348

"Time will show. Come away, Impertinence, and don't shock my family by calling me names before their faces."

"How happy those children seem together!" observed Mr. March after the young couple had gone.

"Yes, and I think it will last," added Mrs. March, with the restful expression of a pilot who has brought a ship safely into port.

"I know it will. Happy Amy." And Jo sighed, then smiled brightly as Professor Bhaer opened the gate with an impatient push.

Later in the evening, when his mind had been set at rest about the bootjack, Laurie said suddenly to his wife, who was flitting about arranging her new art treasures, "Mrs. Laurence."

"My lord!"

"That man intends to marry our Jo!"

"I hope so, don't you, dear?"

"Well, my love, I consider him a trump, in the fullest sense of that expressive word, but I do wish he was a little younger and a good deal richer."

"Now, Laurie, don't be too fastidious and worldly-minded. If they love one another it doesn't matter a particle how old they are nor how poor. Women *never* should marry for money——" Amy caught herself up short as the words escaped her, and looked at her husband, who replied, with malicious gravity:

"Certainly not, though you do hear charming girls say that they intend to do it. If my memory serves me, you once thought it your duty to make a rich match; that accounts, perhaps, for your marrying a good-for-nothing like me."

"O my dearest boy, don't, don't say that! I forgot you were rich when I said Yes. I'd have married you if you hadn't a penny, and I sometimes wish you *were* poor that I might show how much I love you. You don't really think I am such a mercenary creature as I tried to be once, do you? It would break my heart if you didn't believe that I'd gladly pull in the same boat with you even if you had to get your living by rowing on the lake."

"Am I an idiot and a brute? How could I think so when you refused a richer man for me, and won't let me give you half I want to now, when I have the right? Girls do it every day, poor things, and are taught to think it is their only salvation; but you had better lessons, and though I trembled for you at one time, I was not disappointed, for the daughter was true to the mother's teaching. I told Mamma so yesterday, and she looked as glad and grateful as if I'd given her a check for a million to be spent in charity."

"May I ask you a question, dear?"

"Of course you may."

"Shall you care if Jo does marry Mr. Bhaer?"

"Oh, that's the trouble, is it? Not being a dog in the manger, but the happiest fellow alive, I assure you I can dance at Jo's wedding with a heart as light as my heels. Do you doubt it, my darling?"

Amy looked up at him, and was satisfied; her last little jealous fear vanished forever, and she thanked him with a face full of love and confidence.

"I wish we could do something for that capital old Professor. Couldn't we invent a rich relation who shall obligingly die out there in Germany and leave him a tidy little fortune?" said Laurie.

"Jo would find us out, and spoil it all. She is very proud of him just as he is, and said yesterday that she thought poverty was a beautiful thing."

"Bless her dear heart! She won't think so when she has a literary husband, and a dozen little professors and professorins to support. We won't interfere now, but watch our chance, and do them a good turn in spite of themselves. I owe Jo for a part of my education, and she believes in people's paying their honest debts, so I'll get round her in that way."

"How delightful it is to be able to help others, isn't it? That was always one of my dreams, to have the power of giving freely, and, thanks to you, the dream has come true."

DAISY AND DEMI

I cannot feel that I have done my duty as humble historian of the March family without devoting at least one chapter to the two most precious and important members of it. Daisy and Demi had now arrived at years of discretion; for in this fast age babies of three or four assert their rights—and get them, too, which is more than many of their elders do. If there ever were a pair of twins in danger of being utterly spoiled by adoration, it was these prattling Brookes. Of course they were the most remarkable children ever born, as will be shown when I mention that they walked at eight months, talked fluently at twelve months, and at two years they took their places at table and behaved with a propriety which charmed all beholders. At three, Daisy demanded a "needler," and actually made a bag with four stitches in it; she likewise set up housekeeping in the sideboard, and managed a microscopic cooking stove with a skill that brought tears of pride to Hannah's eyes, while Demi learned his letters with his grandfather, who invented a new mode of teaching the alphabet by forming the letters with his arms and legs, thus uniting gymnastics for head and heels. The boy early developed a mechanical genius which delighted his father and distracted his mother, for he tried to imitate every machine he saw, and kept the nursery in a chaotic condition, with his "sewin sheen"—a mysterious structure of string, chairs, clothespins, and spools for wheels to go "wound and wound"; also a basket hung over the back of a big chair, in which he vainly tried to hoist his too confiding sister, who allowed her little head to be bumped till rescued, when the young inventor indignantly remarked:

"Why, Marmar, dat's my lellywaiter, and me's trying to pull her up."

Though utterly unlike in character, the twins got on remarkably well together, and seldom quarreled more than thrice a day. Of course Demi tyrannized over Daisy, and gallantly defended her from every other aggressor, while Daisy made a galley slave of herself, and adored her brother as the one perfect being in the world. A rosy, chubby, sunshiny little soul was Daisy, who found her way to everybody's heart. One of the captivating children who seem made to be kissed and cuddled, adorned and adored like little goddesses, and produced for general approval on all festive occasions. Her small virtues were so sweet that she would have been quite angelic if a few small naughtinesses had not kept her delightfully human. It was all fair weather in her world, and every morning she scrambled up to the window in her little nightgown to look out and say, no matter whether it rained or shone, "Oh, pitty day, oh, pitty day!" Everyone was a friend, and she offered kisses to a stranger so confidingly that the most inveterate bachelor relented, and baby-lovers became faithful worshipers.

"Me loves evvybody," she once said, opening her arms, with her spoon in one hand and her mug in the other, as if eager to embrace and nourish the whole world.

Her grandfather often called her "Beth," and her grandmother watched over her with untiring devotion, as if trying to atone for some past mistake which no eye but her own could see.

Demi, like a true Yankee, was of an inquiring turn, wanting to know everything, and often getting much disturbed because he could not get satisfactory answers to his perpetual "What for?" He also possessed a philosophic bent, to the great delight of his grandfather, who used to hold Socratic conversations with him.

"What makes my legs go, Dranpa?" asked the young philosopher, surveying those active portions of his frame with a meditative air while resting after a go-to-bed frolic one night.

"It's your little mind, Demi," replied the sage.

"What is a little mine?"

"It is something which makes your body move, as the spring made the wheels go in my watch when I showed it to you."

"Open me. I want to see it go wound."

"I can't do that any more than you could open the watch. God winds you up, and you go till He stops you."

"Does I?" And Demi's brown eyes grew big and bright as he took in the new thought. "Is I wounded up like the watch?"

"Yes, but I can't show you how, for it is done when we don't see."

Demi felt of his back, as if expecting to find it like that of the watch, and then gravely remarked: "I dess Dod does it when I's asleep."

352

A careful explanation followed, to which he listened so attentively that his anxious grandmother said: "My dear, do you think it wise to talk about such things to that baby? He's getting great bumps over his eyes, and learning to ask the most unanswerable questions."

"If he is old enough to ask the questions he is old enough to receive true answers. I am not putting the thoughts into his head, but helping him unfold those already there. These children are wiser than we are, and I have no doubt the boy understands every word I have said to him. Now, Demi, tell me where you keep your mind."

If the boy had replied, like Alcibiades, "By the gods, Socrates, I cannot tell," his grandfather would not have been surprised; but when after standing a moment on one leg, like a meditative young stork, he answered, in a tone of calm conviction, "In my little belly," the old gentleman could only join in Grandma's laugh, and dismiss the class in metaphysics.

Meg made many moral rules, and tried to keep them; but what mother was ever proof against the winning wiles, the ingenious evasions, or the tranquil audacity of the miniature men and women who so early show themselves accomplished Artful Dodgers?

"No more raisins, Demi, they'll make you sick," says Mamma to the young person, who offers his services in the kitchen with unfailing regularity on plum-pudding day.

"Me likes to be sick."

"I don't want to have you, so run away and help Daisy make pat-a-cakes."

He reluctantly departs, but his wrongs weigh upon his spirit, and by and by, when an opportunity comes to redress them, he outwits Mamma by a shrewd bargain.

"Now you have been good children, and I'll play anything you like," says Meg as she leads her assistant cooks upstairs when the pudding is safely bouncing in the pot.

"Truly, Marmar?" asks Demi.

"Yes, truly, anything you say," replies the shortsighted parent, preparing herself to sing "The Three Little Kittens" half a dozen times over, or to take her family to "Buy a penny bun," regardless of wind or limb. But Demi corners her by the cool reply: "Then we'll go and eat up all the raisins."

Aunt Dodo was chief playmate and confidante of both children, and the trio turned the little house topsy-turvy. Aunt Amy was as yet only a name to them, Aunt Beth soon faded into a pleasantly vague memory, but Aunt Dodo was a living reality, and they made the most of her, for which compliment she was deeply grateful. But when Mr. Bhaer came, Jo neglected her playfellows, and dismay and desolation fell upon their little souls. Daisy, who was fond of going about peddling kisses, lost her best customer and became bankrupt. Demi, with infantile penetration, soon discovered that Dodo liked to play with "the bear man" better than she did with him; but though hurt, he concealed his anguish, for he hadn't the heart to insult a rival who kept a mine of chocolate drops in his waistcoat pocket, and a watch that could be taken out of its case and freely shaken by ardent admirers.

Gentlemen are sometimes seized with sudden fits of admiration for the young relatives of ladies whom they honor with their regard; but this counterfeit philoprogenitiveness sits uneasily upon them, and does not deceive anybody a particle. Mr. Bhaer's devotion was sincere, however likewise effective—for honesty is the best policy in love as in law. He was one of the men who are at home with children, and looked particularly well when little faces made a pleasant contrast with his manly one. His business, whatever it was, detained him from day to day, but evening seldom failed to bring him out to see—well, he always asked for Mr. March, so I suppose *he* was the attraction. The excellent papa labored under the delusion that he was till a chance remark of his more observing grandson suddenly enlightened him.

Mr. Bhaer came in one evening to pause on the threshold of the study, astonished by the spectacle that met his eye. Prone upon the floor lay Mr. March, with his respectable legs in the air, and beside him, likewise prone, was Demi, trying to imitate the attitude with his own short, scarlet-stockinged legs, both grovelers so seriously absorbed that they were unconscious of spectators till Mr. Bhaer laughed his sonorous laugh, and Jo cried out, with a scandalized face:

"Father, Father, here's the Professor!"

Down went the black legs and up came the gray head as the preceptor said, with undisturbed dignity: "Good evening, Mr. Bhaer. Excuse me for a moment, we are just finishing our lesson. Now, Demi, make the letter and tell its name."

"I knows him!" And after a few convulsive efforts, the red legs took the shape of a pair of compasses, and the intelligent pupil triumphantly shouted, "It's a We, Dranpa, it's a We!"

354

"He's a born Weller," laughed Jo as her parent gathered himself up, and her nephew tried to stand on his head.

"What have you been at today, *Bübchen?*" asked Mr. Bhaer, picking up the gymnast.

"Me went to see little Mary."

"And what did you do there?"

"I kissed her," began Demi, with artless frankness.

"*Prut!* Thou beginnest early. What did the little Mary say to that?" asked Mr. Bhaer, continuing to confess the young sinner, who stood upon his knee exploring the waistcoat pocket.

"Oh, she liked it, and she kissed me, and I liked it. *Don't* little boys like little girls?"

"You precocious chick! Who put that into your head?" said Jo.

" 'Tisn't in mine head, it's in mine mouf," answered literal Demi, putting out his tongue with a chocolate drop on it, thinking she alluded to confectionery, not ideas.

"Thou shouldst save some for the little friend. Sweets to the sweets, *Männling,*" and Mr. Bhaer offered Jo some with a look that made her wonder if chocolate was not the nectar drunk by the gods. Demi also saw the smile, was impressed by it, and artlessly inquired: "Do great boys like great girls, too, 'Fessor?"

Like young Washington, Mr. Bhaer "couldn't tell a lie," so he gave the somewhat vague reply that he believed they did sometimes, in a tone that made Mr. March put down his clothes brush, glance at Jo's retiring face, and then sink into his chair looking as if the "precocious chick" had put an idea into *his* head that was both sweet and sour.

UNDER THE UMBRELLA

While Laurie and Amy were taking conjugal strolls over velvet carpets as they set their house in order and planned a blissful future, Mr. Bhaer and Jo were enjoying promenades of a different sort, along muddy roads and sodden fields.

"I always do take a walk toward evening, and I don't know why I should give it up just because I often happen to meet the Professor on his way out," said Jo to herself after two or three encounters; for though there were two paths to Meg's, whichever one she took she was sure to meet him, either going or returning. He was always walking rapidly, and never seemed to see her till quite close, when he would look as if his shortsighted eyes had failed to recognize the approaching lady till that moment. Then, if she was going to Meg's he always had something for the babies; if her face was turned homeward, he had merely strolled down to see the river, and was just about returning, unless they were tired of his frequent calls.

Under the circumstances, what could Jo do but greet him civilly, and invite him in? If she *was* tired of his visits, she concealed her weariness with perfect skill, and took care that there should be coffee for supper, "as Friedrich—I mean Mr. Bhaer—doesn't like tea."

By the second week, everyone knew perfectly well what was going on, yet everyone tried to look as if they were stone-blind to the changes in Jo's face. They never asked why she sang about her work, did up her hair three times a day, and got so blooming with her evening exercise; and no one seemed to have the slightest suspicion that Professor Bhaer while talking philosophy with the father was giving the daughter lessons in love.

Jo couldn't even lose her heart in a decorous manner, but sternly tried to quench her feelings, and failing to do so, led a somewhat agitated life. She was mortally afraid of being laughed at for surrendering, after her many and vehement declarations of independence. Laurie was her especial dread; but, thanks to the new manager, he behaved with praiseworthy propriety, never called Mr. Bhaer "a capital old fellow" in public, never alluded in the remotest manner to Jo's improved appearance, or expressed the least surprise at seeing the Professor's hat on the Marches' hall table nearly every evening. But he exulted in private and longed for the time to come when he could give Jo a piece of plate with a bear and a ragged staff on it as an appropriate coat of arms.

For a fortnight, the Professor came and went with loverlike regularity; then he stayed away for three whole days, and made no sign—a proceeding which caused everybody to look sober, and Jo to become pensive at first, and then—alas for romance!—very cross. "Disgusted, I dare say, and gone home as suddenly as he came. It's nothing to me, of course, but I *should* think he would have come and bid us good-by like a gentleman," she said to herself, as she put on her things one dull afternoon.

"You'd better take the little umbrella, dear. It looks like rain," said her mother, observing that she had on her new bonnet, but not alluding to the fact.

"Yes, Marmee. Do you want anything in town? I've got to run in and get some paper," returned Jo.

"Yes, I want some twilled silesia, a paper of number nine needles, and two yards of narrow lavender ribbon. Have you got your thick boots on, and something warm under your cloak?"

"I believe so," answered Jo absently.

"If you happen to meet Mr. Bhaer, bring him home to tea. I quite long to see the dear man," added Mrs. March.

Jo heard *that*, but made no answer except to kiss her mother, and walk rapidly away thinking with a glow of gratitude, in spite of her heartache:

"How good she is to me! What *do* girls do who haven't any mothers to help them through their troubles?"

The dry-goods stores were not down among the countinghouses, banks, and wholesale warerooms where gentlemen most do congregate; but Jo found herself in that part of the city before she did a single errand, loitering along as if waiting for someone, examining engineering instruments in one window and samples of wool in another with most unfeminine interest; tumbling over barrels, being half-smothered by descending bales, and hustled unceremoniously by busy men who looked as if they wondered "how the deuce" she got there. A drop of rain on her cheek recalled her thoughts from baffled hopes to ruined ribbons; for the drops continued to fall, and being a woman as well as a lover, she felt that though it was too late to save her heart, she might her bonnet. Now she remembered the little umbrella, which she had forgotten to take in her hurry to be off; but regret was unavailing, and nothing could be done but borrow one or submit to a drenching. She looked up at the lowering sky, down at the crimson bow already flecked with black, then one long, lingering look behind at a certain grimy warehouse with Hoffmann, Swartz, & Co. over the door, and said to herself, with a sternly reproachful air: "It serves me right! What business had I to put on all my best things and come philandering down here hoping to see the Professor? Jo, I'm ashamed of you! No, you shall *not* go there to borrow an umbrella, or find out where he is from his friends. You shall trudge away and do your errands in the rain, and if you catch your death and ruin your bonnet, it's no more than you deserve. Now then!"

With that she rushed across the street so impetuously that she narrowly escaped annihilation from a passing truck, and precipitated herself into the arms of a stately old gentleman who said, "I beg pardon, ma'am," and looked mortally offended. Somewhat daunted, Jo righted herself, spread her handkerchief over the devoted ribbons, and, putting temptation behind her, hurried on, with increasing dampness about the ankles and much clashing of umbrellas overhead. The fact that a somewhat dilapidated blue one remained stationary above the unprotected bonnet attracted her attention, and looking up, she saw Mr. Bhaer looking down.

"I feel to know the strong-minded lady who goes so bravely under many horse noses, and so fast through much mud. What do you down here, my friend?"

"I'm shopping."

Mr. Bhaer smiled as he glanced from the pickle factory on one side to the wholesale hide-and-leather concern on the other, but he only said politely: "You haf no umbrella. May I go also, and take for you the bundles?"

"Yes, thank you."

Jo's cheeks were as red as her ribbon, and she wondered what he thought of her; but she didn't care, for in a minute she found herself walking away arm-in-arm with her Professor, feeling as if the sun had suddenly burst out with uncommon brilliancy, that the world was all right again, and that one thoroughly happy woman was paddling through the wet that day.

"We thought you had gone," said Jo, hastily.

"Did you believe that I should go with no farewell to those who haf been so heavenly kind to me?" he asked, so reproachfully that she felt as if she had insulted him by the suggestion, and answered heartily: "No, I didn't. I knew you were busy about your own affairs, but we rather missed you—Father and Mother especially."

"And you?"

"I'm always glad to see you, sir."

In her anxiety to keep her voice quite calm, Jo made it rather cool, and the frosty little monosyllable at the end seemed to chill the Professor, for his smile vanished as he said gravely: "I thank you, and come one time more before I go."

"You *are* going, then?"

"I haf no longer any business here, it is done."

"Successfully, I hope?" said Jo.

"I ought to think so, for I haf a way opened to me by which I can make my bread and gif my *Jünglings* much help."

"Tell me, please! I like to know all about the—the boys," said Jo eagerly.

"That is so kind. I gladly tell you. My friends find for me a place in a college where I teach as at home, and earn enough to make the way smooth for Franz and Emil. For this I should be grateful, should I not?"

"Indeed you should. How splendid it will be to have you doing what you like, and be able to see you often, and the boys!" cried Jo.

"Ah, but we shall not meet often, I fear. This place is at the West."

"So far away!"

Mr. Bhaer could read several languages, but he had not learned to read women yet. He flattered himself that he knew Jo pretty well, and was therefore much amazed by the contradictions of voice, face, and manner which she showed him in rapid succession that day, for she was in half a dozen different moods in the course of half an hour. When she met him she looked surprised, though it was impossible to help suspecting that she had come for that express purpose. When he offered her his arm, she took it with a look that filled him with delight; but when he asked if she missed him, she gave such a chilly, formal reply that despair fell upon him. On learning his good fortune she almost clapped her hands. Was the joy all for the boys? Then on hearing his destination she said, "So far away!" in a tone of despair that lifted him onto a pinnacle of hope; but the next minute she tumbled him down again by observing, like one entirely absorbed in the matter: "Here's the place for my errands. Will you come in? It won't take long."

Jo rather prided herself upon her shopping capabilities, and particularly wished to impress her escort with the neatness and dispatch with which she would accomplish the business. But owing to the flutter she was in, everything went amiss; she upset the tray of needles, forgot the silesia was to be "twilled" till it was cut off, gave the wrong change, and covered herself with confusion by asking for lavender ribbon at the calico counter. Mr. Bhaer stood by, watching her blush and blunder, and as he watched her, his own bewilderment seemed to subside, for he was beginning to see that on some occasions women, like dreams, go by contraries. When they came out, he put the parcel under his arm with a more cheerful aspect, and splashed through the puddles as if he rather enjoyed it, on the whole.

"Should we not do a little what you call shopping for the babies, and haf a farewell feast tonight if I go for my last call at your so pleasant home?" he asked, stopping before a window full of fruit and flowers.

"What will we buy?" said Jo, ignoring the latter part of his speech as they went in.

"May they haf oranges and figs?" asked Mr. Bhaer.

"They eat them when they can get them."

"Do you care for nuts?"

"Like a squirrel."

"Hamburg grapes—yes, we shall surely drink to the Fatherland in those?"

Jo frowned upon that piece of extravagance, and asked why he didn't buy a frail of dates, a cask of raisins, and a bag of almonds and done with it? Whereat Mr. Bhaer confiscated her purse, produced his own, and finished the marketing by buying several pounds of grapes, a pot of rosy daisies, and a pretty jar of honey, to be regarded in the light of a demijohn. Then, distorting his pockets with the knobby bundles and giving her the flowers to hold, he put up the old umbrella and they traveled on again.

"Miss Marsch, I haf a great favor to ask of you," began the Professor after a moist promenade of half a block.

"Yes, sir." And Jo's heart began to beat so hard she was afraid he would hear it.

"I am bold to say it in spite of the rain, because so short a time remains to me."

"Yes, sir." And Jo nearly crushed the small flowerpot with the sudden squeeze she gave it.

"I wish to get a little dress for my Tina, and I am too stupid to go alone. Will you kindly gif me a word of taste and help?"

"Yes, sir." And Jo felt as calm and cool, all of a sudden, as if she had stepped into a refrigerator.

"Perhaps also a shawl for Tina's mother, she is so poor and sick, and the husband is such a care. Yes, yes, a thick, warm shawl would be a friendly thing to take the little mother."

"I'll do it with pleasure, Mr. Bhaer. I'm going very fast and he's getting dearer every minute," added Jo to herself. Then, with a mental shake, she entered into the business with an energy which was pleasant to behold.

Mr. Bhaer left it all to her, so she chose a pretty gown for Tina, and then ordered out the shawls. The clerk, being a married man, condescended to take an interest in the couple, who appeared to be shopping for their family.

"Your lady may prefer this. It's a superior article, a most desirable showed how happy she would be to walk through life beside him, even though she had no better shelter than the old umbrella, if he carried it. It was certainly proposing under difficulties, for even if he had desired to do so, Mr. Bhaer could not go down upon his knees, on account of the mud; neither could he offer Jo his hand, except figuratively, for both were full; much less could he indulge in tender demonstrations in the open street, though he was near it. So the only way in which he could express his rapture was to look at her, with an expression which glorified his face to such a degree that there actually seemed to be little rainbows in the drops that sparkled on his beard. If he had not loved Jo very much, I don't think he could have done it *then*, for she looked far from lovely, with her skirts in a deplorable state, her rubber boots splashed to the ankle, and her bonnet a ruin. Fortunately, Mr. Bhaer considered her the most beautiful woman living, and she found him more "Jovelike" than ever, though his hat brim was quite limp with the little rills trickling thence upon his shoulders (for he held the umbrella all over Jo), and every finger of his gloves needed mending.

Passers-by probably thought them a pair of harmless lunatics, for they entirely forgot to hail a bus, and strolled leisurely along, oblivious of deepening dusk and fog. Little they cared what anybody thought, for they were enjoying the happy hour that seldom comes but once in any life, the magical moment which bestows youth on the old, beauty on the plain, wealth on the poor, and gives human hearts a foretaste of Heaven. The Professor looked as if he had conquered a kingdom, and the world had nothing more to offer him in the way of bliss, while Jo trudged beside him feeling as if her place had always been there, and wondering how she ever could have chosen any other lot. Of course she was the first to speak—intelligibly, I mean, for the emotional remarks which followed her impetuous "Oh yes!" were not of a coherent or reportable character.

"Friedrich, why didn't you——"

"Ah, heaven, she gifs me the name that no one speaks since Minna died!" cried the Professor, pausing in a puddle to regard her with grateful delight.

"I always call you so to myself—I forgot, but I won't, unless you like it."

"Like it? It is more sweet to me than I can tell. Say 'thou,' also, and I shall say your language is almost as beautiful as mine."

"Isn't 'thou' a little sentimental?" asked Jo, privately thinking it a lovely monosyllable.

color, quite chaste and genteel," he said, shaking out a comfortable gray shawl and throwing it over Jo's shoulders.

"Does this suit you, Mr. Bhaer?" she asked, turning her back to him, and feeling deeply grateful for the chance of hiding her face.

"Excellently well. We will haf it," answered the Professor, smiling to himself as he paid for it.

"Now shall we go home?" he asked, as if the words were very pleasant to him.

"Yes, it's late, and I'm so tired." Jo's voice was more pathetic than she knew; for now the sun seemed to have gone in as suddenly as it came out, the world grew muddy and miserable again, and for the first time she discovered that her feet were cold, her head ached, and that her heart was colder than the former, fuller of pain than the latter. Mr. Bhaer was going away. He only cared for her as a friend; it was all a mistake, and the sooner it was over the better. With this idea in her head, she hailed an approaching omnibus with such a hasty gesture that the daisies flew out of the pot and were badly damaged.

"This is not our omniboos," said the Professor, waving the loaded vehicle away and stopping to pick up the poor little flowers.

"I beg your pardon, I didn't see the name distinctly. Never mind, I can walk. I'm used to plodding in the mud," returned Jo, winking hard because she would have died rather than openly wipe her eyes.

Mr. Bhaer saw the drops on her cheeks, though she turned her head away. The sight seemed to touch him very much, for, suddenly stooping down, he asked in a tone that meant a great deal: "Heart's dearest, why do you cry?"

Now if Jo had not been new to this sort of thing she would have said she wasn't crying, had a cold in her head, or told any other feminine fib proper to the occasion; instead of which that undignified creature answered, with an irrepressible sob:

"Because you are going away."

"Ach, mein Gott, that is so good!" cried Mr. Bhaer, managing to clasp his hands in spite of the umbrella and the bundles. "Jo, I haf nothin' but much love to gif you. I came to see if you could care for it, and waited to be sure that I was something more than a friend. Am I? O you make a little place in your heart for old Fritz?" he added, all in breath.

"Oh yes!" said Jo, and he was quite satisfied, for she folded both over his arm, and looked up at him with an expression that

"Sentimental? Yes. Thank *Gott* we Germans believe in sentiment, and keep ourselves young *mit* it. Your English 'you' is so cold, say 'thou,' heart's dearest, it means so much to me," pleaded Mr. Bhaer, more like a romantic student than a grave professor.

"Well, then, why didn't thou tell me all this sooner?" asked Jo bashfully.

"Now I shall haf to show thee all my heart, and I so gladly will, because thou must take care of it hereafter. See, then, my Jo—ah, the dear, funny little name!—I had a wish to tell you something the day I said good-by in New York; but I thought the handsome friend was betrothed to thee, and so I spoke not. Wouldst thou have said Yes then if I *had* spoken?"

"I don't know. I'm afraid not, for I didn't have any heart just then."

"*Prut!* That I do not believe. It was asleep till the fairy prince came through the wood and waked it up. Ah, well, '*Die erste Liebe ist die beste*,' but that I should not expect."

"Yes, the first love *is* the best, so be contented, for I never had another. Teddy was only a boy, and soon got over his little fancy," said Jo, anxious to correct the Professor's mistake.

"Good! Then I shall rest happy, and be sure that thou givest me all. I haf waited so long I am grown selfish, as thou wilt find, Professorin."

"I like that," cried Jo, delighted with her new name. "Now tell me what brought you at last, just when I most wanted you?"

"This," and Mr. Bhaer took a little worn paper out of his waistcoat pocket.

Jo unfolded it, and looked much abashed, for it was one of her own contributions to a paper that paid for poetry, which accounted for her sending it an occasional attempt.

"How could that bring you?" she asked, wondering what he meant.

"I found it by chance. I knew it by the names and the initials, and in it there was one little verse that seemed to call me. Read and find him. I will see that you go not in the wet."

Jo obeyed, and hastily skimmed through the lines which she had christened

IN THE GARRET

Four little chests all in a row,
  Dim with dust, and worn by time,
All fashioned and filled, long ago,

By children now in their prime.
Four little keys hung side by side,
  With faded ribbons, brave and gay
When fastened there, with childish pride,
  Long ago, on a rainy day.
Four little names, one on each lid,
  Carved out by a boyish hand,
And underneath there lieth hid
  Histories of a happy band
Once playing here, and pausing oft
  To hear the sweet refrain
That came and went on the roof aloft,
  In the falling summer rain.

"Meg" on the first lid, smooth and fair.
  I look in with loving eyes,
For folded here, with well-known care,
  A goodly gathering lies,
The record of a peaceful life—
  Gifts to gentle child and girl,
A bridal gown, lines to a wife,
  A tiny shoe, a baby curl.
No toys in this first chest remain,
  For all are carried away
In their old age, to join again
  In another small Meg's play.
Ah, happy mother! Well I know
  You hear, like a sweet refrain,
Lullabies ever soft and low
  In the falling summer rain.

"Jo" on the next lid, scratched and worn,
  And within a motley store
Of headless dolls, of schoolbooks torn,
  Birds and beasts that speak no more;
Spoils brought home from the fairy ground
  Only trod by youthful feet,
Dreams of a future never found,
  Memories of a past still sweet;
Half-writ poems, stories wild,
  April letters, warm and cold,
Diaries of a willful child,
  Hints of a woman early old;

A woman in a lonely home,
  Hearing, like a sad refrain—
"Be worthy love, and love will come,"
  In the falling summer rain.

My Beth! The dust is always swept
  From the lid that bears your name,
As if by loving eyes that wept,
  By careful hands that often came.
Death canonized for us one saint,
  Ever less human than divine,
And still we lay, with tender plaint,
  Relics in this household shrine—
The silver bell, so seldom rung,
  The little cap which last she wore,
The fair, dead Catherine that hung
  By angels borne above her door;
The songs she sang, without lament,
  In her prison house of pain,
Forever are they sweetly blent
  With the falling summer rain.

Upon the last lid's polished field—
  Legend now both fair and true—
A gallant knight bears on his shield
  "Amy," in letters gold and blue.
Within lie snoods that bound her hair,
  Slippers that have danced their last,
Faded flowers laid by with care,
  Fans whose airy toils are past;
Gay valentines, all ardent flames,
  Trifles that have borne their past
In girlish hopes and fears and shames,
  The record of a maiden heart
Now learning fairer, truer spells,
  Hearing, like a blithe refrain,
The silver sound of bridal bells
  In falling summer rain.

Four little chests all in a row,
  Dim with dust, and worn by time,
Four women, taught by weal and woe
  To love and labor in their prime.

Four sisters, parted for an hour,
  None lost, one only gone before,
Made by love's immortal power
  Nearest and dearest evermore.
Oh, when these hidden stores of ours
  Lie open to the Father's sight,
May they be rich in golden hours,
  Deeds that show fairer for the light,
Lives whose brave music long shall ring
  Like a spirit-stirring strain,
Souls that shall gladly soar and sing
  In the long sunshine after rain.

J. M.

"It's very bad poetry, but I felt it when I wrote it, one day when I was very lonely, and had a good cry on a ragbag. I never thought it would go where it could tell tales," said Jo, tearing up the verses the Professor had treasured so long.

"Let it go, it has done its duty, and I will haf a fresh one when I read all the brown book in which she keeps her little secrets," said Mr. Bhaer with a smile as he watched the fragments fly away on the wind. "Yes," he added earnestly, "I read that, and I think to myself, 'She has a sorrow, she is lonely, she would find comfort in true love. I haf a heart full, full for her. Shall I not go and say, "If this is not too poor a thing to gif for what I shall hope to receive, take it in *Gott's* name" '?"

"And so you came to find that it was not too poor, but the one precious thing I needed," whispered Jo.

"I had no courage to think that at first, heavenly kind as was your welcome to me. But soon I began to hope, and then I said, 'I will haf her if I die for it,' and so I will!" cried Mr. Bhaer with a defiant nod.

"What made you stay away so long?"

"It was not easy, but I could not find the heart to take you from that so happy home until I could haf a prospect of one to give you, after much time, perhaps, and hard work. How could I ask you to gif up so much for a poor old fellow who has no fortune but a little learning?"

"I'm glad you *are* poor. I couldn't bear a rich husband," said Jo decidedly, adding in a softer tone: "Don't fear poverty. I've known it long enough to lose my dread and be happy working for those I love. And don't call yourself old—forty is the prime of life. I couldn't help loving you if you were seventy!"

366

The Professor found that so touching that he would have been glad of his handkerchief, if he could have got at it. As he couldn't, Jo wiped his eyes for him, and said, laughing, as she took away a bundle or two: "I may be strong-minded, but no one can say I'm out of my sphere now, for woman's special mission is supposed to be drying tears and bearing burdens. I'm to carry my share, Friedrich, and help to earn the home. Make up your mind to that, or I'll never go," she added resolutely as he tried to reclaim his load.

"We shall see. Haf you patience to wait a long time, Jo? I must go away and do my work alone. I must help my boys first, because, even for you, I may not break my word to Minna. Can you forgif that, and be happy while we hope and wait?"

"Yes, I know I can; for we love one another, and that makes all the rest easy to bear. I have my duty also, and my work. I couldn't enjoy myself if I neglected them even for you, so there's no need of hurry or impatience. You can do your part out West, I can do mine here, and both be happy hoping for the best, and leaving the future to be as God wills."

"Ah! Thou gifest me such hope and courage, and I haf nothing to gif back but a full heart and these empty hands," cried the Professor.

Jo never, never would learn to be proper; for when he said that as they stood upon the steps, she just put both hands into his, whispering tenderly, "Not empty now," and, stooping down, kissed her Friedrich under the umbrella. It was dreadful, but she would have done it if the flock of draggletailed sparrows on the hedge had been human beings, for she was very far gone indeed, and quite regardless of everything but her own happiness. Though it came in such a very simple guise, that was the crowning moment of both their lives, when, turning from the night and storm and loneliness to the household light and warmth and peace waiting to receive them, with a glad "Welcome home!" Jo led her lover in, and shut the door.

HARVESTTIME

For a year Jo and her Professor worked and waited, hoped and loved, met occasionally, and wrote such voluminous letters that the rise in the price of paper was accounted for, Laurie said. The second year began rather soberly, for their prospects did not brighten, and Aunt March died suddenly. But when their first sorrow was over—for they loved the old lady in spite of her sharp tongue—they found they had cause for rejoicing, for she had left Plumfield to Jo, which made all sorts of joyful things possible.

"It's a fine old place, and will bring a handsome sum—for of course you intend to sell it," said Laurie as they were all talking the matter over some weeks later.

"No I don't," was Jo's decided answer.

"You don't mean to live there?"

"Yes I do."

"But, my dear girl, it's an immense house, and will take a power of money to keep it in order. The garden and orchard alone need two or three men, and farming isn't in Bhaer's line, I take it."

"He'll try his hand at it there, if I propose it."

"And you expect to live on the produce of the place? Well, that sounds paradisaical, but you'll find it desperate hard work."

"The crop we are going to raise is a profitable one." And Jo laughed.

"Of what is this fine crop to consist, ma'am?"

"Boys. I want to open a school for little lads—a good, happy, homelike school, with me to take care of them and Fritz to teach them."

"There's a truly Joian plan for you! Isn't that just like her?" cried Laurie, appealing to the family, who looked as much surprised as he.

"I like it," said Mrs. March decidedly.

"So do I," added her husband.

"It will be an immense care for Jo," said Meg.

"Jo can do it, and be happy in it. It's a splendid idea. Tell us all about it," cried Mr. Laurence, who had been longing to lend the lovers a hand, but knew that they would refuse his help.

"I knew you'd stand by me, sir. Amy does too—I see it in her eyes, though she prudently waits to turn it over in her mind before she speaks. Now, my dear people," continued Jo earnestly, "just understand that this isn't a new idea of mine, but a long-cherished plan. Before my Fritz came, I used to think how when I'd made my fortune, and no one needed me at home, I'd hire a big house, and pick up some poor, forlorn little lads who hadn't any mothers, and take care of them, and make life jolly for them before it was too late. I see so many going to ruin for want of help at the right minute. I love so to do anything for them. I seem to feel their wants, and sympathize with their troubles, and oh, I should *so* like to be a mother to them!

"I told my plan to Fritz once, and he said it was just what he would like, and agreed to try it when we got rich. Bless his dear heart, he's been doing it all his life—helping poor boys, I mean, not getting rich; that he'll never be, money doesn't stay in his pocket long enough to lay up any. But now, thanks to my good old aunt, who loved me better than I ever deserved, *I'm* rich, at least I feel so, and we can live at Plumfield perfectly well if we have a flourishing school. It's just the place for boys, the house is big, and the furniture strong and plain. There's plenty of room for dozens inside, and splendid grounds outside. Then Fritz can train and teach in his own way, and Father will help him. I can feed and nurse and pet and scold them, and Mother will be my stand-by. I've always longed for lots of boys, and never had enough; now I can fill the house full. Think what luxury—Plumfield my own, and a wilderness of boys to enjoy it with me!"

As Jo waved her hands, and gave a sigh of rapture, the family went off into a gale of merriment, and Mr. Laurence laughed till they thought he'd have an apoplectic fit.

"I don't see anything funny," she said gravely when she could be heard. "Nothing could be more natural or proper than for my Professor to open a school, and for me to prefer to reside on my own estate."

"She is putting on airs already," said Laurie. "But may I inquire how you intend to support the establishment? If all the pupils are little ragamuffins, I'm afraid your crop won't be profitable in a worldly sense, Mrs. Bhaer."

"Now don't be a wet blanket, Teddy. Of course I shall have rich pupils also—perhaps begin with such altogether; then when I've got a start, I can take a ragamuffin or two, just for a relish. Rich people's children often need care and comfort, as well as poor. I've seen unfortunate little creatures left to servants, or backward ones pushed forward, when it's real cruelty. Some are naughty through mismanagement or neglect, and some lose their mothers. Besides, the best have to get through the hobbledehoy age, and that's the very time they need most patience and kindness. People laugh at them, and hustle them about, try to keep them out of sight, and expect them to turn all at once from pretty children into fine young men. They don't complain much—plucky little souls— but they feel it. I've been through something of it, and I know all about it. I've a special interest in such young bears, and like to show them that

I see the warm, honest, well-meaning boys' hearts in spite of the clumsy arms and legs and the topsy-turvy heads. I've had experience, too, for haven't I brought up one boy to be a pride and honor to his family?"

"I'll testify that you tried to do it," said Laurie, with a grateful look.

"And I've succeeded beyond my hopes; for here you are, a steady, sensible businessman, doing heaps of good with your money, and laying up the blessings of the poor instead of dollars. But you are not merely a businessman—you love good and beautiful things, enjoy them yourself, and let others go halves, as you always did. I *am* proud of you, Teddy, for you get better every year, and everyone feels it, though you won't let them say so. Yes, and when I have my flock, I'll just point to you and say, 'There's your model, my lads.'"

Poor Laurie didn't know where to look. "I say, Jo, that's rather too much," he began. "You have all done more for me than I can ever thank you for, except by doing my best not to disappoint you. You have rather cast me off lately, Jo, but I've had the best of help, nevertheless; so if I've got on at all, you may thank these two for it," and he laid one hand gently on his grandfather's white head, the other on Amy's golden one, for the three were never far apart.

"I do think that families are the most beautiful things in all the world!" burst out Jo. "When I have one of my own, I hope it will be as happy as the three I know and love the best. If John and my Fritz were only here, it would be quite a little Heaven on earth," she added more quietly. And that night, when she went to her room after a blissful evening of family counsels, hopes, and plans, her heart was so full of happiness that she could only calm it by kneeling beside the empty bed always near her own and thinking tender thoughts of Beth.

It was a very astonishing year altogether, for things seemed to happen in an unusually rapid and delightful manner. Almost before she knew where she was Jo found herself married and settled at Plumfield. Then a family of six or seven boys sprang up like mushrooms, and flourished surprisingly, poor boys as well as rich; for Mr. Laurence was continually finding some touching case of destitution and begging the Bhaers to take pity on the child, and he would gladly pay a trifle for its support. In this way the sly old gentleman got round proud Jo, and furnished her with the style of boy in which she most delighted.

Of course it was uphill work at first, and Jo made queer mistakes; but the wise Professor steered her safely into calmer waters, and the most rampant ragamuffin was conquered in the end. How Jo did enjoy her "wilderness of boys," and how poor dear Aunt March would have lamented had she been there to see the sacred precincts of prim, well-ordered Plumfield overrun with Toms, Dicks, and Harrys! There was a sort of poetic justice about it, after all, for the old lady had been the terror of the boys for miles round, and now the exiles feasted freely on forbidden plums, kicked up the gravel with profane boots unreproved, and played cricket in the big field where the irritable "cow with a crumpled horn" used to invite rash youths to come and be tossed. It became a sort of boys' paradise, and Laurie suggested that it should be called the "Bhaergarten," as a compliment to its master and appropriate to its inhabitants.

It never was a fashionable school, and the Professor did not lay up a fortune; but it *was* just what Jo intended it to be—"a happy, homelike place for boys who needed teaching, care, and kindness." Every room in the big house was soon full; every little plot in the garden soon had its owner; a regular menagerie appeared in barn and shed, for pet animals were allowed; and three times a day Jo smiled at her Fritz from the head of a long table lined on either side with rows of happy young faces, which all turned to her with affectionate eyes, confiding words, and grateful hearts, full of love for "Mother Bhaer." She had boys enough now, and did not tire of them, though they were not angels by any means, and some of them caused both Professor and Professorin much trouble and anxiety. But her faith in the good spot which exists in the heart of the naughtiest, sauciest, most tantalizing little ragamuffin gave her patience, skill, and, in time, success; for no mortal boy could hold out long with Father Bhaer shining on him as benevolently as the sun and Mother Bhaer forgiving him seventy times seven. Very precious to Jo was the friendship of the lads; their penitent sniffs and whispers after wrong-doing; their droll or touching little confidences; their pleasant enthusiasms, hopes, and plans; even their misfortunes, for they only endeared them to her all the more. There were slow boys and bashful boys; feeble boys and riotous boys; boys that lisped and boys that stuttered; one or two lame ones; and a merry little quadroon, who could not be taken in elsewhere, but who was welcome to the Bhaergarten, though some people predicted that his admission would ruin the school.

Yes, Jo was a very happy woman there, in spite of hard work, much anxiety, and a perpetual racket. She enjoyed it heartily, and found the applause of her boys more satisfying than any praise of the world; for now she told no stories except to her flock of enthusiastic believers and admirers. As the years went on, two little lads of her own came to increase her happiness—Rob, named for Grandpa, and Teddy, a happy-go-lucky baby who seemed to have inherited his papa's sunshiny temper as well as his mother's lively spirit. How they ever grew up alive in that whirlpool of boys was a mystery to their grandma and aunts; but they flourished like dandelions in spring, and their rough nurses loved and served them well.

There were a great many holidays at Plumfield, and one of the most delightful was the yearly apple-picking, for then the Marches, Laurences, Brookes, and Bhaers turned out in full force and made a day of it. Five years after Jo's wedding, one of these fruitful festivals occurred—a mellow October day, when the air was full of an exhilarating freshness which made the spirits rise and the blood dance healthily in the veins. The old orchard wore its holiday attire; golden-rod and asters fringed the mossy walls; grasshoppers skipped briskly in the sere grass, and crickets chirped like fairy pipers at a feast; squirrels were busy with their small harvesting; birds twittered their adieux from the alders in the lane; and every tree stood ready to send down its shower of red or yellow apples at the first shake. Everybody was there; everybody laughed and sang, climbed up and tumbled down; everybody declared that there never had been such a perfect day or such a jolly set to enjoy it.

Mr. March strolled placidly about quoting Tusser, Cowley, and Columella to Mr. Laurence while enjoying "The gentle apple's winy juice." The Professor charged up and down the green aisles like a stout Teutonic knight, with a pole for a lance, leading on the boys, who made a hook-and-ladder company of themselves, and performed wonders in the way of ground and lofty tumbling. Laurie devoted himself to the little ones, rode his small daughter in a bushel basket, took Daisy up among the birds' nests, and kept adventurous Rob from breaking his neck. Mrs. March and Meg sat among the apple piles like a pair of Pomonas, sorting the contributions that kept pouring in, while Amy sketched the various groups, and watched over one pale lad who sat adoring her with his little crutch beside him.

Jo was in her element that day, and rushed about with her gown pinned up, her hat anywhere but on her head, and her baby tucked under her arm, ready for any lively adventure which might turn up. Little Teddy bore a charmed life, for nothing ever happened to him, and Jo never felt any anxiety when he was whisked up into a tree by one lad, galloped off on the back of another, or supplied with sour russets by his indulgent papa, who labored under the Germanic delusion that babies could digest anything, from pickled cabbage to buttons, nails, and their own small shoes. She knew that little Ted would turn up again in time safe and rosy, dirty and serene.

At four o'clock a lull took place, and baskets remained empty while the apple-pickers rested, and compared rents and bruises. Then Jo and Meg, with a detachment of the bigger boys, set forth the supper on the grass, for an out-of-doors tea was always the crowning joy of the day. The land literally flowed with milk and honey on such occasions, for the lads were not required to sit at table, but allowed to partake of refreshment as they liked—freedom being the sauce best loved by the boyish soul. They availed themselves of the rare privilege to the fullest extent, for some tried the pleasing experiment of drinking milk while standing on their heads, others lent a charm to leapfrog by eating pie in the pauses of the game, cookies were sown broadcast over the field, and apple turnovers roosted in the trees like a new style of bird. When no one could eat any more, the Professor proposed the first regular toast, which was always drunk at such times: "Aunt March, God bless her!" A toast heartily given by the good man, who never forgot how much he owed her, and quietly drunk by the boys, who had been taught to keep her memory green.

"Now, Grandma's sixtieth birthday! Long life to her, with three times three!"

That was given with a will, as you may well believe, and the cheering once begun, it was hard to stop it. Everybody's health was proposed, from Mr. Laurence, who was considered their special patron, to the astonished guinea pig who had strayed from its proper sphere in search of its young master. Demi, as the oldest grandchild, then presented the queen of the day with various gifts, so numerous that they were transported to the festive scene in a wheelbarrow. Funny presents, some of them, but what would have been defects to other eyes were ornaments to Grandma's— for the children's gifts were all their own. Every stitch Daisy's patient little fingers had put into the handkerchiefs she hemmed was better than embroidery to Mrs. March; Demi's shoe box was a miracle of mechanical skill, though the cover wouldn't shut; Rob's footstool had a wiggle in its uneven legs that she declared was very soothing; and no page of the costly book Amy's child gave her was so fair as that on which appeared, in tipsy capitals, the words "To dear Grandma, from her little Beth."

During this ceremony the boys had mysteriously disappeared, and when Mrs. March had tried to thank her children and broken down, the

Professor suddenly began to sing. Then, from above him, voice after voice took up the words, and from tree to tree echoed the music of the unseen choir as the boys sang, with all their hearts, the little song Jo had written, Laurie set to music, and the Professor trained his lads to give with the best effect. This was something altogether new, and it proved a grand success; for Mrs. March couldn't get over her surprise, and insisted on shaking hands with every one of the featherless birds, from tall Franz and Emil to the little quadroon, who had the sweetest voice of all.

After this, the boys dispersed for a final lark, leaving Mrs. March and her daughters under the festival tree.

"I don't think I ever ought to call myself 'Unlucky Jo' again, when my greatest wish has been so beautifully gratified," said Mrs. Bhaer, taking Teddy's little fist out of the milk pitcher, in which he was rapturously churning.

"And yet your life is very different from the one you pictured so long ago. Do you remember our castles in the air?" asked Amy, smiling as she watched Laurie and John playing cricket with the boys.

"Dear fellows! It does my heart good to see them forget business and frolic for a day," answered Jo, who now spoke in a maternal way of all mankind. "Yes, I remember, but the life I wanted then seems selfish, lonely, and cold to me now. I haven't given up the hope that I may write a good book yet, but I can wait, and I'm sure it will be all the better for such experiences and illustrations as these." And Jo pointed from the lively lads in the distance to her father, leaning on the Professor's arm as they walked to and fro in the sunshine deep in one of the conversations which both enjoyed so much, and then to her mother, sitting enthroned among her daughters with their children in her lap and at her feet.

"My castle was the most nearly realized of all. I asked for splendid things, to be sure, but in my heart I knew I should be satisfied if I had a little home, and John, and some dear children like these. I've got them all, thank God, and am the happiest woman in the world." And Meg laid her hand on her tall boy's head, with a face full of tender and devout content.

"My castle is very different from what I planned, but I would not alter it, though, like Jo, I don't relinquish all my artistic hopes, or confine myself to helping others fulfill their dreams of duty. I've begun to model a figure of Baby, and Laurie says it is the best thing I've ever done. I think so myself, and mean to do it in marble, so that, whatever happens, I may at least keep the image of my little angel."

As Amy spoke, a great tear dropped on the golden hair of the sleeping child in her arms, for her one well-beloved daughter was a frail little creature and the dread of losing her was the shadow over Amy's sunshine. This cross was doing much for both father and mother, for one love and sorrow bound them closely together. Amy's nature was growing sweeter, deeper, and more tender; Laurie was growing more serious, strong, and

firm; and both were learning that beauty, youth, good fortune, even love itself, cannot keep care and pain, loss and sorrow, from the most blessed, for

> "Into each life some rain must fall,
> Some days must be dark and sad and dreary."

"She is growing better, I am sure of it, my dear. Don't despond, but hope and keep happy," said Mrs. March, as tenderhearted Daisy stooped from her knee to lay her rosy cheek against her little cousin's pale one.

"I never ought to while I have you to cheer me up, Marmee, and Laurie to take more than half of every burden," replied Amy warmly. "He never lets me see his anxiety, but is so sweet and patient with me, so devoted to Beth, and such a stay and comfort to me always, that I can't love him enough. So, in spite of my one cross, I can say with Meg, 'Thank God, I'm a happy woman.'"

"There's no need for me to say it, for everyone can see that I'm far happier than I deserve," added Jo, glancing from her good husband to her chubby children tumbling on the grass beside her. "Fritz is getting gray and stout; I'm growing as thin as a shadow, and am thirty; we never shall be rich, and Plumfield may burn up any night, for that incorrigible Tommy Bangs *will* smoke sweet-fern cigars under the bedclothes, though he's set himself afire three times already. But in spite of these unromantic facts, I have nothing to complain of, and never was so jolly in my life. Excuse the remark, but living among boys, I can't help using their expressions now and then."

"Yes, Jo, I think your harvest will be a good one," began Mrs. March, frightening away a big black cricket that was staring Teddy out of countenance.

"Not half so good as yours, Mother. Here it is, and we never can thank you enough for the patient sowing and reaping you have done," cried Jo, with the loving impetuosity which she never could outgrow.

"I hope there will be more wheat and fewer tares every year," said Amy softly.

"A large sheaf, but I know there's room in your heart for it, Marmee dear," added Meg's tender voice.

Touched to the heart, Mrs. March could only stretch out her arms as if to gather children and grandchildren to herself, and say, with face and voice full of motherly love, gratitude, and humility:

"O my girls, however long you may live, I never can wish you a greater happiness than this!"